THE RECKONING

MARTINA MURPHY

CONSTABLE

CONSTABLE

First published in Great Britain in 2023 by Constable

A CIP catalogue record for this book
is available from the British Library.

ISBN: 978-1-40871-883-4

Typeset in Bembo MT Pro by Initial Typesetting Services, Edinburgh
Printed and bound in Great Britain by Clays Ltd, Elcograf S.p.A.

Papers used by Constable are from well-managed forests and
other responsible sources.

Constable
An imprint of
Little, Brown Book Group
Carmelite House
50 Victoria Embankment
London EC4Y 0DZ

An Hachette UK Company
www.hachette.co.uk

www.littlebrown.co.uk

For Tom, the best uncle in the world. (And that's a fact.)
And for Pat and Jack – sadly missed.

Glossary

AFIS	Automated Fingerprint Identification System
APT	Assistant pathologist
Cig	Short for Cigre. A common nickname for detective inspectors, as 'cigre' means 'inspector' in Irish. Pronounced 'kig'.
DDU	District Detective Unit (unmarked cars)
DG	Detective guard
Debs	A graduation dance attended by sixth-year students before they go on to college.
DI	Detective inspector. Often referred to as 'cig'; 'cigre' being the Irish word for 'inspector'. Pronounced 'kig'.
DS	Detective sergeant
GNECB	Garda National Economic Crime Bureau
IP	Injured party
IRC	Incident room co-ordinator

NSU	National Surveillance Unit
SIO	Senior investigating officer
SOCO	Scene of crime officers
SO	Suspected offender
TE	Technical examination

Prologue

It is a risk but one he is prepared to take. That bitch had destroyed what mattered to him. Now he will do the same to her.

To anyone looking, he is a middle-aged bloke, a bit hipster, scattered, longish hair and a beard. Haversack hitched high on his back, sleeping bag. Stout walking boots. He is a fitter man than he'd been when she'd come into his life. Stupid wagon.

He is clever too.

He'll stay close to her. Watch her.

Strike when the opportunity presents itself.

He has an easy way about him, people say.

Those who don't know him trust him.

Achill is a godforsaken kip but she is here now, and it being so . . . remote might make things easier.

Thoughts of her make his breath hitch.

He'd never understood before that love was just as destructive as hate. How loving someone could eat you up. How losing someone could tear you open. And all the sorts of bad things that came from that.

Including what he is about to do.

He pulls a picture from his jacket pocket. Old now, faded, but never forgotten.

He will avenge.

1

The bar is hopping, which is surprising because it's mid-January, six months off tourist season and dreary as hell outside. It's also not the most popular bar in Westport, serving mostly locals and those who just want a quiet pint. Tonight, there seems to be some sort of party going on. The level of chat is high and the sound of someone strumming a guitar floats around the room. All the tables except one are taken up with young people, laughing, shouting, swilling back pints or doing shots while four elderly men crouch around the remaining table in the corner eyeing the interlopers in annoyance.

Larry, Ben, Dan and I are at the bar, there being nowhere else to go. We're celebrating the closing of a case that had led to the conviction of two men for assault and robbery. They'd plagued the locality for close to eight months before their granny had finally turned them in. She was sick, she declared in court, of trying to get them on the right path.

'To the right path,' Larry raises his pint, 'and to Granny Ryan.'

'To the right path,' we chant, clinking glasses, 'and to Granny Ryan.'

'To Granny Ryan,' a tipsy red-headed woman to our right shouts, having overheard us.

'And to all who sail in her,' someone else chimes in, amid laughter.

The redhead chortles loudly, in a frantic sort of way.

There is something familiar . . .

'Lucy, d'you hear what I just said?' Larry asks. He follows my gaze, screws up his face. 'I'm not into redheads.'

Larry is a total player. I'm just waiting for the day when some woman will break his heart but it's looking increasingly unlikely.

'I doubt that redhead is into arsehole narcissists.' I pull my gaze away from her and refocus on the lads. For some reason, while I've been mentally congratulating myself on my clever comeback, they've suddenly developed an air of nervous apprehension. 'What?'

Larry won't meet my gaze as he mumbles, 'I, eh, well, hmm, Larissa McKenna died. Isn't she the one . . .?'

He doesn't finish his sentence. Instead his eyes slide right into his pint glass. I know what he was about to say. Isn't she the one who threw acid in your face?

'Did you draw the short straw on having to tell me that, Lar?' I ask.

All three have the grace to look abashed.

'I tried to tell you,' Dan says, 'but there was no right time.'

'I told him to just say it out straight,' Larry says. 'But he's a bloody pussy.'

'Sorry.' Dan winces.

'Thank you for your sensitivity in choosing this pub to break it to me,' I say. 'It's so the right place.'

'You're welcome.' Larry totally misses my sarcasm.

'You all right?' Dan asks.

I think I am. It's a relief to be honest. I'd known she was released a couple of years ago and had always wondered where she was. In all my years on the force, her attack had been the most traumatic thing that had ever happened to me. She'd been the wife of one of my informants who had turned state's witness. He'd gone on to witness protection while she had refused to go, unwilling to uproot her child. She had walked into the Dublin station where I worked at the time and accused me of robbing her of her husband.

I suppose I had.

The next thing I remember was pain. Searing, burning, horrific pain. And the surgeon telling me that there was only so much he could do and that I'd have to live with a huge scar down the left side of my face.

It was as if the bottom had fallen out of my world.

'Cancer,' Larry says then. 'Liver.'

'Lucy Golden, hey!'

The voice breaks into our conversation. It's the red-headed woman again. I should know her, I think. She's older than she first appears, a little younger than me maybe, attractive, her hair a riot of corkscrew curls, framing a thin face with over-large green eyes. She's wearing red jeans and a yellow top, the clothes making her stand out in this packed but dreary pub. Her make-up is bright too, scarlet lipstick that clashes with the hair.

The three men make room for her to squeeze in, Ben giving her a not-so-subtle once-over.

'It's me,' the woman says, her voice bright as a new penny, 'Sandra Byrne. Megan's sister?'

Of course.

'Don't you remember? I—'

'Yes, I remember you.' I attempt a smile. 'Blast from the past.' I shift, a little uncomfortable, not sure how to broach the subject in the packed pub, but knowing I should. 'I was so sorry to hear about your mother. I couldn't make the funeral. My mother went, though. She said it was lovely.'

'Thanks.' Sandra's bright smile dips and she blinks rapidly. 'It was awful, totally unexpected.' Bright smile again. 'How are you?'

'Grand.'

She looks expectantly at me, wanting an introduction to the lads.

'Ben.' He pre-empts me. 'I'm a detective, I work with Lucy, and this is Larry and this is Dan.' He offers her his most charming smile.

She laps it up.

'Oh, a de-tec-tive,' she says. 'That must be dangerous work.'

'It can be.' Ben's voice is unnecessarily grave and Larry rolls his eyes.

'Ripe for the plucking is our Ben,' Dan whispers in my ear.

'Ripe for the fucking,' I whisper back, and Dan snorts a laugh, which he quickly tries to turn into a cough. Ben is separated about two years now from his ultra-glamorous, ultra-young, ultra-pain-in-the-hole wife.

'Ben got beaten up by an old woman once.' Larry adopts the same grave tone as Ben. 'A packet of frozen peas, right in the face.'

'Piss off, that's not true,' Ben says quickly, with a glare at Larry. 'He's just messing. I was involved in that case last year when the girl was found in the suitcase in Achill.'

'Never!' Sandra is good, I'll give her that. If Ben was an apple, he'd have ripened right up.

'Let me buy you a drink and I'll tell you about it,' Ben says, gently leading her back to her seat. He wants us to butt out, which we do. As Larry sensitively puts it, Ben needs to get his hole and fast.

Ben doesn't need to know that when Sandra was fifteen she'd given birth to a boy and, much to the horror of the older locals, had refused to name the father. He doesn't need to know that at sixteen she'd got a job in a shop in Dublin and left her son with her older sister Megan – my long-ago best friend – and her husband. He doesn't need to know that to all intents and purposes, according to my mother, she'd abandoned her child, never coming back for him. 'Though,' my mother always says, 'Devon was probably better off. Sandra would never have been able for him with all his illnesses. And her own problems.' Mental Sandra Byrne, she'd been christened in those less sensitive times. And it had been an apt moniker.

No, I think, Ben just needs a good time. Sandra too, maybe.

An hour later, with his arm about her waist, Ben leaves with Sandra. By ten the next morning, Sandra is dead.

2

Devon, her son, was the one who rang 999. I spot him as I make my way towards the scene. I tell Dan to go on ahead and I approach Devon, who is leaning against the bonnet of his dilapidated car, which nevertheless is polished to a high shine. It's obviously his pride and joy. He's a small man, at least a head shorter than Luc, though almost everyone is shorter than Luc. He has inherited his mother's curly red hair, which pokes out from under his hat, and his face is nut brown from summers on the beach. He wears a thick tracksuit, a blue beanie hat and blue runners with an Adidas logo. He recognises my voice behind my mask and greets me as 'Luc's mother'.

'How are you doing?'

'All right.' His tone is flat, eyes expressionless. Shock.

'Me and my colleague are just going into the house now,' I tell him. 'That's what this is for.' I hold up the sealed bag containing the dust suit. 'When I come back out, I'll talk to you, okay?'

'All right.'

'I'm so sorry,' I add.

'My auntie Megan is on her way over.'

'Good. Get some sweet tea into you.' I attempt some sort of comforting smile, but he doesn't react. 'See you in a bit.'

I change into the suit, which is, as usual, bloody enormous. Pulling the mask on, I join Dan, who is waiting for me at the front door. 'Are we all right to enter?' I call out.

'Come on in, Lucy. Dan, stay outside for now, talk to the SOCOs, see if there's anything.' It's William, the DI. As senior investigating officer, or SIO, he oversees all our cases down here. A man without the ability to small-talk, he terrifies most of the team. I don't mind him at all: I like that he's so direct because I have to know where I stand with people and William does not pussy-foot around.

His voice comes from upstairs, and after we give our names to the garda on the scene, Dan moves to the side of the building, following the safe path marked out. I enter, mindful to step only on the plates that the SOCO team have placed on the floor. They can be slippery sometimes, especially on tiles, and I'm relieved to see that these are the metal ones, which are a bit sturdier than the plastic.

With great care, I make my way down the hall towards the stairs. Flock wallpaper, dado rails, brown pictures of hunting scenes. The smells of bacon and cabbage and stew permeate the place, but underneath is a smell I recognise, faint now but if left, it will smother all other odours with its sweet, rotten heaviness. Four brown doors open off the hall and, peering briefly inside, I catch glimpses of the SOCO team tagging and bagging any-thing they think might help the investigation. Unfortunately, the place appears to be a hoarder's paradise, and while some of the rooms seem to have been cleared out into boxes, others are full of clutter. Shelves of heavy ornaments and photograph frames cover every surface. Cups and glasses and dinner plates spill from the kitchen. Empty wine bottles stand to attention just about everywhere I look.

This place will be a nightmare to gather evidence from.

Climbing the stairs, I pass boxes labelled 'Mammy's clothes', 'Daddy's clothes', 'religious pictures', 'ornaments'. At the top, I steel myself to approach the bedroom where the body is. Through the open door, I see William standing at the foot of a bed while a garda photographer takes pictures of the body from every angle. The pathologist, Joe Palmer, has been and gone with promises to get an interim report to us by the conference this evening. He's a cranky bastard, always ready with a barb or two. I'm glad to have missed him.

The bedroom, where the body lies – or 'the injured party' as Sandra will be known from now on – is caught in a nineties time warp. It must have been either Sandra's or Megan's at one time. Posters of Oasis and the Spice Girls are pasted crookedly on the swirly-patterned wallpaper. An old radio sits atop a brown chest of drawers. Heavy blue curtains, in need of a good wash, hang in the window, which also needs cleaning. A cup and glass have been smashed and lie scattered near the door.

There is a strange stillness in the space, even though the broken body of Sandra lies splayed out across the floor, face down, blood pooling on the carpet from a head wound. You don't have to be a pathologist to guess that that's probably what killed her.

'Palmer says it looks like the blow to the head was the fatal wound,' William says. 'We haven't found a murder weapon yet. Early indicators point to her having a tussle with the suspected offender. She tried to escape, was struck with an object, fell, and was struck again.' He points at the walls, where the blood has made a classic impact spatter pattern. 'See?'

'Yes.' I finally turn to Sandra. Last night she'd been alive, tipsy and flirty, and now, ten hours later, she was dead, her body already showing signs of rigor mortis. She looks tinier in death than she did in life and I wonder who the hell has done this and if they are still on the island.

She is barefoot, an oversized black pyjama top covering her upper body to just above her knees. I squint slightly, the better to see. 'John,' I call to the SOCO, 'what's that?'

John crosses over, leans in.

'See there.' I point to what looks like a reddish-brown hair on her black T-shirt. 'See that?'

'Try to get it, John, will you?' William orders.

'Good spot.' John, using tweezers, takes the hair from the T-shirt. He turns it this way and that, before bagging and tagging it.

'No sign of a break-in,' William goes on. 'This was done by someone she opened the door to or by someone who had a key.'

Shit, I think. If Sandra had been murdered in a break-in, Ben would have been in the clear. Only there hasn't been a break-in. Shit. I have to tell William that Ben may be a suspect. 'Cig,' I begin, not knowing how to say it, feeling I'm betraying a man I've grown to know very well.

'We need as much as we can on the IP before tonight,' William interrupts. His gaze flits from me to take in every detail of the room. 'We'll have the usual team, if they're available. I hear Matt is off in the Canaries with that Stacy one. I've a good mind to pay him to stay there, keep that reporter out of our hair.'

'I'm sure Matt would oblige, Cig,' I say. 'They're engaged now apparently. Look, there's something—'

'Marvellous,' William interrupts again. 'Just what we need,

a guard in love with a reporter. Hopefully they'll break up.'
He means it, too, I think in amusement. 'Mick and Susan are
available, Pat's around, Kev's raring to go. And Larry's free too.'
He pauses and I wait because I know it's coming. Without even
glancing at me, he asks silkily, 'Were you ever going to tell me
that Ben was in a relationship with our IP, DS Golden?'

Shit. He never calls me by my rank. 'Just now, only you inter-
rupted me,' I say, then add, a little defensively, 'I wouldn't actually
call a one-night stand a relationship, Cig.'

'He was the last person to see her alive,' he says. 'As far as we
know.'

A silence develops. I fall right into the classic garda trap.

'Yes . . . well, I know. I know that. But Ben? Come on . . .'

'He's going to be a suspect.'

'Ben would never—'

'Most people would never.' William snaps his head around,
and I cringe. 'Most people don't go out to murder someone,
Lucy. Have you not realised that by now?' His voice is ice. 'Most
murders just happen.'

'That's assuming she was murdered,' I say. 'She could have just
tripped and banged her head off the bed or whatever. There's a
lot of wine bottles about the place.'

'There was one by the bed.' John speaks up. 'Along with a
glass.'

'Point taken,' William says, though he knows that neither of
us really believes she banged her head. He turns to me, his eyes
hard. 'If you have information, you bloody well tell it sooner.'

'Yes, William. Sorry.'

John sidles from the room, throwing me a sympathetic glance
behind William's back.

'Get out.' William dismisses me with a scathing look. 'Go on. Tell Dan, if he's finished, to go back and sort out the incident room. Make sure we have everything we need. You, go and talk to the son.'

3

Chastened, kicking myself for my hesitation, I give Dan his instructions and am about to change out of my dust suit when I'm approached by Louis, one of the SOCOs. 'Come and have a look at this,' he says, and I follow him around to the side of the house.

'See the windowsill here,' he says, and I notice that it's covered with what looks like blood. At my unspoken question, Louis nods. 'Blood all right,' he says. 'But it hasn't come from inside the house, as far as I can tell.'

The whole windowsill is covered with it, almost like it was poured on. How weird. 'Can you take a sample of that as soon as possible, Louis?'

'Yes. We're on it.'

'Thanks.' Disposing of the dust suit, I head towards Devon. Someone has given him a tea, but he's not drinking it. Instead, his gaze is focused somewhere beyond the house, across the brown-gold scrubby landscape to the rise of the hill, dark against the grey sky. There is loneliness in the image he presents. A biting wind sweeps in from the Atlantic, and the sound of the waves slapping against Dugort Pier is carried across on the air. It's desolate. This is a road travelled only by those using the pier and by the few people who live along this stretch. It's just a step up from a narrow dirt track. The pier itself is tiny, functional. I zip up my jacket against the chill.

As I approach him, Devon is joined by a stout woman, who lightly presses his arm. It makes him flinch, liquid slopping over the rim of the mug onto his hand. The woman gently takes the tea from him, setting it on the ground, before wrapping him in her arms, whispering to him. He looks stiff in her embrace, but she holds him hard. Then she pulls away and stares into his face, says something else and he signals agreement.

It's Megan, I realise. Sandra's sister and my teenage friend. She's got plump and round and . . . the only word I can think of is *womanly*. Her clothes are square, a big square black padded jacket, black trousers with straight legs. Functional black shoes. Her hair is buried underneath a black hat, which is pulled down low over her forehead. She looks like the person she was always going to be. Sensible. Homely.

I wait a moment, observing, then cross towards them. 'Hello,' I say. Then, 'Megan? I'm so sorry for your loss. Losses,' I amend.

Megan releases Devon and turns to me. There is such savage sadness in her eyes that I feel suddenly ashamed of myself for losing touch with her. 'Thanks,' she says. A pause, before she turns to Devon saying, 'Devon, this was my best friend in school, Lucy Golden.'

'Luc's ma, I know,' he says. 'Luc was in my school.'

'And your aunt and I, we were good friends.' I half smile. 'Megan, can I talk to Devon? You can stay if you like.'

'You want to talk to him here?'

'If you don't mind. The sooner we get a statement the better.

It's surprising how things get forgotten with shock and that, you know.'

'Of course.' Megan shoves her hands into her overlarge jacket. 'Are you all right with that, Devs?'

'Sure.'

'I just need you to take me through how you found the . . . how you found your mother.' I pull out my notebook and pen and look at him.

He drops his gaze before removing his hat and running a stubby hand through his hair. 'I just came to help with the clear-out,' he mumbles.

'Clear-out?'

'Mammy died a week ago,' Megan explains. 'We've been clearing the house out to sell it. Sandra was helping. She said she'd stay until it was done.'

'Of course.' That explains the boxes. 'I'm sorry I didn't make your mother's funeral,' I say. Then I add, because it's expected, 'My mother says it was a lovely one.'

'It was,' Megan agrees, swallowing hard. 'She would have approved. All her favourite hymns and that.' I watch her battle back the tears. 'Sorry,' she apologises, flapping a hand. 'I still can't believe . . . and yet she was old, not in the best of health. I mean, it was almost a relief when she died, in a way, not that I don't miss her,' she tacks on hastily. 'But Sandra . . . that . . . that is—'

'A relief too,' Devon says flatly, and Megan flinches. He looks at me and his eyes, green like his mother's, are desolate. 'It's just hypocrisy to pretend we're sad about it. It is a relief.' A tear slides out of the corner of his eye. He doesn't notice. 'I mean, she came back for the funeral and then caused trouble at the afters.'

My mother had mentioned nothing about trouble.

Megan is at a loss as to what to say. After a moment, she shrugs, says to me, 'You know what Sandra was like.'

'Not really,' I answer. 'But maybe you'll be able to tell me. For now, though, Devon, can you go through the events of earlier? Tell me as much as you can remember. What time you arrived, how you got in, what you did, all that sort of thing.'

He shivers, twists the hat in his hands, 'Em . . . I got here, eh, about ten, because there was loads of work to do. My nan had a lot of stuff in that house and Auntie Megan and me, we were sorting it into boxes. Sandra was meant to help but she wasn't, said it was too upsetting.'

Sandra, not Mam. *Interesting.*

'It was better that way, pet,' Megan says. 'You know that.'

Devon flicks her a look but doesn't acknowledge the comment. 'So, I got here about ten and I went in and she wasn't up and I called out to her to see if she wanted tea and there was no reply and, see, she was normally all over me because she thought by being nice to me it would make up for dumping me when I was a kid and—'

'Devon,' Megan chastises gently, looking a little alarmed.

'Don't!' Devon snaps at her. 'Just don't.' They eyeball each other until, finally, Megan slumps a little, which he takes as his cue to continue. 'Like I said, she was normally all over me, and when she didn't answer, I knocked at her bedroom door and looked inside and . . .' He stops. This time it's a while before he says softly, 'And there she was.'

He looks at me.

'How did you get into the house, Devon?'

'Sorry, front door. I had a key.'

'And you say you just found her. What did you do then?'

'Nothing. Like . . . I knew . . . I knew she was dead, see. It was . . . like . . . obvious, so I did nothing. Just called the ambulance and the guards and that.' He shudders. Squeezes his hat harder.

'All right. Can you remember, Devon, if you saw anything unusual this morning on the way here or even in the house?'

'I don't think so.'

'Anything disturbed in the house? Anything missing?'

He winces. 'There's a lot of stuff.'

'Fine. One of our members will be in touch to show you some pictures of the house and contents. See if you can spot anything that might look amiss. Or things that are missing.'

'There was so much,' Megan reiterates. 'We might not know.'

'Just try your best. Now, could either of you tell me if there was anyone who would want to harm Sandra?'

'We barely knew her,' Devon says, bitterness laced with un-acknowledged grief. 'She wasn't exactly in our lives. She had bigger fish to fry than her own family, that was for sure, and—'

'Devon,' Megan says, almost like she could cry. 'Just . . . don't. Please.'

He gives her a look that I can't quite fathom before shaking his head and walking off. We watch him go, pulling his hat back on, zipping up his jacket and striding away towards the road.

'He gets upset,' Megan says. 'And he's right, he didn't really know her.'

'How was she since she came home?'

'Difficult,' Megan answers, with a hint of bitterness. 'Like she always was. You know yourself.'

'What she was like years ago has no bearing on what she was like today,' I state firmly. 'I barely remember her. So, tell me, what was she like? Explain why she was difficult.'

18

Megan flushes slightly under the rebuke, but the truth is, I can't have what I knew of Sandra colouring this case. I can only work on what I have now. It's why I should have told William about Ben before I'd even got to the scene. 'She was . . . selfish for one,' Megan says. 'She only came swanning back to see what she could get out of Mammy's death. Oh, she was upset, too, but it was the money she came for. She caused trouble at the afters. I don't know if it was drink or what but she verbally abused Dom, started interrogating the new priest on religion or something. Maudie had to take her home. I mean, for Christ's sake.'

I haven't met the new priest, but apparently, he's a fine thing. My mother said that if the Church was hoping to get the young girls back, they were going the right way about it.

'Any reason she might have abused Dom?' Dom is her uncle, her mother's brother.

'Sandra doesn't need a reason.'

I wait, see if she says any more.

'You'd have to ask Dom, I don't know.'

'All right. So is it fair to say that neither you nor Devon welcomed her back?'

'I was glad to see her,' Megan says, a bit defensively. 'Relieved, if I'm honest, because we never knew where she was. Oh, she sent us her address from time to time but didn't phone us or . . .' a flush '. . . answer our calls. I think Devon, though you'd have to ask him, I think he's embarrassed by her. But he loves her too, I'm sure,' she adds hastily.

'And you're positive you don't know if anyone would want to harm her?'

'She tended to annoy people so . . .' Her voice trails off. She looks towards the house and shudders. 'I don't know.'

'Did she say anything about her life beyond here?'

'I think she was working in a shop, but I get the feeling that she'd ditched it – she seemed determined to stay here for a while. To be honest, I've only seen her a couple of times since Mammy's funeral. I'm just . . . well . . . I was just so angry at her for the afters. Maudie saw her more than me – she might know more.' A moment, before she adds, 'Once or twice she helped with the packing up but most of the time she was out gallivanting, drinking her head off, bringing men back. She fell a few days ago, Maudie said, so Leo put a solar light in the garden. Not that she gave him any thanks. I don't think she even noticed. And have you seen the mess the house is in? She never tidied. Mammy would have been so upset to see her house in that state.' Then she stops, covers her mouth with her hand. 'Oh, God, I'm sorry. I'm so sorry.' A sudden tearing up.

'It's all right.'

'She was my *sister*. My baby *sister*.' And she starts to cry, shoulders shaking, little black hat bobbing up and down. 'I don't know how it got to this. I did love her.'

I'm swamped with pity for her: she looks so forlorn, hunched over, sobbing on a Baltic January day, in her dull square clothes. She was the kind one, I remember suddenly. The one who always had the plaster in the handbag, or safety-pins, or tablets for a headache. She'd be the one who'd sit with the pissed-drunk party-goer, holding their hair as they puked up. She deserves better than a murdered sister, a dead mother.

'Take your time.' I know from the job that sometimes, when a relationship is bad and the person who has made it so dies, there is a lack of closure for those left behind. And it's hard for people to live with that. Things will always remain unsaid. Moments that hurt will never be examined or explained. 'I know it's difficult. I'm sure she knew you loved her.'

She cries harder at that and I see, from across the way, Devon look over. Then he turns again, unable to cope with her grief as well as whatever he's feeling. I let Megan cry herself out until, at last, she stops, like a car running out of petrol. 'I'm sorry,' she says again, wiping her eyes, which are red and swollen. 'What was it you were asking?'

'Just about anyone who might have held a grudge against your sister.'

'I don't know.'

'What about Devon's dad?'

'Sure none of us knows who he is.'

'She never said or gave a hint?'

'No.' It's abrupt and final. 'She wouldn't talk about it. All I remember was that my poor mother was up to here,' she taps her forehead, 'with the whole thing. Poor Maudie was in bits.' And then she starts to cry all over again.

'Maudie?' That's Sandra's aunt. 'Why would Maudie be so upset?'

'Sandra lived with her and Uncle Dom after Daddy died. Mammy couldn't cope with her.'

That's right. I remember now.

I wait again until she's calmer, then ask, 'Would you have an address for Sandra? Where did she live when she wasn't at home?'

'I can't remember the exact address, though it was nearer here. I know she wrote it down for me to give Devon and I told her . . .' Her voice hitches and she swallows. 'I was mean and sure now . . .' She wipes her face with the sleeve of her jacket.

I wait for a moment before asking if she could hunt down the address for me. 'And any other addresses you have for her.'

'I'm not sure, I could have thrown them out.'

'When did you last see your sister?'

'Yesterday. I was in the house yesterday. About four.'

'And was she all right?'

'Jumpy, the usual. Unable to settle.'

'And Devon?'

'Devon,' she calls across, 'when did you last see Sandra and how was she?'

He crosses back to us, shoots a look at his aunt, hesitates, mutters into the collar of his jacket, 'Maybe two days ago at home.'

'That's right,' Megan agrees, 'after she called and moaned that someone had been messing about in the garden.' A sniff. 'As if she'd even pay attention to the garden.' Then a swallow. 'I'm sorry.'

I jot the details down and tell them I'll be in touch.

I'm leaving for the station when my phone rings. 'DS Lucy Golden.'

'Aren't you awful official!' Dan laughs. 'I was setting up the incident room here and Jordy came in. He said something interesting.'

Jordy is the oldest guard in Achill. Shambling, unkempt, with a constant fug of cigarette smoke around him, he's also pretty sharp in a very lackadaisical way. He can drop vital bits of information into an investigation without seeming to realise their value. And he knows everyone in the place, even better than my mother does. 'Go on,' I say.

'He recognised our IP and not because she was once a local but because she was into the station on Saturday making a report.'

'Yeah?'

'She told him she thought someone was watching her.'

4

When I get back to the station, the whiteboard has been set up in the incident room with a blown-up picture of our IP taken from her Instagram page. She looks stunning there. Photoshopped and filtered, her skin is reduced to a creamy white, the masses of freckles deadened. Her hair hangs in loose, tumbling curls around her shoulders and her teeth are a bleached white. Her eyes, though, have a strangeness about them, as if she's not quite present. As if nothing about her is real.

Most of the team have assembled, which I'm glad to see. We've worked two big cases together in the past eighteen months or so, the last of which is still unravelling as more and more money and evidence are uncovered by the Garda National Economic Crime Bureau. I like the guys on the team. Mick, skinny, nervy, jangly as ever, leans against the window. I haven't seen him since our last case. He's laughing at something Larry is saying about some GAA team or other. Larry is the stereotypical cop: he's full of macho arrogance, a player, a breaker of hearts but a whiz on CCTV. He has the focus to spend hours upon hours looking at cars going up and down roads or people window-shopping. Dan once joked with me that it was because there is nothing else in

Larry's brain and sometimes I think it's true. Dan, my best friend in the force, is there, setting up the room with Kev, who's hoping to be appointed to detective officer in the next few months. He'll get it too. Kev is one of the smartest guards I've come across in my time in the force. And he's prepared to put the work in. A buckshee detective, he goes above and beyond, is worked like a dog, but seems to love it. As he and Dan set up the laptop and attach the wires, I hear him telling Dan about this girl he's just met online. Her name is Kylie and she's from Ballina. 'I think she likes that I'm a guard,' he says, 'because she gets me to send her photographs of me in my uniform.'

'I'm no expert on heterosexual relationships,' Dan says back, flicking on the laptop, 'but isn't it more normal to swap pictures of ye both with your clothes off?'

The room erupts in laughter.

Kev blushes to the tips of his hair. 'Have some respect,' he snaps. 'Kylie isn't that sort of girl.'

'What? Normal?' Larry calls across.

'We're not all sex maniacs,' Kev says. 'And I'm not telling ye any more about her.' But he's grinning.

Now some hotshots from the National Bureau of Criminal Investigations arrive in. Murder is always news and sometimes you'll get people coming into the first murder conference to hear details or just to offer a hand. While I'm grateful to see them, I don't want them trampling all over us either.

'Is Jordy around?' I ask Larry.

'Here,' Jordy calls, shuffling over with a slim file in his hands. It's the report that Sandra made yesterday. 'I just had a quick reread of it there.'

'Good job recognising her,' I say, taking it from him and

24

carrying it to one of the tables to read it for myself. Jordy stands by my shoulder, his breathing laboured.

I glance at him in concern.

'Just ran up the stairs,' he says, patting his stomach for some reason. 'I'm not fit.'

Of course it's nothing to do with the chain-smoking, I think in semi-amusement. I turn back to the report. Jordy's writing is small and cramped and he doesn't seem to believe in keeping it on the lines. I have to not-see it to see it. 'Is this up on Pulse?' I ask. 'It might be easier to read.'

'Not yet.' He winces. 'It was only yesterday evening and I didn't have time.'

This station is not exactly busy.

'I was going to do it this morning but Marie Mullen called,' he says, picking up on my thoughts. 'You know her from Dugort. She's the daughter of James Mullen, who played for Mayo in the sixties. Well, didn't her husband come back from the pub drunk out of his head last night, roaring and shouting. She wanted me to be with her today when he woke up, so I drove over there and had breakfast and, sure, he was still asleep and then she gave me lunch and—'

I hold up my hand. 'Enough.'

'And I'm managing the station on me own what with Matt off on his winter holiday.'

'All right.' I pass him the report. 'Can you summarise it at conference?'

'I can.'

'Thanks.' I move up the room to join Dan. 'William is on his way,' I say. 'He should be here about—'

I don't get to finish because William appears. He chats briefly to some of the detectives on the door before greeting our team with a quick 'Hello,' even including Mick in it, which must show he's finally forgiven Mick and Susan for fecking up in court a few years back. Come to think of it, where is Susan? My eyes slide to the door. It's not like her to be late.

'All right,' William says. 'You're all very welcome. I just—'

There's a commotion as Susan, red-faced and gasping, pushes her way in.

William stops talking.

The whole room turns to stare.

Susan freezes like a rabbit about to be run over by a truck.

'You're late,' William says pleasantly.

'Yes, sorry.' She flushes. 'I had trouble parking. I'll just . . .' She scurries to a seat. 'Sorry.'

He waits another moment or two, just enough for us all to grow uncomfortable and Susan to blush harder. 'As I was saying,' William goes on, 'you're all welcome. I just want to give a run-down on what we have so far before we kick off, make sure we're all on the same page. This morning, at five past ten, the body of a thirty-nine-year-old woman was discovered by her son in a house near Dugort Pier.' He points to the picture of Sandra, alongside a blown-up map of the area. 'Her name is Sandra Byrne and she has been living off the island for approximately twenty-four years. Her family, including her son, had very little contact with her, as far as we know. She had come home for her mother's funeral and was living in her mother's house until it sold. The last sighting of her was last night at approximately twelve forty-five in a taxi. She was accompanied by a man whom we have traced and who has voluntarily agreed to be interviewed tomorrow in Westport.'

I'm glad he hasn't mentioned Ben's name, I'd have a hard time believing that Ben is the culprit. His wife was a weapon, and although the split was acrimonious, there was never a sniff of violence. Though one thing I have learned in this job is that you never know what goes on behind closed doors. Still, Ben . . .

I tune back in as he gives a briefing on how our suspected offender might have travelled to Sandra's property. 'He could have come on foot, by car or indeed by boat. We'll be harvesting CCTV from everywhere on the island. Unfortunately, there is none at the pier so we'll need interviews with anyone who uses it to see if they spotted anything unusual. Now, Dan, if you could read Palmer's preliminary PM report, please.'

Standing, Dan reads, '"On Friday the thirteenth of January last, at ten-oh-five a.m. I examined, in situ, the body of a woman, late thirties, in the back bedroom of her house in Dugort, Achill Island. She was positioned on her stomach, her head turned to the right. There is bruising to her left wrist and what appears to be sharp force trauma to the back of the head, which had bled profusely. Due to the nature of the bleeding, I can conclude that these injuries were sustained peri-mortem. From the state of decomposition, I estimate the time of death to be between seven o'clock the previous evening to five o'clock the following morning, as rigor mortis was not complete. Lividity was consistent with the IP having died in situ. The PM will take place once the body has been moved to the mortuary."' Dan sits down.

'I'll be attending the PM along with Kevin,' William says.

Lucky Kevin, I think wryly, stealing a glance at him.

He doesn't seem all that bothered, just nods and gives the Cig the thumbs-up. No one else would get away with doing that and, indeed, William stiffens slightly beside me but doesn't mention it.

Instead, he turns to me. 'Lucy, could you give everyone a sum-mary of what you managed to find out this morning?'

'Sure.' I stand now and run through what I saw at the crime scene and how the blood sample from the windowsill is gone for forensic analysis, as is the hair found on the T-shirt. I move on to my interview with Megan and Devon. 'In short,' I finish, 'Megan maintains that they had very little contact with Sandra over the years, though obviously she was in their lives a lot in the past week, helping pack up the house after their mother's death. Megan thinks that Sandra had recently moved to some-where more local. She will provide us with any addresses she has for her as soon as she can. Once Sandra's image is released to the media, I'm sure we'll be able to trace her present address. Megan was also under the impression that Sandra worked in a shop but that she may have left it.'

'We retrieved her phone from the scene, and it's being exam-ined now,' William says. 'It might give us more information to go on. Anything else?'

'Yes. Apparently, she came into the station yesterday to make a complaint. She thought she was being watched.' That causes a stir. 'Jordy?'

Huffing, puffing and snorting, Jordy gets to his feet. He sniffs loudly, coughs chestily, then picks up his report. 'Right. Well, Sandra Byrne came in at four yesterday, and she appeared to be a bit agitated, sort of all over the place, her mind not quite settling on anything, d'you understand me,' Jordy says, but it's not a ques-tion. 'It was hard trying to get any sort of an account out of her but, anyway, this is what I took down. "Sandra Byrne, presently living in Dugort Pier House, Achill Island, arrived into the sta-tion at sixteen hundred hours on the twelfth of January. She stated that she was being watched. She said that at first she thought she was imagining it, but then she started taking a note of all the little things that were happening."' Jordy pulls out a list. 'This here is the list she made.' Once more he bends to read it. '"Jan seventh, shrubs pulled up during the night. Jan eighth, a broken window when I came back from a night out. A dead cat in the driveway. Jan tenth things moved in the house."' Jordy looks up. 'Then when I asked her if she had any idea who it might be, she said she thought she knew who it was, but when she checked his social media, it wasn't. Honestly,' he says, 'I didn't take it seriously. Up there, people throw stuff from passing cars all the time. The cat could easily have been run over by someone and just pushed in off the road. And she admitted that the window that broke had been cracked anyway. I did tell her I'd be out today to have a look around and I would have . . .' He heaves a sigh. 'Maybe I should have moved on it yesterday.'

'None of us would have done anything different,' I tell him, and although he knows it, it's going to hit him hard if it turns out that she was being watched. As I say it, something shakes loose in my head. Something Megan said that doesn't add up. I'll be calling out to her again anyway and will ask her about it then.

'If anyone was watching her, there should be evidence of some sort around the house and grounds,' William says. 'I'll ask SOCO to keep it in mind and also check any reports in the area. In the meantime, if this turns out to be foul play, I want to know everything about this woman. What did she do on her last day? Who did she meet? Who did she talk to? I want to know where she lived before this. I want to know about her job, her relationships. Everything. This was a person who only last night was out having fun.' He turns to Larry. 'If we manage to get Sandra's locations from her phone, I want you to harvest CCTV from everywhere she went in the twenty-four hours. We know she spent her last hours in the Seafarer pub in Westport, so request CCTV from the pub as well as from any business in the area. We'll put out an appeal for dash-cam footage. We know she was alive at twelve forty-five this morning so we're fortunate in that the window for the time of death is narrow. Was she being followed? If so, let's see if we can spot it.'

'On it,' Larry says.

'Mick?'

'Yes!' Mick is startled at being addressed so early on and his 'yes' comes out as a shout. A titter runs around the room.

William ignores it. 'Tic-tac with Forensics. Put the pressure on. Anything you get, bring it to me or Lucy. It's likely they might have something by tomorrow.'

'Yes,' he says again, slightly more muted.

'Pat, I want the IP's phone records examined and anything significant reported to Lucy or myself. If there was a fitness app or a location app, give the details to the incident room so they can job it out.'

'I'm on it already,' Pat says smartly. 'The text and phone records came down about an hour ago.'

'Good.' William flashes a rare smile of approval. 'There will be a press conference tonight at seven in time for the nine o'clock news. Lucy and Dan, I want you both there. As for now, until we get CCTV and anything Forensics or the phone records throw up, door-to-door is our best bet. Susan, you're trained on door-to-door?'

'Yes.' Her face drops a bit.

'Get started on that as soon as possible. Bring the questionnaire to Lucy before you go haring off. I want all houses within a three-mile radius in all directions canvassed for starters. Brian, I want you answering phones as well as whatever is on your job sheet, all right?'

'Sure.'

'Kev,' William goes on, 'I want you down to the Seafarer pub to talk to staff. See if they can remember anything. As before, Jim D'arcy will be incident-room co-ordinator. You'll get the job sheets from him and return them to him when the job is completed. Having worked with ye all before, I know I have no need to say that all information here will be shared, no keeping juicy bits for yourself. And I know I have no need to tell you all not to assume anything.'

'He's telling us, though, isn't he?' Dan whispers.

I splutter out a laugh, which causes William to turn towards me.

'Something you'd like to add?' he says.

Christ, he has it in for me today. 'Actually, yes,' I say, surprising him and shocking myself.

William, an eyebrow quirked, signals, with the tiniest hand gesture, for me to go ahead. I stand up slowly, aware that I need to claw back a bit of respect from this man. I need him to believe that I can do this investigation without any prejudice. I buy a few moments, looking at my colleagues, the team William has assembled over the past eighteen months. The man who rarely smiles, the man looking right at me with his ice-blue eyes, has brought us all together, shaped us, made us a unit. 'Detective Inspector William Williams is right,' I say, somehow finding the right words despite my panic. I ignore the sniggers of the blow-in guards who haven't heard William's full name before,

31

'There is no need for him to tell you these things. We've handled two challenging cases so far and the work has been impeccable. I know that you won't assume. I know that you won't hoard. I know that this will be an exhaustive investigation run to the highest standards. If this woman was murdered, we owe it to her family to find out how and why and bring a criminal to justice.' I let the words settle, then sit down, half afraid to look at William and definitely not wanting to catch Dan's eye.

'We'll meet again tomorrow night,' William's voice cuts through the ensuing silence. 'But in the meantime keep tic-tacking with each other with anything you find out. Lucy, Dan, Larry, come with me.' So saying he stalks out of the room, shiny shoes making clipping sounds on the old wooden floor.

5

William always uses the front room on the top floor of the garda station as his office when he comes to Achill. It's the biggest space with a killer view towards the ocean. On a clear day, you can see Saula on the east of the island. Today, though, the weather is grey and spitting rain, tiny flecks of which land silently on the window outside and streak down, like tears. It's the sort of dull go-nowhere day when island living can be particularly depressing. The office is bare, as if William hasn't unpacked himself into it yet. The only thing on show is his travelling bonsai tree, which sits proudly in the centre of the windowsill. It's grown a bit in the last six months, which was when I last saw it. Its tiny branches spread outwards; its gnarled trunk twists every which way.

When we make it to the end of this investigation, I swear I'll ask him what the hell it means to him. He's never told anyone as far as I know.

'Sit,' he says, and, like obedient puppies, the three of us plonk down onto the three chairs that face the desk. William studies us all for a second, then leans across the desk towards us, hands clasped. 'This is tricky,' he says. 'As you know, Ben has admitted that he was with Sandra Byrne until almost one a.m. on the night she died. He maintains that he left her at home and only spent ten minutes in the house. He's going to be interviewed in Westport tomorrow by two detectives from outside the area. Lucy and Dan, ye might as well look on, see if you can offer anything.'

'Grand,' Dan agrees easily.

'I need your assurances that you'll all handle this case without prejudice.' He looks at me. 'We follow the facts, not our hearts.'

That is aimed at me because of my hesitation earlier. I flinch.

'We'll treat Ben like any suspect,' Larry says. 'It's no secret we all like the guy – hell, I've worked a few cases with him – but we're professionals, you know that.'

'Lucy?'

'Of course I'll be professional,' I answer, a bit sharper than I meant to. 'And just FYI, the sister, Megan? She was a good friend of mine growing up. We lost touch years ago, but I was fond of her and I'll do anything to get justice for her. I'm not going to prejudice the case.' Then I realise how that sounds. 'In either direction,' I clarify. 'For Ben or for her and—'

'Fine,' William interrupts. 'I'll see you and Dan at six thirty down at Dugort Pier, suited and booted and looking like proper detectives. Larry, go and harvest the CCTV.'

We all hot-foot it out of there.

6

Before the press conference, Dan and I grab a bite to eat in McLoughlin's bar in Achill Sound. As we wait for our food orders to arrive, I tell him I want to go back and talk to Megan again to double-check what she told me that morning.

Dan frowns. 'You think she could be a suspect?'

'The families are always suspects, aren't they?' I say. 'And, by the sound of things, she and Sandra had grown apart. Both she and Devon admitted that they're half relieved she's dead, which is awful, isn't it? We need to check their alibis anyway.'

'What's the story with her? How do you know her?'

'She's Achill, like me. We hung about together in secondary school.'

The waiter arrives then, a spotty, gangly youth, with a beaming face. 'Burger and chips for you,' he says cheerily, laying the plate before me. 'And a ham sandwich for you.' After giving Dan his food, he bounces back up the room in squeaky white runners.

'A ham sandwich? Are you not hungry?' I pick up a tomato-sauce sachet and begin to do battle with it.

'Fran has made a curry for when I get in,' Dan answers.

'You'd eat a curry late at night?' I squirt tomato sauce onto my chips, pick up another sachet.

'Best time to eat a curry.'

'If I ate a curry late, I'd be up half the night drinking Gaviscon.' More squirting of sauce. Yum.

'If I ate that much tomato sauce, I'd be up half the night worrying about the planet's supply of tomatoes.'

'Ha-ha.'

Dan chuckles and we turn to our food. In two bites, his sandwich is gone. I catch him looking longingly at my chips.

'Just take some,' I grumble, as I pour half of them onto his plate.

'Ta.' He throws me a wink. 'Did you like her?' he asks, popping a chip into his mouth. 'Megan?'

'Back then, I did. I barely know her now.'

'And Sandra?'

I shrug. 'I didn't know her at all. She was five, six years younger than us, the annoying kid sister always getting into trouble.' I think about this. 'Maybe we'd call it ADD, these days. But from what Megan said earlier, she doesn't seem to have changed.'

'We can't just go on what she says.' Dan chews the last chip on his plate. 'You know when you go back home it's like you revert.'

'I must be permanently reverted,' I mutter. It comes out a little bitter. I didn't mean it to.

'Aw, now, stop. Your ma is fantastic.' Then, with bite, he adds, 'You don't need to revert. She lets you be who you are.'

As opposed to Dan's parents, who can't accept that he's gay. And though I know it hurts him still, he's normally chill enough about it, mostly brushing it off with a joke. 'Who's pulled your chain?'

'Nobody.' He glowers at his empty plate. 'I just . . . Well, you're lucky, that's all.'

I wait a couple of moments, sipping my water, letting the silence develop. 'I am,' I admit. 'So, what's happened?'

He glances up, huffs out a sigh, 'I suppose you'll find out some-time,' he says. 'Me auld fella is dying. My sister rang me yesterday.'

'Aw, Dan . . .'

'Lung cancer, apparently. Not surprising since he smokes about sixty a day.'

'I'm sorry.'

He shrugs, seems about to say something, then thinks better of it. Instead, he glances at his phone. 'We'd better get going. Can't be late for the press conference.'

So saying, he jumps up and heads for the door.

The fine drizzle has turned into steadier rain, and along the pier, the wind is brewing up a storm. The slap of water against the sides of the two boats berthed there, along with the clinking of moorings, carries across to where William, Dan and I are facing into a blaze of TV lights and microphones. It's a dark night but the moon rides high and I can't help thinking that the effect will be quite ghostly on the late-evening news.

'All right,' someone says. 'Are we ready?'

I'm never ready for these things. I become way too conscious of my facial expressions. Obviously I can't look happy, but when I try to be serious, I just end up appearing dour and ridiculously rigid, like a figure hewn from granite. There is no way anyone would approach me with sensitive information. They'd rather take their chances with a hungry shark. I always try to hide in the background. Tonight, though, William wants me at his left shoulder and Dan by his right. I can only admire his grace and poise as he stands, totally at ease, in front of the camera. He's wearing a suit and doesn't even have the warmth of a coat. I'm shivering already.

'All right,' someone says. 'We're rolling.'

'The woman's body found today in a house in Dugort, Achill, has been identified as Sandra Byrne.' William holds up a picture of Sandra. 'It is important to state that, as of yet, we do not know how Sandra died. This will change with the results of the post-mortem tomorrow. However, we would appeal to anyone who knew Sandra or who has been in contact with her in the past while to call our confidential line.' He gives out the number. 'Or indeed call into Achill garda station. We are anxious to establish a timeline for Sandra's movements in the hours and days before she died. We appeal to anyone who thinks they may have information to come forward. Thank you.'

And that's it. Thankfully, it's done in one take, and as the press disband, after they've taken their pictures and tried their best to get extra information from us, I can go home.

It's been a long day.

Just as I'm about to leave, William's phone pings. He reads the text, 'Blood on the windowsill is animal in origin,' he says to me. 'And recent.'

'Interesting. Maybe put there to freak her out. And if it was recent, maybe whoever put it there was present when she was murdered.'

'We need to find out who had a grudge against her. Dig into her as deep as you can.' He pockets his phone and tells me to get on home.

7

'Sandra Byrne,' my mother says to me, as I almost crawl with tiredness through the door. 'Sandra Byrne.'

'I know.' I take my coat off. 'Any chance of a cuppa?' I head for the kitchen as she follows.

'And in Pauline's own house,' my mother goes on, as if I haven't just been investigating the case all day. 'And Devon the boy that found her, and poor Megan having to go and identify her.'

'Yes, it's terrible.' I flick on the kettle.

'And there you were, only telling me last night that one of your guard friends went home with her, and how you and all the other guards were laughing about it. Wouldn't he be a suspect now?'

My hand stills on the mug I'd been about to pull out of the press. I close my eyes, try for calm. 'You haven't been going saying that around the place, have you?' I turn to her.

She's standing there with her mouth open, looking a bit guilty. 'Well . . . I'm not sure . . . you were the one . . .'

Deep breaths, Lucy, I tell myself. 'Tell me you didn't go about telling all and sundry that maybe a guard was the last person to be seen with Sandra?' I am appalled. I should have thought of this, of course I should. I'm suddenly weak. 'Jesus, I have to sit down.' I stagger to a chair and place my head in my hands. 'Who have you told?'

'Not all and sundry,' she says. Then, in a watery voice, 'I probably only told Frank at the butcher's when I went in to get some sausages. I only went to Frank because the sausages I got in the other place last week were—'

'You told Frank?' Frank is probably the biggest gossip on the island. Well, no, his wife probably is. No, actually, my mother bloody is.

'I might have,' she clarifies, sliding into a chair opposite me, a bit stricken. 'We talked for a while, sure the news was all over the place. And poor Sandra, murdered in her mother's house.'

'We don't know that she was murdered.' It's my own fault, I should never have told her about Saturday night, but there is always a high when cases make court and I'd been only too eager to share details of Ben because, truth be told, I was delighted for the poor sucker. His wife, whom I'd never met, was a horrible woman by all accounts: she'd seduced him, bled him dry, taken his children from him, and it was good to see him with someone. And now . . . I rally. 'Mam, you can't tell anyone else about Ben,' I say. 'It's not fair on him. He might have done nothing. It'll prejudice a trial as well if it gets out. And you'll have to go and tell Frank to keep his trap shut.'

'I didn't realise it was a big deal. And, well . . .' She swallows, and I know more bad news is heading my way. 'Well, I think there might have been a few people in the shop at the time, when I said it, so you know . . .'

'Oh, God.'

'I'm sorry.'

I can't speak. William will go ballistic.

'I can make you a sandwich if you like.'

I'm unsure if the sandwich is part of the apology or not but, feck it, there's nothing I can do. The damage is done. 'Grand. Thanks.'

She stands up. 'I am sorry, pet. I suppose what with it being Megan's sister and she being such a great friend of yours and—'

'Back in the day,' I say. 'I barely know her now.'

'Aw, she hasn't changed. Still the dependable one. Sure, she had to be with her parents drinking day and night.'

'What?'

'She's the dependable one.'

'No. What you said . . . her parents drank?'

'Do you not know this?' At my blank look, she flaps a hand. 'Sure how would you, I suppose. You were only young that time and no one really talked about it. But Pauline and the husband were both terrible for the drink. Sure isn't that what happened to him? Fell down the stairs, half cut. And sure that made Pauline drink all the harder. It's a wonder Megan turned out as well as she did. But then, sure, after the death, Pauline couldn't manage Sandra and Megan was about to get married, so Maudie and Dom took over and found it terrible hard going.'

Maudie and Dom, Sandra's unmarried aunt and uncle, lived in the family home. Maudie, a secondary-school teacher, had terrified me when she'd taught me business for the Leaving. She'd told me to let her know whenever I opened a business because, in the interests of public safety, she would advise people not to touch it with a barge pole. I'd hated her. She'd been engaged to be married when I knew her but that had fallen apart sometime afterwards. Dom, a one-time fisherman, had left the house years ago to work up in Dublin somewhere. He hadn't married either, as far as I knew.

'Maudie and Dom were terrible good to poor Pauline at that time, taking little Sandra in,' my mother continues. 'Still, I'd say it was hard on the child, being handed over.'

And yet Sandra had done it to her own son. Talk about history repeating itself.

'I never knew they drank.'

'Pauline straightened out in recent years. I think it was for the benefit of the young lad. He was the makings of her. She adored that boy.' She shakes her head. 'Poor Megan. First her mother dies, then her sister. And, sure, poor Devon too. I called Luc to let him know, but he said he'd seen it on the internet.'

Luc, my son, is in his second year at college. There was some uncertainty about him going at all because he is the father of a two-year-old adorable messer frighteningly called Sirocco. But his girlfriend's mother, Katherine, and my mother, take turns caring for her during term time so that both Luc and Tani can get their degrees. I mind her whenever I can, which isn't that often as the job swallows everything. Still, after a hard day in work, returning home to Sirocco is one of the joys in my life, even if she does scream when she doesn't get her own way, and say, 'Shit!' really loudly if she drops something. Luc, my mother and I think it's hilarious, Katherine not so much. Tani's father, Johnny, helps out too, though he's recently taken up residence in a grotty rented apartment in Westport, having been kicked out by Katherine for sleeping with a work colleague. He tends to take Sirocco for day trips, feed her full of shit and return her, bloated and cranky, to his wife.

But there is no doubt that Sirocco makes us all better people.

I think about that as I chew the cheese and ham sandwich my mother places in front of me along with a cup of tea. It's what having Devon as a grandchild had obviously done to Pauline Byrne. She'd stopped drinking because Devon had come into her life. Or at least tried to stop drinking: I'm sure it hadn't been as easy as that.

'Luc says he'll be back for the funeral whenever it is,' my mother says, as she puts the ham, cheese and mayo back into the fridge. 'He says he'll call Devon, which I thought was nice.'

My mother thinks everything Luc does is great.

'Enjoy the sandwich and good night.' My mother bends to kiss the top of my head. 'And don't worry about Frank. I'll tell him I made a mistake.'

'Don't. You'll only make it worse.' My mother is not a good liar. She'll end up over-explaining. 'Just leave it.'

'All right, if you're sure.' She sounds incredibly doubtful.

'I am.'

'Okay.' Still that doubt. 'I'll be off to bed so. I'll see you tomorrow.'

'See you.'

And I'm left alone for the first time that day, the silence of the night pushing against the walls of the house. The faint heave of the sea out beyond the road.

I fall asleep at the table.

8

She had done him a big wrong all them years ago, he thinks, as he slides into his tent, pulling his sleeping-bag up around him. The breeze cuts sharper than a knife, but once he zips up the bag, he feels warmer. As he stares up at the fabric, which dips and moves in the wind, he inhales deeply. It relaxes him, the breathing. He'd learned that during his stint in prison. Breathe deeply into your stomach, through the nose. Breathe out through your mouth. Relax. It was a handy thing to know.

It had begun, he thought, the reckoning. People always had to pay for making other people suffer.

And he had only begun to take his revenge. Slow and steady.

Slow and steady wins the race.

Years he'd been planning this. Ever since he was young and she'd messed with his head. Ever since he was denied watching his boy grow and thrive. And though some might argue that it hadn't really been her doing, he knew it was. She was to blame. Her and that other fellow.

He'll do it through the son. That was where it would hurt most, he reckoned.

9

14 January

The next morning, my stupid car won't start for me. I suppose it's hardly surprising seeing as it's failed every annual NCT test at least twice before passing third time lucky. It's failed on brakes, on lights, on seatbelts. It never sounds quite healthy, even when it does get going, but I'm stupidly attached to it. Getting rid of it is an affront to me, this car that has served me well just abandoned to the scrapheap. I pop open the bonnet and stare bemused at the engine. Quite why I've done that, I'm not sure.

There is a wire poking loose, though I don't know what it's meant to be attached to, so I give it a bit of a prod and slam the bonnet closed again.

'Mam,' I head back into the house and knock gently on my mother's door, 'can I take your car this morning? Mine is out of action. If you get a chance, will you call Barney at the garage and ask him to take a look at it for me?'

'I might ask him to take it away too,' she grumbles, sitting up in the bed, rubbing her eyes. 'Honestly, Lucy, that car is a death trap.'

'Thanks.' I blow her a kiss and am gone.

My mother has always had a thing for cars. Hers is a nifty little top-end Fiesta with satnav and air-con. I don't even have to slam on the brakes to get the car to stop. I hadn't realised how bad my fifteen-year-old Micra was. Despite the angry black clouds rolling in over the sea and the spatter of fat raindrops on the windscreen, it's quite the pleasure to drive it from Achill to Westport. The heater in this car actually blows out hot air, and the volume on the radio can be adjusted. The wipers glide silently across the windscreen without making a fuss. Driving this car is like going from a student bedsit to the Burlington Hotel.

The roads are quiet as I leave the island and drive towards Mulranney. Fields, burned brown and winter orange, lie long to my left, and to my right the smash of the ocean, like a hungry monster, always waiting to be fed. Up ahead, the road stretches like a ribbon, the horizon of tarmac meeting with the black march of the clouds. In parts, the road criss-crosses with the Greenway, but no one is on it today. I always think that this time of the year, just after midwinter, is a great time to see the west, because the skies are a drama all their own.

I drive into Newport, over the Newport river, passing the playground and on. The news at eight, and Sandra Byrne is the top story. To my relief, there is nothing on a member of the force being interviewed about her. If Ben was to be identified on social media, there would be a field day. Once again, the appeal for people to come forward is made, William's voice calm and in control. The item is followed by the price of heating your home this winter. The road narrows and widens again. The rain gets heavier and the car is buffeted by the wind. I eventually arrive in Westport, the statue of St Patrick barely visible through the rain. Another statue had once stood atop that plinth, but during the civil war, the free-state troops had taken pot shots at it and blown off its head. Now St Patrick stands proudly up there, covered with bird shit. I park the car and, rain-jacket over my head, I leg it into the station.

This is where I usually work from.

'DG Ben Lively is due in for interview in thirty minutes,' the sergeant in charge tells me. 'Dan is just gone in ahead.'

'Do we know who is interviewing him?'

He thumbs through some paperwork. 'DS Peter Glynn and DG June White, both from Dublin.'

I don't know those detectives, which, I suppose, is good for the investigation. I grab a cup of coffee and join Dan in the obser-vation room. He's nursing his own coffee, staring through the one-way glass into the room that Ben will shortly be led into.

Neither of us say anything, both of us feel shit for Ben, but he knows it's procedure. I'd expect to be treated the same if I was a suspect. To my surprise William arrives in a few moments later.

''Bout time you got a new car,' he says, as he takes a seat.

'You got a new car?' Dan looks affronted that I didn't run it by him first. 'I could've—'

'It's my mother's,' I interject. 'Mine is off the road today.'

Thankfully, before either of them can make a smart remark on my decrepit car, Ben is led into the interview room. He looks scattered - though, in fairness, he always looks a bit scattered. Trousers too big, shirt hanging out. Tie askew. He sits and rubs a palm over his unkempt hair.

The two detectives take a seat opposite. Peter Glynn looks familiar and I flinch when I recall that he was one of the detec-tives who was on the investigation with me when it turned out my own husband, Rob, was the perpetrator. How could I have forgotten that? Although there's a lot about that time I'm sure I've blanked from memory.

I don't know June White at all. She's young, eager and fresh-faced. I'd imagine the lads at the station think they can run rings around her: she's got this sweet innocence, even in the way she moves. It probably works to her advantage in interviews because she's obviously not like that or she wouldn't be here.

Peter is all business and, after flipping on the DVD, he introduces himself and June before cautioning Ben in a brisk, no-nonsense way. 'Tell us about the night of the twelfth of January, Mr Lively, in your own words.'

Because Ben is a guard, he knows how to give a proper account. So, he takes the night step by step, naming us, naming the bar, meeting Sandra. 'She seemed like a bit of a laugh,' he says, 'and she was good-looking, plus she seemed interested in me, so when she suggested that we go back to her place, I thought, Yeah, great, why not? It was only about midnight. Neither of us was fit to drive so we caught a taxi back to her mother's house. She'd been buried a week before that, she told me. Taxi Joe's was the firm I called. Just down the road there. I didn't catch the driver's name, but it was a black Passat. He was young enough, I'd say thirties. He had red hair, shorn, and there was some kind of a mole or freckle on his left cheek. He drove us to Dugort – that's where the mother's house was. Sandra said they were in the process of packing it up. The house was about five hundred metres from the little pier, isolated enough. The taxi driver let us out, just at the gate of the house, and drove off. I walked with Sandra up her driveway. She was staggering a bit and had trouble getting her key in the door. It was dark, the porch light was broken, so I got out my mobile phone and put on my torch

48

for her. She was actually very drunk so I had to take the key from her, put it in the lock and let us in. At that stage, I was having doubts. I mean, she was pretty bad, could hardly stand up, you know?

'Anyway, next thing is, she directs me to the sitting room, saying she was going to grab a bottle of wine from the fridge. I told her that maybe she'd had enough, that maybe we both had had enough but she got all upset and said it was important that I stayed. I had to stay, she said. I said maybe I'd just have the one, maybe that I'd see her tomorrow. She said she was going to get the wine anyway and that I could fuck off if I wanted and, sure, I didn't quite know what to do then. I ended up just standing, half in, half out of the sitting room and watched her storm off into the kitchen. Then I went into the sitting room, wandered around it for a bit, looking at stuff. Then I came out, made the decision to leave when I heard a lot of noise coming from the kitchen. I thought I'd better have a look. She didn't notice me. She was just pulling all sorts of things out of the press. And then she screams and puts her head into her hands and I thought, Jaysus, she's totally out of it, and so, well, I just left.' He stops.

'What do you mean, you just left?' Peter asks.

'I mean that I waited until she seemed to have forgotten I was there and then I snuck out.' He looks down at his hands. 'I'm not proud of it, but it was better than sleeping with her. That would have been wrong. Honestly, I thought she'd taken some sort of a drug at that stage.' His eyes dart towards the reflective glass, where we are and I involuntary pull back, much to Dan's amusement. 'She was going a bit mad in the kitchen.'

'Was she?' Peter taps his fingers on the table. 'Let's get this straight, then, shall we? You're saying that you and Sandra left the Seafarer pub at a quarter to midnight and caught a taxi from Taxi Joe's?'

'Yes.'

'What time did you arrive at Sandra's house?'

'Her mother's house,' Ben corrects. 'It's about an hour at the best of times so I'd say about twelve forty to one o'clock.'

'How long were you inside the house?'

Ben shrugs. 'About fifteen minutes.'

'I see.'

I know what he's thinking. I'd be thinking the same. It's enough time to assault someone.

'She was in the kitchen destroying the place when I left her,' Ben says again. 'I never laid a finger on her.'

'You're saying that the kitchen was not destroyed in the assault?'

'I don't know what the kitchen looked like after the assault. I just know she was going ballistic tearing it apart when I left.'

Peter nods affably. 'I see.' A moment. 'How did you get home?'

'I didn't. Not that night. I walked to a friend of mine who lives in Tonregee.'

'That's a long walk.'

'About twenty K or so. It took me around three hours.'

'You walked for three hours?' Peter looks sceptical. 'Why?'

'My phone died, so I couldn't ring for a taxi. I would have tried to hitch, but the roads were quiet. I knew my friend had a shed in his back garden and I made for there. I slept in it and he drove me back home the next morning.'

'So, you have no alibi at all for that night?'

'No, other than hoping that some cars or CCTV at the bridge might have spotted me on the road.'

Oh, shit, Ben, I think.

'Would you have the name and address of that friend?'

'Sure.' Ben rattles it off. His posture is easy, though, relaxed as much as he can be. His eye contact looks good, but then again, he knows what we look out for.

'And the clothes you were wearing that night, where are they?'

'I brought them in yesterday when I called into the station. Unfortunately, my friend's wife had washed them because they'd taken a soaking. I showered in their house and borrowed some of my friend's things.'

'And your shoes?'

'I threw them out. They were destroyed by the rain.'

Peter says nothing. June continues to scribble down the interview. And I know that if it was me in there, I'd be thinking, *Convenient*. Because Ben knows, like we do, that while DNA is great evidence, it's not always possible to get it. It's not foolproof. Clothes that have been washed, shoes that have been thrown away. If only he had kept the shoes, the lack of DNA might have helped him, because it would have been impossible to kill Sandra without getting blood on his shoes.

'Where did you dispose of the shoes?'

'I fired them into my friend's bin, which was collected yesterday morning.' Ben huffs out a sigh. 'I know how it looks. I know what ye're thinking, but I swear I never laid a finger on her. I'm a bloody detective, for God's sake.'

Peter says nothing to that. What is there to say? Sometimes people become guards just to learn how to commit crime. And they've always blended in. Mostly . . .

'All right,' Peter says. 'Let's go back to when you left the club with Sandra. You spent an hour with her in a taxi, right?'

'Yes.'

'Did you talk about anything?'

Once again Ben darts a look towards the reflective glass. 'Not much. But she did say something I thought was weird, but sure then I just let it go. She said that her mother was dead and that finally she was going to do what she had to do.'

'And what was that?'

'I don't know. I didn't ask. It wasn't my business.'

'Can you describe what Sandra was wearing?'

Ben does and Peter takes a note of it.

As far as I know, those clothes were located by SOCO and sent for forensics.

'Did Sandra say anything else?'

'No. Nothing else of note anyway.'

'We'll be the judge of that.'

Ben stills, and although I've only worked with him on a couple of cases, I know this is a sign that he's pissed off. 'I'm a detective,' he says, the words grinding out. 'I know what's important.'

Peter waits a moment, to let Ben's rage simmer down a bit. 'Ben Lively, as of last night, you are a person of interest in this case. What else did you talk about in the car?'

'The driver will tell us anyway,' June chimes in, her voice like a silver tinkling bell.

'Fine.' Ben shifts slightly, darts another look at the reflective glass. 'She commented on how big she thought I was going to be and I asked her if she had a ruler and she said I could be her ruler in bed and then . . .'

As Ben continues, the comments growing increasingly filthy. Dan, unable to hold it in any longer, snorts out a laugh.

'Grow up, Brown,' William says witheringly.

It's William's disapproval that sets me off and soon the two of us are giggling like schoolkids at a circus.

Still deadpan, Ben delivers the final comment, about Sandra fucking him upside down, after which he calmly folds his arms on the desk and stares at Peter.

'I'd say you were raring to have sex at that stage,' Peter says.

And bang.

Dan and I stop laughing.

William arches an eyebrow. 'You couldn't see where all that was leading?' he says to us.

In the room, Ben closes his eyes, knowing he has let emotion sink him. 'I was but I don't tend to find drunk-out-of-their-head women that arousing. I had no idea how bad she was until she tried to get into her house.'

'I see.' A pause. 'You are married, is that right, Mr Lively?'

'Separated. We're divorcing.'

June jots it down. They'll be interviewing Miranda, Ben's wife, about him.

'Bad separation?' Peter asks.

'Isn't every separation bad?' Ben asks back.

'All right, Mr Lively. June will read your memo back to you, if you agree to it, sign it please.'

While June reads, I watch as Ben, who has, up to now, sat upright and rigid, bends forward and buries his head in his hands. He knows how bad it looks for him. His DNA will be all over that house. Hopefully, it won't be in the bedroom because, according to Palmer, that was where she was murdered.

William strides from the room. 'I've a PM to attend,' he calls from the door. 'I'm sure you two have jobs on.'

In the room, Ben signs his name to the memo and is told

that he is free to leave, but if anything else comes up, he will be invited back in. I love the word 'invite': it sounds so polite and civilised but it's basically like having a choice to go to Hitler's birthday party or be shot.

Dan looks at me. 'The ex-wife will try to hang him,' he says.

He's right. 'Which is why we need to explore everything else in this case, starting with Megan and Devon.'

'Lead on, boss.'

10

Megan lives in a miserable-looking bungalow, set square in the middle of a scraggy, boggy field, with a pot-holed, stony drive-way leading to it. Our car rocks from side to side as we drive up. Sheep stare at us from tattered fields, turning back to graze on the non-existent grass. Not even the stunning beach view to the front or the spectacular view of the Booster, a.k.a. Mount Minaun, to the rear can alleviate the air of desperation about the place. Somewhere a dog barks and the sound is lonely as it whips across the landscape. The sky is the flat white of a cinema screen. Rain starts up.

How does anyone survive here?

As we park and get out of the car, feet crunching on gravel, the barking of the dog grows more furious. Someone tells the animal, 'Shut up.' It's a vicious command, born of frustration. Grief, maybe.

Devon strides around the side of the house, his hand on the dog's collar. A large breed of indeterminate nature, it strains wildly, all the while wagging its tail and howling. It looks wel-coming enough.

'It's grand,' I say, so Devon lets the dog go and the animal launches himself towards me, all eager friendship. It plants enormous paws on my chest and slams me to the ground.

The pain in my arse is instant.

'Shit! Shit! Sorry.' Devon rushes to help me up, but Dan gets there first.

'You'd want to control that animal,' he says, though I notice he's fighting hard not to laugh. I'm covered with muck and dog hair. 'You can't let it go hurling itself at people.' He pulls me up. I wipe myself down. Oh, God, my arse!

'*Tá brón orm.*' Devon does look sorry. 'Madra, sit.' The dog sits. Barking stops. It looks expectantly at Devon for a pat, which doesn't come. 'Sorry,' he says again to us. Then his eyes unexpectedly fill with tears.

Dan shifts, uncomfortable, and then, with a knack I don't have, he crosses to the dog and pats it. It wags its tail, docile now.

'Don't worry yourself over it,' I blabber. I give Devon a moment to get himself under control. And I wonder if he might say something, then think, How awful is that? To hope I can use his grief against him.

It's the job, though. It's the job to find out if the grief hides something more sinister. But if it doesn't, there's no better way to feel like a heel. After a moment, when it's clear he's not going to speak, I ask, 'We were wanting to talk to Megan?'

'She's inside with Uncle Dom. And a couple of the neighbours.'

'We'll go on in then, if that's okay?'

'Sure.' Devon holds hard to Madra as we pass.

'We can talk to Dom now too,' I say to Dan. 'Save us a journey.'

Megan is sitting at her kitchen table, surrounded by three neighbours and her uncle. They each have a cup of tea in front of them, in good china cups on good china saucers. Plates of biscuits and cakes are set out. As we walk in, conversation stops and all eyes turn in our direction. I notice that the place is stuffed with Tupperware containers of various shapes and sizes – they fill the windowsills and counter tops. It's obvious that people have been dropping food in because they feel unable to help in any other way. It's the Irish for 'I'm here if you need me'.

I have a sudden sharp memory of when my father died. I was only eight, and I really didn't have a clue what death was. I only knew that he was gone, that his body was in the front room and that everyone was having a grand time looking at him but he wasn't joining in. The pang of grief takes me by surprise. I haven't thought of Daddy in years, and if I do, it's mostly because my mother brings him up in conversation. It's the sight of the neighbours, all that food and the cups of tea that bring it back to me.

I shove the emotion down and glance about the kitchen. It's a sad affair. It looks like it hasn't been done up in years, the floor covering, a sort of beige and white lino, curling at the edges. The cooker doors are discoloured from years of use, the once yellow walls a darker yellow. It's a bit like Megan, old and square and just about functional. A trophy cabinet stands incongruously in the corner, groaning under large and small trophies. By far the biggest one is at least two foot high, with a large silver cup on top of it.

'One of Dev's,' Megan says, following my gaze, breaking the silence, 'for athletics when he was in school.'

'I heard he was good,' I say, though I hadn't.

Megan smiles.

Dan takes over. 'Hi, everyone,' he says pleasantly. 'I'm Detective Dan Brown. Me and Detective Lucy Golden have a couple of questions for you, if that's all right, Megan? Dom, too, if ye have a minute.' A nod of apology to the three neighbours. 'Sorry to disturb ye, ladies.'

'It's fine,' Megan says. She looks . . . I can't put my finger on it. She looks different, though I can't pinpoint exactly how. She's still wearing the odd square-shaped clothes, her hair is still unkempt, and she hasn't applied make-up. And yet she . . . blooms. That's the word. A chill creeps across my shoulders, into my scalp. I study her more closely.

I wonder where her husband, Leo, is. She had chased him for years before he'd finally asked her out. I'm not quite sure they'd ever suited each other. Megan was soft, biddable, and I'd often thought that Leo's cocksure confidence would swamp her. But what did I know? I'd married con man *extraordinaire*, the aptly named Rob.

'All right, we'll move on out of your way,' one of the neighbours says, pulling on a royal blue coat. 'Take care of yourself, Megeen, pet.' And she bends over and clasps Megan to her. 'Call me if you need anything.'

'I will, Daisy, thanks.'

The other two women do the same and soon all three are on their way, silently, shaking their heads over the tragedy.

Now it's just me, Dan, Megan and her uncle.

'Lucy, I haven't seen you in an age. How are you?' Dom says. He's not the bright-eyed man I remember from years back. He looks hollowed out now, first the death of his sister and now his niece.

'I'm grand, Mr McCoy, thanks.' I slide into a seat.

'Dom, please,' he says. 'Isn't this a terrible business? My heart is broken.'

'We'll do our best for her.'

'Thank you.' He says it with a quiet sincerity. 'What is it you want to know?'

'We'll need to interview you all separately,' Dan says.

'Do Dom first,' Megan stands up. 'I know he wants to pop in to Maudie on the way back to Dublin.' She bends over and gives him a hug, winding her arms about his neck, 'Thanks for coming.'

He reaches up and clasps her hands. 'Anything, pet.'

I turn my face away from the raw emotion. Life can be so unfair. Megan leaves, the door clicking closed behind her.

Dom perches on the chair, hands clasped between his knees, breathing hard. 'What is it ye want to know?'

'When was the last time you spoke to her?'

His eyes tear up and, for such a big man, it's hard to witness. 'Last time I spoke to her she was giving me grief. Isn't that terrible now?' He pulls a hankie from the sleeve of his shirt and mops his eyes. 'Sorry now, sorry, but my heart is broken.'

Dan darts a quick look at me. That confirms what Megan told me yesterday.

'Why?'

'She had this – this idea. She thought, you see, that I had let her down. And maybe I had. Maybe I had.'

'I'm not following you,' Dan says.

'Sorry, sorry. I'm shocking nervous.' His voice trembles. 'Years back, Sandra came to live with me and Maudie. 'Twas after her father died and we promised to mind her. I always got on great with her, even when she was raising hell. But then didn't I get this job in Dublin and I took it. Sandra was not in a good place at the time. Her dad had died, her mother had given her away, she was pregnant with some louser's child.' A pause. 'Sorry, Devon is a great boy but . . . Anyway, she went wild after I left. She never forgave me for it.' He sounds like he can hardly believe it himself. 'But I needed that job. This place,' he shakes his head, 'there's nothing here. It was a good job.' A pause, then almost to himself, 'I did my best. We all did.'

Dan asks him where he was at the time of the murder.

'Back up in Dublin, with friends, having a few drinks.'

'Who can confirm this?'

'Two friends. I work with them. I can tell you the bar we were at if it helps.' Without needing to be prompted, he reels off the name, the time he got there, what he drank, when he left. And the names and numbers of his friends.

'That sounds like you rehearsed it,' Dan says jokingly.

'No. It sounds like I was at the pub with friends.' He sounds offended.

Dan nods. 'All right. That's it for now. Thanks.'

'Can you send Megan in?'

He gets up, knees creaking, pulling his jacket with him. We hear him call out to Megan that he's away. Megan bids him goodbye before she joins us in the kitchen.

'That was quick,' she says. She gestures at the table. 'Help yourselves to a biscuit. I've a lot of food to get through.'

Dan doesn't need to be told twice. He takes two chocolate digestives from the plate in the centre of the table.

'After you question me, you can take your dinner home with ye,' Megan says, with a bit of a laugh, then stops. 'Oh, God.'

'Times like this you find out who your friends are,' Dan says, with a sympathetic smile. 'People are good, bringing all this food.'

She nods, tears bright.

'I've just a couple of questions,' I begin. 'I was reading over the interview I did with you yesterday, Megan, and you told me that the last time you saw your sister was on the day she was killed, at around four. Have I got that right?'

'Yes.'

'It's just that, according to one of the lads in the garda station in Achill, she was there talking to them at that time.'

'What?' Megan is taken aback. 'What was she doing there?'

I sidestep that for the moment. 'I just need to know when you last saw your sister.'

Megan's mouth drops open. 'Maybe it was the day before that then,' she blabbers. 'I mean, it was definitely four o'clock. Yes, actually, that could have been the day before. I'm trying to think now, like. With the shock of everything yesterday, I most likely made a mistake.'

'Most likely.'

'Yes. Yes. Most likely.'

'Have a think, and when you remember for sure, get back to me about whether you saw her at all on Thursday.'

'I might not have.'

'That's okay.'

'Why was she in the garda station?'

I'm about to answer with a question when a small wiry man enters. I recognise him immediately because, although his hair has greyed, he hasn't changed a lot. He was always muscular but now there is not a spare ounce of fat on him. His step is quick as he crosses towards the table, all pent-up energy.

'Aw, Leo, your boots,' Megan says. They have left muddy prints across the ragged lino.

Devon, who has followed him, removes his shoes but not before shooting a poisonous look at Leo. 'I'll wash my hands, Megan,' he says, quite pointedly, I think. 'Then I'll heat up some soup.'

'Thanks, love.' Megan brushes his sleeve as he passes.

'Lucy Golden.' Leo sits on a chair opposite, arms folded, studying me from top to toe. 'Megs said you were working on Sandra's case. Thanks.'

'I'm glad I can do it. This is Detective Dan Brown.'

Leo dips his head in a hello to Dan. 'It's terrible. I mean, I know Sandra was a . . .' he lowers his voice a little, darts a glance to where Devon has gone '. . . fruit cake but—'

'Leo!' Megan winces.

'Sorry,' Leo mutters, 'but sure the whole place always said it. That doesn't mean it's not terrible. And it's shocking on Dev.'

'They weren't close,' Megan says.

'At the end of the day, she was still his mother.'

Megan flushes.

Is there is a barb in it somewhere? Did he want to take care of Sandra's kid? Were they just landed with him? Not the best start to a marriage.

'Lucy says she was down at the garda station the day she was killed,' Megan says to him, pronouncing it 'kilt'.

'Was she?' Leo looks mildly interested. 'What was wrong this time?' He makes it sound like Sandra had a habit of complaining.

'What *was* wrong?' Megan asks. Then she calls out to Devon, 'Sandra was down in the garda station the day before she was killed.'

'Yeah?' Devon has arrived back in, drying his hands on a faded blue hand-towel. He opens the fridge and takes out a carton of soup. Pouring it into the saucepan, he lights the gas. 'What was wrong?'

All three look at me.

'Did she ever say anything about feeling watched while she was in the house?' Dan asks.

Leo barks out a laugh, as if to say, 'See? A total fruit cake.'

'Nope,' he says.

Megan is slower to answer. She eyes us warily, then says, 'You wouldn't be believing her, see.'

'How do you mean?' Then I remember something else, something Devon said yesterday. 'Didn't Devon mention she complained that someone was messing about in the garden?'

'Oh, please.' Megan looks embarrassed. 'She hated being on her own. Even as a child, she imagined that people were out to get her. It was just her overactive imagination.'

Devon turns away, stirs the soup.

'What exactly did she say to you about it?'

'It wasn't real,' Megan insists. Then, seeing I'm serious, she says on a sigh, 'She just said she felt she was being spied on, that someone was messing about with Mammy's plants. Honestly, she wouldn't have known what plants were where.' After a moment, she goes on, 'She started to hang sheets in the window in case there was someone peeping in. I took them down. It was all non-sense. Tried to tell her to take deep breaths, but it was . . .' she bites her lip '. . . useless.' She turns around. 'Sorry, Dev.'

He shrugs, puts a bowl of soup in front of her, hands her a spoon and takes his own bowl to sit on a small sofa in the corner of the kitchen.

It must be half cold.

'It'd be better if we talk to you all separately,' I say.

'You want us out?' Leo looks indignant. 'But I'm in for my lunch. I'm starving.'

'Devon has just done soup.'

'I hate soup,' he snaps. 'Liquid food. I'm not eighty.' He cackles at his own joke as Megan flushes in embarrassment. Taking a plate from the press, he leans across Dan and plucks some biscuits and cakes from a plate. 'Come on, Devs, we'll make ourselves scarce.'

Devon slowly unspools himself from the sofa and, without looking at Leo, he follows him from the room.

'Going back to the stalker,' Dan says to Megan. 'Was there something about a dead cat?'

'It was probably thrown into the garden by someone who knocked it down on the road,' Megan says. 'But, yes, there was a dead cat in the garden. No one took her seriously. She was always scared of something.' Then she stops. 'Do you think . . .?'

'We don't know,' I say gently. 'It's just a line of enquiry we're pursuing. Tell me about the funeral.'

Megan does, echoing her uncle almost word for word. She also adds again that there was some trouble with the priest, and Maudie had had to bring Sandra home. 'I think Maudie said she was flirting with him or making a nuisance of herself. I don't know. I just didn't ask because . . .' a shrug '. . . honestly, I was . . .' another shrug, followed by a long pause '. . . tired,' she settles for.

'And the night she was killed can you tell us what you were doing between twelve forty-five a.m. and five a.m.?'

'I watched a film, me and Devon. Both of us. And, eh, then we went to bed.'

'The name of the film?'

She rattles off a title, the time it started and finished, and at what time she got a glass of milk, and how she fell straight asleep.

It's quite . . . pat. 'And Leo?'

She hesitates, glances towards the door. 'He was out, I don't know . . .' A look at me. 'He was probably, though he wouldn't admit it to me in a million years, out with Sam Summers.' It's bitter.

Sam runs card games. It's common knowledge but we turn a blind eye. I sense it's hard for Megan to disclose that.

'When did he get back?'

'About . . . well . . .' She stumbles. 'I was asleep. I don't know. He was there when I got up for the milk. I don't know what time that was.'

'All right. Thanks. Will you get Leo?'

She half stands up, then sits down. Leaning towards me, she says, a little desperately, 'He didn't . . . wouldn't . . . none of us . . .' A pause. Then another attempt: 'You know Leo of old. He wouldn't. I—'

'Just get him,' Dan says. 'Please.'

'I'm just saying . . .' She looks imploringly at me and, feeling shit about it, but knowing it's necessary, I stare impassively back. Realisation that I am not her ally makes her pull away. Slowly she stands. Then, without a backward glance, she leaves the room, head high.

I let out a slow breath.

'You can interview me but I'll be eating while you're at it.' Leo bursts into the room a few seconds later. 'I've been working all morning and I'm bloody hungry.' He takes some sandwiches and, leaning back, tipping the chair up on two legs, he starts to munch.

I ask him the same questions as Megan. And he denies meeting up with Sandra at all, except at the funeral. He doesn't know who would hurt her.

'Any chance ye could tell us where you were on the night of the murder, between twelve forty five a.m. and five a.m?'

Leo glares at us. 'Are we under suspicion?'

'In cases like this we have to rule out the family so if you could just tell us. It's routine.'

There is a small pause, and finally he says, 'I was in Amethyst Bar with some lads until closing and then we went off to play cards in Sam Summers's, just a few harmless games. We were there until three in the morning. You can check with him.' He pulls out his phone, scrolls and calls out Sam's number.

'How did you get home?' Dan asks.

'Walked. I left his place, took me an hour to get back here.'

I know where Sam lives. The route could conceivably have taken Leo past Sandra's but it would have taken more than an hour to get home if he'd diverted. That's if he did walk.

We ask him a little more about Sandra but he insists that he hasn't heard from her in years.

Devon slides in next, looking apologetic for even thinking of taking up space. There's something about him. I can't quite get my head around it. He seems upset, and yet it doesn't strike me as a grief. I decide to go for it. Shock him. 'What were you doing on Thursday night, Devon? In particular during the hours between twelve forty-five and five in the morning?'

'Watching a film with Megan and then I went to bed.'

'Would you remember the name of the film or what happened in it?'

He stares at his hands.

'Devon?'

His head jerks up. Something chases its way across his face before he mumbles, 'Some stupid RTÉ film. A romantic thing. Stupid. I went to bed after it.'

'A romantic film on a Thursday night?' Dan says. 'Really?'

I know what Dan's thinking. He's thinking that it's a load of bullshit. Devon is twenty-four, and it's highly unlikely that he'd have watched a stupid romantic film with his aunt on a Thursday night. Most lads would be out with their mates or on their laptops.

'Do ye normally watch movies together?'

'No.' He hops up. 'Can I go now? I've to be in work for two.'

'So why that night?'

'Leo was out, and Megan wanted company.'

There's a ring of truth there somewhere. A world of bitter.

After that he just tells us what he'd said the previous day.

There's nothing left but to get fingerprints from them for elimination purposes.

As I'm taking Megan's she hands me a slip of paper. 'Sandra's last-known address,' she says. 'Main Street, Crossmolina.'

She'd lived an hour up the road.

As I fire up the engine, Dan busies himself picking dog hair from his trousers and flicking it out of the window. 'How's the backside?'

'I may never walk properly again.'

He laughs, flicks some more hair out of the window.

'Dan, just leave it a second,' I say suddenly. I hop out of the car and get an evidence kit. Very carefully, I take tweezers and place a sample of the hairs into the bag and tag it. 'It looks similar to the hair I found on Sandra's T-shirt yesterday. It might have fallen from Devon when he was at the scene.' And yet, I think, the positioning of the hair on the T-shirt would not fit because Devon said he didn't enter the bedroom at all.

'That family is all sorts of weird,' Dan remarks, once we get going.

'Yep,' I agree, trying to navigate the potholed drive. 'And Megan is lying about that alibi. I don't think Devon was watching TV. Or, at least, not the whole film.'

'Me neither. Though it might be hard to prove if she backs him up.'

'If he was out we'll find it.' I say it with more confidence than certainty. If he was out on Achill, we might never find it. It's a CCTV black spot.

We slump into silence, until Dan says, 'I never thought I'd say it, but I prefer when relatives are more upset. I can get a better read of them.'

'Me too. But in their favour, at least they're honest, which makes me think they're in the clear and yet . . .'

'Who wouldn't be upset if a family member died? I mean no matter how much . . .' Dan stops, realising what he's about to say. 'Apart from me and those people.' It's a joke but it falls flat.

I leave a bit of a conversational gap before I ask, 'What does Fran think about it all?' Fran is Dan's partner.

'Last I looked he wasn't a detective.'

I keep my eyes on the road and don't respond.

'Aw, come on, Luce. You know Fran. He loves everyone and everyone loves him. He'd have me up in Dublin playing nurse to me da if he could.'

'That's only because he'd like to see you in the uniform.' As Dan chuckles, I take the turning for Achill Sound. The rain turns to hail and it bounces off the windscreen, coating the road white in seconds. 'Does your dad have long left?'

'A few months apparently.'

'Take a day out, go up. I'll clear it with William.'

For the briefest moment, I think he's considering it, but then he says, 'Aw, I don't think so.'

He's certain to regret it but I don't push it. I've made the offer and there's nothing else I can do. 'Devon isn't Leo's greatest fan, is he?'

'No.' Dan seizes on the subject change, like a man drowning, 'The look he gave him for walking in with muddy boots, did you see it? There's something there, all right, but whether it has to do with our case or not . . .'

'There was something odd about Megan today. She was different.' He doesn't reply, and I remember he hadn't spoken to her yesterday. 'Maybe she is relieved . . .' Then I think, How could she be? Sandra hadn't bothered them in years, so she was hardly a burden. But there was something . . .

'Did you see the state of the kitchen?' Dan says. 'Not a lot of money in that house.'

'No. Still, they were probably due to inherit. Let's see if we can get a look at the will. Maybe Sandra got a big share or something. I'd say Megan would have found that grossly unfair, seeing as she brought up Devon and spent all her years running and jumping after the mother.'

'Yes. And if we pull bank accounts we might uncover debts. If Leo is out betting at Sam Summers's, chances are they might be in financial trouble.'

And yet I can't see it. Megan had loved Sandra once, been very protective of her, but maybe she'd had enough. People snap.

Dan puts in a call to Pat, our document whiz, and while he's doing that, my phone rings. It's William. 'Can the two of you get back out to the house in Dugort? SOCO have found something.'

11

There's a roadblock up ahead. Well, as much of a roadblock as you can get on this godforsaken island. Two guards – one old, overweight with a red face and a uniform that looks as if it was made for a man two sizes smaller, and the other young and eager, ears sticking out under the hat, a long pale face – hold up cars as they make their way across the Matt Talbot bridge onto the mainland. He wonders if they'll let him by without questioning him because, after all, he's just cycling.

But, no: the older one indicates for him to stop while the younger one continues to chat to the motorists. He hears the young lad talking away about the weather to one of the drivers. What kind of idiot guards are these?

Still, idiots or not, his heart starts up a steady rhythmic pound. He takes a breath, forces a look of concern. 'Hi, Guard, what seems to be the problem?'

It takes a second before the guard reacts, his watery blue eyes studying him. A trickle of fear tickles like a feather, but he damps it down. There is no way . . .

Finally, the auld lad says, 'There was a woman assaulted and killed in the early hours of Friday morning. 'Twas on the news. You didn't hear about that, no?' The guard cocks his head to one side.

His pulse slows. *Breathe.* 'No. That's terrible. I'm on holidays, and I never listen to the news when I'm away. That's shocking.'

'It is surely,' the guard agrees, with a slow wheeze. 'Anyhow, we're checking everyone coming in or off the island. Can I have your name, please?'

'Liam Hand.' He pulls out a driver's licence. *Thank God for the false name,* he thinks. 'All I can say is that I never saw or heard anything, Guard. The poor woman. Where did it happen?'

'Beyond in Dugort.' A moment. 'We don't get too many tourists here in January.'

He's a suspicious little bastard. 'I come for the light,' he answers. 'I take pictures of it. Paint it.' To prove it, he holds up the camera slung around his neck. *He hopes the bastard doesn't want to check what's actually on it.*

'Where are you staying, Liam Hand?'

'I'm camping near Keel. I'm just on my way to get some supplies.'

'When did you arrive?'

'Last Wednesday.' *If the bastard checks, at least it'll be the truth.*

'This assault happened the following night. Were you around Dugort at all on the Thursday?'

'No. I'd cycled from Westport on the Wednesday. The weather was terrible, and I was knackered, so I was. I just collapsed into the tent and didn't surface until yesterday lunchtime. You can ask the site manager. I was asking him the way to Keem.'

'Keem?' he says. Then stops. *Again that look.* Then he says, 'That's a great beach. I wouldn't cycle to it in this weather.'

'I'll bear that in mind.' *He had, though. He had cycled there. There was something he needed to see out there.* 'Is that all, Guard?'

'Yes, thank you. How long of a holiday have you here?'

As long as it fucking takes, he thinks. 'Another week.'

'Enjoy.'
He hops back up on his bike and pedals away.
He doesn't look back.
He'll be hot-footing it out of Keel now, that's for sure.
Better to be safe.

12

We arrive at the cottage twenty minutes later. The narrow road is still jammed up with garda vans and cars, crime-scene tape still up from yesterday, which isn't surprising as the house is full of clutter: it will take ages for SOCOs to go through the lot to see what might help the investigation and what won't. After signing the logbook to be allowed onto the scene, the guard on duty lets us through. We don the dust suits and booties, and John, a scene-of-crime officer, greets us by beckoning us forward. 'William said he'd send yez on. Come, have a look at this.'

He leads us up a marked safe path towards the back of the house. The garden is basically a reclaimed part of the hill that rises back from the house. It's long and overgrown, hedgerows boarding it on every side. A small round patio table and two chairs are positioned on a small, concreted area. They've rusted and the red colour has seeped into the concrete, like blood. Light is leaking into the day now and a shaft falls through the wall of clouds in the sky. The sudden effect on the garden and the mountain backdrop is startling. Shadow and light vie with one another for dominance. The rain is a steady drip. The whole world smells of damp earth. The tramp of our feet seems loud in the quiet of the landscape.

John leads us to the edge of the cordon, to where rhododendron bushes have grown wild. These plants can be found over great parts of the island. In summer they look eye-poppingly beautiful with their purple foliage but their spread is killing the native flora. Today, though, early January, the bushes are bare but large. 'Here's the interesting thing,' John says, leading us around the back. 'See.' He points to where the bushes have been hacked away. 'Cut, right into the centre.'

The ground inside the bushes has been trampled on. 'A den,' I say.

'Yep. William told us yesterday to look out for something like this so we extended the cordon. Someone was watching that woman. See here.' He points to where a small hole has been forged in the bushes. 'A pair of binoculars through that and you're looking into the kitchen and back bedroom of the house.'

Dan gives a low whistle.

'We found an empty wine bottle close by, which we've sent off, and this place will be forensically examined as a matter of urgency,' John says.

'Great stuff,' I say.

Dan takes out his phone and starts snapping a few pictures for the conference this evening. It's always good to have a few images to show the team. It works better than trying to describe something verbally.

'I'll keep William informed on what we find,' John says.

We thank him and follow him out. Looking back, from halfway down the garden, the rhododendron bush appears intact. You can't even see the spy-hole. I imagine Sandra moving about in the house, the nights growing dark, and some fecker out here, spying on her. He would have needed night-vision binoculars to do it, though, I think. It's dark by five thirty now. It's something we should look out for in a search. I make a mental note of it.

'Anything interesting turn up in the house?' I ask John, as we exit the cordon and start to take off the dust suits.

'No murder weapon we can identify,' he says, 'though there were some interesting boot prints in the hallway. We're sending pictures over to you later. Lots of fingermarks which you can run through the system, see if you get a hit.'

'I've asked for elimination prints to be taken of the immediate family,' I say, 'so at least we can match theirs up if we get any. Anything else?'

He shakes his head. 'Nothing that jumps out, unfortunately, unless you count old teeth and bits of hair.'

'What?'

'Baby teeth. One from Sandra and Megan and one from Devon. Seems to have been a bit of a family tradition.'

'I get that,' I say, as Dan wrinkles his nose. 'I have Luc's first tooth and I bought him a box for Sirocco's.'

'Gross,' Dan mutters.

'And hair,' I continue. 'I have his first curl and my mother has mine.'

'All my mother kept was my bad school reports.' Dan rolls his eyes.

John laughs. 'Anyway, aside from that, nothing. We'll keep in touch.'

'Thanks, John, appreciate it.'

'Good luck.' He waves his hand in goodbye, and leaves us.

'So, she's not as crazy as her family think,' Dan says, pulling the booties off his super shiny shoes. I wonder, not for the first time, how long it takes him to polish them like that. The black leather gleams like a mirror.

I tear my glance from his footwear, gaze once again towards the back garden. 'Not crazy at all. Someone was watching her, someone was moving things about in her garden, pouring blood on her windowsill and throwing dead cats in off the road. The question is why and who?'

'To scare her, make her leave, only she doesn't?'

'If she was due to inherit money, scaring her off wouldn't mean she couldn't inherit.'

'To make her leave, then?'

We're walking back towards the car.

'She would have had to leave at some point. The house was being sold.'

'So why stalk her? Just to scare her? Or to kill her?'

I think about the scene. It didn't look like the killer had been particularly organised, not someone who had plotted and planned it, and if the killer was a stalker of some sort, that's exactly what he would have done, unless, of course, she surprised him in some way. 'It doesn't make sense,' I say. 'There's bits missing.'

Dan looks at his watch. 'We're not going to solve it today,' he says, 'but we can solve the problem of being hungry.'

'You're always hungry.'

'I've only had porridge, eight biscuits and a coffee today. Let's grab something in the Beehive, then head to the station after for the conference.' He looks at me hopefully.

I jangle the car keys. 'Right, come on.'

13

When we finally arrive at the station, having had, in Dan's words, 'a great feed' in the Beehive, a few of the team are there already, Larry faffing about with his mobile phone, Kev chomping on a huge sandwich, which is leaking bits all over his trousers. Susan, Pat and Ger, who must have been drafted in since last night, are huddled together, talking about some TikTok-er who has gone viral. No sign of Jordy: he probably got called out on something else.

'How'd the PM go today?' I ask, as I pass Kev. His mouth is full of the leaky sandwich so he has to chew furiously and swallow before he can answer. He ends up going a bit purple in the face, thumping his chest, and saying, 'It feels like a whole load of food just got stuck there.'

'A whole load of food was swallowed, so technically that could happen,' Dan says, passing by. Kev looks a bit panicked and thumps himself again.

'My mother was always telling me not to swallow like that and she was right.' Kev gives his chest another thump for good measure. Then, after a few test swallows, he decides that all is well. 'The PM went well, Lucy. We got quite a bit off the body.'

William enters with a bang of the door and strides up the room. There's a newspaper clenched in one hand and he looks like he wants to hit someone with it. The silence in the room is immediate. I sit down quickly and Dan, with a nervous look at me, sits down too. I wonder who or what has rattled William's cage.

William waits until we are all suitably terrified, then slowly unfolds the paper. 'We will start the conference in a minute,' he says, his voice low, his gaze like ice, as he sweeps the room. Susan looks ready to wet herself. And then, as he holds up the paper, I think I might actually wet myself.

GUARD MAY BE INVOLVED IN BRUTAL SLAYING, screams the headline.

Oh, shit.

'This is the piece of crap that is the local rag.' William shakes the paper like a dog would a rabbit. 'This piece of crap has somehow managed to scoop the nationals with this piece-of-crap article. Now, I want to know how the fuck that happened.'

He glares at us. No one meets his gaze.

Did it start with my mother? I wonder. Then I think, It fecking has to have. How else could the story have got out there?

'Does it name the guard?' Dan asks.

'Is it true?' Susan asks, her mouth agape.

'Is it Ben?' Kev asks. 'I was wondering why—'

'Listen here now,' William snaps. 'It doesn't matter who the hell it is. It doesn't even matter if it's true. What matters is that we do our bloody job. Now, someone leaked this to the paper. Someone who knew.' He eyeballs me, Dan and Larry, then moves on. 'I will not be sidetracked and tormented by this sort of crap. Anyone who rings, anyone at all, anyone who approaches you, refer them to the garda press office. And I want no speculation between you lot here. I want nothing to be said outside. The member has been interviewed and has given a statement. Following on from that, more interviews will be conducted. This is a separate strand in the investigation. If our enquiries lead us to this man, you will be informed. Larry, Dan, Lucy, I want to speak to ye afterwards.' He slams the paper on the desk, its lurid headline in red, like a blaring beacon. I feel sick.

'Let's get on with the conference. Kevin and I attended the PM today,' he says. 'And we can safely say that we are looking at a murder here. Joe Palmer will state in his report that our IP was killed by sharp-force trauma to the back of the head, causing our IP to pitch forward onto her face. She was then dealt another blow. From the angle of the first blow, Palmer believes that her assailant was mostly likely taller than Sandra, which wouldn't be hard as the IP was five feet one, though the angle of the blow suggests that the assailant was a maximum five feet seven or so. It does not appear that she was sexually assaulted in the hours before her death or indeed had had any sexual intercourse. Her stomach was empty, which suggests that she had not eaten in at least twenty-four hours. Though it could have been longer.' Without missing a beat, he snaps out, 'Lucy, Dan, reports, please.'

I push my panic to the back of my mind and give a run-down of where our investigations have led us. 'After talking to the family, I do think we need to look at them a little closer. I've asked Pat to see if he can get eyes on the will, see if there was any potential for dispute there. He's drawing up orders to access all their bank accounts, including Sandra's. We have a last-known address for her, which we can check out tomorrow morning. Dan and I went back to the cottage today, after receiving a call from John. Dan?'

Dan stands up and, after a bit of faffing about, hooks his phone to the projector and the pictures of the den are blown up for everyone to see. It looks even more sinister as a still photo, eerie, waiting for its occupant. 'It's being forensically examined as a matter of urgency.' I repeat John's line. 'So, we might have something in the next couple of days.'

'Good,' William says curtly. 'Larry?'

Larry rubs a hand across his military haircut and heaves a sigh. 'There is fuck-all, Cig,' he says. 'Like, it's the quietest piece of road - very few people live up that way. I harvested CCTV from all the areas I could. All in all, there were twelve cars heading in that direction from ten the night before to ten o'clock that morning. However, though the CCTV shows cars moving in that direction, there was no CCTV close enough to see any actually turning off towards the house. However, I will try and trace those cars. Not all the registrations are clear and it's very dark, but I'll do my best, see if anything jumps out. Pat passed on Sandra's locations over the last twenty-four hours of her life, which he gleaned from her mobile phone. It was mostly Westport and Achill, which is good for us. I'm harvesting CCTV from those areas to see if we can trace her and who she might have met. I'm still awaiting the CCTV from the bar in Westport.'

'Hurry that up. Mick, you were tic-tacking with Forensics?'

'I was, Cig. It's early days. Nothing much has come back yet. You know yourself.'

'I know myself? What do I know?'

Mick doesn't seem to know how to respond to that. His ears pink up and he looks down at his hands.

'Tomorrow. I want you to have something for me by tomorrow. Right?'

'For sure, Cig.'

William mutters something like 'Jaysus' sake' under his breath but moves on. 'Pat?'

'Like Larry said, I got into the IP's phone, Cig, and passed on her location information. I'm checking out any phone numbers she used in the past three weeks. A number of recurring ones I'll track down first. Nothing is jumping out so far – a couple of calls to a sailing club in Sligo who have no record of a Sandra Byrne ever having dealings with them. The receptionist said it might just have been an enquiry for a sailing tour. A couple of calls to a "D". No answer on that as yet. Now, one thing of interest popped up in the texts. In the week before she died, she got several text messages from a Richard, which go unanswered. From the nature of them, it appears Sandra and Richard had a row of some sort. I rang the number and it was answered by a man calling himself Richie. I asked if he knew Sandra Byrne and he said he did, that she was his partner. I asked him for his address and he gave it to me but he demanded to know what was going on so I had to break the news to him on the phone.' Pat pauses for a second. 'He was shook up when I told him she'd been found dead. He doesn't watch TV or follow the news apparently. He's expecting someone to call out tomorrow. Is that last-known address you got from Megan Main Street, Crossmolina, Lucy? Because that's where this Richie character lives.'

'Yes, that's right.' Megan had said nothing about Sandra having a partner. Maybe she didn't know.

'Same place so,' Pat says. 'I'll show you the texts later. Other than that, nothing much. Regarding the bank accounts for the family, I'm on that and also I'm hoping to talk to Shea Levin, the one and only solicitor on the island, to see if he's willing to identify the executors of Mrs Byrne's will. If they give permission for us to examine it, it'll be a lot quicker than jumping through the paperwork hoops.'

'What if she didn't go through Shea Levin for the will?'

'Everyone on the island uses him, and if she didn't, he'll be the one who'll have made the calls to locate the will for the family. He'll know where it is.'

'All right. Just make sure, whatever you do, it'll stand up in court.'

'As always,' Pat says, with a bit of an edge that William ignores. 'Susan?'

'I was doing door-to-door with the regular guards, Cig, and as Larry said, that part of the island is largely unoccupied, though there's a number of holiday homes about five hundred metres away. They face Dugort Strand, at right angles almost to Pauline's house. All in all, fifty houses that might have seen something. We called into fifty and got answers at twenty-five. And nobody saw anything or heard anything.'

'What do you mean? Surely they heard the ocean, the birds . . .'

She looks confused. 'Well . . . I don't think . . . like . . . with all respect, Cig, that a bird murdered her.'

The room erupts in laughter.

'What I'm trying to say,' William cuts through the mirth, 'is that you have to ask people what they did hear, what did they see, not what they didn't.'

'That's exactly what we did, Cig,' Susan says, sounding a little offended, 'and they all answered that it was quiet out there. That they heard nothing. If there was something to be heard, they would have heard it. I know Jordy and another guard talked to people going on and off the island today, too, and nothing came up there. Of the houses, we have twenty-five to revisit, so maybe one of those. And three of those houses are closer to the IP's place of residence.'

'Kev?'

He reports that while the staff of the pub remembered Sandra, mainly due to her bright clothes, none of them mentioned anything out of the ordinary about her. One was observant enough to notice that she left the pub with a 'slobby-looking fella'.

Poor Ben, I think.

'So, we have one interview lined up for tomorrow? Other than that, a great big fat zero?' William glares at us. 'No CCTV, no forensics until first thing tomorrow,' he pointedly says that to Mick, who pinks up again, 'nothing on door-to-door and—'

At the back of the room, a hand shoots up. It's Brian's.

'Cig,' he says, interrupting William's ire, 'I might have got something on a call.'

'You got something and you're only telling us now?'

'Go ahead, Brian,' I say. This is all my fault. William is never as unreasonable as this. 'What have you got?'

Brian looks to William for confirmation that he can speak, sees nothing to dissuade him, and says, faltering, 'A man rang this morning, a Mr David McLean. He says he employed Sandra until early January. She worked in his garage shop but one day she left, never said why, just never came back. I told him someone would be out to him tomorrow. I have his number here.' He holds up a slip of paper.

William looks mollified. 'Good work. We'll get him interviewed tomorrow too. Right, all, get your job sheets today. And I want something better by tomorrow. This case isn't going to solve itself. Lucy, Dan, Larry.' So saying he exits the room, leaving the newspaper behind.

I reckon it'll be less than five seconds before they've all crowded around it. I barely have time to think this before Dan says, in an undertone, to me, 'It was you, wasn't it?'

'Sorry?'

'Who leaked the story.'

'I didn't leak—'

'Whatever you did, you jumped when you saw that headline. William isn't stupid. He knows, just own it, and it'll—'

'Lucy, Dan!' William calls from his office.

He's waiting at the door and holds it open as we enter. Larry is already sitting and Dan and I join him.

'I want to know how it happened.' He stays standing.

I take a breath. 'It might have been me, Cig.'

'Might have been?' He quirks an eyebrow.

'Look, I told my mother, Thursday night, that Ben had gone home with Sandra Byrne. I didn't know she was going to end up dead the following day. My mother said last night that she went and told the butcher, who is the worst gossip on the island and obviously, from the headline, it looks like he went and told everyone else.'

There's a silence after I finish.

Larry and Dan are gawking at me. Whatever it was, they hadn't expected that.

William walks slowly to the window and looks out.

The silence grows bigger and more oppressive.

'Can I go?' Larry asks eventually. Then, at my look, 'Well, it's nothing to do with me, is it?'

'Go,' William says.

Larry shoots a rueful glance at me and Dan and hightails it out.

Still William says nothing.

'In fairness,' Dan starts up, 'Lucy wasn't to know that—'

'Stop!' William says, his back to us. 'Stop there, Dan. You can leave, please.'

'Well, I just think—'

'Now.'

Dan half stands. Then sits, then stands again. It's almost comical and I have an urge to giggle. 'Just go,' I tell him, and he leaves.

I don't even try to apologise. What is there to say?

'Aren't you going to apologise?' William finally turns around.

'Will it do any good?' He looks a bit startled. 'Honestly, I know I messed up. I should have copped that she might go telling people and headed it off but I didn't.'

'It's going to be hard to explain to the chief that the leak came from a seventy-year-old woman talking to her butcher.'

I bite my lip. Oh, shit, it's not funny.

'It's not funny.'

'I know.' Then, 'I'm sorry. I really am.'

'I'm sure you are.'

'She won't be saying any more.'

'She'd better not.'

In the ensuing silence, I want to ask if I can go but I'm a bit scared to. 'Eh, can—'

'By the way, Jordy will not be on the case for the foreseeable.'

'What? Why?'

'You are not in a position to question, Lucy, but if you must know, he's following up on something else that I'm interested in. For now, you and Dan go and talk to the boyfriend or whatever he was. Get me something.' He dismisses me with a wave, turns back to the window.

As always, I think he cuts a lonely figure, the man with no family that I know of, who carries a bonsai tree from case to case. Where does he go after work? Does he have a girlfriend or partner or—

'Are you still standing there?'

I'm gone.

14

Though Larry and Dan have gone home, Pat is waiting for me when I get back to my office. He's sitting on my desk, the transcript of texts from Richie to Sandra with him. 'I've highlighted the highlights,' he says, handing them to me.

> *4 January 2021 21:05*
>
> **Richard: Sorry. Please come back. Love you**

> *4 January 2021 22:05*
>
> **Richard: Come on. Let's talk about this. I said I was sorry.**

> *5 January 2021 12:06*
>
> **Richard: Why aren't you replying? Come on . . .**

'It goes on like that,' Pat says, flipping over a page, 'And here's the last text of that day.'

> *5 January 2021 02:16*
>
> **Richard: If you want to end it, don't ghost me. Tell me 2 my face. I know I was a dick.**

'If you go through all Richie's texts,' Pat says, 'they gradually, over the course of the week, get more and more desperate or threatening, whichever way you want to read it. But safe to say that this guy is sending twenty to thirty a day. And she doesn't reply to any of them. This here,' he flips to the last page, 'sent two days before the murder. This you should read.'

10 January 2021 3:16am

Richard: I've had it now. I won't be treated like this. I have my pride. I know where you are and you will NOT walk away until we are done.

'Ouch,' I say.

'Will you bring him in?' asks Pat.

I think for a second. 'Naw, we'll just go soft, see if he brings them up. If not, we can dig into him, bring him in later to ask about them under caution.'

'Sure thing. I'll keep on trying the other numbers and if I get anything I'll come back to you. She didn't have much of a social life if her phone is anything to go by.'

'Great work. You'll get a big shiny star from William tomorrow.'

Pat laughs and agrees that tomorrow's conference has to go better than today's.

15

15 January

Richie lives in a row of terraced houses just outside Crossmolina on the Ballina road. It takes an hour to travel over – the road winds and twists. We find parking two doors down from him, which is a bonus, though Crossmolina is a sort of nothing place. The house looks neat, a little old-fashioned, with net curtains hanging in the windows, the sills painted a bright blue and the door knocker polished to a high shine. It's not really the sort of place I'd have pictured Sandra living. It seems too settled for her, too normal.

I damp down that thought: I'm still referencing the wild child I remember. The one who jumped into the water one cold after-noon to swim to Inishbiggle, through a stretch of one of the most dangerous currents. Her rescue had made headlines around the country. What hadn't been reported, my mother later told me, was that the child had been drunk out of her head. Teenage Sandra allegedly slept with half the men in Mayo. She ran away from home on a number of occasions, one memorable time when Megan and I found her halfway up An Sliabh Mór or Slievemore as some call it. She was passed out. Megan had broken down, screamed abuse at her sister and I'd stood there, like a tool, wanting to thump Sandra for putting my friend through this. We'd half walked, half carried her down the mountain and my mother had driven to meet us, then taken her back to our house in Achill Sound, where she'd sobered her up, and fed her.

Thinking back now, I should have guessed that it wasn't normal behaviour, that maybe Sandra was reacting to events at home, but I was a teenager myself, oblivious and probably consumed with thoughts of my school crush, Johnny Egan. In my mind, she was just a nuisance, and anytime I'd thought of her since, that was how I remembered her. But I need to start thinking of Sandra as the IP I'm learning about, the same way I learn about all my cases. Sandra must have matured, though last Saturday night, in her too-tight, too-short clothes, drawing too much attention to herself, it didn't seem as if she had changed that much. And yet this house . . .

'I'll get Ger to run that reg through Pulse.' Dan points to a silver Toyota parked outside Richie's house. 'See if it's his.'

He's just hung up on Ger when the front door is opened. A small man stands in the doorway. 'Guards,' he says, 'I'm Richie. Come in.' His voice is all Dublin.

Richie has to be about ten years older than Sandra, a man already fading away from middle age, though trying desperately to cling to it. He's around five eight, thin, a hoop earring in his right ear. Grey hair, sparse, tightly shaved. Slow enough on his feet, he shuffles his way from the hall into the front room. He wears jeans that showcase skinny legs, shoes with no socks and a T-shirt with a slogan I don't understand. The place smells a little of pot. The house is quite the spectacle, painted in *über*-bright colours with clashing furniture. There's an empty Carlsberg bottle on a red coffee-table, which he removes and puts of sight, before he perches on a yellow and red sofa. He's been crying, I think. 'Is it true?' he asks, before we can say a word. He speaks quietly, grey eyes searching our faces. 'Is she . . .' He swallows hard. 'She's not dead, is she? Has there been a mistake?'

I take a seat opposite him, on a royal blue, very uncomfortable chair. Dan remains standing, leaning against the pale green door frame. The walls in this room are a blue-green. Cheap ornaments vie for attention on the mantelpiece. I take my time answering: I want to get a proper feel for this guy. 'There's been no mistake, I'm afraid, Richie. She was found by her son—'

His head shoots up. 'Son? She didn't have a son. You must have it wrong. She—'

'No mistake,' I say gently but firmly, hating to quash the momentary hope that had sprung up in him. 'Sandra Byrne had a son called Devon. He was being raised by her sister, Megan.'

'No.' He shakes his head. 'No, it's . . . No.'

'She never said?'

He looks at me blankly. 'No.'

I glance at Dan, who takes out his notebook.

'Richie, I have to ask you a few questions, I'm afraid. Do you feel up to answering them?'

'Sorry . . . what?' Another blank look.

I repeat myself.

'Sure. Whatever. A son?' Then, 'How . . . What happened to her?'

'Someone hit her with a sharp object in the bedroom of her mother's house, we think.'

'Her mother's house?'

'Yes.' Is he getting any of this? I wonder. 'Where she was living since her mother died.'

'Her mother died years ago.'

'Just over a week ago, actually.'

'What?'

'Richie, I have to ask, how well did you know Sandra?'

He stares at his hands and says nothing. It's like he's lost somewhere inside his head.

'Richie?' I prompt.

His head jerks up. 'I . . . well . . . I thought I knew her. She had a mother? Still alive?'

'Died just over a week ago.' I leave it a moment. There's nothing to be gained by going full tilt at this guy. He's obviously had a shock. And yet he sent that last semi-threatening text to Sandra. I watch as he slowly absorbs the news, the look of confusion being replaced by a dawning realisation that things have shifted and he has to catch up. 'Tell me how you met Sandra.'

There's a slight hesitation. Wariness. Then he says, 'At an AA meeting.'

Oh . . . That explains a little.

'Where was the meeting?'

'Dublin.' He stops, remembering.

'And?' I prompt.

'In the city centre,' he says. Then more hesitation, before he continues, 'I was sober two years by that stage. Doing well. I had a little apartment and I was earning a few bob as a plumber. I had done all my apologising to whoever I had to apologise to for my drinking. I'd done the whole nine yards, like, you know.'

'Yes. And you say you met Sandra one night.' I get him back on track.

'About eight months ago. She was there and she'd never been there before and she was . . .' An expression of pure grief and regret crosses his face. 'She shone,' he says simply, eyeballing me.

'She had just moved to the area and had given up alcohol a few months before and she was just attending the way you do to keep on the straight and narrow, and she told her story, and she told it in such a way that we laughed. She made us laugh.' He says it with wonder, with affection, with grief.

'And what was her story?'

He looks at us. 'We're not meant to talk about it.'

'This is a murder investigation. You can talk about it,' I say.

He doesn't seem convinced.

'We need to know, Richie, if we're to find her murderer.'

He flinches at that, though whether out of guilt or because the news is sinking in, I'm not quite sure.

'I can't tell it as well as she did,' he says hesitantly.

'That doesn't matter.'

'Sandra always says I have a tendency to make even the most exciting stories boring.' He peers anxiously at us. 'So, you know, she was better at telling it.'

'It really doesn't matter,' I say, feeling a twinge of pity for him. He probably thought he'd won the jackpot to attract Sandra's attention. He's a strange-looking man, too skinny by half with a precision about him that doesn't tally with the clothes. 'Go on,' I say.

'Okay.' A pause before he plunges in: 'Well, the bare facts are that she said she started drinking when she was nine. She did it because she liked the taste. Then when her dad was murdered and she lost her mother she just went at it like there was no tomorrow. She lost everything. At one stage she borrowed from a money lender but did a runner when she couldn't meet the repayments. Finally, though, she got sober again, found a job in a hotel and rented a room in an apartment.'

There is a moment before Dan says what I'm thinking: 'That was funny?'

'I told you I wasn't a good storyteller,' Richie mumbles.

'All right. So she arrives at the AA meeting, tells her story, and then what?'

'After these meetings, there's, like, tea and biscuits and that and we all talk and she picked me to talk to.' He says it with pride. 'And, like, at first our chat was all normal, above board, we didn't see each other outside the meeting, but then one night she just asked me. Asked me if I wanted to go for a coffee, and you know what, I did. And then a week later she moved into my apartment, and I'm a realist, I knew she was stuck for somewhere to stay but I didn't care. Then a few months back, around last October, she said she'd like to live in the west, where she was from, and I thought, Why not? We sold my apartment and bought this place and she made it her own.' He waves his arm about the multi-coloured room. 'She just . . . shone.' He breaks down, shoulders heaving, sobs tearing out of him, palms planted in his eyeballs. To all appearances, he seems like an utterly broken man.

I let him cry without saying anything. Finally, the sobs cease and he rubs his fist over his eyes, like a kid. 'Sorry,' he says.

'That's all right. It's understandable. So, you moved down here and then what?'

'She was so happy. We both were. She had all these plans and I liked to see her all fired up, and I thought we were good, stable, you know, but then something changed a couple of weeks back. She – she came home early from work and she got all weird on me and then next day she just packed her bags. She said she was leaving and I still didn't know if she was leaving me or, like, going on a holiday.'

'When you say something changed?'

'She was . . . I don't know . . . Something had got to her. She was in a bit of a state and . . .' he stops, examines the frayed edge of his T-shirt '. . . well, she said she was fine. Then she left me.'

'Did you ask her why she was going?'

'Of course I did.' He sounds cross at that question. 'But she was in one of her moods and she wasn't talking, and I wonder if it's something I did but I can't think of anything. So, I figure, I'll let her go and then go after her.' He starts to sob again. 'I should have stopped her. I should have just stopped her.'

'How did she seem when she was leaving?'

'Fired up,' he says.

'And you're positive you don't know what prompted her to go?'

'No.' He answers almost too quickly, his eyes sliding to the side.

'No rows or anything?'

At that his head jerks up. 'No,' he says. 'Just like I said . . . She was upset over something but she didn't say what.'

Dan flicks a look at me.

'Did she tell you where she was going?'

'No.' Then, with a shrug, 'But, like, when I bought her her phone, we installed this app to find it if it ever got stolen or went missing – she was always losing things – so when she left, I went on my laptop and tracked it. I knew she was in Achill.'

'Did you not want to go after her?'

'I thought she'd come back.' His voice cracks and he waves his hand around the room. 'I gave her everything. She had nothing when I met her. I just figured she'd be back.'

'Did you contact her at all?'

'Course, but she didn't answer so then I sent texts asking when she was getting back, stuff like that, and she never replied.'

'I see.'

There's a moment, the 'weighing-up' moment, when you know someone is considering saying a little more.

I let the silence do its work.

'I suppose as well . . . they were, you know, cross texts. I was annoyed and that.'

'I'd say you were,' I inject sympathy into my voice. 'Did you go to see her?'

'No.' He gulps. 'I wish I had. I wish I'd gone and dragged her back. Why didn't I?' He looks at us. 'I should have.' He doesn't wait for us to answer. 'I even . . . I even went and apologised to her and I didn't even know what I was apologising for. I thought that would make her come back but I should have just . . .' He lets the words die away.

That was neatly done, I think.

'Do you normally do that? Apologise for things you haven't done?'

'No.' That's made him cross.

'All right, so let me get this straight.' I repeat his story back to him, finishing, 'Then one day she comes in from work, upset, and just leaves you?'

'Uh-huh.'

It makes no sense. 'Sandra worked in Dave's Garage, didn't she?'

'She was getting a lot of hours there before she . . . I dunno . . . didn't go back.'

'The day you say she came in upset from work, you're saying she never went back after?'

'No.'

'And you don't know what upset her?'

'I already told you, no.'

I wonder if she'd heard anything about Richie in her work. Had she come back to confront him over something?

'Had she any friends? Besides you?'

'We were both wary of people. There comes a time when you have to let them know who you are, where you come from. A lot of the time we kept to ourselves.'

'So, are you saying she had no friends?'

'None that I knew of, and sure, we've only lived here about four months so none here, bar the neighbours to say hello to.'

Poor Sandra.

I run through all that Richie has told us again and he confirms I've got it right. Then, with a quick look to Dan, who pockets his notebook, I stand up. 'All right, Richie, we'll be in touch. A family liaison officer will be assigned to you today. She'll help you process this awful event. And if we need to talk to you, we'll be back, all right?'

'Okay.'

'One more thing,' Dan says casually, turning in the doorway, 'Last Thursday night, where were you between the hours of one a.m. and five a.m. Friday morning?'

If Richie is suspicious at the question, he does a great job of hiding it. 'Here. Reading a book.'

'Alone?'

'Yes. I don't get out much. Neither of us do . . . did. I told you.'

'You did.' Dan nods, as if he's just been reminded. 'Any chance I could get a look at your phone to prove that?'

Richie flinches.

'Like, just to prove it,' Dan says. 'It'll show if you were here.'

'Is that not, like, an invasion of privacy?'

Dan says nothing, just looks all innocent.

'Don't you need a warrant or something?'

'You don't want to give me the phone?'

'I am not comfortable with that, no.' Richie's eyes are narrowed. His voice dips.

'Sure, no bother, see you now.' With a pleasant smile, Dan opens the door and we leave.

Outside, Ger rings to confirm that the car parked outside his door belongs to Richie and Dan tells him to ask Larry to see if he can spot it crossing onto the island during the day.

One good thing about investigating a crime on Achill: by road, there is only one way in and one way out.

16

'Reading a book, that's convenient,' I splutter, as we sit back into the car. 'We can't even check that. Do you believe him?'

'I dunno,' Dan says. 'He came clean about knowing where she was and the texts—'

'Which he neatly explained,' I scoff.

'I caught that too,' Dan agrees. 'But maybe it's the truth. Maybe he did apologise to her to keep the peace. I mean, he was playing out of his league there, wasn't he?'

'Maybe she was unfaithful to him.' I float it. 'She was all over Ben in that taxi. Maybe he caught her with someone.' And then I remember what Pat had said at the last conference. 'That might be the "D" in Sandra's contacts.'

'Could be and, let's face it, Sandra appears to have had form. And, Jaysus,' he laughs a little, 'he says he loved her. He barely knew anything about her, for Jaysus' sake.'

'And something must have happened between them to make her up and leave like that. You'd imagine if work had upset her, she would have told him.'

'She didn't tell him much, did she? He thought she'd no family.'

'She told him nothing,' I say. 'Her father murdered? Her

mother dead? No other family? Christ.'

'Maybe Richie found out she'd lied to him,' Dan says.

'Yeah, it's possible too. We'll have to dig into Richie, and we'll also need to investigate what he told us about her saying in the AA meeting that she fled town because she owed money to a money lender.'

'Even though the rest of it was bollix?'

I heave a sigh. It seems like such a waste of time. 'I think so. We'll suggest it to William anyway.' I flick through my note-book. 'Next up it's David McLean, owner and manager of Dave's Garage. Let's see what he has to say for himself.'

I pull out of the car-parking space.

'He played the grieving partner very well.'

'He did.'

'Get on to the sergeant in Crossmolina garda station,' I say. 'See if he can spare a few of the regular lads to talk to Richie's neighbours. Nothing much happens out here so I'd say they'll jump at the chance to investigate. If he was acting oddly, or if they'd been fighting, it'd be noticed by the neighbours, especially with him not being a local.'

As Dan talks to the powers-that-be in Crossmolina, I drive into the town centre to locate the garage Sandra worked in. It's one of the new shop-garage-coffee places that are springing up all over the country. Small but compact. There's a sullen teenager working behind the till in the garage part. A Goth, dyed black hair, lipstick and a nose ring, she glances dispassionately at our ID cards, then brings a lazy glance upwards to us. Her name badge says 'Joy'.

'You don't look like guards,' she says, pulling at an earring and sounding disappointed.

'Jeez, we're sorry about that,' Dan quips. 'Can we talk to David McLean, your manager?'

'Maybe you're not real guards,' she says, head cocked sideways, studying us. 'And if you're not, I'd be in trouble for wasting— Excuse me.' She looks beyond us to where a customer has entered. 'What pump number?' she calls out to him.

'Five,' the man says.

Dan holds up his hand. 'No one will be served until you get your manager. Now.'

She assesses us.

'He means it,' I say brightly.

With an enormous sigh that comes from her black Doc boots, the girl heaves herself off her chair and trundles away to get her boss.

'Is this about the carjacking that took place here last week?' the customer says, joining us at the counter. 'Only my wife was in at the time and she said that—'

'It's about a murder,' Dan answers shortly, and the man's mouth snaps closed, only to open again two seconds later.

'Is it the murder of that girl in Achill? Aren't they saying one of your own was involved? I hope you won't do a big whitewash and—'

'Here they are,' Joy says to a tall man, who is following her. 'They wouldn't let me serve this customer until I got you,' she adds a bit defensively.

'That's all right, Joy.' David smiles at her. 'I've been expecting them. Guards, if you'd like to come with me, my office is over here.' We follow him through the shop, which sells a mish-mash of sandwiches and cakes, key-rings and postcards. There's a hot counter to the left with wedges, chicken wings and sausages on display. 'Can I get you a coffee or anything?' David asks.

'I'll have a coffee and some wedges,' Dan says.

'A coffee for me,' I say. 'Thanks.'

David barks out an order and another long-haired disinterested teenager jumps to attention. Then, with our coffee and food in hand, he leads us into his office. It's the size of a cupboard, but still manages to contain a desk, a computer and two chairs. 'One of you will have to stand, I'm afraid,' David says, taking a seat behind his desk and blocking all the light from the tiny window behind him.

Neither of us sits. 'We won't keep you long. We're just looking for some information on Sandra Byrne. You rang the station to say she worked here?'

'She did.' He screws up his eyes, swivels a little in his chair, thinks, clicks a mouse, presses a few keys on his computer, reads the screen: 'She was here for about three months,' he says. 'So, from October the fifth to the third of January. And on that day, she left me high and dry, just abandoned the till.'

'Any reason why she did that?'

'I asked a couple of the staff about it,' David says, 'after I heard that she was . . . murdered.' He shudders at the word. 'One of the girls, a French kid, Chloé, she was with her that day, said she freaked out with a customer or something. Here,' he pushes over a card, 'that's her number, you can ring her.'

'Great, thanks.'

'And we hold the CCTV for a month, so I have the CCTV of that day too, if you want it?'

Does a fish want water? 'That'd be fantastic,' Dan says, trying hard not to grin, I think.

A few minutes later David hands it over. 'It's not the best,' he says, 'but I'm sure you have all the gadgets to make it better and that.'

If only . . .

'I haven't looked at it but I've checked the rotas and she was on the early-morning shift that day, so just view it from the start.'

'Thanks,' Dan says, taking it from him. 'Can I ask if she had any friends on the staff?'

'Unlikely. She was about twenty years older than most of them. I employed her because I thought she'd bring a bit of maturity to the job. But I could be wrong.' He shrugs. 'Interview the rest of the staff if you like.'

'We will. How many workers have you?'

He tells us that he has five full-timers, all of them young.

'Can we have their numbers, please?' Dan asks, popping the final wedge into his mouth.

As David puts the list together, Pat calls me.

I excuse myself and take the call in the small corridor, which is only slightly wider than I am. A smell of garlic and coffee wafts up from the shop floor and my stomach rumbles. 'Pat,' I say, 'what have you got for me?'

'The number Sandra called a bunch of times during her last couple of weeks came back. The "D" in the phone book? I think I hit a bit of pay dirt.'

'Go on.'

'Donna Kilbride.'

That is so not what I expected. '*The* Donna Kilbride?'

'The one and the same.'

Christ, I think. 'Did you contact her? Does she know Sandra Byrne?'

'She knew her and, what's more, she's agreed to talk with you both.'

'Brilliant, Pat. Thanks. Have you got an address there?'

'I'll text you it. She says she can meet you at the centre.'

'Great work, thanks.'

Pat disconnects and I lean up against the wall to wait for Dan.

I think about what this means. Certain things that should have been obvious are slotting into place.

I wonder if Megan knew, and if she did, why hide it?

And I think, Of course she'd hide it. Megan has never set foot off the island. She is entrenched in the mindset of—

Dan comes out, pocketing a list. He thanks David, who wishes us luck.

Something in my expression must give Dan a hint that a piece has cracked open.

'What?' he asks.

'Come on,' I say. 'We've got a very interesting place to be.'

17

When he drinks he remembers how they met because it blots away the pain, and he can think about her without making a show of himself. In better days, he'd spin the story out for his friends, make more of it. Some friends a lot of them turned out to be. Shallow, deserting bastards. He'll deal with them if he manages what he has come here to do.

The story had gone like this. He'd seen her, queuing for a curry, in some nightclub he was working in as a part-timer. And in those days, for the bar to keep serving, they had to dish up a meal to the punters. Though 'meal' was pushing it. It was usually skanky chips or some cheap curry but the hordes descended on it like there was no tomorrow. He was putting himself through college, and to earn a few bob, he doled out the food to the punters and sold them a few Es. He wasn't proud of that bit. It wasn't something he would ever have told people in later years, had he made his life work, but it did help with the bills. God knew his parents couldn't have afforded to bankroll him, and the job in the nightclub barely paid for his travel to college. Selling the drugs was a fucking lifeline.

Anyway, that night, there she was, too young to be in the bloody club, but the management didn't give a shit, queuing up, frilly white shirt and red skirt. He'd told her that he liked her legs – those were the days when you could compliment a woman without having a hashtag invented for you

– and she said if that was the case, then maybe he'd give her more curry. He'd given her the extra and watched as she'd sashayed back down to her clatter of mates, skirt swishing against white thighs. He'd had a hard-on just looking at her. Then, at the end of the night, when he was working the cloakroom, he'd seen her again. Her coat was leopard print, very sexy. He asked her if her legs would go for a drink with him the next day and she had tossed her mane of curly hair and said that they probably would, and that was how they met. That was his story anyway. But story aside, she had been the love of his bloody life.

Then it had all gone to shit. Fallen like ashes from 9/11 all around them. And she had bailed. Deserted him.

And now she was dead.

He'd done his research. He knew how to play this. No one would ever trace anything back to him.

One woman was dead and another payback death would follow.

18

The journey from Crossmolina to Castlebar can be a bit heart-in-the-mouth, especially for someone like Dan, who doesn't 'do' the Mayo roads. There's a spot, the Windy Gap, that cuts through the Ox mountains. A Formula One driver would be hard pressed to navigate it, with its hairpin bends and its narrow roads. The landscape is one of desolation, with sheep roaming the bogs, and on a foggy, dreary day like today, it's as if nothing else exists except the vast stretch of land and the towering mountains. The silence out here is absolute. Today, Dan barely notices the danger because we're both slightly pumped by the information that Sandra Byrne was in contact with Donna Kilbride or, to give her her correct title, Dr Donna Kilbride.

I think talking to Donna might unlock a lot for us. That's if she's prepared to hand over pertinent information. Doctors are always a bit tricky.

After some hairy driving, we arrive in Castlebar. The clinic is located just outside the town in what was once a large, sprawling country manor, a red-brick, porticoed affair, which is reached by traversing a long driveway, lined with tall trees. After parking in a designated space we make our way to the front door. A tasteful plaque to the side reads, *Welcome to New Beginnings*.

We are buzzed in to a large foyer, which is dominated by an enormous circular reception desk, like something out of the Starship *Enterprise*. An air of quiet efficiency permeates the place.

I flash my badge at the receptionist. 'We're here to speak with Donna Kilbride.'

'Is she expecting you?' If she's surprised at us being here, she doesn't show it.

'Yes.'

'Wait over there.' She waves us to a couple of blue chairs. 'I'll give her a call.'

Dr Donna Kilbride is a TV doctor, known all over the country for her no-nonsense advice on mental health. Her age is hard to determine, but as my mother says, 'She's fierce well preserved'. Once a week, she appears on an RTÉ afternoon show, she writes a column for a Sunday newspaper, and a couple of years back she had a book out that apparently sold zillions. Most of her advice consists of telling people to take exercise, eat well and breathe. She's the founder and director of this clinic, which treats addiction in young adults.

A framed poster on the wall, beside the chairs, reads, 'Happy humans have to work at it.'

'Is "people" a banned word now?' Dan rolls his eyes as he takes a seat. 'Humans, Jaysus.'

'Tani called Sirocco a "little human" last week,' I confess, as Dan laughs. 'She said her little human was now able to climb the stairs. Me and my mother had to use everything we had not to comment on it.'

'Guards, if you'd like to come in now, please do.'

We hadn't noticed Donna approaching – some detectives we

are. Dan throws me a wry grin behind her back as we follow her across the foyer and down a corridor to a door that reads *Director*. Donna has one of those quick, competent, no-nonsense walks. She's smaller than she appears on TV and not half as glamorous. I'm a bit disappointed.

And her office is a disappointment too. I don't know what I was expecting but I certainly didn't think it would just be an *office*. A crappy grey filing cabinet, a loudly ticking clock, a brown desk, pale walls and some battered beige cabinets that, I guess, are used for storing files. A number of certificates hang on the wall to the side of the desk, the frames polished to a high shine.

'Thanks for coming, Guards.' Donna takes a seat behind the desk. Her voice at least is the same as on the telly, warm and sweet. Like caramel.

'No problem.' My own sounds flat and sharp. 'Thanks for agreeing to meet with us. Anything you have on Sandra Byrne will help.' I am still scrabbling with my image of her versus the reality. 'And whatever you have, no matter how insignificant, tell us.'

'I have her file here.' She taps a large brown one on the desk. 'I had a brief read of it before you came. I'm not sure how much of this is relevant to your case and, under the general data protection regulations, I don't want to disclose anything that might compromise Sandra's right to privacy.'

Oh, fuck's sake, I think. GDPR is the bane of my bloody working life. 'Look, Donna, we can apply for information from you under section forty-one of the Data Protection Act, and if you want us to, we will. But it would only hold things up. In my opinion, as we're investigating the murder of your patient it would be in her interest to release the information to us. And as her murderer is still at large, it is also in the public interest to tell us what you think would help catch him.'

Beside me, I know Dan is holding his breath. All this fecking paperwork gets in the way of what we do best.

After a few agonising seconds, Donna gives in. 'All right. Yes. What you're saying makes sense. I won't give you the file, though. You can apply for that if you still want it.'

'Thank you,' I say, relief at her decision trickling through me. 'So, what can you tell us?'

'Where to start?' Donna frowns. 'I've known Sandra for a long time – she was one of the first patients here.' A flash of sadness before she rallies. 'I started this place along with two other therapists, and in the beginning we could accommodate five young people. It was a three-month residential programme. Sandra was sixteen at the time. She'd just had her baby and there were issues with alcohol. Over the following years, I've seen her on and off when she was struggling. And up until a couple of weeks ago, I hadn't heard from her in over a year, so that's why . . .' Her voice trails off.

This is a woman who chooses her words carefully, weighing the precise value of each utterance. I always admire that quality, especially when it's a person on our side. If it's someone I'm hoping to prosecute, that's not so good. Dan and I wait but she seems caught in the memory.

'Can you remember the date she contacted you exactly?' I ask, to get her back on track as Dan pulls out his notebook.

'Yes, it was the fourth of January and she was . . .' Donna frowns. '"Upset" is too easy a word. She was intense, maybe?' She looks at us as if we'd know. We gaze blankly back. 'Intense,' she settles for. 'She wanted to book an appointment with me. Now

I don't do clinics or sessions any more because I find the fact I'm on TV gets in the way with clients, but for patients like Sandra, whom I've previously treated, I occasionally oblige because it keeps my hand in and they've learned to trust me. I booked her in for the next day. Now, over the years, Sandra has relapsed. You know, she'd get sober, then fall off the wagon because she'd lost a job, or a romance had gone sour, things like that. And about a year ago, maybe a little more, I told her that unless she fully confronted the issue that was at the root of her drinking, she would never fully recover.' She opens the file, turns to a report, scans it. 'She stormed out of the office and didn't come back, and I didn't hear from her at all until, as I said, the fourth of January. She was . . .' she shakes her head '. . . she was not good.' Regret leaks into her voice.

We wait.

'She was stressed, pin-balling from one topic to another, but from what I could make out, she'd been trying hard to confront her issues, trying to be honest, and I told her I was proud of her for that. She said it had been going well. She had moved closer to home, had managed to hold down a job, but then she said that the day before she'd seen someone from her past and it had sent her spiralling.' Donna pauses. Then, 'She said, and it stuck with me, that it had found her again.'

The words are chilling.

Yet my initial reaction is followed by 'Is it true?' which makes me feel instantly bad. But Sandra is a person who had lied to a room full of alcoholics. Who had told them that her mother was dead, her dad murdered. Who had omitted to tell her partner that she had a son. Why not lie to her counsellor as well?

'Did she say who it was?'

112

'No. She was upset, I mean really upset, and I couldn't push her.' She reads from the file. '"I saw this man and even though, at the time, I tried to push it away and get on with my life, I realised it hadn't gone away. It all came back. Everything. Everything that ever happened and I know even the things I'm trying to do won't help me escape it.'"

'So, what did you do?' I ask, thinking I'd never make a counsellor. I'd be pushing to find out who he was. Determined to send him scurrying.

'I asked her to describe to me how he made her feel. To write it down, there and then. And she did.' More turning of pages. 'Yes, here we are.' She reads, '"I got a shock but I'm not a kid any more. I have my own power now." So I asked her what she could do with that power and . . .' Donna shifts in her seat, her confidence seeming to waver '. . . she said she was going to tell this man how she felt. She was going to post the letter to him.'

The words, so innocent, slam into me like a freight train. 'And did she?'

Donna shrugs, face pale. 'I don't know.'

'Do you have the note?'

'No.'

Damn. 'Can you remember if it revealed anything about this man or what had happened?'

'I don't think so. Even if it had, I might not remember. That's not my job. But as far as I recall, it was all "I can't keep this secret any more" and "I know you think it was all right but it wasn't" and "You made me feel".' Donna closes the file and rests her hands on it. 'When she left here that day, she really was determined to reclaim herself.' A second before she adds, 'But she never got the chance.'

So many times I've heard that in this job. All the wasted opportunities because we think we'll have more time. It hits me again and again.

Maybe Sandra had confronted this person and it had gone badly wrong. But this whole thing could be a pointless rabbit-hole. She was murdered in the middle of the night. We don't yet have any record of her meeting or rowing with any man. But the timing ties in with what David said about a customer scaring her in the garage and with what Richie said about her coming home from work early one day.

'Did you believe her?'

'I did.' Then, after a slight hesitation, 'But it's a good question. Sandra never really told me anything. She was always evasive. I think she'd been lying her whole life and it was a habit. It was as if she never wanted to be known.'

'Did she ever confide in her family?'

'Unlikely. She didn't seem that close to them.'

'Her mother must have worried, though, if she sent her here. It couldn't have been cheap.'

'Her aunt paid – she had a few bob. And back then, it wasn't as expensive as it is now.'

'Did Sandra say where she saw this person?'

'No.'

'But it was recent, and you last saw her on the fourth of January?'

'Yes.'

'Did she say anything about her partner or relationship?'

'Partner? She told me she wasn't in a relationship.'

Oh, Christ.

It's like trying to catch smoke.

How can you investigate a crime when there's a trail of gossip and lies? When the IP's story changes from person to person.

I look to Dan and know that he, too, believes there's nothing more to be gained here. Not yet anyway.

'I really hope you get the bastard who did it,' Donna says, as we stand. 'She was a lovely person. All she wanted was to learn how to live.'

Those words hit me hard. 'We'll do our best,' I say.

19

We eat a quick lunch in Castlebar and are on our way back to the car, tossing ideas about, wondering if the alleged sighting of this man is even relevant to the case, when I look up and there he is. Coming straight at us.

'Aw, no. Aw, no.'

'What?' Dan asks.

I can't even answer: I am so starkly, horrifically aware of how pristine he looks in his dark jeans, sparkling white runners and expensive jacket while I'm plodding about in a too-large blue raincoat, black woolly hat and curiously misshapen trousers.

I pray that he'll cross the road or change direction but no . . . He's seen me, too, and on he comes.

Fuck him, I think. With grim determination, I continue walking, too.

'Luce?' Dan asks.

'Rob,' I hiss. 'At twelve o'clock.'

'Oh, shit. We can cross the—'

'No bloody way.'

'But—'

Five feet away.

Maybe he won't say anything.

Four feet.

I won't if he won't.

Three feet.

Same lazy-arse walk.

Two feet.

He looks the same too. Bastard.

Level.

'Well, well.' Rob stops and give me a big, cheesy, white-toothed grin. 'If it isn't my charming ex-wife.'

And that does it.

'Well, well,' I counter, with my own grin, though my teeth aren't half as good, 'if it isn't my cheating, robbing fraudster husband.' I think I speak a bit too loudly because the people who have just passed us turn to look back.

Beside me Dan lets out an involuntary 'Oh.'

Rob laughs, as if it's a big joke. Then, to Dan, 'Don't break any laws or she'll turn you in. She has no loyalty whatsoever.'

'He's a work colleague,' I grind out, 'not that it's your business. Now excuse—'

'Aw, you haven't replaced me,' he says, hand on heart. 'That must mean something.'

'Yeah,' I answer, aiming for cool and sounding anything but. 'It means I had such a shit experience with you that I never want to go there again.' And even as I say it, I think, Why am I bothering? Why couldn't I just have walked on? But, nope, honestly, if I thought I'd get away with it, I'd plant him.

He actually has the nerve to look wounded. 'It wasn't all bad. Just the bit at the end and—'

'Rob, much as I like standing here assassinating your character,

I really have to go. Dan, come on.' I make to walk past.

'How's the young lad?'

There's something raw in the way he asks, a vulnerability in his expression. I'm about to reply that Luc is fine, that he's at college, when I'm slammed with the knowledge that this is ROB. Master manipulator. Who knows what he'd do with any information I give him? This man caused people to lose their life savings and didn't once express remorse. 'You lost the right to know when he told you to stay out of his life,' I say instead.

'Aw, come on. Please.'

'Let's go, Dan.'

This time I get three steps away before he calls, 'When did you become such a bitch?'

'Hey, that's enough,' Dan snaps.

'Ooooh.' Rob sniggers. 'Is that meant to scare me?'

'No, but this is.' I advance upon him. 'I became a bitch when I was left to rear a son on my own. I became a bitch when I had to tell him that his dad was in prison for fraud. I became a bitch when you destroyed my career. I became a bitch when I got sent down to Mayo to police. I became—'

'That worked in your favour,' he interrupts, in a loud voice. 'I've read about you solving all these murders. Bit rich, isn't it, when you couldn't solve a fraud case in Dublin or a child kidnap case or—'

'With all due respect,' Dan pokes his face into Rob's, 'fuck off.'

One of the bystanders claps.

'Yeah, fuck off, Rob,' I chime in.

Someone laughs. We've attracted quite the crowd. The polite ones are standing around in little groups pretending not to look. Others are openly staring.

'Ladies and gentlemen,' Rob says, like a showman, doing a twirl, 'your garda force.'

'If I were you I'd turn around and leave, right now,' Dan says, up in his face.

You don't mess with Dan when he looks like that: there's an expression in his eyes that can be chilling.

Rob holds his ground for a few seconds more before curling his lip and dismissing Dan with a half-laugh before walking casually away.

'Nothing to see here,' Dan says to the onlookers. 'Come on.' He grasps my arm and hurries me away. 'Don't upset yourself over that gouger.' He takes the car keys from me and ushers me into the passenger seat. 'Wanker,' he says, as he sits into the driver's side and slams the car door. 'Total wanker.'

'I'm not upset,' I say, but the shake in my voice gives me away. 'I'm angry, is what I am. There he is.' I pull down the passenger mirror to see what I looked like to Rob. 'Oh, Christ,' I flip the mirror back up and continue my rant: 'There he is swanning about, taking his photographs, getting clapped on the back for it, having his work exhibited, talking the talk, everyone thinking he's great, while you and me, better people entirely – entirely,' I emphasise this point by jabbing Dan in the arm, 'grind out an existence, only ever seeing the very worst people can be, hearing about rapes and death and murder and trying to stop the unstoppable.' I swallow hard. 'I am angry is what I am.'

There is the briefest pause in which Dan inserts the key into the ignition, before turning to me and saying, 'It's good, though, yeah? Trying to stop the unstoppable.'

It's a question no one has ever asked me before. Is it good? Is it good for me? I have spent years getting to where I am, years sacrificing time with my boy to see the dead bodies and hear about the rapes and the terrible things people do to each other. And for what? 'There are times, Dan,' I haul in a deep breath, 'when I wonder what it would be like to be untouched by it. To know it's there but not . . . I don't know.' And then, to my utter shame, I start to cry. Huge, gulping, unattractive sobs, tears tracking down my face like big snail trails. 'Oh, shit,' I scrub my eyes with my fist, 'shit, sorry.'

Dan says nothing, just sits there, staring out of the windscreen. Then, 'Feck sake, Lucy, stop, would you? I don't know what I'm meant to do.'

'I thought you gay people were good at being sensitive and consoling.'

'That would be called stereotyping and could get you cancelled,' he says mock-gravely.

I choke out a laugh. Swallow a lump in my throat.

We sit there for a moment or two as I get myself under control. 'Sorry,' I eventually mutter. 'I don't know why that happened.'

'Seeing that gouger, that's why.'

'Yeah. And the awful thing is he looks exactly the same. How can a man who spent a decade in prison look the same? And me,' I think the tears might come again, but I swallow hard, 'I certainly don't look the same.' I don't have to say it, but Dan knows what I mean. In the decade Rob was away, I got the fine big facial scar for myself.

'You look different because you were out doing the right thing. You were bloody living. He looks the same because he did fuck-all.' He inhales, says again, crossly, 'He did fuck-all. Right?'

He has a point. 'Yeah.' And then I repeat, with more conviction, 'Yeah. Thanks, Mr Sensitive Gay Man.'

He laughs loudly. Then, firing the ignition, he says, 'So, do you think this guy is relevant to the case?'

And we're off, tossing theories about like confetti all the way back to the station.

When we arrive in Achill, I take a hasty look at my eyes in the passenger mirror. 'Shit,' I mutter.

'Tell them it's an allergy,' Dan advises.

'We're going into a room full of detectives,' I snap. 'Do you really think they'll fall for that?'

'They'll want to,' Dan says, with certainty. 'It's either that or ask you why you were crying.'

That is a fair point.

Matt is back.

'I thought you were on holidays,' I say.

'Matt's charms were apparently no competition for Sadie's journalist quest to uncover the truth wherever she goes,' Larry says, with a laugh. 'Isn't that right, Matt?'

'She is senior journalist on *Island News*,' Matt says to me, ignoring Larry. 'And when she heard that a guard was being questioned about this latest murder, she had to come back. It's her job.' He tries and fails to look happy about it. 'Did you hurt your eyes, Lucy?'

'Allergy.' I bat it away. 'Are you cleared to be on this investigation?'

'No, he isn't.' William arrives in. 'I heard you were back, Matt, but you've been assigned to work with Jordy.'

'Aw, Cig!' Sounding dismayed, Matt hauls himself to standing. He's actually slightly taller than William but you'd never think

121

it because he's a lot scrawnier and he looks like he should be in a school uniform. 'I'm not going to tell Stacy anything. Like, she can do whatever she wants to get it out of me but I swear, Cig, I won't tell her.'

'What sort of a thing would she do?' Larry asks, sounding interested. There's a splutter of laughter from the room.

'Talk to Jordy,' William says again to Matt, pointing at the door. Then, obviously feeling a bit sorry for him, he adds, 'Look, Matt, if there was a leak, you'd be the first one suspected.'

'Or Lucy's ma,' Larry pipes up, and I want to brain him. 'Or the butcher. Or the woman who bought the chops off him or—'

'All right, enough,' William raises his hand against the laughter. 'Matt, go. Jordy has work for you.'

'Yeah, Marti Brown's dog pissed in Mrs Jones's garden and—'

'That's enough, Larry,' William says, though without rancour. He's obviously in a better humour than he was yesterday. I wonder if something's happened with the case. And then I think it must have, because Larry is beaming and Larry is not a beamer. He generally prowls around the edges of an investigation, staring at CCTV and throwing in his tuppence-worth with the air of a man giving diamonds to paupers. He does not usually have a restless edginess that he can barely control. Thank God someone has something, or William would lose it altogether.

When Matt has left the room, William says, 'Right, let's get started.'

There's a shuffling to chairs and a general quietening.

'DS Peter Glynn,' William says, 'has a report for us into the investigation of DG Ben Lively.'

If anyone is surprised to hear Ben's name, they don't show it.

Most of them probably figured it out when he wasn't included on the team.

Peter ponderously makes his way to the top of the room, standing right in front of William and blocking him from view. 'My team have been tasked with the investigation of the detective involved,' he says, in a big, booming voice, as if he's auditioning for a job as a ringmaster. 'For those of you who don't know, Ben Lively was with our IP the evening before she was murdered.' He outlines Ben's account of the night, and hearing it aloud makes it sound even more suspicious. If I put aside my own feelings, he'd be a person of interest, no doubt. But there is no motive, no reason why he would have murdered her. 'Following this,' Peter continues, 'we interviewed a Ken Johnson, that's Ben Lively's friend, who confirms that, yes, indeed, Ben did sleep in his barn that night. He was unable to confirm from what time but he corroborated Ben's account that his clothes were washed by his wife on his wife's insistence. She insisted that she noticed nothing suspicious about his clothes. She does not remember seeing blood or anything of that kind. Bear in mind, however, that they are his friends. We've sent his clothes for forensic analysis. We were also tasked with talking to Mr Lively's ex-wife, a Marisa McDaid. She and Mr Lively separated just over a year and a half ago, quite acrimoniously, she says. They have two children. Marisa McDaid told our officer that Ben was incredibly difficult to live with, that he had a temper when challenged. When she was asked if there were any specific issues of domestic violence during the time they were married, she said she left before it could go that far. She—'

'That is utter bollix,' Larry shouts, standing up. 'That bloody woman is poison.'

'Sit down.' William's voice crackles like a whip. 'Sit the hell down, Larry.'

'I'm just saying—'

'Sit. Down.'

Larry takes a moment to glare at Peter, who stares back impassively. Then, very slowly, he sits.

I'm glad it's not just me who finds this hard. Ben is a decent guy. He's a great detective. There is no way—

'Anyone who can't look at the evidence dispassionately needs to walk away now,' William says. He waits. No one moves. He's furious, I can tell from his tone and the small tic at the corner of his lip. William isn't a man to shout or roar. He doesn't need to. 'Look, lads, this is hard on all of us but the investigation process is all we have. Bias has no place in it, ye know that. If Ben is innocent, we'll find that out. Understood?' A moment as his gaze sweeps the room. 'Larry?'

'Yes.' The bantering Larry of a few minutes ago is gone. 'Grand.'

'Good. Go on, Peter.'

'Marisa said she left the marriage in fear,' Peter repeats. 'Having said that,' he eyeballs Larry, 'there are no reports of any complaints made by her. There were no complaints to social workers about the children, and their teachers say they seemed very well adjusted. We'll talk to friends and neighbours in the coming days.'

'Thank you, Peter.' William turns to me as Peter strides from the room. 'Lucy?'

I outline what we found out that morning. 'To finish, the station in Crossmolina have agreed to interview a few of Richie's neighbours to find out if there was anything they might have seen or heard on the night in question or indeed on the nights before Sandra left. It's interesting that she told Donna Kilbride she wasn't in a relationship. Dan and I wondered if maybe she'd been involved with someone else and that had set Richie off. According to Richie, he spent Thursday evening at home reading a book.' After that I recount Sandra's meeting with Donna and how Sandra claimed to have met someone from her past. 'We have CCTV for Larry to look at, and we hope to interview the staff member who says they were with Sandra when this man came in. Donna, Richie and David's accounts of this encounter seem to tally, so it must have happened.'

'Do we believe her?' William asks. 'What she told the counsellor?'

'Well, the stories tally, as I said, so I think we need to investigate it, even if just to rule it out. If it is true and she met a man she was determined to oust for whatever reason, we need to trace her movements from the fourth of January to the night of her death and find out as much as we can about who she met during this time.'

'Let's see if we can identify this man first,' William cautions. 'We can't go using resources if it's a wild-goose chase. Anything else?'

'That's it for now.'

'Pat?'

'Bank accounts will be through tomorrow, Cig. And one of the executors of the will, an aunt of Sandra's, Maudie McCoy, states that Sandra was not due to inherit anything. It was all going to Megan and Devon. I'm seeing the will first thing.'

'That rules out a dispute over money on Megan and Leo's behalf,' William says, once again showcasing his extraordinary memory for every detail of a case. 'But it doesn't rule out Sandra disputing the will. We need to find out how she felt about that. If she knew. Anything on her phone, Pat, to indicate she was involved in another relationship?'

'Nothing.' Pat looks at us. 'Sorry.'

Damn.

'Susan?'

Susan reports that they managed to call into a few more houses, including the ones nearest to Sandra's mother's house, and that one neighbour, who lives facing Dugort Strand, thought she heard raised voices around half three or four in the morning. 'The woman's dog was barking,' Susan says, 'and when she told it to shush she says she thought she heard people shouting. She went out and when she realised it was coming from the direction of the Byrnes' house and Sandra was there, she assumed it was some kind of a drunken party.'

This whole place, I think in horror, this whole community, has certainly done a number on Sandra. And I'm as bad. For years, like everyone else, I accepted her as the troublesome sister of Megan. I hadn't bothered to wonder why. And she must have been struggling to have taken to numbing herself with drink. And the toll it must have cost her to leave her baby and get treated for alcohol addiction, never to see him grow or hug him. And then finally to come back and be murdered in a grotty bungalow down by a pier.

I will find out who did this, I vow.

'The same neighbour said that in the past couple of weeks she'd spotted a light up beyond Pauline's house,' Susan says. 'Not every night, but once or twice as she was going to bed late. She said it could've been a torch. She's not sure if she saw it last Thursday.'

'Up from the house?' William says. 'In the garden?'

'Further up, Cig.'

'Could it have been a walker? Did she hear voices?'

'No voices, and she didn't think much of it until I asked her if she'd seen anything unusual in the past while. She also added that the light didn't move. It was just there.'

'Could she be more specific with where this light was?'

'I did ask but there's a lot of land up behind that house. It'd be impossible to pinpoint a position. I told her to call me the next time she spots it.'

'Grand. Anything else?'

'The priest who performed Sandra's mother's funeral also lives up that way so I took the opportunity to ask him about the funeral.' She looks up at William. 'I hope that was all right?'

He's dubious. 'Depends on what you asked.'

'Right. Well,' Susan's hand trembles a little as she flips pages in her notebook, 'I asked him about the funeral because, you know, there is a story about Sandra flirting with him at the afters and having to be hauled away. He's happy to make a proper statement if needed. He basically told me that Sandra came over to him during the afters, that she started talking to him about forgiveness, that she seemed genuinely interested in the concept. That she got a little emotional when he said if you were truly sorry you could be forgiven and she wanted to know what truly sorry was, like how you do truly sorry. That's what he said she said. He told her it depended on what you'd done but making reparation was a good start. She got more emotional. He supposes she had a little drink taken but wasn't terribly drunk, but Maudie insisted that she go home with her. I asked what Sandra's reaction was to this but as far as he remembers she just went with Maudie. I said there was a suggestion that she had been flirting with him but that made him cross.' A pause, before she adds, 'He got quite annoyed with me.' Then she says, 'But if she was flirting, it would be very believable.'

The room erupts in laughter and catcalls as Susan says indignantly, 'I'm just stating facts.'

'And what facts are these?' William asks.

'Basically,' Susan says, with spirit, 'if I was to rate the guys here, it'd be three out of ten tops. He's a ten.'

To booing she sits down. Larry, I note with amusement, is not happy at all.

William smiles slightly. 'All right. Thanks for that. Next thing for you is to talk to a few fishermen, ask who might use that pier or if anyone was using it recently.'

'I'll get on to it tomorrow.'

'Ask them about any unusual lights, see if they spotted anything. They'd be the ones to see a light at night if there was one. In the meantime, we'll put a call out and see if anyone was walking in the area at that time of morning. Next?'

Mick hops up.

'Two things of note from Forensics,' Mick says, 'First off, some shards of glass were found in the house, in Sandra's bedroom, which we think were brought in on the shoes or boots of the SO. And these boot prints, which were sent over early this morning.' He presses a button and a large bloody boot print appears onscreen. 'We are working on size and make,' Mick says, 'but also, Forensics said that in the blood, there were some particles, which must have been on the soles of the SO. They'll have a look at those as soon as. Nothing else of major significance, a few fingerprints we can't identify, but there's no way to say how fresh they are. No murder weapon has been uncovered, though a couple of items have been tested. Oh, yeah, the hair found on Sandra's T-shirt was most likely a dog hair. And as she has no dog, it most likely came in with the SO.'

'Has it been compared to the one I sent in yesterday?' I ask.

'Not yet,' Mick says. 'I'll press for it.'

'See you do, Mick,' William says. 'Now, as well as forensics, I want you to go through open sources on this Richie fella's social-media accounts, see if you can spot anything amiss. If you can't access them, get a section sixty-three order. Let's try to locate a girlfriend, a friend or two who might talk to us about Richie and Sandra as a couple. Larry?'

Larry doesn't bother to stand. 'I've been spectacularly unsuccessful in finding CCTV for Dugort Pier,' he says. A glance at Susan. 'So you're on your own with that. And we've not got any dash-cam footage either as nobody in this place seems to bother with that sort of thing. There are very few visitors at this time of year, too, so I drew a lot of blanks. I did actually do a check for boats coming into Dugort, but it's only a small pier. One boat came in that night, though. The guy rang us, he docked at eight, a Ned Needham, but he was gone again by ten. So no joy there. I then switched my attention to our IP to see if I could trace her movements on the day she was murdered. And I found this.'

He flicks on the CCTV and it shows the area in Achill Sound, just opposite the door of Sweeney's supermarket. My mother loves those shops, few though they are, because they don't go for 'all the fancy names'. The signs over the doors read: 'Books. Clothing. Household. Giftware. Internet. Clothing.' My mother maintains it's nice to go into a shop and know exactly what you're getting.

'This is four forty in the evening,' Larry says, 'so it's getting dark, but this here, I believe, is Sandra. Jordy confirmed that this looks like the jacket she wore into the station that day.'

The video is grey and grimy and seems to jump about a lot. After a moment, a woman in a pink sparkly jacket comes into view. She's a bright patch in a dreary landscape. We can only see her from the back as she waits to cross the road. The traffic coming across the bridge is light but steady. Finally, she takes her chance and runs. Reaching the other side, she stops, then quickly moves off in the other direction. As she disappears out of shot, another familiar figure comes into it. Who is it? The figure seems to be hurrying after Sandra, calling out.

Larry presses a button and we get some footage from another premises. This time the woman has caught up with Sandra and Larry stills the video, zooming in on their faces.

'Sandra and Maudie,' I say. Then, at the blank looks, 'That's Sandra's aunt. She is down to be interviewed by me and Dan in the coming days.' It's not an interview I'm looking forward to: that woman could deep freeze you with a look. She has a way with her that makes you feel about twelve.

Larry lets the video run again. 'Now watch.'

Sandra pulls her skimpy jacket a little closer about her. She's in a too-short skirt and heels. She must have been freezing. Her hair is whipped about her face by the wind. 'We're working on the assumption that this is just after she left the station,' Larry says. 'This is where it gets interesting.'

My pulse quickens as I watch Maudie call to Sandra, who turns around. Sandra rears back. Maudie goes in on her and, from the body language, it looks like a row. Then Sandra seems to gather herself, breaks away and walks off. Maudie stays, staring after her, before walking in the opposite direction.

'Those two passers-by need to be identified.' Larry points to two teenagers, who have stopped to watch the drama.

William takes a note of it. 'She never came forward to say she had met Sandra that day,' he says. 'I want her interviewed under caution tomorrow.' He looks at me. 'Find out what that row was about.'

'Will do.'

'All right, good,' William is pleased. 'Kev?'

'I got the footage from Westport, Cig. I know Larry is going to have a look at it.'

'All right. For tomorrow, give Susan a hand talking to the fishermen, yeah? Brian, any calls of note?'

'It seems Sandra checked into a B-and-B on the fourth of January for two nights, Cig. In Castlebar. The woman who runs it was away and only saw the papers today. She recognised Sandra immediately. She says Sandra arrived with a suitcase, came down for breakfast and she didn't see her much after that.'

That causes a bit of a stir.

'All right, great.' William rubs a hand on his jaw. After a moment, he says, 'So, the timeline is looking like this. Sandra goes to work in the garage on the third, sees someone, reacts badly, comes home early. On the fourth she's at a B-and-B for two nights.'

'She visits Donna on the fourth,' I pipe up, 'and leaves galvanised, ready to confront her past.'

'On the fifth, Cig,' Pat says, 'there's a call from her sister, Megan, on her phone, which goes unanswered. That's followed by a text to say their mother had taken bad. So she left the B-and-B on the fifth and came to Achill.'

'Let's make sure that's what happened. Good work. Can someone brief the night unit?'

At that moment, my phone buzzes and I leave the room to take the call.

It's the sergeant in Crossmolina. 'Hi, Lucy,' he says, sounding full of the joys. 'I had a couple of the lads talk to some neighbours of Richie Fisher, like you requested. Thanks for asking us – there's not much happens around here. Great to be involved.'

It's endearing. He makes it sound like I invited him and his lads to a party.

'Now, the house to the left of Richie is vacant at the moment, apparently the old dear died a few months back, but the lady who lives on the right said she felt that though they seemed like a lovely couple there was a bit of fighting now and again, and a couple of weeks ago there was, in her words, "a humdinger of a row between the two of them" and she says she hadn't seen Sandra since. However, she states that Richie was a lovely fella, though when pressed, she admitted she only thinks that because he helped her in with some heavy bags of shopping one day.'

I laugh slightly, 'That's great, thanks. Any idea what the row was about?'

'No, but it was bad.'

'Any date for when the row happened?'

'No. Early January, though.'

Interesting. 'Thanks.'

'No bother. We'll keep at it. I'll email you the report from the neighbour now.'

He hangs up and a couple of minutes later my phone pings. The report is surprisingly well written and details everything I would have asked. The picture the neighbour paints of the state of the relationship gives us leverage to haul Richie in and question him.

People have begun to leave the conference and I wait in the hallway until William emerges. He's talking to Peter, so I hang about until they're finished.

'What is it?' He turns to me, eyebrows raised. He looks knackered.

'I'd like to bring Richie in.' I hand William my phone with the reports from Crossmolina.

He glances at it, sharp eyes taking in the pertinent points. 'What are you thinking?'

'That maybe they had a row too many. Would she have had a falling-out with Richie? Is that why she was in a B-and-B? And is it also why she told Donna she had no partner? Maybe it was a big enough row to split them up. Then after she came to Achill, he tried to text her, which we know he did. She didn't respond, he snapped, came after her.'

He thinks about this. 'You said in conference that he admitted he knew where she was. That he had tracked her phone. That he had sent angry texts. Would he say that if he killed her?'

'He knew we had her phone and that we'd find out anyway,' I say. 'Admitting it makes him look good.'

After a moment, he hands my phone back. 'Look, let Mick have a dekko at his social media, maybe talk to a girlfriend or two, and see if we can get more on him. But if we can't, we'll ask him to come in voluntarily. Give it until tomorrow afternoon, all right? We've failed to find his car on CCTV.'

'Fine,' I say, with a bad grace. Tomorrow afternoon when he could be getting rid of evidence right now.

'Do you not think Mick is up for it?' William asks. 'You're always championing him and Susan, and here I am, doing my best to give them a try-out. Letting them interview people and all.'

I think this passes for teasing in William's world but I'm not in the mood. 'You wouldn't give them that responsibility unless you thought they were up for it, Cig.' I pocket my phone. 'I'll wait until tomorrow afternoon so.'

A grin. 'Go home. Get some sleep. You look like you need it.'

Charming as always.

20

Sirocco is staying overnight. She's my two-year-old granddaughter and the light of my life. My mother insists she told me she was coming for a sleepover but I don't remember.

'That job makes you forgetful,' my mother mutters, as she follows me down the hallway. Then as I push open the door into Luc's bedroom, she whispers loudly, 'Don't wake her'.

I wish I could. I want to scoop her up, squish her to me and inhale her. I spend a second just standing at the door of the darkened room, listening to the rise and fall of her breath, before I cross to the cot we've placed in Luc's room for her. Luc is away in college but due back at the weekend. I love him coming home with all his washing and tales of new friends made, but by Sunday, he's generally succeeded in annoying me so much that I'm glad to see him head off again. Sirocco, though, I could have to stay for ever. My heart tips in my chest as I stare down on her. She's lying flat on her back, hands curled into soft fists on either side of her head, like a little boxer celebrating a victory. Her pyjamas are pink and fluffy and have a pattern of a cartoon character. She is the most beautiful thing, with her curly dark hair and long eyelashes.

'Katherine has to get her hair done tomorrow,' my mother whispers from the door. 'If you ask me there's a new man on the mat.'

'No one is asking you,' I whisper back. Katherine is the other grandmother. She and her husband Johnny separated about eighteen months ago. If she has a new man, fair play to her. I've never got back on that horse since Rob let me down so badly.

I tiptoe out of the room and follow my mother to the kitchen, where she hands me a plate of sausages and chips. My go-to comfort food.

'Thanks.'

As I eat, she slides into the seat opposite. 'She didn't say she had anyone now,' my mother continues the non-conversation of two minutes ago as she pours herself a cup of tea, 'but why else would she go to all that trouble? She's going shopping too, she told me. A whole day out for herself.'

My mind is still on Sirocco, and on the case, and on something cementing in my head.

'Isn't she great?' My mother stirs a large spoonful of sugar into her tea. 'I could never even think of replacing John.'

'Well, in fairness, Dad didn't cheat on you or get your daughter to lie for him about where he was going.' Johnny Egan, my first love and Katherine's husband, was a total arsehole where women were concerned.

'That's true, but he was no saint. He was an awful man for the pub after a day at sea. We used to have terrible rows over it, especially after you were born.' She says it in the way of someone recalling a particularly fond memory.

'You always told me he was great man.'

'He was,' she says. 'He was fantastic.'

'But you just said—'

'I said he liked his drink and the pub and that we fought. So what? No man is perfect, Lucy. You should know that by now, working in that awful job of yours.'

She has both a high and a low opinion of my job. And while she's proud of the work, she's right. It is awful: you never meet people at their best. Though when you convict someone and bring justice home for a victim, there's something deeper than happiness in that. A satisfaction in yourself and in everyone who helped convict that person. The knowledge that most people are sufficiently appalled by a criminal act, that they will turn up to do jury duty when asked. 'I just never knew he was a drinker.'

She flicks a glance at me, then looks down into her cup.

'What?'

'What?' Trying to pretend she doesn't know what I mean.

'You were going to say something.'

'I wasn't.'

'You were so.' I lean back and fold my arms. 'Go on, say it.'

'I will not. It'll only end in a row.'

'You were going to say that that was nothing compared to marrying a con man, weren't you?'

'I was not. I would never say a thing like that.'

'Hmm.' I stab a few chips onto a fork and shove them into my mouth. Maybe that was a bit harsh, but I know it was something along those lines. She just can't help herself. There is silence for a few moments.

'I was actually going to say,' she sounds all defensive and self-righteous now, 'that every man has faults, and that if you're waiting for one with no faults to turn up, you'll have a long wait.'

'And what's that supposed to mean?'

I'm expecting her to say it means what it means, but instead, she says, all calm, 'You've let Rob put you off meeting anyone and that's sad. I mean, there's loads of lovely men here on Achill for you.'

I almost choke on a chip. There is literally no one in about thirty miles of this place. 'I do not want a man.'

'Rob was a terrible choice, there's no two ways about that, but he's not the only fish in the sea.'

'He's not even a fish. He's the pollution that kills the fish.'

Her silence at my comment speaks volumes.

'I'm happy as I am,' I say. 'I've got Luc and you and Sirocco, and I don't need any more.'

'The reason I never replaced your daddy is that there was no one good enough for me afterwards. You haven't met your good enough yet, Lucy.' And with that, before I can even retaliate, she sweeps out of the door with 'Good night'.

How long has she been waiting to say that to me?

Then she calls, 'Oh, by the way, your car is unfixable. Barney said that wire should never have come out, that it was a death trap. That it looked like you cut it with scissors. You can have mine for the next couple of weeks but then you'll have to get your own. I need to get out now and again.'

Bollix.

I don't sleep well. My mother's words are tumbling around in my head. Is my car really unfixable? Have I really steered clear of relationships just because of Rob? Have I given him that much power over my life? His smug, white-toothed face swims in and out of my mind, the way he asked after Luc today, trying to gain a foothold back in. But I had loved that man, been blinded by—

The shrill ring of my phone makes my thoughts scatter and I'm glad of it. There's nothing I hate more than self-examination. It's four in the morning and the night is pitch dark.

It's Matt. He sounds tired. 'Luce, sorry about this but I thought I'd better call you. I'm at the hospital here. Megan Blake's young lad, Devon, he tried to kill himself tonight.'

'What?' I'm out of bed and dragging off my pyjamas. 'How? When?'

'I wouldn't have called only they're part of the investigation and—'

'Aw, no, poor Megan, she must be up the wall. Where is she?'

'Mayo General. Look, if you're going—'

'Of course I am.' I know I haven't been friendly with Megan in years, but she's like a mother to Devon. I couldn't not go. And, as Matt said, she's part of this investigation and it's odd that this should happen now.

'William says to try to get a read off them. See if there's any reason he would do that.'

His mother was murdered. It's a lot for a young man. But maybe there's more. 'Tell William that yes, yes, I will.'

21

16 January

The hospital is quiet at this time of night, and after I identify myself at Reception, I'm directed to a waiting room. Megan and Leo are inside, with Matt, who looks like he could do with a good sleep. He must have been called out before the end of his shift.

'I'm so sorry,' I say, crossing to Megan. 'How is he?'

She looks surprised to see me. 'Lucy,' she says. 'I didn't think . . .' Then, 'He's alive, anyway.' She looks so fragile, standing in the middle of the room, while Leo, in his own private island of shock, sits on a chair in the corner staring at his hands.

'Good. I'm glad.' I decide that the best thing I can do is come clean. I take a seat along the wall and Megan follows my lead. 'But I have to ask you both if you think that this has anything to do with our investigation?'

Leo's head shoots up. His eyes are red, but the expression in them is suddenly furious, 'Of course it does. His mother died and—'

'She was not a mother to him. I was,' Megan says, and she sounds on the verge of hysteria. 'Me! I was. How could he do that?'

'Because he's upset,' Leo grinds out. 'And it's our fault. We encouraged him—' He stops abruptly, his mouth snapping closed. He covers his face with his hands and his shoulders start to shake. I think he's crying.

Matt looks at me and I give him the signal to leave.

'Devon is in the best place here,' I say, as Matt makes a bolt for the door. 'And he's alive so there's hope he'll recover.'

There is silence after that and I let it settle like feathers all around us. The sounds of the hospital seem to fade into the background and all I can hear is Leo's ragged breathing and Megan's sniffles. I've asked the nurse to keep people out of this room for a few hours until I get some kind of a story from them. Some way of telling if it's related to the investigation. 'Can you tell me exactly what happened, Megan?' I ask, after she appears to have regained some composure.

'I don't know.' Tearful. 'Looking back, he was quiet all day.'

'He's always quiet,' Leo says.

She shoots him a bitter look. 'Quieter than usual,' she amends. 'Then he said he was going off to his friend's house. Conor Quirke, you know, from down the road? They work in the glass shop in Westport together.' She doesn't wait for me to answer, just goes on, 'Anyway,' her voice catches, 'I texted him when it got late to see if he had a key - he's an awful lad for going out and not having a key - and I got no reply and that's unusual because he always replies. So I rang him and he didn't answer, and that was when I started to panic, which I know is an overreaction.' A look at Leo, who is still hunched over in the chair, heels of his palms pressed to his eyes. 'But it was just as well I did because Conor's mother said that Devon had left Conor over an hour ago. And so me and Leo get in the car and start to drive along the road

141

looking for him and next thing we see all this commotion on the beach and I just knew. I just knew.' She starts to sob.

'Knew what?' I ask gently. My heart breaks for my one-time friend.

'Knew it was him.' A sob tears itself out of her. 'It's like I was always waiting for it.'

'Don't talk bollix,' Leo says. 'You can't say that.'

'I can because it's how I always felt.'

'You never said it to me.'

'Would you have listened?' At his lack of response, she makes a *pft* sound. Turning back to me, she says, 'I was always on edge. You know, just in case.'

'What would make you think like that?'

'Because of Sandra and—'

'I've had enough of this.' Leo hops up and walks out, slamming the door behind him.

'I'm sorry about him,' Megan says, like she's used to apologising for her husband.

'It's fine. He's upset.' I wait another few moments before asking, 'What did you mean you were always expecting it?'

'Because of Sandra and what she was like.' Then, at my blank look, she explains: 'You know when my dad died, Maudie and my uncle Dom took Sandra in because my mother couldn't manage her. Sandra was terrible upset over it and I used to tell her that Mammy would take her back once she got better. Mammy was . . .' She flushes. 'She drank, Lucy. Her and Daddy. I never told anyone, though I'm sure everyone knew.'

'I didn't. Not back then anyway.'

'And you call yourself a detective.' She gives me a watery smile.

What a terrible childhood. My own father died when I was

young but at least my mother was together enough to provide for me.

'Anyway, I just think Mammy drinking and the way her and Daddy went on, always fighting, affected Sandra dreadful. I was better able for it. I had Leo.' She gives a bitter little laugh. 'He was my escape. My out. Sandra was . . . well, she was too sensitive. And I was afraid Devon would be the same. He takes things hard, so he does.'

'But Sandra never attempted suicide.'

'She tried to drown herself, didn't she, all them years back? Oh, I know people said she fell in but she didn't. She knew full well what the currents were like around there because she sailed, didn't she? And that day, she took a rake of drink because she wanted to drown. And didn't she climb Slievemore in the winter? Brennie Walsh saved her the first time. And you and me found her the second.' Tears hang bright in Megan's eyes.

And there it is. Not some stupid troublemaker as everyone believed, but a seriously depressed youngster who got no treatment. 'Has Devon ever tried anything like this before?'

'No,' Megan says.

'Could it have been the murder of his mother that sparked it? The shock of it?'

'I'm his mother. They weren't close.' She says it like she's trying to believe it herself. 'But I don't know. Maybe . . . I don't know. I don't.'

'All right. I'll have a chat with him when the nurse lets me in and see what he says, if that's okay?'

She flinches. Rallies. 'Yes, but it's got nothing to do with the murder. I think just seeing his mother . . . well, it made him realise . . . He hasn't been himself since she came back here. He just wanted her gone.' A gulp. 'From the island. Not dead. And I think he felt guilty for the way he treated her, these last few days, and now she's really gone. Please don't go upsetting him.'

'I won't. What way did he treat her the last few days?'

'Just ignoring her. Not talking to her when she talked to him, that sort of thing.'

'And did you encourage him to do that?'

'No!' She's defensive. 'Sandra left him. What other way could he react?'

'Did she leave him? Really?'

Megan flushes. 'She never came back,' she counters. 'She could have and she didn't.' At that moment her phone rings. She holds it up. 'It's Maudie. I called her. Do you mind . . .?'

'You go ahead. I'll be back in a minute.'

I leave her tearfully explaining the situation to Maudie.

Out in the corridor, I make a quick call to the night unit to leave a note for Mick to ask Forensics if they can get the glass found at the scene matched up with anything in the glass shop where Devon works.

Now it's time to find Leo.

22

I walk the building looking for him. I eventually find him sitting on one of the planters, just outside the main door, having a smoke. He seems to have recovered some equilibrium and he gazes impassively at me as I cross towards him.

'Finished talking to her, then?' he says, and there is such hostility in his voice, I wonder if he ever loved his wife. 'Filled your head with rubbish, has she?'

'You and Megan encouraged Devon to hate Sandra, didn't you?' I say.

He doesn't flinch from the question. Instead he studies me, his head to one side. 'That's what it feels like now, all right,' he says, with a sigh, as he drops his cigarette and crushes it under his foot. 'Though at the time, they all made out like it was for the best.'

'They?'

'The coven.'

I wait.

'Pauline, Maudie and Megan. Jesus, one down, two to go.' Then he stops. 'Sorry, that's horrible.' He doesn't sound too sorry.

'Tell me how it happened.' I'm fishing now, not sure it makes a difference knowing, but sometimes you need a big picture to see the smaller stuff. You need to see how people relate to each other. What they will do for or to each other. And a shock like he's had tonight will shake all sorts of things loose.

'How what happened? How we ended up with Devs?'

'Yes. Start there.' I sit alongside him on the planter and he offers me a cigarette. He seems calmer away from his wife.

'No, thanks.'

He pulls out a smoke for himself and tucks the packet back into his jacket. Lighting up, he takes a drag. Exhales. After a few seconds, he says, 'Sandra left, that's what happened. She was sent for treatment apparently and then to a school to keep her away. It was all hushed up at the time. Still is, I suppose. Maudie paid for it all. Said Devon would be better with me and Megs and maybe that was true, but I think it suited Pauline and Maudie. They didn't want Sandra around embarrassing them. That was it, plain and simple.'

I believe him. Years back, mental illness or odd behaviour was swept under the carpet for fear anyone would find out. For fear it would reflect back on the family. And Sandra's behaviour, drinking and trying to drown herself and getting pregnant, would not have been looked on too kindly.

'And you and Megan just fitted into this?'

It takes a moment, but finally he says, 'Megan loved Sandra, she did. And I loved that she was so kind to her but, you know, by then, I think . . . she was burned out by her so when Sandra went away there was almost like a relief, if you know what I mean.'

I nod.

'So even if it was unfair that she was . . . I dunno . . . banished maybe, Megan just hadn't the energy to fight for her. And I think it destroyed Megan, destroyed us, really. And,' he gulps, 'around that time we discovered we couldn't have kids. My fault. Mumps.' A bitter laugh. 'And Megan was great about it. She said nothing even though I know she was devastated. So, when the idea was floated about us raising Devs, I agreed because I could make her happy. And as the three of them told me, Sandra knew it was in Devon's best interests to keep away. Plus, the way she was, she wasn't able for stress, so after school, after the treatment, Maudie paid for her to do a course. I think it was Maudie anyway – Pauline hasn't that much money. Anyway, it was a win-win. Sandra gone and we had our kid.' He inhales again, before breathing out a long, slow stream of smoke. 'And then sure, Jesus, Pauline died. And I'm told to meet Sandra from the bus. I think Megan wanted to make sure she was acting normal and all that. Anyway, she was grand. She looked well, if a bit shook. You know yourself, Pauline's death was unexpected. Anyway, I'm driving her and she asks me about Devon and I say that he's doing good, and I'm thinking, If you really wanted to know you could have made an effort to contact him or that. And next thing is she starts to cry and she says that she hopes he'll talk to her, but as he'd never replied to her letters, she would understand if he didn't. I said nothing because I thought, like, she was stirring it, but then, a couple of days after the funeral, I heard Megan telling Devon not to feel guilty about blanking Sandra because Sandra had blanked him for years, so I told Megan what Sandra had said in the car. And she said that that was a lie but I knew she was the one lying. And eventually she admitted that, yes, Sandra had written every two weeks for the last ten years. Ten years! Like, Megan *knew*, and she and her mother and Maudie had never bloody mentioned it to Devon. The kid had grown up thinking his mother didn't care about him. She had spent ten years thinking he didn't care about her. I was – I was raging, is what I was. Raging.' He jabs his cigarette in my direction and his eyes blaze. '"You don't do that," I said to her. "What in the hell has to happened you?" I said to her. And she said that Sandra might have come and stolen Devon off her and I said, "So what? She's his mother, she has a right." Anyway, we haven't talked much since.' He drops the cigarette and crushes it viciously with his heel.

That explains the atmosphere between them, I think.

'And then Sandra is murdered,' I say softly.

'Yeah. And Devon is all mixed up because he ignored her since she came. He's devastated and yet he's angry. And I thought . . . aw . . . I shouldn't have . . .'

I wait, and Leo brings his gaze to meet mine.

'I told him – I never thought it through – I told him that his mother hadn't abandoned him, that she had written to him. I wanted to make him feel better. I wanted to do it for Sandra. I felt bad about it all, you know. I mean, Devon wouldn't look at her. It was all a mess.'

'When did you tell him?'

He looks at me. 'Last night.'

'Ah.'

He closes his eyes. 'I didn't think it'd make him do this.' A look up at me. 'I should have thought it out.'

Yes, he should have, I think. He basically destroyed Devon's trust in Megan, to whom he seemed particularly close when I interviewed them. 'How do you get on with Devon otherwise?'

He shrugs. 'Up and down. He's a young lad, isn't he? Last few days, he's been annoyed with me for fighting with Megan, though he hadn't a clue what it was about. He always takes her side – she has him brainwashed.' He says it bitterly and I wonder suddenly if he didn't go telling Devon about his mother to damage Megan. Maybe he was pissed off always being cast as the bad guy. 'I never thought,' he swallows, 'never thought he'd go and do anything like this.'

It seems a bit extreme, all right. Unless, of course, he was already depressed or he had a bit more motivation. Maybe he was so angry at Sandra that he . . .

My phone pings. I pull it from my jacket. A text from Megan. *Devon awake.*

'Looks like your son is awake now,' I say, standing up. 'Come on, you should go and see him.'

He follows me back into the hospital.

23

While Devon's family are in with him, I call Dan. It's now six in the morning and I know he'll curse me, but I want another body with me when I interview Devon. Afterwards, it'll be good to bounce ideas and theories off each other to see what sticks. A lot of possibilities and motivations for Sandra's killing are opening up now.

'Yeah,' he says, voice clogged with sleep.

I explain the situation and before I finish, I hear him moving about, pulling on clothes. He says he'll pick up a District Detective Unit car from the station and see me soon.

An hour later, he joins me outside the main door of the hospital, and we head up to where Devon has been put into a private room at our request. 'Rough night,' Dan says to me, as we make our way along the corridor. Looking at him, I'm not sure if he means me or himself. For the first time I can remember, Dan looks less than pristine. His shoes aren't polished to their usual high shine and the shirt he's wearing looks like the one he wore yesterday. His eyes are falling out of his head with tiredness. I don't have time to ask him about it, though, as I have to brief him properly about Devon and what happened the night before.

After that, I locate Devon's doctor and ask if it's all right to interview Devon. To our relief, he nods. 'We've assessed him and he'll be discharged in a day or so,' he tells us. 'He's adamant that he doesn't want to go home so we have to see what other arrangements can be made for him.'

A few minutes later I push open the door into Devon's room. 'Hi, just us,' I say breezily. 'The doctor says we can have a chat with Devon, just to get a picture of what happened last night.'

Maudie, or Miss McCoy, as I used to call her, is there and she offers me a clipped smile of greeting. I smile back and wonder if she'll be so cordial later on when we interview her. I observe her whisper something to Megan, causing Megan to flick an anxious glance at me and Dan. Leo stands behind them, appearing well and truly in the doghouse. Devon, paler than the sheets on his bed, is listless, his eyes focused somewhere on the wall opposite.

'We won't be too long,' I say, by way of hurrying them out of the room.

Megan presses Devon's hand in hers but he fails to respond. 'Don't go upsetting him,' Megan says to me, as she lets his hand go. 'I don't care what happened now or why. I just want him to be all right.'

'Sure.' However desperate she was for a child, if what Leo says is true, what she did to Sandra was unforgivable.

When they've gone, Dan and I cross to the bed. 'Hey,' Dan says. 'Lucy's arse is still sore from the other day when your dog knocked her over.'

There's a flicker of life behind the blank eyes.

'Don't mind him,' I say, making a face. 'He's only trying to embarrass me.'

Nothing.

I wait a moment or two before saying, 'I'm glad you're all right, Devon. Now, I just have a couple of questions for you in relation to last night. Dan will take notes. All right?'

An almost imperceptible nod.

'Can I ask if what you did had anything to do with your mother's death?'

In my mind, you don't walk into the sea unless something is weighing very heavily on you, especially if you've never done anything like it before.

A slow, silent tear slides from the corner of his left eye, down his cheek and plops onto the shoulder of his hospital gown. 'Yes,' he whispers, his voice barely audible. 'I felt terrible bad about it.'

'How so?' I have that prickling sensation under my skin, the one warning me not to get too ahead of myself.

'That she died and I never . . .' He swallows hard. 'I was horrible to her.' More tears slide out. I don't think he notices.

'In what way, buddy?' Dan asks.

'Just – just not talking to her and being mean and then . . . and then she was dead.' He looks at me. 'I was horrible about her and all.'

Dan flashes me a look that says maybe he did just walk into the sea out of remorse, but it niggles. Yes, it's a huge loss when you believe you've been let down by someone and then find out too late that you had it all wrong and you never get the chance to talk it over, but at the same time, is the guilt big enough to drive you to such lengths?

'Are you saying that you were upset about how you treated your mother?'

'Yeah.' He glances at the door. 'And it's all Megan's fault. She

152

made me believe . . .' He doesn't finish – his words get all choked up. 'Sorry.' He scrubs his face.

I pull up a chair and sit down. 'You've had an awful few weeks, Devon,' I say. 'First your nana dies, then your mother, and it's hard when we don't get to say to someone that we still care a little about them, despite what we believe they did. But you know what? Sandra knew you were happy and cared for and, take it from me, that's all a mother wants for her son. She wouldn't hold what you did against you. Don't go throwing your life away over it.'

He stills, looks hard at me, like he's weighing me up. I sense he's on the verge of saying something and then, like watching a cap catch in the breeze, it's gone and I can see it spinning away from me as he physically shuts himself off. 'Thanks,' he says.

'Was there something you wanted to say?' I ask.

He swallows. 'Nope.'

I lay my card beside him. 'Just in case you change your mind.' Nothing.

'I'll send your family in now.' I stand up, still hoping, but nothing. 'The night your mother was murdered, Devon, where were you?'

Silence for a long moment. 'Watching TV,' he says. 'Like we already told you.'

The chance is gone.

We leave and catch up with the family who are down the corridor, staring into cups of dark brown coffee. They turn as we approach.

When we draw level, Dan says, 'Devon's talking anyway,' and after they've expressed relief at this, he says, 'Maudie, we'll be interviewing you later. What time suits?'

If she's surprised, she doesn't show it. 'I'll be leaving here soon. You can find me at my house.'

'Why do you need to talk to her?' Megan says.

'Routine,' Dan says back, which basically means nothing. 'Catch you later, Maudie.'

We head for the hospital car park. Passing a vending machine, Dan slots in a couple of euro and grabs a bar of chocolate. He breaks it in half to share it with me. 'I haven't enough cash to buy two,' he says.

I'm glad of that. The last thing I need at eight in the morning is a whole bar. I pop a square into my mouth. 'This is more than remorse for how he treated his mother. Either he did something to Sandra or he knows who did and it's someone he cares about.'

'Megan would have had motive, especially if she thought Sandra was a threat to her relationship with Devon.'

'She loved Sandra, growing up, so I can't believe she would go that far.'

'It did look like a spur-of-the-moment murder,' Dan offers.

'Yeah.' We arrive at the car and I lean on the bonnet. 'And though Maudie looked like she was arguing with her in the video, would she have had the physical strength to carry out a murder? And I wouldn't say Sandra would exactly have invited her into the house, not after they had words on the bridge that day.'

'True. Leo?'

'Again, we can't rule him out. Yes, he was very forthcoming today but in the process he managed to paint his wife and aunt-in-law in a very bad light. Maybe it was to take himself out of the frame, though his alibi is strong.'

'And why would he kill her anyway?'

'I don't know. It can't have been financial gain because Sandra wasn't getting anything in the will. And he told Devon that Sandra had written to him, so he wasn't trying to hold on to Devon as tightly as Megan.'

'Maybe he killed Sandra for Megan and now he regrets it?'

'I doubt either of them would do anything for each other.'

'So?' Dan looks at me. 'Where are we?'

'We need to hurry Pat up with the financials and the will. We need to double-check Leo's alibi and check for any CCTV of Devon that night. That's all we can do with them for now. Their DNA will be all over that crime scene as they were in and out of the place all the time so it'll tell us nothing if that turns up.'

'Great. Now, let's get breakfast and some good coffee before we talk to Maudie.'

I hesitate. 'This is Castlebar. I don't need to go bumping into Rob again.'

'Let's go somewhere further out of town,' he offers. 'On the way.'

Now that I can agree to.

24

Gielty's do a grand fry, so they do, he thinks, as he ponders for the thou-sandth time why the bitch had left in such a hurry a few hours back. Since prison, he hardly sleeps and since he was let out, he's formed the habit of walking and wandering until tiredness takes him. He'd watched her drive out of sight and she hadn't even noticed him as she sped by. It was as if he'd never existed. Anger flamed in his chest and, like heartburn, it spread out until he was shaking with it.

It had made him do something a little reckless, but it'd be worth it if she got even a little spooked.

He stabs his fried egg and it bursts yellow all over his plate.

The boy hated soft eggs, he remembers suddenly. He's tried, over the years, not to think of him too much because it hurts. It hurts mainly because of the brutal way he'd been taken from him. He would have made a good father, he knows that. When she told him she was pregnant, he'd panicked, he let her down with that initial reaction, but then, he'd rallied. Told her it would all be all right. That he would sort things out for her. He'd get money. He just needed his college degree first. He just needed time. If he had time, he'd support her and the child.

And she'd agreed. She wanted that.

And then that bitch had got in the way and ruined it all. Had changed the course of everything. And his boy had grown up without him. And the only thing he could remember now was that he looked like him and that he hated soft eggs.

And then nothing.

He is aware suddenly that the barman is looking in his direction. He realises that he's been stabbing his egg over and over.

'Sorry,' he calls, all sheepish. He dips his voice, approaches the bar. 'I have . . . eh . . .' deep breath, shaky sigh '. . . a condition. Please excuse me.'

The barman flinches. Doesn't know what to do with the information. 'Not at all,' he says, with a self-conscious smile. 'It's your egg.'

He smiles back.

Returns to his breakfast.

Jaysus, they do a good fry in Gielty's.

25

Before we go into Maudie's, I ring Mick. 'Any news for me on Richie?' I ask.

'His Facebook is public,' Mick says, 'which he hasn't been on in a while. I'm just compiling a list of people that feature most on it right now. There's one girlfriend he seems to have had and then she goes off the radar. I'll try to get hold of her.'

'William says we can haul Richie in this afternoon, so keep on it. Find out what you can as soon as you can.'

'Absolutely.' Mick hangs up.

I tap the phone. 'I think what we have is damning enough but William needs more,' I grumble to Dan.

'Someone to back things up would help our case, though,' Dan says. 'No point rushing things.' He hops out of the car. 'Coming.'

Maudie, who has failed to answer any of our calls, answers the door to us with a very disgruntled expression. 'I was in bed,' she says. 'I needed some sleep after that traumatic night.'

I ignore the rebuke in her voice and ask after Devon.

'He's shaken but he'll survive,' she tells us, as she leads the way to the kitchen. 'When Megan rang me, I had a flashback of

Brennie dragging his mother half dead from the waters around Inishbiggle. It was like history repeating itself.'

Her place, which is her mother's old home, is not at all what I expected. Somehow, I had formed the impression that it'd be poky and full of little rooms with lots of clutter. But, unlike Pauline, she's had work done, having extended out the back, creating a large light-filled kitchen. The furniture is funky and modern and puts my place to shame. But then again, this woman was always about show.

'Pauline loved it here,' she says, as she indicates for us to sit down on one of her hard, colourful chairs. She looks rough, her hair dry and brittle and sticking out every which way despite her best efforts at patting it down. Her face is devoid of make-up, her eyes are tired and bloodshot. She has thrown on a patterned top, beige cardigan, dark brown trousers and a pair of incongruous fluffy bunny slippers. Sitting down opposite us, her bony hands clasped together, she says, 'We'd spend nights just looking out the big window at the sunsets.' Her voice is tinged with grief, and it feels real. 'Tea?'

'No, thanks. We won't be long,' Dan says. 'We've just got a few questions for you that have come up as part of our investiga- tion.' His gaze is steady but she doesn't flinch. 'And I have to tell you that you are not obliged to say anything, however whatever you do say will be taken down in writing and may be given in evidence. Do you understand?'

She splutters out a disbelieving laugh. 'Is that the caution? Am I under arrest?'

'You're not under arrest,' Dan says. 'Do you understand the caution?'

'I'm not stupid. Yes.' Another laugh.

'Okay. Tell me about your relationship with Sandra.'

He's easing her in gently, letting her talk, getting her comfortable. I've warned him about her, about my experiences of her in the classroom. How she could appear full of charm, reel you in and then, BAM!, wrongfoot you. Maybe it was just that I wasn't good at her subject, but I always found her deeply unsettling. I take notes as she goes through the whole story, the 'Sandra story', as I've taken to calling it in my head. Trotting out exactly the same narrative as everyone else we've talked to. Troublemaker Sandra. Devoted aunt wading in to help. Pregnant. And on. 'Dom and I soon discovered that Sandra was a handful. Oh, we tried to get help for her but nothing worked. She was drinking all the time. She'd tried to drown herself the year before and my Brennie saved her. But our relationship, mine and Brennie's, didn't last when she came to stay with me. Two months later he'd gone, unable for it all and Dom couldn't cope either, so he fecked off to Dublin leaving me on my own. And though I wouldn't say it to him, he abandoned that child. She adored him. He left because it suited him to leave. And, of course, then I find out she's pregnant and it's too late to do anything about it. The rest is history, she had the baby. Then she left and sure Megan took Devon in and it was best all around, and even Sandra thought so because she stayed away. The last we heard from her she's billing us for therapy sessions with some TV personality.' An affectionate roll of her eyes.

I bristle. Talk about rewriting the story.

'Lucy there will remember what she was like.' She smiles across the table at me.

'It was all a long time ago,' I say flatly. 'And we have it on good authority that Sandra didn't leave, that you booked her into a clinic and paid for her to attend with Donna Kilbride.'

She jerks and I suppress a grim smile.

'Haven't you been digging around,' she says.

'It's our job,' Dan answers.

'And, yes, it's true. I did pay. I paid for everything in that family,' she says. 'I don't go shouting from the rooftops about it.'

'Bringing it up to date,' Dan switches subject, 'when was the last time you saw your niece?'

She hesitates, obviously wondering what we know. Donna Kilbride has made her wary. She glances down and picks some imaginary fluff from her cardigan. 'I think it was on the day she died,' she says slowly.

'Oh.' Dan quirks his eyebrows. 'Did you not think to report that to us? We put a call out.'

'I didn't kill her so I saw no need.'

'Tell us about that day.'

More hesitation. Do we know or not? she's thinking. 'I need a cup of tea.' We watch as she calmly moves about her kitchen, boiling the kettle, taking one china cup from a press, tossing a teabag into a small pot, letting it brew before pouring the liquid into the cup crossing back to the table. 'I can't bear people who just throw a teabag into a cup,' she says, as she sits. 'Such an ignorant thing to do.'

Dan raises his eyebrows at me. I see what you mean, he's saying. I know he'll relish this. The schoolgirl in me is half afraid, half excited to see the fireworks go off. 'Now that you've got your tea,' he says, 'perhaps you'll tell us about the last day you met Sandra.'

She shoots him a look that is pure poison. I think it's on the tip of her tongue to rebuke him for being cheeky, but she holds back. 'Sandra making a drama out of nothing, that's what.'

161

'You'll need to be clearer.'

I can tell by Dan's tone that he's getting annoyed.

A long moment before Maudie answers, her voice a world of weariness. 'I had a row with her that day. It was the same old row since she came home. Sandra wanted money, as usual. Asked to meet me and then asked me for a loan against whatever she was set to inherit. However, as an executor of her mother's will, I knew she wasn't due to inherit anything, so I refused. You can check that out because one of your lot asked for a copy of the will only yesterday. Anyway, Sandra didn't take it well. I told her that we'd paid her rent over the years, we'd paid for her treatment and a lot of other things, and she had the cheek, the cheek to say that we'd done that in payment for Devon. Paid her to stay away. She felt she was owed.' There is real venom in her voice. 'She felt that Megan and Leo and I owed her. The cheek! She was the one owed us. I saved her. I used my money to help her. Always to help her. And the only thing Pauline had left was her house and a few thousand in savings, which Megan is well entitled to.'

She's getting worked up, her words tumbling over each other, the volume rising, bitterness lacing every word. 'Megan stayed. Megan minded Pauline, minded Devon, asked nothing in return. Leo put up with another man's child in his house.' She reins herself in but bursts forth again: 'The cheek of her.' Spent, she takes a gulp of tea and unclenches her fists.'

'Why did she ask you for a loan?'

That stops her momentarily before she launches back in. 'Because I have money. I saved. I wasn't fortunate enough to have a child or a family and she became a child of sorts for me. I loved her until I couldn't. I tried to help. But that day, that day, I was done. The bit I have, I was not giving it to that trollop. Even

162

if she was due money, I wouldn't have helped her out. She made all our lives a misery with her carry-on.'

'Yes, but what did she want the money for?'

'Herself! What else?'

'So let me get this straight,' Dan says. 'You and your sister paid Sandra to stay away and—'

'We did not. We helped her out if she needed it.'

'On condition that she didn't come home?'

A beat. 'She agreed. It was better for Devon. Less confusing.'

Her arrogance is astounding.

'So now that she had come home, were you still planning on paying her?'

'No, I was done.'

'Is that why she decided to stay? Did she want money to leave the house?'

'She was only in the house until it sold.' Maudie purses her lips. 'Only there thanks to Megan's generosity. I would have turfed her out.'

'There was no need for that in the end, was there?' Dan says.

Maudie pulls back and studies Dan. 'I don't like where you're going, young man,' she says. 'And unless you have proof, I wouldn't go about implying things like that. If Sandra wanted to stay for ever in that house, it was no skin off my nose. She wasn't taking anything from me. I have nothing to gain by her death.'

And therein lies the truth of the matter. Even if the girl embarrassed her, that really isn't a strong enough motive.

It makes Megan look bad, though.

'Did Sandra say anything when you told her she wasn't in the will?'

'A lot of rubbish.'

'What sort of rubbish?'

'What anyone would say.'

We wait.

'She said she'd contest it. That she was entitled to something. That Devon was her child. I said to her that the only reason she tried to connect with him was because she wanted his money. Yes,' she raises her eyebrows, 'that's what it was. She tried to get in touch with him this last while because she wanted his money. A money-grabber. What a . . .' She can't find the word to express her outrage. 'I told her to let it go, to have some dignity, but she didn't know the meaning of the word. And then I walked off.'

And then Sandra was murdered.

We don't say that, though we both think it.

'So what you're saying is that, in the early days, you and your brother took Sandra in to help her mother out after her husband died and—'

'Yes.'

'—and that she went off the rails—'

'I didn't send her off the rails!' she snaps. 'I hope that's not what you're suggesting.'

Dan waits a moment. 'I'm just summarising. She went off the rails and, between the jigs and the reels, she got pregnant, had Devon, was sent off to a clinic followed by a boarding school.'

'Yes.'

'And she never came back.'

'Yes.'

'And she never tried to come back.' Dan is trying to get a handle on how compliant Sandra was with these plans.

'No. Never. She did not love that boy.'

'Did she ever try to make any other contact with Devon?'

A long, long moment as she carefully puts down her cup. It clinks softly against the china saucer. Her gaze meets Dan's. 'She wrote to him,' she answers. 'Telling him anytime she moved. Giving him her address, her phone number. But her letters were . . . weird. Pauline and Megan thought it would confuse Devon so we never told him.'

'I see.' She has extradited herself nicely out of that one. 'If she didn't love him, why would she give him her address?'

'I have no idea. Maybe she thought he'd want it. As if!' She tosses out a laugh.

'Did you think it was a good idea to keep the letters from him?'

'What has this to do with Sandra's murder?'

'Can you answer the question?'

'All right. Yes, yes, I thought it was a good idea. That boy is better off without his mother. We all are.' Then she realises what she's said and flushes. She closes her eyes and brings a hand to her face. Outside, it starts to rain, big spatters hitting the window. The wind picks up. She looks at us. 'She was a beautiful little girl,' she says, 'a joy. Then . . .' a shrug and a few tears spark her eyes '. . . then she wasn't.' A moment, her voice turns bitter. 'Then she wasn't.'

And then she wasn't.

Only it can't be that simple.

'Maudie,' Dan says, 'going back to the row you had with her the day she was murdered—'

'Do we have to?'

'You say Sandra asked to meet you?'

'To get money, yes.'

'Lucy, can you roll that video, please?'

I open my laptop and play the CCTV video. I watch Maudie watch it. Watch her calculating where this is going. When it finishes, she pulls back. 'Yes?'

'It appears that you followed Sandra there, not that she was waiting for you?'

Maudie shrugs.

'Would you not agree? The time stamp is four forty. By our reckoning Sandra was just leaving the garda station. Did you follow her?'

'She asked to see me, I told you.' A gesture towards the laptop. 'Do you have sound for that?'

'No.'

'Then it's my word against yours, isn't it?'

'She asked to see you on a public bridge to discuss delicate financial matters?'

'That was Sandra.'

'What it looks like to us,' Dan says, 'is that you confronted Sandra over something. Run it from the start, Lucy.'

I press play and it can clearly be seen that Maudie calls to Sandra, who turns and rears back in fright or surprise. I freeze the picture at that moment.

Two bright red spots appear over Maudie's high cheekbones, even as her face pales. 'I shall not go over it again. The girl asked to see me.'

I leave the picture frozen on the screen as the interview continues.

'Tell me about Pauline's funeral,' Dan says.

She's back on comfortable ground now. Her posture relaxes and the colour comes back to her face. She even takes a sip of tea as she describes how she had to 'haul Sandra off the poor priest'.

'She was flirting with him, no boundaries, but he was very gra-
cious about it. A nice man, the new priest. He gave a lovely
sermon last Sunday.' A look to me. 'I never see you at mass, Lucy.'

'When you hauled her off,' Dan says sharply, 'what happened?'

'I had to bring her back to her mother's. Poor Pauline would
have been rolling in her grave at the carry-on of her. I told her to
get some sleep and to sober up. And I left.'

'Did she ever say that she was being watched or stalked?'

And she hesitates once more. 'No,' she says finally. 'Not to me.
Megan told me that she was going about saying these ridiculous
things.' She leans towards me and Dan, 'Sandra was an anxious
person. Over-reactive. No one was watching her.'

'How do you know?'

'For God's sake. With all due respect, Detective or Guard or
whatever you are, you didn't know Sandra. I did. I tried to bring
her up. I spent money on her. No one was watching her.'

'We found a makeshift den out her back,' Dan says. 'Someone
was.'

That takes the wind from her sails. I can't gauge her as a range
of emotion seems to play across her face. Mostly I think she is
puzzled, confused. As if she is so sure of her own view that to find
out she is wrong shakes her world.

'Finally,' Dan says, in the tone of one who has had enough of
bullshit, 'where were you between one a.m. and five a.m on the
night Sandra was murdered?'

'I was in bed, Detective. I usually go to bed at ten and sleep
through until nine the next day. That night I was in bed earlier
than usual as I'd hiked up Slievemore with my hiking group.'

'Can anyone confirm this?'

'The hiking club can confirm the hike but, no, I live alone, so no alibi for that.' A small laugh, filled with patronising overtones. 'I hardly think I'm physically capable of killing anyone, do you?'

'That'll be all for now,' Dan says, as I close my laptop and we pick up our jackets. 'We'll be in touch.'

We leave her, staring after us, in her fancy kitchen.

And it's only when I'm out of the door that I begin to breathe properly.

'Imagine having her for an aunt,' Dan says, as he climbs into the car. 'Jaysus.'

And we laugh.

'She kept glancing at the laptop. Did you notice?' I say.

'I did. It definitely made her uncomfortable. But she's right. She had nothing to gain by Sandra's death, and even if she had, she couldn't have done it herself.'

My phone rings. It's Mick. 'Hey, Luce,' he says. 'I just might have something here. There was a girl in Richie's social media. A Robyn Gray. There were various pictures of the two of them together, posing outside shops, walking in parks, all that sort of thing. Anyway, I messaged her early this morning and she just pinged back now. And this is what she says.' A moment while he calls it up. '"That tosser,"' he begins. '"Yes, I've plenty to say. I'm around about four today if you want to talk to me."' He then reads out her address, which is on the Galway-Mayo border, about an hour's drive away. 'I talked to the Cig for ye,' Mick says, 'thought I'd save yez the call and he says to get her interviewed and then, if she has anything of significance to add, to arrest Richie as soon as. Leave the interview with the garage employee until Richie is dealt with.'

'Thanks, Mick. That's great. We'll head over to her now.'

26

Robyn's mother answers the door and, leaning towards us and lowering her voice, she hisses, 'I don't want her upset. She's doing so well. The last thing she needs is—'

'I want to do it.' A waif-like woman stands in the doorway of what is the front room of the house, her oversized cardigan and big fluffy socks making her appear even smaller than she is. 'I'd like to do it, Mammy.' She's pinched and thin, and even from here, I can see that her teeth have the brown of a serious addict. Her face is etched with lines that tell a story of hardship and she looks older than the person she calls mother.

Her mother turns and looks anxiously at her. 'I don't want it to—'

'It won't set me back. This is good for me, Mam.' Her voice slurs. A very serious addict, then.

'Do you want me to sit in with you?'

'No.'

They do a sort of silent eye battle but eventually her mother pulls away, and I'm reminded of how I felt leaving Luc on his first day at school. You have to trust and let go. 'We're not here to upset your daughter,' I tell her. 'We just need some information from her.'

Her mother doesn't respond, just walks by Robyn, squeezing her shoulder as she passes.

Once again, I wonder at the morality of upsetting this girl's life to get what we want out of her. But as William would no doubt say, she's an adult, she's consented, it's her choice. Still, he's not a parent.

'Come in here.' Robyn walks into the room and we follow her. It's a tiny, cosy space and the telly has been muted. It's switched to one of those afternoon shows. Some celebrity chef has cooked what looks like vomit on a plate and the presenters are digging in and raving about it.

'That food looks rank,' Dan says, which causes Robyn to giggle slightly.

'This chef always makes horrible stuff. I think he does it to see how far he can push the presenters. There's some kind of insect in that dish.'

'Jaysus.' Dan looks pained.

'Sit down,' Robyn says, as she folds herself like a bird onto a chair that seems to swallow her small frame. She tucks her legs in under her and, without any more preliminaries, she says, 'You want to know about Richie Fisher, is that right?'

'Please. What can you tell us about him?'

'That he is one sick wanker,' she says.

Dan chuckles. 'I'm not sure that would stand up in court. Tell us how you met him and why he's a sick wanker.'

A timorous chuckle. 'I met him at Narcotics Anonymous. I was off the gear about three weeks and I thought I'd just, you know, give it a go and go along to a meeting. Supposed to be good for you and all that. Anyway, there he was and he's a weird-looking fella so you notice him and sort of feel sorry for him all in one go. And, anyways, I tell me story and everyone nods along and then he tells his story and it's like my story. His auld fella had beat him up and his mother had to move into a shelter and run from him. Just like us. And I think that this fella knows – he knows what it's like. He gets it and so, after, we get talking. And then a bit after that, we start going out and we move in together and then, right,' she sniffs hard, rubs her hand over her nose, coughs, continues, 'one night I come back to the flat, early, like, and he's with his mate and they're drinking. And I say,' her voice breaks a bit, 'I say, I say, "Richie, you're not supposed to be drinking," and he jumps up and looks all guilty, and his friend laughs and he tells the friend to shut up and his friend says to me, "Has he not told you yet?" and Richie says, "Shut up," and I say, "What?" and Richie says, "Nothing," and the friend says, "Richie isn't an addict, you stupid bitch. He just goes there to pick up needy women," and then he laughs again, and then Richie says, "Well, I was going to tell you," and then he laughs, like it's a big joke or something. I feel like shite. Like shite. And I want to cry but instead I pick up Richie's glass and I throw his beer in his face, and he lets out a roar and he pushes me hard and I hit my head, right here.' She points to her temple.

'Did you go to the hospital?' I ask. It'd be good if it was on record.

'No. I couldn't. Because they were right. I was needy, like a dog that wanted a rub, you know. I felt stupid. I just walked out of the room and packed me bags and left.'

'Best thing you could've done,' I say. 'Did you ever hear from him again?'

'No.' She shrugs. 'That hurt more than anything.'

'He never came after you?'

'No.'

'Any communication at all?'

'Nothing. Like I wasn't even worth a text. I should've told the NA crowd at the time but I didn't, so when Mick contacted me, I thought, This is my chance to make people aware of him.'

'And we appreciate it.'

She bends her head, unpicks a thread on her cardigan.

'Just to clarify, you're saying that Richie Fisher uses NA meetings to pick up women.'

'Yeah.'

'And that he assaulted you?'

'Yeah. A push. Just the once, though.'

'Once is enough,' I tell her. 'Now, just to check that we're talking about the same man, can you identify him for us?' I open my laptop and click on Viper, a programme we use in lieu of identity parades. I've uploaded a picture of Richie, and Viper has generated eight other pictures of people who look like him, showing their front, and side profiles. It's a fairer system and a lot less hassle for us. 'Just look through the whole parade and when you spot Richie, please let us know. He might not be here, either,' I say, though I know damn well the little fecker is.

After she has examined all the photos, she points out picture two.

'The witness has circled image two,' I say, and Dan notes it down. 'Thanks, Robyn. That'll be very helpful.'

'What will you do now?'

I don't tell her we're investigating him in conjunction with the Achill murder, so I say, 'We'll probably arrest him, ask him about this among other things.'

'And will he go to jail?' There's so much hope in her voice. I've

172

seen it before, these people who screw up the courage to testify, to have their experiences validated. It might be the first time they have ever felt heard, and it's so important for us to take that on board, but we can't make promises.

'Honestly,' I tell her, 'I don't know.'

She bites her lip and swallows hard.

'But one thing I can promise you,' I say, 'is that he'll get a right shock when we hammer on his door first thing tomorrow and arrest him.'

Her lip quivers and big tears stand in her eyes. 'That'd be great. Thank you. Thank you so much.'

Dan taps his notebook. 'No, Robyn, thank *you*. If he is put in jail, it'll be because you helped put him there.'

'Good.' She wipes her eyes. 'Good.'

Dan stands up. 'Right, we have to hit the road, get the bad guys before they all skip town.'

I love Dan for this. He's got an easy way about him that people warm to. Robyn is openly smiling at him now as she stands up and leads us into the hall. 'The guards are going now, Mam,' she calls, and her mother appears in the kitchen doorway. The relief on her face takes years off her. She joins Robyn and the two women watch us as we pull out and head for home.

William is in his office when I get back. We've missed the conference, so I go in to check if there have been any developments and to fill him in on what we learned from Robyn. He tells me to arrest Richie tomorrow morning and see what we can get out of him. 'Whether he did it or not, he sounds like a complete gouger,' he says. Then he fires off the bullet points of today's conference. 'Mick has had no luck on forensics. Honestly, that boy needs to learn to kick some arse. It's all please and thank you. Christ on a bike.' He rolls his eyes. 'Susan has tracked down a fisherman who, she assures me, knows everything there is to know about piers in Achill and who uses them. Pat has confirmed that Sandra was not due to inherit anything, and also that Megan got a loan two years ago for kitchen improvements and is paying it back.'

'Kitchen improvements? There were no improvements when we visited, Cig. She must have spent it on something else. Maybe she needed to pay off gambling debts – Leo is a bit of a player apparently. I'll get Pat to ask.'

'Do,' he says. He heaves a sigh. 'Larry is still going through CCTV and has spotted her in Westport heading into the pub, but there is nothing on the video to arouse suspicion. He has Ben and her leaving as well and, again, no one seems to follow them or be interested in them. And they're all over each other.'

Great.

'He'll be looking through the CCTV from the garage probably tomorrow. That's about it.' He sits back and folds his arms, 'What's your gut feeling on this, Lucy?'

I squirm a bit. I've never quite trusted my gut since I married a con man and thought he was the love of my life. 'If I had to take a punt on it, I'd say the answer lies somewhere in that family. I mean, Richie looks good for it—'

'Ben looks good for it,' he says.

I close my eyes. 'I know.' Then: 'But there's a weird dynamic among those people, Cig. I can't figure it out. I don't know if Megan and Leo hate or love each other. I don't know how Devon feels about anyone, and Maudie . . .' I shiver. 'I'm probably biased, but she was my business teacher and I hated her. And they've lost two members of their family in a short period and it's like . . .'

I frown '. . . it's like they can't grieve because they're all doing their best to hold everything together.' I shake my head. 'Sorry, I'm not making much sense. Maybe tomorrow we'll haul Richie in and he'll confess. Case closed.'

William laughs slightly. 'We can only hope. Have you eaten yet?'

'No. I'll get chips on the way home.'

'Come on.' He jangles some change in his pocket. 'I've to eat too. I'll buy you some chips.'

'Sure. Thanks.' I pull on my jacket and wait as he goes about tidying up his office, aligning his files, turning the bonsai plant so that another part of it faces the window, slipping on his jacket and zipping it up, all before he turns off the light and closes his door. There's usually no night unit in Achill but when something happens there's always a skeleton crew hanging about. As William and I go by, heads are swiftly bent towards desks and people become suddenly engrossed in their computer screens.

'Is it hard to breathe?' I try out a joke.

'Sorry?' he says.

'You know, in the air of authority?'

He looks at me blankly for a second or two, then raises an eyebrow. 'That was pathetic.'

The chips are good, and he buys us a tin of beer each in the local shop. Though it's blustery, the rain has stopped and we're both well wrapped up, so we stroll towards Achill Sound proper. Standing alongside the wall where Sandra and Maudie had their argument, we turn to face the raging Atlantic. 'It must have been nice to be brought up by the sea,' William observes, looking slantways at me.

I lean against the wall and take a slug of beer. 'Yeah and no. Yeah for the beaches, and no because everyone here expects you to be a bit of a water-baby. I hate boats and surfing or even swimming come to that.'

'Oh, what a disappointment you must be to your mother.'

'Well, she doesn't mind, though my dad, if he'd lived, might have. He was a fisherman. He died at sea.'

'Ah, right,' William mutters, sounding a little uncomfortable.

And I take my chance. Fair's fair. He's asked about me, after all. 'What's with the bonsai?'

I might as well have asked him to strip naked, such is the look he gives me. But, ever the guard, it's fleeting and someone else might not have noticed it. 'I don't understand the question.'

I have to flounder on when really I just want to tell him to forget it. If I was ever guilty of a crime, I'd just confess. I'm useless under pressure. 'It's just . . . you bring it everywhere. That's what everyone says. They even christened you William and His Travelling Bonsai Tree.'

'William and His Travelling Bonsai Tree?'

'Yeah. It's a sort of joke. Forget it. Doesn't matter.'

'All right. We'll forget it.' He turns back to the sea and the camaraderie of a second ago vanishes.

I'm a bit pissed about that, actually. What makes it acceptable for him to poke his nose into my life, ask questions and expect answers and unacceptable for me to do the same? I drain the last of my beer and roll up my bag of chips. 'I'll get going. See you in the morning, Cig.'

He doesn't look at me. 'Yeah. See you, Lucy.' Then: 'Make sure and get a taxi, right. You've been drinking.'

I don't dignify that with a response.

27

17 January

Dan almost eats himself laughing. He's chomping on a banana as we get into the DDU car to pick up Richie, and almost chokes. 'You did not tell him about William and the Travelling Bonsai Tree comment,' he splutters. 'Aw, God, aw, Jaysus! You,' he points a finger at me, 'will never, ever, ever be promoted ever again.' Then he thinks. 'Though maybe you might get the George Cross for bravery.' And he's off again.

'They don't give out the George Cross here,' I tell him, as I snap on my seatbelt. I start the car, pulling out of the station. Behind me, the search team moves out as well. They've been briefed on what to look for in Richie's house. I cannot wait to see the look on his face when we turn up at the door.

'Well, they should,' Dan says, 'because you've earned it.' And he laughs again.

Richie answers the door in a pair of boxers with images of Minnie Mouse all over them and a slice of toast between his teeth. He immediately attempts to cover himself up by crossing his skinny arms about his chest.

'Jaysus, what the—' His toast falls to the floor and he scrabbles to pick it up. It's covered with fluff but he takes a bite and backs away from the door. 'I'm having me breakfast,' he says, waving the toast about a bit and looking at us all assembled and ready to move in.

'Richard Fisher,' I say, 'I'm arresting you on suspicion of murder. You are not obliged to say anything, however whatever you do say will be taken down in writing and may be given in evidence. Do you understand?'

'Understand? No, no, I don't understand. I haven't murdered anyone.' The look of shock on his face is satisfying. 'This is ridiculous. Piss off.' And he tries to close the door on us.

Dan jams his foot in it, and I wince for him as Richie opens it wide only to slam it again. 'I wouldn't do that,' Dan says. 'Here's a warrant.' He holds it up so Richie can see. 'We have the authority to break in, and you don't want a bill for a new door to worry about, do you? Now, go and put some clothes on. I'll come up with you.'

'No, you bloody well won't, you perv.'

'I will, and these lads,' Dan indicates the search team, 'they're going to come in and search the place.'

'No.' A panicked look crosses his face as he takes in the men gathered on his doorstep. 'They'll wreck the house.'

'Can you get dressed, please?' Dan says.

'We don't have all day,' I chime in.

He glares at me and I glare back.

'Richie, Richie pet.' An elderly woman with fluffy white hair and a shopping bag that advises people to 'Put your faith in God but your money in the bank' pushes her way through the throng. Ignoring Dan, she peers into Richie's face, 'How are you holding up, pet?'

'Aw, sure grand, Patti, grand,' Richie says.

'I only heard yesterday. If there's anything I can do, anything.' She pats his arm, seemingly unfazed by his state of undress. Then she turns to us. 'Mind him now, won't ye?'

'Absolutely,' Dan says.

'Good. Good.' Another look drenched in sympathy before she takes her leave.

'She thinks you're my friends.' Richie sounds anguished. 'God, come in then, if you have to, while I get dressed.'

We step into the garish house, which smells even more strongly of pot today. Dan clambers up the stairs with him and I stand in the hallway, waiting while the search team, in pairs, begin looking for anything that might tie Richie to the crime. The door to the kitchen lies open and I see through the gap a small round brown table with two spindly chairs. On top of it there is a laptop with a bunch of what looks like bills stacked beside it. Someone has visited because there are Tupperware containers full of food on the countertop.

In the hallway, where we wait for Richie, a couple of framed photographs hang on the wall. There's a small one of Richie and Sandra looking as happy as can be, the way people do in pictures. Cheek to cheek, they're outside the St Stephen's Green shopping centre in Dublin. The other photograph shows Richie with a pint of Guinness in what looks like . . . I peer more closely. Luc has a picture much the same in his room. Well, well.

I snap that. I don't know how we missed it the other day.

Richie skips down the stairs, light on his feet. He's wearing skinny dark jeans, black Dr Martens and a blue woolly jumper under a leather jacket. Standing in front of us, he asks, 'Is this something I'd need a solicitor for?' It's obvious he's screwed up his courage to even broach the subject.

'You can get one if you like. Up to you.'

'Will I look guilty if I get one?'

I shrug. Dan shrugs.

'I won't so,' he says.

He follows us to the car and sits in the back, behind the passenger seat, Dan sits behind me.

A few hours later, having been processed, a solicitor-less Richie is settled into an interview room in the Achill station. He's got a cup of tea in front of him and a Mars bar. He's been finger-printed, photographed, DNA'd and had his phone taken from him. Right now, he's quite subdued, realising, maybe, the shit he's landed himself in.

We've turned on the DVD recorder and introduced ourselves and I've cautioned him again. Much more cooperative now than he'd been on his doorstep, he meekly recites the whole story of how he met Sandra, how she 'shone', how he was captivated by her and how she approached him after the meeting. And then of how she suddenly upped and left him. Dan and I let him talk, colouring in his narrative, saying very little in response. Finally, he finishes: 'And the next thing was the guards knocking on my door, telling me she had a mother and son and that she was dead.' He gulps hard. 'I still can't really believe it. That she lied like that.'

'It's desperate to be lied to, all right,' I say, trying not to sound sarcastic and I must succeed because, looking wounded, he nods along.

'Thanks for that,' I continue. 'Now, we have a few questions for you, if that's okay?' I'm interviewing him because we reckon he most likely hates women being in charge so he picks on the vulnerable. He might just lose it with me if I push him hard enough.

'I don't mind,' he says, as he breaks off a piece of chocolate and lets it melt between his fingers.

'You admit you knew where Sandra was?'

'Yes.'

'Did you go after her?'

'No.' He sounds impatient. 'How many times?'

'Tell me what you did Saturday night again.' I pretend I've forgotten.

'I read me buk.' He means book.

'Which one?'

'I made a vow to read all the classics this year. I'm on Jane Austen now. *Persuasion.*'

I've never even read one Jane Austen. And I wouldn't have put him down as an Austen fan. 'Impressive.'

He curls his lip, 'If you say so.'

Smart little feck. 'We found a couple of things at the scene that we'd like to ask you about. The first was Sandra's phone.'

He stills. 'Yes,' he says, sounding careful.

'And we have your phone too, so we'll be checking that.'

He's watchful, like a cat waiting for a mouse.

'There were a number of calls and texts from you on Sandra's phone.'

'She was my partner, wasn't she? Be weird if there weren't.'

'Fair point,' I agree. 'Now for the record . . .' I wait while Dan pushes a page across the table to Richie '. . . I am showing Richard Fisher exhibit SB1, text messages from him to Sandra Byrne. This message here,' I jab the transcript, the one where Richie says he was going to track Sandra down and that she won't walk away from him, 'can you explain that?'

Richie reads it and shrugs. 'Look, she'd left me. I didn't know where she was. I was angry, right. I already told you this.'

'You did.'

'And who wouldn't be angry?'

'I get that.' I am sympathetic. 'She just ups and leaves and you don't know where she is. Did you not think to report her missing?'

'She wasn't missing, was she?'

'You knew that for a fact, did you?'

'Sandra wasn't the type to do something stupid.'

'You were tracking her all along, weren't you? Not just when she came to Achill?'

'So? I knew she was punishing me, that's all.'

Too late, he realises he's pushed the door open for us.

'Why would she punish you?'

He glares at me, folds his arms.

'What did you do?'

'Nuttin'.'

'We heard from a couple of your neighbours that you seemed to row quite a bit.'

Richie half laughs. 'Have you seen the age of my neighbours? Half them are deaf, the other half probably have Alzheimer's. We hardly ever rowed.'

'One of the neighbours stated that in early January, there was, her word, a "humdinger" of a row and that she didn't see Sandra after that.'

He's wrongfooted now.

'We hardly ever rowed,' Richie says. 'But, yeah, Sandra had a temper.' Then, 'And if we did row, it was a lot of noise but it was harmless. Yous saw the house. She got her own way in everything. You hardly think I like those colours?'

'That must have been hard on you.' I observe lightly, 'no say in your own house.'

'I had plenty of say,' Richie says, 'so don't try and pin that on me. Sandra was a great girl, but I found out she lied to me. I don't know how I feel about her right now.' Another injured expression.

'Going back to the AA meeting where you met her,' I say, 'how long were you attending that before Sandra came?'

'A couple of weeks.'

'And what is your story, Richie? How did you end up on the sauce?'

'Is that relevant?'

'I think so.'

'Well, I started drinking young, when my parents died, to cope with the grief and, eh, it made me do ridiculous things, like one time I had to go to the shops for my foster mother and I ended up spending the money she gave me on drink. She had no money for the week. And they couldn't cope with me, and my foster father was a brute.' He swallows hard, his lip wobbling.

God, he's good.

'Do I have to go on? It's a bit upsetting.'

'No, it's fine. Sorry to have put you through that.'

'It's all right,' he says weakly.

'It's just odd,' I say casually. 'I can't quite make sense of things now.'

Richie leans forward. 'What things?'

'We talked to an old friend of yours yesterday and they told us that your father used to beat your mother and that you had to move from house to house to escape him.'

There's a tiny flicker of unease. He pulls back. 'That's not right. Whoever said that is mistaking me for someone else. Was it an AA person? They don't have the best memories.'

'No. It was an NA person.'

'I never took drugs. I was just an alcoholic.'

'This girl is one hundred per cent certain it was you. Robyn Gray. Ring any bells?'

'Robyn Gray?' he says, and he's like a person on a bike trying to back-pedal to fix the chain. And, clink, he does. 'She is one hundred per cent drug-addict mental.' He makes a circle with his finger against his head. 'For the birds. You wouldn't want to be believing her. She latched onto me at a meeting once and never let go.'

Looking at him, it's hard to imagine anyone becoming obsessed with him.

'I went there because I thought it was AA, see?' He rolls his eyes. 'I felt a right eejit when I discovered I was in the wrong place.'

'Robyn says you had a relationship with her.'

'Not true.'

Dan, without prompting, pushes across pictures taken from Richie's Facebook. It's him, arm around a beaming Robyn. The caption reads: 'Me and the bird (Robyn) having the craic (not the drug type) LOL'. 'Exhibit SB8.'

'That post doesn't mean I went out with her,' Richie says. 'It was just a pun on her name, see?'

'There are a lot of pictures with you and her on this Facebook account,' I tell him. We'd searched other social-media sites, but as he's hitting fifty, Facebook is his platform of choice. 'I can show you them all day. She alleges you go to AA and NA meetings to pick up women.'

'No.'

'Did you read *About a Boy*?' I ask. 'Where the man goes to the single-mothers meetings. Is that where you got your idea?'

'No.'

'Funny, because the book was in your house.' I push across an image of the book on his shelf.

'Haven't read it.'

It's a truth that you can't get anything from a liar unless you can make the ground shift under their feet. And even then, when it all falls apart, they will stick to their stories. 'Last night,' I say to Richie, 'we trawled your Facebook page. There were two other women we contacted who also met you at AA and who went on to have a relationship with you. Can you tell me about that?'

He shrugs. 'Happens to me a lot. Women saying these things.'

I rein in my frustration. 'How would you describe your relationship with Robyn?'

'I didn't have a relationship.'

We'd tried to track down the friend who had been there when he'd pushed Robyn but we hadn't been able to.

'She alleges that you pushed her when she threw drink in your face.'

'She have any proof?' He raises his eyebrows before laughing slightly. 'No, thought not.'

'Are you an alcoholic, Richie?'

'Yes.'

'And yet,' the picture I snapped in his hallway is pushed across, 'you have this picture of you framed in your hallway.'

'To remind me not to drink,' he says, making an attempt at sounding righteous.

'I don't know if you can see the background in that picture,

Richie, but it's the beer festival in Munich, two years ago, isn't it? We had our guys look at it and they enhanced it. And see here?'

Dan pushes another picture towards him. 'This was the new attraction for that year, wasn't it? Did Sandra find out you had lied to her? Is that what happened?'

'I just held the pint. I didn't drink it. I used that picture as a way to motivate me and Sandra.'

'Remember at the start when I said we'd be checking your phone? Well, we'd already started and, sure, we came across a few videos taken while you were there. So, I'll ask you again, are you an alcoholic?'

He swallows hard. 'Whether I'm an alcoholic or not, it doesn't matter because I never killed her.'

And, unfortunately, he's right. I lay it out for him, how bad it looks for him. 'You knew where she was, you sent her messages that appear threatening, we have evidence to say you used AA to meet her and that you chose her because she was needy. You tailored your AA story to match hers. It's all very predatory. Have a think about it. Oh, and the day we first met you, you were drinking a bottle of Heineken, which you attempted to hide.'

'I loved her,' he says, with passion, as we gather up our things. 'I fucking loved her. I did not kill her.'

'Interview stopped at sixteen forty,' I say into the tape.

The DVD is signed and Richie is led back to his cell. As the slam of the door reverberates in the hall, Dan turns to me.

'Bollix,' we say together.

At the end of the detention period, we have exhausted everything we have and we have to let the little shit go. We'll just have to hope for a print to show up or find a dog he minds whose hair matches the one found on Sandra, or something else to tie him to the scene. And the search of his house has yielded nothing.

We are there when he pulls on his jacket and signs for his things. With a smirk, he says, 'Aside from all this, I can't stop thinking . . . Her son . . . would he like some of her stuff? You know, 'cause he missed out and maybe it'd help him?'

Dan and I stare at him. Is this fellow for real? 'We can ask,' Dan says, in a clipped voice. 'But don't worry, we'll be in touch, Richie.'

'Sure.' Another smirk as he walks out, using his phone to call a taxi.

'He lied about everything,' I say, as I join Dan in the office. 'Absolutely everything. They had a row, she left. She must have told him it was over if she told Donna she wasn't in a relationship. Plus she moved to a B-and-B.'

Dan sits on the edge of the table. 'Even if it turns out he's lying, we still can't prove he killed her. There have been no boots found in his house that match the ones at the scene, no prints, no pets. Nothing.' A sigh. 'Much as it kills me, we'll have to leave him in the wind for now. Who else is looking good for it?'

'Devon is the top of my list. He works in a glass shop – did you know that? And there was glass found at the scene.'

Dan winces. 'Jesus, I hope the kid didn't do anything stupid.'

'You and me both.' Something strikes me suddenly. I pull out my notebook and flick back to my first conversation with Devon. 'If he wasn't talking to his mother why would he be offering to make her cups of tea?'

'What?'

'That's what he said to me the day he found her body.' I hold my notes towards him. 'He asked her if she wanted tea.'

'Thin but weird,' Dan muses. He glances at his watch. 'Chloé is expecting to meet us in Crossmolina in half an hour. We'd better make tracks.'

'We should have asked Richie to share the taxi with us.'

'I'd rather eat my head,' Dan jokes. 'Come on.'

On the way out, I pass Mick. 'Push for that glass analysis, will you, Mick? Kick some arse, all right? Thanks.'

And we're off again.

28

Chloé has agreed to meet us in a café on Crossmolina's main street. For a small town, it's quite an impressive coffee shop. Chloé takes a seat and when Dan asks her if he can get her a coffee, she orders chips and a chicken vol-au-vent with cake to follow and a cappuccino. 'Thank you,' she says then, in her attractive French accent, and with that, she has consigned us to paying for her.

What she has for us better be good, I know Dan is thinking.

I make small-talk with her until Dan returns with coffee for me and him and the full works for Chloé. We might get something when we've finished talking to her. It's five already: I'm starving and so tired I could drop.

Just as Dan divvies out the coffees and Chloé begins to dig into her mountain of chips, my phone rings with a call from my mother. I'm tempted to leave it but she never contacts me at work unless it's important. I excuse myself and move away and Dan begins to make the exact same small-talk to Chloé that I just have.

'Flowers came for you,' my mother says, sounding quite accusatory. 'You could have told me.'

'Told you what?'

'That someone was sending you flowers and me going on last night about—'

'Mam, I'm about to interview a witness here. And those flowers aren't for me. There must be a mistake. Ring the shop and get them to take them back.'

'No, the man—'

'Bye, Mam.'

Honestly, what is she thinking? I'd love to have been a fly on the wall when those flowers were delivered. I'd say she'd have been giddy with excitement. 'Sorry about that,' I say to Chloé, taking my seat. 'Dan, why don't I take notes and you ask the questions?' I suggest it because Chloé is eyeing Dan approvingly. He looks like shit today but even on a shit day Dan still appears rather sharp. I am a mess due to lack of sleep and the need of a good shower.

'Sure.' Dan starts off by asking about her shifts, what hours she works and what it all entails. When she's at ease, he moves on to Sandra.

'Nice lady,' Chloé says, polishing off her last chip and licking her fingers with gusto. 'I only work one or two afternoon with her. She normally worked ze morning, you see?'

Dan nods.

'She is funny and she tell me all about her life and about Richie, the man she love.'

Dan glances at me. That's new.

'She said she loved Richie?' Dan says.

'Very much. How he,' she screws up her face, 'put up with her,' she says hesitantly, 'she do not know. That is what she say.' Throwing her arms into the air and making a fair stab at a Mayo accent, she says, 'How he put up with me, I do not know.'

'Great.' Dan smiles and Chloé returns it with interest, dimples appearing in both cheeks. 'Now, you told another guard that there was a day Sandra reacted to a customer. Would that be right?'

'That is correct.' Chloé takes a huge bite out of her cream cake. Filling squirts everywhere and she exclaims in French. Putting the cake down, she touches a fingertip to her lip, dabs at the cream and sucks it off the finger, cheekily looking at Dan. He grins back. Dan is merciless: he will use anything to get him what he wants.

After she has disposed of the excess cream, Chloé starts talking again. 'This day, the one I talk about, Sandra was serving – on till, I mean. I was – *qu'est-ce que c'est?* . . . how to say it? – stacking cigarettes up. I was behind her and my back to shop and zis man, he walk in to pay for petrol. He say, "Fifty worth of petrol," and nothing happen. All is . . .' She can't find the word, so she puts her fingers to her lips and mouths, 'Ssh. So, I surprise. I turn about,' she moves her head to show us what she means, 'and zere is Sandra, all like zis.' And she mugs a scared look.

'You're telling us she looked frightened? Or angry?' Dan asks.

'Yes, yes, fright. She get a fright. Her back is up against the wall where the drink all is. And she shakes. And she try to talk and cannot. I think at first that she is having . . . illness. And then man look at her all funny, like he shock too, but then he say, all . . . normal . . . he say something like "Is all right." And how he did not think she was in Mayo and then Sandra just run to staff-room and leaf and I am left to do shift on my own.'

'When did this happen?'

She bites her lip, ponders, runs a finger around the rim of her cappuccino mug. 'Only a little bit ago. New Year. After bank holiday because we have laff over that. Richie make resolution to get fit but try to run in big heavy trousers. Very funny, she tell the story.'

'That's really good, Chloé,' Dan says. 'Now, don't answer immediately. I want you to think back to that moment, when you turned around and saw this man. Close your eyes if you like.'

'Mm.' Chloé raises her eyebrows at the suggestion and immediately shuts her eyes, long lashes, which have to be fake, brushing her cheeks.

'All right, so you're at the cigarette machine. Tell me what you're doing exactly.'

She describes how a cigarette machine is stocked in excruciating detail. She's a girl who tells a story the long way around, I think.

'Okay,' Dan says, when she's finished. 'Next thing you hear this man. What did he say?'

'Fifty worth of petrol.'

'What did he sound like?'

'Oh.' She flaps a hand. 'Just like man. I cannot know Irish accents but from here, maybe. I don't know . . .'

'Not to worry. So, you're turning around now and you see him. Describe him.'

'Not good-looking,' she says, as if it's somehow his fault. 'A face like,' she scrunches up her own, 'squash. He thin, no hair, shave or bald, I cannot know. Rich. Old. Older than the woman detective.'

Gee, thanks, you twenty-year-old French freeloader, I think, as Dan smirks at me.

'He wear trainers, white, expensive. Nike. Brand new, like Christmas present. Jeans and a jacket. Red with,' she draws a circle just over her left breast, 'yellow circle with words, I don't know.' Her eyes pop open. 'That is it.'

'All right,' Dan says. 'A couple more questions. How did he pay?'

'Cash. Nice new money. I remember that because I hate dirty money. I hate it.'

'Right. And how did you figure he was rich?'

'They have shine, *comprenez*? Rich people have a shine. And,' she continues, 'I look out after him when he go and he has big black car. All shiny.'

'Make?'

She looks blankly at Dan.

'What type of car was it?'

'Big. Black. Shiny,' she repeats.

'Okay. Now this circle you say was on the jacket. What did it look like? Words? Picture? What shape was it?'

Chloé heaves a sigh, straight from her boots, 'I don't know.' She sounds bored now. She eyes the cake counter. 'That was nice cake.'

Dan ignores the hint. 'What did he say after Sandra left?'

'Easy,' Chloé says, like she's doing a quiz. 'He say, "Was it something I said?" and he laugh, but it not a real laugh. He was not happy either. He pay and then he leaf.'

'Did you talk to Sandra about it afterwards?'

'When she on her way home, I try. I say, "Who was that man? Why are you so . . ."' She mugs the frightened face again. 'She just say sorry and leaf. I feel this man is bad man.'

Dan passes her his card. 'If you think of anything else, give me a call, would you?'

'I will,' she says, with a bat of those long eyelashes. 'I will think *very* hard.'

'Yeah . . . good.'

I'm amused to see now that he's a little uncomfortable with the admiration he has unleashed.

Standing up, Dan tells Chloé to enjoy the rest of her coffee and we leave before she can sting us for anything else.

29

While I drive us back to the station, Dan googles red jackets and yellow crests. 'If the man is from down here, it's most likely a GAA club jacket,' he says, calling up a list of GAA clubs in Mayo. I keep my eyes on the road as he scrolls through them and after about ten minutes he shakes his head. 'Nothing here. I'll try soccer clubs.'

'He might not have been from Mayo,' I say. 'Sandra has lived in at least five places, so he might have just been passing through. Try GAA clubs in Ireland.'

'That'll take for ever.'

I manage a laugh. 'Call the GAA headquarters, dumbo. They're bound to have lists of club colours or be able to put you in touch with someone who knows.'

'Yeah . . . sorry. No sleep, early start, that's what happens.' He bends back to his phone and starts looking up who to ring.

In the silence, I start to try to fit the pieces together. We have a man calling to the petrol station. Sandra leaving in a fright. Getting home early and unexpectedly to Richie. Maybe she caught him at something. Maybe she caught him drinking. Or maybe she told him about this man. Either way, they had a row,

195

she left, stayed in a B-and-B, went to Donna, came away determined to take action on whatever was bothering her, and then
on the fifth heard her mother was dying but got down too late.
Had a bit of a spat at the funeral. My mother never mentioned it.
I wonder if many people even noticed or was it all blown up by
Maudie? After that, she was brought home. Rowed with Maudie
over the will. Or had she? For some reason, though it's a plausible
explanation, I'm not buying it.

I put a call through to Larry.

'Yo!'

'That is such a professional way to answer the phone,' I say.

'I knew it was you.'

'Exactly,' I say, and I hear him chuckle. 'Have you got the
CCTV from Dave's Garage up yet?'

'I'm looking at it now. It's a pain in the hole because it just
shows a view from the front door. The camera pointing at the
till just shows the till so would only catch someone leaning in or
jumping the counter.'

Damn. 'Look out for a man in a red jacket with a yellow crest
entering.'

'I hate to break it to you but it's black and white. I suppose there isn't much trouble there so they didn't invest in the
colour.'

'Great. Right, bald man, thin, wiry. I'll be back soon anyway.'

'Sure. No bother. How'd the interviews go?'

'Not bad. But there is such a thing as having too many theories.'

'Well, as you subtly reminded me two seconds ago, you are the
boss so good luck with that.'

'That fella gets worse,' I mutter, but Dan isn't listening, he's
waiting for his call to go through.

Finally, he connects with someone and puts in a request to be called back.

'Have we made any progress on tracking down that money lender Sandra said she owed money to?' I ask.

'I think Ger said he was on it. Maybe the guy in the garage was the money lender.'

'That's a possibility. We might ID him from the CCTV even if it is black and white.'

'It doesn't feel like that kind of crime, does it, though? 'Dan says. 'It's more . . . personal. To go into her house early in the morning. We're missing something.'

'Maybe we are,' I say quietly. 'Maybe it was someone who didn't intend to kill but knew how to clean up a scene.'

He doesn't reply, both of us cowering from the thought. But, yes, Ben has to be a major suspect.

'We need to trace this guy at the garage, see how he fits in. We still have to get forensics back on the den out the back garden. I mean, that wasn't Ben - he didn't even know her. And that den is pretty disturbing.'

'It is.'

But so is the thought that, if I didn't know Ben, he'd be my number-one suspect.

There's a pink-haired punk with a nose ring in the station when we get back. I didn't think they still existed.

'There he is now,' Matt says cheerily to her. 'I told you he'd be here soon.'

The girl can only be Dan's sister. Even though their dress sense is massively different, she has his high cheekbones and fine nose. Even their eyebrows are the same shape.

'I thought I'd come and say goodbye,' the girl says to Dan, standing up, the chain around her neck jangling. She's tall and willowy and has a certain presence about her. 'Thanks for putting me up the last couple of nights. It was good to meet Fran.' Her gaze falls on me. 'You must be Lucy.'

'Yep. And you are?'

'Lois. Dan's twin. I'm called after Spiderman's girlfriend, if you can believe it.' She rolls her eyes. 'He's called after Desperate Dan in the *Beano*.'

'Right.' That's a lot of information, I think in amusement. I never knew Dan had a twin. She looks younger than him. 'Desperate Dan, eh?'

'Not something I go around telling everyone,' Dan answers, slightly mortified. To her, 'Is Fran driving you to the bus?'

'Yeah.'

'Good. Come back anytime, right, yeah?' His accent has gone even more Dublin in response to hers. 'I—'

'I won't be back unless you come up,' she interrupts firmly. 'None of us will ever come down here to see you.'

In one swift movement, Dan takes her arm and escorts her out of the station.

The door slams behind them.

'What the hell was that about?' Matt asks, as we stare at them out the front of the building having what looks like a good old-fashioned under-the-breath argument.

'No idea.' Then, seeing as I've got him on his own, I ask, 'What has William got you and Jordy working on?'

Matt startles slightly, then tries to recover but overcompensates with a huge guffaw. 'Eh . . . just a thing,' he says.

I let him grow uncomfortable, which is mean, I know. Then I

ask, 'What sort of a thing?'

'All right there?' Jordy arrives out, scratching his belly, and looks from me to Matt. Then he screws up his eyes and gazes out to the car park. 'Is that Dan arguing with someone? Is that his girlfriend?'

'Dan is gay,' I say.

Jordy laughs. 'Christ, that's right. I forgot. You'd sort of forget with him, wouldn't you?'

'What are you and Matt doing working for William?'

'That's something you'd have to take up with the boss man,' Jordy says, not as intimidated by me as Matt. 'Not for us to say.'

Just as I'm about to order them to tell me, Dan arrives back. He claps his hands together, looks a bit startled at the sound they make. 'All done staring?' And he stalks off up the stairs.

'I never knew you had a twin,' I run to catch him up.

'I do and she arrived down last night to tell me that Da only has weeks left and that I'd better go up or I'll regret it and I said no. Simple.'

'That's why you looked so wrecked this past couple of days, your clear conscience.'

He just keeps walking.

He heads towards the kitchen and I think it's better if I don't join him. Besides, I have a CCTV date with Larry. He, Dan, Ben and I all share the same office space when we are on the Achill team. It's usually cramped and stuffy, no matter what the weather does outside. With Ben missing now, there's a little more room but it doesn't feel right.

Larry beckons me over. 'I've the CCTV all loaded up and ready to roll,' he says. 'What are we looking for?'

I join him at the desk and stand at his shoulder as he calls up footage from the morning of 3 January. He presses play. It's so boring, I don't know how Larry does it, watching people come in and out. We spot a shoplifter an hour into it but that's as exciting as it gets. The footage from the till shows two women, Sandra and Chloé, alternately taking payments from the customers. It's dire, though: we can't get an eye on anyone they serve, save from an oblique angle to the side. Two hours in, I glance at Larry and he's still staring at the screen with the same intensity he started with. 'Stop looking at me,' he says. 'I'm not interested.'

'Hilari— Hey.' I jab a finger at the screen. 'Stop - stop it there.'

He does.

I lean in. A man, head bowed, walks jauntily through the doors. White runners, jeans and a lighter shade of grey jacket, which might be red. Head dipped, pulls out his wallet and takes out some money. We watch him as he turns and makes his way out of shot. I ask Larry to rewind. Then to play it forward slowly and to freeze. 'There.' I point to a spot, just visible on the jacket. 'Would you say that's a logo?'

Larry magnifies it. It pixilates but, peering closer, he says, 'Yeah, it is all right.' We turn to the counter footage now. We watch as Sandra crosses to the till and freezes, then presses herself back to the wall. We can't see the man: he's just out of shot. Sandra runs off and we watch as Chloé moves in to take payment.

'Whoever installed that security system should be shot,' Larry mutters, as he studies the screen, then zooms in on the side of the till, which I notice then is reflective, but it yields nothing. He runs the video and we get a slightly better view of the man as he leaves the shop and turns into the forecourt.

'Anything on the forecourt?'

Larry pulls up the footage and we groan as the man's car pulls in at the furthest pump from the camera, giving us its wheels and side. Though I'm not sure any pump would have given us a great view.

'Black mid-sized car,' Larry says.

The driver's door opens and a man gets out. The footage is shite but we watch as he fills up.

'Petrol car,' Larry notes.

The man is not as tall as the pump, so of average height. When he's finished, he turns around and we get a full, though very grainy, look at him. Larry freezes the picture and zooms in. 'Shit,' he says, as the picture pixilates and goes out of focus. 'Bollix.' He zooms back out. 'I'll see if I can work on it,' he says. He lets the video run on.

The next piece of footage shows him coming out of the station, climbing into his car and driving off in the direction of Ballina.

'Let's harvest any CCTV we can from along the route. See if we can pick up the car anywhere else.'

Larry looks pained.

'I know. But at least we have a date and a time. If we can get a clearer look at the reg we'll be cooking.'

'Clearer?' Larry laughs. 'Any sort of a look at the reg would be nice.'

'I know.'

As Larry gets back to work, Dan enters carrying two cups of coffee and hands one to me.

'Ta.'

'Any luck?'

I fill him in.

'I talked to the guy in the GAA,' he said, 'and he really wasn't able to help. There's a club called Newcastown who play in yellow and red stripes but their crest is red and green. I've called the soccer and the rugby clubs now to see if we can identify it.' He pauses. 'It could be a uniform of some sort. I mean, would you wear it all the time if it was a club jacket?'

'Good point. Maybe we should put out a call describing the jacket, see if anyone can identify it?'

'Kev has been roped in to do *Crimecall* so he can talk about it on that. Just run it by the Cig,' Larry says. A smirk that promises trouble. 'Are you heartbroken, Luce, not to be doing *Crimecall*, you going viral and all the last time?'

The two lads laugh, and Larry, with lightning dexterity, pulls up the picture of me when I did the show about eighteen months ago. I'd picked a tree with the most phallic-looking branches to stand beside during the recording and as a result I'd been christened Penis Tree Girl on Twitter.

Still, it had been the report that had broken open the case.

'Enough of this hilarity.' Larry winks at me as he turns back to run the footage again.

Ten minutes later, I'm on the phone to Ger, who is indeed following up on the money-lender theory. 'I've a list here from the central bank,' he says, 'and I've even got a list of those who've had their licences revoked in the past couple of years, but so far no one has lent a Sandra Byrne anything. Not that they're saying anyway.'

'Grand. Keep on it.' I'm doubtful that Sandra would have been able to outrun a legitimate business, though, or indeed if a legitimate business would have gone so far as to murder her late at night, but it needs to be ticked off.

Just as I hang up, Larry sucks in his breath. 'Well, well, well, hello there,' he says, as he zooms in on the tiny piece of car we saw in the footage.

'What is it?'

Larry presses a few buttons and the side of the car is enhanced. Larry focuses on a piece to the upper left and blows it bigger again. 'A scratch,' he says, in satisfaction. 'Quite a deep one too. See?' He points it out to us and I admit that I never would have noticed.

'And that's why the Lar is the best in the business,' he crows, as he prints out the page.

'Excellent. So, our driver had had an accident. What might have caused it, do you think?'

'It doesn't look like it resulted from a collision.' Larry studies the printout every which way. 'But I'm no expert. I'll get on to the boys and ask them what they think.'

'Great work, Lar.'

'Yeah, I know.' But he's joking. 'Thanks.'

30

'Unless we have something to report, conferences will take place every second day from now on,' William says, to a packed room. 'I still want all information brought to the table promptly.' He looks a bit harried. 'Now let's get this hurried on. It's late. Lucy, Dan, where are you at?'

Is he being a bit short with me? I give him the run-down of our day, leaving the CCTV reveal to Larry. 'In short, we have five persons of interest.' I pin a shot of the petrol-pump guy to the board. 'This mysterious guy at the pumps because she seemed scared of him. We're in the process of trying to track him down. Larry will give ye the run-down on that. We've Megan,' I point to her picture taken off Facebook, 'Sandra's sister, who had plenty of motive - her fear of Devon being taken away, Sandra lodging in the cottage and refusing to move on thus holding up her inheritance, Sandra maybe contesting the will though whether they're strong enough motives, I'm not sure. There is Devon,' another picture, 'Sandra's son. His suicide attempt was certainly out of character. He says he felt guilty for how he treated his mother but, in my experience, out-of-character behaviour like this hints at larger concerns. We also have Richie—'

'What about the husband?' William interrupts. 'Leo, is it?'

'His alibi is solid,' Kev pipes up. 'He wouldn't have had time to leave his friend's house, murder Sandra and get back home by four a.m. I walked the route on my lunchtime today.'

'Was he definitely home by four?' William asks.

'Yeah. A neighbour going out to work saw him on the road.'

William beams in approval. Kev never leaves a stone unturned.

'There's also Richie,' I continue. 'He admits he sent the texts, that he was pissed off with Sandra. And his alibi is quite weak with no one to back it up.' I give the room the run-down on our interview with him yesterday. 'He has form with violence, according to Robyn, but no prints from Richie were found at the scene.'

'Though absence of evidence is not evidence of absence,' William says.

'And, of course, there's Ben Lively, though he's part of a separate investigation.'

'Five persons of interest.' William raises an eyebrow. 'Is that some kind of a record?'

'You said you wanted something and now you've got it,' I mutter, under my breath, to Dan, who kicks me to shut up.

'Pat?'

'I talked to Megan yesterday, Cig, about the ten-thousand-pound loan that was down as kitchen improvements. She admitted that the loan was taken out to clear her husband's gambling debts. Seeing as he was out playing cards on the night his sister-in-law was murdered, I thought I'd check with the bookies and the local card sharps and they confirm that Leo has racked up another two grand since then. So, this inheritance is badly needed.'

'A lot of motive there then,' William muses. 'And if the girl was going to contest the will, it would hold everything up.'

'Susan?' William says. 'You were talking to the fisherman?'

'Yes,' Susan says. She pulls her notebook out of her top pocket and flicks through it. 'I . . . eh, well . . .'

'You, ah, eh, well what?' William asks, eyebrows raised.

'I'm finding the exact words here, Cig, just so I get it right.'

'What part of "Let's get this hurried on" didn't you understand?'

Susan huffs out an exasperated sigh, which takes us all by surprise. 'All right,' she says, and she sounds cross. 'I talked to a Dotsy McGuire and—'

'Who?' William looks pained.

'A Dotsy McGuire,' Susan says.

'Dotsy.' William's face is a picture. 'Dotsy?'

'Do you want me to continue?' Susan asks, and I have to bite my lip not to giggle.

William waves her on.

'So, Dotsy said that no one really uses Dugort Pier, not really. And even if they did, there is no record-keeping or anything like that. It's mainly for locals. Plus, he said that it would be impossible to navigate it at night without lights. That no one would dare.'

'Lights?'

'Yes.'

'But sure a boat would have lights,' William says.

'He meant transit lights,' Kev pipes up.

'What?'

'My dad was a fisherman,' Kev says. 'Dotsy was saying that without transit lights you'd find it impossible to dock.' At our blank looks, he goes on, 'A transit is a guidance system for boats to make it into pier. In a place like Dugort, there wouldn't be an official transit, so most lads would use local knowledge. Say, during the day they might line up two navigation marks or two

206

ocean buoys or a lighthouse and a headland light, and the captain has to keep them in line at all times as he makes his way to port. Sort of like lining up the sights on a rifle. But at night you can't see those things, so you'd need to line up two lights. They call them leading lights.'

'And would the fixed light that the neighbour saw be one of those?' William asks.

'Could be, Cig,' Kev nods. 'Though to dock you'd need a second light.'

William nods. 'Right. Ask Dotty—'

'Dotsy.'

'—what lights would be used at night for Dugort, and if any fishermen have seen them on recently. If it was Devon, Megan or Ben murdered Sandra, they'd hardly be sailing,' William says. 'They'd have walked. Does Richie sail?' He looks at me.

'I don't know.'

'Check it out. And as for our petrol-pump man, well—'

At that moment Mick barges in at the door.

'Sorry, sorry,' he says, not sounding at all apologetic. 'I was waiting on tests to come back from Forensics, Cig, and I might have something.'

All our attention is suddenly focused on him and he balks. It better be good, I think, or he might be in for a bollocking.

'It's the glass,' Mick says, without being invited to speak. 'Remember there was glass found at the scene? Well, Forensics just got back to me and said that there were shards of glass found in the den as well. They ran a preliminary comparison and they match, so it looks like our stalker was in the house.'

'Good, but we don't know who the stalker was or if he killed anyone,' William says.

'That's the exciting bit.' Mick looks like he's about to burst. 'Yesterday Lucy told me that Devon works in a shop that cuts glass for tabletops and cabinets and that. She asked if I could compare the glass found in the house to any that Devon had come into contact with. Anyway, his manager told me that on the Saturday, Devon and another employee dropped a large pane of glass when they were loading it onto the van. The lab rang about ten minutes ago. Analysis of this glass matches exactly the one found in the house so, by the laws of logic, it must also match the one found in the den.'

'Brilliant, Mick,' Susan calls, then clamps a hand over her mouth.

'That is brilliant,' William agrees. 'Did Forensics say when they might issue the official report?'

'Later on.'

'Because I won't believe it until I see it. Lucy and Dan, let's do some background, get things in motion and arrest Devon Byrne. Let's see what he has to say for himself.'

My heart sinks at another few hours' work, but the fact that we've made this much progress is fantastic. Still . . . Devon? For Megan's sake, I hope not.

'Fast track that dog hair for us too,' William says. 'Is it Devon's dog or not?'

'I'll draw the warrants up,' Dan whispers to me. 'You're knackered. Go home and get some sleep. You'll need all your wits tomorrow when we arrest the kid.'

'Thanks.'

He winks and then we tune back in to hear Larry modestly claim that he should be able to ID petrol-pump man in a few days.

★★★

When I get home, my mother is asleep. A bunch of dead flowers is displayed in a vase on the kitchen table. Dead fecking flowers? And she put them in a vase?

Who on earth . . .?

There's a note beside the vase – *I rang every shop. None of them remember the order. They must be lying because they don't want to replace them.*

The thought slithers through me and I shiver.

It's Rob.

What the hell is he playing at?

I push it to the back of my mind. I'll deal with him tomorrow.

I take the flowers and, opening the back door, I hurl them out into the night. With any luck the wind will blow them straight into the Atlantic.

31

19 January

Two days later, Dan and I settle into dilapidated chairs in front of the television monitor, which feeds into Interview Room Two. There are two cameras, one pointing directly at Devon, so that we can see every grimace and tic of the boy while another camera gives a wide-angle view. A visibly shaken Devon sits at the table while Larry and William sit opposite him. The previous day, it had been confirmed that shards from all three locations were an exact match. The dog hair unfortunately didn't match Devon's dog. But we had enough. Larry and William had then worked out an interview strategy and Dan and I had arrested Devon at his friend's house, where he'd been staying since his discharge from hospital. After that a team had gone in to search his room.

Simultaneously, a team had been sent to Megan and Leo's house. Apparently, Megan had been distraught when the boys had arrived and, according to one of the lads, she'd grown hysterical when she'd heard that Devon was under arrest. Leo had wrapped his arms about her, and she'd sobbed hard into his shoulder. So, there was some affection between them, I was glad to hear.

Devon has been assessed and has been deemed mentally fit to

be questioned. Right now, though, he looks like a man on the edge. His leg is jiggling up and down and he constantly drags his hand through his hair. He looks scared and, yes, guilty. He has refused an offer of tea or anything to eat. 'Please,' he says, 'just get on with it.'

William starts off gently, getting Devon to confirm his name for the purposes of the tape, explaining the caution to him, asking him does he understand the charge, to which Devon nods. He asks Devon about his dogs, about the farm, to which Devon mutters some terse answers.

Finally Devon snaps, 'Look, just stop. You lot think I killed Sandra, but I didn't.'

'All right.' William sounds encouraging. 'Sure, you'll be able to put us straight then, won't you?'

'Uh-huh.'

'Tell me how come you live with your aunt and uncle.'

'Not any more.' It's bitter.

'But how did you come to live with them before?' William rephrases.

'You know how. Everyone in this place knows how.'

'I'm not from this place. I'm a Limerick man, born and bred. Every time I come down here I get asked if I windsurf or sail and that.' He rolls his eyes. 'Jaysus, I wouldn't know one end of a boat from the other.' He smiles and it's quite extraordinary to see. 'How about you?'

Devon shrugs. 'Anyone from here knows how to sail,' he says. 'I'm not much into it, though. Leo taught me.' He spits Leo's name out, then adds, 'I prefer sport.'

'A man after my own heart,' William says, and I wonder if it's true. We know virtually nothing about him. 'Let me see if I got it straight. I heard that your mother left you with an aunt. Is that right?'

'I guess.'

'How do you feel about that?'

'I didn't kill her.'

'Were you angry?'

'I was a baby but, after a while, yeah. Who wouldn't be? I always thought that Megan and Leo cared for me. I trusted them, like.' He sounds angrier now.

William says nothing.

'I always thought that Sandra was this person who only cared about herself, but no such thing. She wrote me, she wrote every two weeks.' His gulps, trying not to cry, I think. 'I didn't know. She rang too, I heard, looking for updates, but Megan used to tell her I didn't want to talk to her. I mightn't have wanted it but I was never offered it. She never offered. Now it's too late.' He swipes at his cheeks where some tears have tracked down.

'Yeah. That's hard.' William leaves a silence before he asks, 'You must have felt betrayed by everyone.'

'Pretty much, yeah.'

'And did you speak to your mother at all in the days before she was murdered?'

'No.' He says it with so much grief that my heart twists.

'Nothing?'

'I ignored her, all right?' He says it with ferocity. 'I feel . . . terrible about it.'

'All right.' William's voice is gentle. 'The day your mother was killed, Devon, can you talk us through what you did?'

'The whole day?'

'Yeah.'

'It was a Thursday, so I got up at eight and was in work for nine. I had lunch at one in the back office. Then I left the place at five thirty – no, it was six that day. Then I drove home to Megan's. I helped Leo feed the animals and then he went out. I watched TV with Megan and went to bed.'

'Tell me about work. How was your day?'

He shrugs. 'A bit shit, actually. Grumpy customers and then, sure near the end, didn't I drop a piece of glass for a tabletop that was being loaded in the van. The boss went mad, and I had to stay back and sweep the lot up.'

'Would it be safe to say that this is the item you broke?'

'Exhibit SB2,' Larry says. 'A picture of a glass tabletop, heat-tempered glass.'

Devon looks a bit surprised that William and Larry know this. 'That's it. It broke into all these shards. 'Twas lucky no one was hurt.'

'And your boss told you to tidy the place up?'

'Aye. I had to brush myself down and then I left, drove home.'

'And you had tea and watched a film?'

'That's right.'

'Now we'll move on to the day you discovered your mother's body, if you don't mind. Is that all right?'

'Aye.'

'Tell me about it again.'

And he does. It's almost too perfect, as if he's learned it off. He even includes the fact that he asked his mother if she wanted tea. I'd alerted William to that anomaly.

'Can you describe the clothes you wore that morning?' William asks.

'My black jacket. I had a hat too and blue jeans.'

213

'Footwear?'

'A pair of Adidas runners.'

'Good,' William says. 'Larry?'

Larry calls in the exhibits officer, who holds up a number of sealed bags containing clothes.

'Exhibit SB6, SB20, SB21, SB25,' Larry calls out. 'Are these your clothes?'

'Yes.'

'A small question,' William asks, 'why would you ask your mother if she wanted tea if you were ignoring her?'

It catches him on the hop. 'What?'

'You told us you were ignoring your mother and yet you asked her on the day you found her if she wanted tea?'

'What? No . . . I didn't ask her.'

'You did,' William says. 'You said it in your first interview and you said it again just there. Larry, can you read it out?'

'"I asked my mother if she wanted tea and when I got no answer I went and knocked on her door and then I pushed it open and I found her."'

'Yeah, well, I always ask people if they want tea when I'm making it for myself, so I must have done.'

'Even someone you're ignoring because she abandoned you when you were five months old?'

He swallows hard.

William moves on. A pair of work boots is shown to Devon. 'Exhibit SB3. These work boots were recovered in a search of your friend's house. Are they yours?'

'Yeah.'

'And when would you wear them?'

'I wear them to work.'

214

'And were you wearing them on Thursday the twelfth of January when the glass broke?'

'Yeah. I wear them to work. That's what I said.'

'Good.' William pushes an image across the table. 'Exhibit SB7. Can you tell me what that is, Devon?'

'It looks like a shard of glass.'

'It is,' William agrees. 'Now, Devon, I'm giving you the chance to tell me the truth before I put this next question to you, all right? Where did you spend Thursday night?'

And there it is again, the hesitation I saw in the hospital, before it shuts down. 'Home, I told you,' he says unconvincingly.

'Oh, Devon, Devon.' Dan sits back in his chair, which squeaks alarmingly. 'This is going to be like watching one of those nature programmes about a lion stalking its prey before totally destroying it.'

And it is. Though Devon doesn't know it, William has him tied up in knots. It's only when he starts to tighten the noose that Devon will feel the ropes. William has put away far bigger fish than a twenty-year-old kid.

'This particular piece of glass was found down Sandra's back garden in a sort of den. SB5.' A picture of the den is shown to Devon. 'Do you recognise that place?'

He rears back from the table. 'No.'

'I don't know if you're aware of it, but your mother reported to us that she had a stalker. We reckon this is where his den was and this piece of glass was found there.'

'So?'

'It matches the glass from that pane we showed you earlier, the one that broke.'

'Glass is glass,' Devon says, with an unmistakable tremor in his voice. 'It could have come from anywhere.'

'That's not actually true,' William explains, like a kindly teacher. 'Every piece of glass has different properties, unique properties. This is the same glass as the pane that you broke.'

'Maybe it is. That doesn't prove anything. I could have walked down that garden on that day.'

'Did you? It's just I remember you saying that after you broke the glass you brushed yourself down, swept up and went home.'

Devon stares at him. 'Maybe I went over to there. Maybe I just omitted to say it.'

'Did you?'

Devon says nothing. He's already said he ignored her so he can't now say he called in. Of course, he doesn't know what's yet to come.

'Let's move on.' William is pleasant, gentle. 'We also found the same type of glass inside your mother's house after she was dead.'

'It was my nana's house and, anyway, I went in the next morning, didn't I?'

And bang. William knew he'd say that.

'But in completely different clothes, not your work clothes or your work boots.'

Devon's eyes widen.

'And this glass, Devon, it was found in the hallway and in your mother's room, in the blood on the floor. So, tell me, how did that happen?'

Devon says nothing.

'There was also a partial boot print found near the window-sill where the animal blood was found. It matches these boots. Where did you get that animal blood, Devon?'

He glares at William.

'And there were blood stains found on the boots, which we are confident will be either your mother's or from the animal blood or both.'

William waits but Devon doesn't answer.

'Look,' William goes on. 'You're bound to have been angry – no one would blame you. It was an anger that got out of hand. I mean, the only way this all fits,' William spreads his hands wide, 'is if you did indeed go over to your mother's that night, and hung around in the den at the back, trying to . . . what? Frighten her to go back to her own life? Make her leave Megan alone? You alone? Maybe you poured blood all over her windowsill and then for some reason you went inside her house and confronted her. That's the only thing that makes sense.'

'I actually did call in to her after work,' Devon says suddenly. 'I didn't want Megan to find out and be hurt, so that's where I went.'

'But your aunt Megan says you were back by six. Your uncle Leo said the same. Your car was spotted on the road home at that time. Glass was found in the blood, Devon. In the blood. In the bedroom.'

Devon lets out a half-sob. 'I did nothing,' he says.

William leans towards him. 'The way I see it, you were angry. You'd a nice life and then she came back and tried to make up for all the shit she put you through. I heard she had to be taken home from the afters of the funeral. No one wants their mother to be the talk of the town. Did you want her gone?'

My phone rings, jerking me out of that room. It's Kev on the front desk. 'Lucy, you won't believe this but we have Megan Blake here. She's confessing to the murder.'

32

I hotfoot it down to the front desk where a very agitated Megan is, Leo by her side. He looks shaken.

'She says she did it,' he says. 'But I don't believe it.'

'They're tearing my house apart.' The words wrench themselves from Megan. 'You've taken Devs. He did nothing. How could you? I thought you were my friend. It was me! It was me, all right? You have to let him go. He tried to kill himself not even a week ago. This could—'

'Megan—' Leo tries to intervene.

'Shut up! Shut up! If you weren't spending money all around you, things might be different. But they're not! They're not! Shut up. Here.' She holds out her hand. 'Cuff me. I did it. Cuff me.'

'Megan, slow down here,' I say firmly. 'Come with me. Leo, stay there or go home. I'll call you, all right?'

'I'll wait.' He takes a seat, and as I leave with Megan, I hear Kev ask him kindly if he'd like a coffee.

I lead Megan into Interview Room One and tell her to take a seat. 'Deep breaths,' I say. 'Come on. Calm down. We'll talk when you're calmer.'

She does as I say, but the tears still spill down her face and she wipes them with the sleeve of her tatty jumper. 'Sorry. Sorry. But you took Devon. He did nothing. Please.'

I wait, and finally, after a bit, she calms. Her breathing eases and I take a seat opposite her.

As gently as I can, I ask, 'Are you saying you want to confess to Sandra's murder?'

'Yes.' Her tone broaches no argument. 'Yes. I did it.'

'And are you prepared to give a voluntary statement?'

'Anything. I just can't let Devon do time for something I know he didn't do.'

It sounds as if she's trying to convince herself that he did nothing. I think back to the interview in the kitchen when I asked where they were on the night of the murder. How Megan had jumped in, including Devon in her alibi. She'd been protecting him, I think. He hadn't been home. Or maybe, the thought worms its way into my head, she'd been using Devon to protect herself. Maybe she was guilty. But it still wouldn't explain away Devon being in the garden that night.

'If this is an attempt to save Devon,' I say to her, 'it won't work. If he did it, we will find out.'

'He didn't!' It's vicious and feral and has all the hallmarks of a mother trying to save a cub. She reins herself in. 'He didn't,' she repeats. 'Now put your cuffs on me or whatever it is you have to do. I'm guilty.'

'I won't cuff you. But I'm going to caution you and arrest you.' I give her the caution and tell her I'm arresting her. 'Once I get you processed, you can tell me what happened.'

I pop back out to the front desk. When I enter Leo jumps up, coffee spilling from what I recognise is Dan's mug. It's the only clean one in the place. Dan will love that, I think wryly. 'She'll be a while yet, Leo,' I say, and he sits down. Turning to Jordy, I ask, 'Will you process Megan Blake, please? I'm going in to talk to William.'

'Sure,' Jordy says, and then in an undertone, 'Do you believe her?'

'No, but I'll keep an open mind.'

He lumbers off to get the forms. I rejoin Dan in the observation room. Referring to Devon's interview, I ask, 'What's happening in there?'

'William has him on the run, though I think he's about to wrap things up for half an hour to let him stew. If you're going to interrupt, do it now.'

'You what?' William says, as he joins me in the corridor.

'Megan Blake is in Interview Room One. She says she's guilty of killing her sister. She wants to make a full statement.'

'She's trying to save the young lad, isn't she?'

'I'd imagine so.'

William's phone rings, and as he listens to the caller, he grows more animated. 'That's grand. Sure, get it tested, will you?' He disconnects and puts his phone back into his top pocket, tapping it as he does so. He stares over my head, biting his lip, thinking. 'That was one of the search team. They've found a number of sharp-edged trophies in the house, in a display cabinet. One looks like it has traces of blood on it.'

I remember seeing that cabinet. Chock-a-block with trophies.

'What's the plan?' I ask.

He thinks for a moment, then says, 'The best way to proceed, I think, is if you get the confession from Megan and, for God's sake, challenge her on it. We don't need to be accused of using the confession to get the boy to confess, so make sure Megan knows exactly what she's doing. If she still goes ahead, I'll go back to Devon and tell him his aunt has confessed to the crime. It might break him.'

'It might not,' I say. 'He's pretty angry with her right now.'

'We'll still get a statement from him. Then we can ring DPP and set a direction to charge.' A pause before he asks, 'Is there any chance it could be her?'

'I don't think so. Nothing has been found bar fingerprints to say she was there that night. But then again, her alibi is weak.'

William groans, massaging the back of his neck with his hands. 'I had the super on my back only yesterday asking what the hell was happening and now we have a plethora of potential murderers.'

I don't ask what 'plethora' means.

'You go, grab Dan and prep for the one with Megan. Larry and I will watch that, and then we'll go back in to Devon.'

'Grand.'

33

There are a lot of people buzzing about the house, cars everywhere on the narrow road, voices carrying from inside to the roadway where he stands. He walks slowly by and tries his best to see what's going on but the house is up a bit of a driveway and to go any closer would only draw attention to himself. And since he's been here before, he doesn't need to be recognised. He can't see the old woman – she always seems to be around, helping out, smiling away like she hasn't a care in the world. He'd like to punch her, so he would. A left and a right. Bam! Bam! He might get to do it yet.

A car comes up behind him. Nearly nudging him up the arse. He tries not to look, just to keep his face to the road, but it's bloody impossible.

'Hello, there,' someone calls from the car. 'Are you all right?'

'Sorry, yes.' He turns. A garda car! What the hell . . .? A young guard with sticky-out ears waves cheerily at him. He'll just bet this fella got bullied in school, probably was asked if he could get satellite TV with them ears or something. He knows that this young fella went into the guards to give himself a bit of importance. But, still, he pulls his anger back and tells the guard, very respectfully, that yes, he's grand. Just on a bit of a walk, you know how it is when you're waiting around for a partner to give you a lift home. He indicates with a small wave of his hand towards the house. 'Lots going on in there,' he says.

The guard nods. 'What's your name?'

Something about the way he asks makes him wary. 'Adam,' he says. 'Adam Greene.'

Before the guard can say any more, he walks quickly away. When he glances back, the guard is on a call.

His step quickens until he's running.

34

Jordy leads Megan back into the interview room at four o'clock. She seems more together as we take our seats. I inform her that I'll be taping the interview.

'Good, because I just want to confess everything. It's been playing on my mind, and I can't let Devon take the blame for what I did.'

'Fine, so.' Dan pops three DVDs into the recorder and checks that it's working. He and I introduce ourselves and she says her name for the purposes of the tape, and also states that she doesn't want a solicitor. I remind her that she's under caution.

'I understand, Megan,' I begin, 'that you wish to tell us something about the murder of your sister, Sandra Byrne.'

'Yes. I want to say that I did it. It was me. I'm guilty.' She looks at me expectantly.

'Can you be more specific, talk us through the night in question?'

'What?'

'In order to satisfy ourselves that we have the right person for the crime, I'm going to need more from you. Just talk me through what happened that night, please.'

She hasn't been expecting this and she looks from me to Dan as if for inspiration.

'Okay. Well, like I already said, I watched a film on the telly with Dev and then we both went to bed. And then, well . . . at about two in the morning, when I was certain Devs was asleep, I got back up and snuck out. I just wanted to talk to Sandra, you know. To ask her to move on. She was upsetting Devon and that upset me terrible, so it did. And I wanted to tell her that she had to get out of the house because it needed to be cleared for the sell-ing, and no matter how much stuff Devs and I packed away, she would take it all out again. And, anyway, when I got there, she was asleep and I was cross about that, her being able to sleep and me not, so I woke her up and I had it out with her and she pushed me and screamed, so I pushed her back, but I pushed her hard and she hit her head and when she tried to get up I . . . I grabbed the trophy that was there and I hit her with it and she fell. And she stopped moving. And I saw that her head was bleeding really bad and I knelt down and I tried to stop the blood but it was pumping and . . .' she grows upset and I glance at her in surprise because suddenly it's as if what she's saying is true '. . . I put my hand on it, I tried to stop it, I did but she just . . . went.' She stops, like she's remembering. 'It was an accident.' A tear falls. 'I never meant it.'

'Okay,' I say, scrambling to get my shit together. I started off not believing her, and yet the way she was at the end, it was almost . . . real. And mention of a trophy . . . We hadn't told her that. 'I've just got a few questions to put to you about what you just said, all right? Just to make things clear for me and you, all right?'

'Yes. Sure.' She looks relieved. Almost unburdened.

'We'll go back to the beginning. What time was it when you got to your sister's house that night?'

'Three maybe?'

'Okay, and you say you wanted to talk to your sister. Is that right?'

'Yes.'

'Why did you choose three a.m. to do that?'

She freezes. 'I just . . . you know . . . didn't have time during the day and, well, you know, lying in bed, you start to think, don't you, and I just got up. I didn't worry about the time. I just wanted to have it out with her.'

'Did you text Sandra that you were coming over?'

'You have her phone. You know I didn't.'

'Why?'

She gives a bit of a laugh, stops. 'I already said. I wasn't thinking straight. Yes, I should have told her. I should have confronted her during the day. But I didn't.'

'Describe to me what you wore over that night.'

'I wore black jeans and a black jumper and my black coat. I had runners on too. And I cycled. I cycled over.'

'Have you still got those clothes?'

'No.'

'Where are they?'

'Burned in the stove, and I put the ashes onto the fields at the back of the house.'

'When?'

'In the last few days. Look, does it matter? Arrest me, would you?'

It's her desperation for me to believe her that makes me doubtful, along with most of her story. She looks right now a woman on the edge, red eyes, hair askew. Her face is etched with years of hardship. What happened to the girl I used to know?

I gaze at her, say calmly, 'I'm not sure I believe you, Megan. First off—'

'You have to accept my confession,' she says. 'I killed my sister. I saw her dead body.'

'Really?'

'Really,' she grinds out. 'She was in this big man's T-shirt. And she lay on her face, so you couldn't see it.' Her voice breaks. 'And her poor head was bleeding and there was spatter all up the wall and on the floor. I saw her.'

Beside me Dan shifts while I try to keep my face from betraying my surprise. How would Megan know what Sandra wore that night? How would she be able to describe the way her sister was found, unless she'd been there? She hadn't gone into the house on the Friday morning: I remember her not being there when I arrived at the scene.

'See?' Megan says. 'I know. She was at the end of the bed, and she bled out and . . .' She swallows a sob. Tears fall from her eyes, like water from a squeezed sponge. 'She was my baby sister. I always took care of her. I always did. I tried . . . I did, and then . . .' She buries her head in her hands and starts to sob. I push over a box of tissues lying on the desk.

'Did Devon call you over that night?' I ask gently. 'Did you go to help him?'

'No!'

'We just want the truth, Megan,' I say softly.

'I was there that night,' she says, her voice muffled. 'I killed her.'

'Megan, I'm going to stop the interview here,' I say. 'Have a think about what you're confessing to. We'll return you to the cell and have another interview with you later. If you still want

227 .

to plead guilty, Dan will read your statement back to you for you to sign. Is that all right?'

'Yes.' She scrubs her eyes with her fists, like a kid. 'Yes,' she repeats.

'Interview concluded at sixteen forty.' I flick off the recorder. Jordy arrives in to take Megan back to her cell.

We meet William in the observation room.

'She was there that night, all right,' I say. 'Have we checked Devon's phone?'

'Yes. According to Pat, Devon rang Megan at around two fifty that morning. The call lasted five minutes. I think he called her. She came out to Sandra's and they agreed to cover it up until the next morning.'

'They probably took the murder weapon home and cleaned it off.'

'Yes.' William heaves a sigh. 'At least it puts Ben in the clear.'

'Yeah, and it gives us the chance to tell DS Peter Glynn to piss off back to Dublin.'

William splutters out a laugh. 'I happen to hold him in very high esteem.'

'As do I, Cig.'

He laughs again and is about to say something when Larry arrives up carrying a pile of files. 'Are we set to go back in there, Cig?'

'Yeah. We'll ask him about that phone call to Megan at two fifty in the morning, see what he says. Try to squeeze a confession out of him before we take our chance and tell him his aunt has confessed.'

'And if he lets her take the blame?' Larry asks.

'I don't think he will,' William says. 'He might have murdered Sandra, but he's not a bad lad. Either way, as I said to Lucy, we'll get a statement from him, and if it turns out that the blood on those boots matches Sandra's, we can haul him in again.'

There is a fair crowd in the observation room when I get there. Dan and Susan have grabbed the chairs. Kev is sitting on the side of the desk, eating an enormous tuna sandwich and the smell is all over the place.

Onscreen, William is kicking off a new interview.

'I don't think he's guilty,' Kev says, through a massive mashed-up mouthful. 'Like all the evidence is there but—'

'Can you not breathe all over me when you're eating your disgusting food.' Susan makes a face. 'Honestly, Kev, you're like a flipping bin truck.'

'My girlfriend says I'm too skinny so I'm bulking up on protein,' Kev answers. 'It's chicken tomorrow.'

'Quiet,' I snap. 'I want to hear this and, Kev, next time eat your lunch in the kitchen. That's what it's for.'

He flushes, not used to being rebuked. He's the big shiny boy on the team. 'Sorry, Luce, I just wanted to—'

'Quiet.'

There is silence then as we turn our attention to the screen. William starts by asking Devon why he called Megan at ten to three on the morning of Friday, 13 January.

'Did I?' He's not the best actor. 'Well . . . oh, yeah . . . I woke up and went down for a glass of water and I noticed that Leo didn't seem to have come in – he sleeps on the sofa if he's had a late night and I got worried so I called Megan to ask where he was.'

'Really?' William says, eyebrow cocked.

'Yeah.'

'But she was in the house with you, wasn't she?'

'Eh . . . yeah. But, like, I didn't want to go into her bedroom.'

'You didn't by chance call her as she was out of the house?'

'No, no, she was in the house.'

'I see.'

Here it is.

William steeples his hands and looks at Devon, who does his best to stare back. His eyes are too wide and his upper lip twitches. 'It's only that we've got your aunt Megan in the other room there,' he thumbs towards the wall, 'and she's saying that she killed Sandra. So is it—'

'No way.' Devon shakes his head furiously. 'That's a lie. I'm not believing that.'

'By law,' William speaks calmly, 'we are not allowed to tell you anything untrue. We can't say we've got evidence when we haven't. We can't pretend to know more than we do. Isn't that right, Detective Lynch?'

'Yes,' Larry agrees.

'This is all on DVD,' William taps the machine, 'and Larry is writing it all down, so if we did anything illegal, if we said anything that was untrue, your solicitor could get everything here thrown out. It would ruin our case. When I say that your aunt is in the process of confessing to this crime, I am telling you the truth. So, you are now free to go, unless of course you have anything else to say.'

'She didn't do it.'

'She says she did.'

Devon looks as if he has been plunged into liquid nitrogen and has frozen on the spot. He stares and stares at William, but I don't think he really sees him. The silence in the room stretches and widens and tightens. It builds and builds so you think it might explode. The four of us watching hold our breath and without even being aware of it we draw closer to the screen.

'She said no one would believe me,' Devon punctures the quiet, 'and she was right because she didn't believe me. I know because she took the trophy home and washed it and put it in the cabinet and I knew then if she didn't believe me no one would. Oh . . . fuck, fuck.' And he lays his head on the table and sobs, his shoulders shaking and heaving.

William looks at Larry and finally William says, and he probably shouldn't but he does, 'Do you want a solicitor?'

'Yes, yes, please,' Devon says.

'Interview concluded at four thirty. DI William Williams and DG Larry Lynch leaving the room.'

In the observation room, we all cheer.

35

An hour later, Devon, solicitor in tow, commences another interview with William and Larry.

'My client is ready to co-operate fully with the investigation,'
the solicitor says. She's young and prim and I've never seen her
before. She looks like she just graduated from secondary school,
never mind law school.

'Are you prepared to tell us exactly what happened on the
morning of the thirteenth of January last?' William asks Devon.

'Yeah. You can't arrest Megan. She's only trying to save me.'

'Let's hear what you have to say.' William waves a hand. 'In
your own time.'

Devon glances at his solicitor, who indicates for him to talk.
Swallowing hard, Devon says, 'Look, everything was good with
everyone until Sandra came back. Maudie was up in a heap
altogether. She didn't even want to tell Sandra that my nan was
dying. She didn't want Sandra near the place. She said trouble
would follow, but Megan said we had to. That was the first argument. Maudie said it would end in tears, that if Sandra came
back it was just for money. That she'd soon be dragging every
man in Achill into bed. She said that Sandra would have her

own agenda and it was true because she made a show of herself at Nana's funeral, all over the priest and fighting with Dom. Like, there she was going on about sinners and saying there were big sinners who didn't deserve forgiveness and all stuff like that.' He swallows. 'Like, in front of my friends and all. And Megan and Leo had this big row about her, and they stopped talking to each other. And she's causing all this trouble and still having a good time, living in my nana's house and saying that she is going to stay until it sells and I just . . . I just wanted rid of her.' Tears stand out bright in his eyes. 'I didn't want her there where everyone could talk about her and know she was my mother. I wanted her gone. Megan said I should just ignore her and not be bothered with her, that she was like a wasp, she would leave eventually once she'd had a nose around and wasn't swatted. But, like, I heard people talking about her when I went into the shops, and when they'd spot me they'd stop and turn away or give me this look of pity and I couldn't bear it. So I thought, you know, that if I could just make her go it would be better for everyone. I didn't want to talk to her, so . . . like . . . I thought maybe if she was frightened she would pack up and leave, and that things would get back to the way they were. So,' he swallows hard, 'I started to do stuff.' He stops, remembering.

In the interview room no one moves for fear they'll break the spell of confession. Larry waits, pencil held aloft.

Finally, Devon continues, his voice trembling, his hands clasped hard together. 'Stupid stuff, like I found a dead cat on the road and I threw it into the garden. I broke a window when she was out of the house. I pulled up plants. And, yeah, I did make that den and spied on her, and whenever she went out at night, I did something. I thought, you know, someone doing things at night would be scarier. When she was out, I'd take the key to the house and go in and move stuff around, or I'd pour all the drink out of her bottles and leave the empty ones standing at the sink. And she was freaking out and accusing people of doing it. But she never once thought it was me. But back then, I believed she never thought of me ever anyway.' Silent tears fall now and, for a moment, he seems lost. Finally, gathering himself up, he goes on, 'And then one of Leo's sheep caught itself on wire and bled out before we could get to it. I found it and took the chance of putting some blood into a water bottle. And I thought if I used it, it'd send her mad completely.' He shakes his head. 'What was wrong with me? I can't believe I even thought of something like that.'

His solicitor pushes a glass of water towards him. He picks it up, takes a gulp and starts to cough and choke. When he has recovered, he says, sounding a bit dazed, 'Where was I?'

'Do you need a break?' William asks.

'No. Where was I?'

'You had got the blood.'

'Yeah, that's right, and I thought, you know, that it would scare her. That she would leave for sure, that she'd think it was a threat or something. So, that night, I watched some of that film with Megan, that bit is true, but then, after Megan went to bed, I pulled on me boots and jacket and snuck out. When I got to the house, about maybe two o'clock or so, the place was dark but I heard voices so I snuck around the back, to the place where I spied on her. There was a light in the bedroom, at the back, and the curtains weren't pulled, just like the blinds, and I could hear voices coming from the house. Then, like, I heard raised voices, but I don't know what they're saying or anything – it's hard to

234

hear way back where I am. And then it all goes quiet. And I wait for like, I don't know, not too long, until I'm sure it's going to stay quiet, and I creep down the garden and I see this guy down the driveway, running. Just like the back of him, like the shape of him, and he doesn't see me because he's like twenty feet away and running. Then, when he's gone, I sprint around to the sitting-room window and pour the blood all over the sill and next thing I see that the front door is wide open. And I thought, That's weird, because it's a cold night, and I'm thinking that it's not safe and that maybe she's too drunk to close it, or the guy forgot or whatever, so I go to pull it closed and I don't know, it was all too quiet or something. Like this man had run off and I would've expected her to be crying after him or shouting or something. And I get this feeling, a terrible feeling, and I want to run but I can't. I thought, Maybe she's after falling over and hurting herself or something, and so, though I know I should leave because if anyone came and saw the blood they'd know it was me and I'd be in trouble, but I can't, it's too quiet, so I go in.'

Dan looks at me. This is not what we expected. Shit.

And he's switched tenses. Past to present. He's remembering all right.

'And it's real quiet and I go into the kitchen and there's nothing, just like . . . mess, like stuff had been pulled out of the drawers and the sitting room is the same. So I thought, maybe she did go to bed, but I still thought . . . It's just weird. It's too quiet for someone having just left, and so I go up the stairs, down the corridor and the door is open and . . . Oh, God.' He looks at William and Larry, like he can see it all over again, and I'm sure he can: these images are not easily erased. 'She's lying on the floor and the big trophy, the one I won for running – Nana used to have it on the fireplace because she liked it – well, that's there, too, and blood everywhere. And I know she's dead. I know but I go over anyway and say her name and nothing, and I feel for a pulse and nothing, and I don't know what to do. Like she's *dead*.' He says it like he can't believe it. 'And I can't just walk out and ring the guards because I'll be in trouble, like how will it look, and so I ring Megan and I tell her, I say, "Sandra is dead," and at first she doesn't believe me but then I start to cry, I think. I can't remember much after that but when she comes I'm outside on the grass and she goes in and I hear her cry out and then she asked me what happened and I tell her, I tell her everything, but then she says we have to get rid of the evidence, that we have to bring the trophy home and wipe everywhere I touched and all that, and I tell her I did nothing but she says no one will believe that. And so she thinks it's best if we report it in the morning. And we make up a story and it seems to be for the best because neither of us did anything.' A pause. 'Only she thinks it was me, but I swear it wasn't.'

In the observation room, Kev is open-mouthed with shock, a masticated bite of sandwich on display. Dan is gawking in disbelief and all I can think of is that if this is true and, to be honest, it makes sense, he seems credible, then Ben is right back in the frame.

Shit.

I know William, despite his professionalism, will be thinking the same thing. He remains composed, though. 'What you're saying, and correct me if I get anything wrong, is that you began a campaign of terror against your mother in order that she move out. One night, when you were watching her from the den in the back garden, you heard an argument between her and an unidentified person. When all was quiet, you moved out of the den, up the garden and saw that person flee. You poured animal blood on a windowsill before noticing that the front door of the house was open, thought it odd, went inside, where you discovered your mother's body. Knowing you might get in trouble, you rang your aunt Megan, who cleaned up the scene and advised you to wait until the morning to report it.'

'She was protecting me. I know she thought I'd done it. But I hadn't.'

'Are you alleging that this unidentified person killed your mother?'

'Who else could it have been?' He looks beat, spent, but the tension has gone from his face.

'What time was this?'

'About three in the morning.'

'All right. I want you to put yourself back there. Close your eyes.'

He does so with a weariness that comes from having nothing left to lose.

William gets him to talk through his whole journey to the cottage.

'When you arrived at the cottage, with your bottle of blood, what did you see on the road outside the cottage?'

'Nothing. It was mostly dark.'

'All right. Now you're walking up the driveway. Anything there?'

'Just plants and gravel and grass. A light Leo put in the garden so Sandra wouldn't fall. An old bit of a tree trunk. Nothing else.'

'You're sure?'

'Yeah.'

'What happened next?'

'Eh, I come up the driveway, straight up. At first I think it's all quiet but I can hear voices. Not loud at first. So I steal up the back garden.'

'Go on.'

And he does, telling the story over again, until he reaches the part where he hears the voices arguing.

'Describe the voices.'

'Faint, because I'm up the back of the garden. But I know it's an argument. It's a man – the voice is deeper than hers. That's all.'

'Keep going.'

He does.

'Describe the man you see in the driveway,' William says.

'It's dark. I can't see him right.'

William waits and uses the silence expertly.

'His back is to me. He's medium height, he had a hood up. He can move, he's fit, and I think he's wearing some sort of soft shoe because I can't hear him on the gravel, really.'

'Good. Any smells, anything like that?'

'No.'

'All right. Think hard now. This man runs off. In what direction?'

Devon shakes his head. 'I didn't look at him for that long. He just ran and I turned back to the house. And that, honest to God, is the truth. Tell Megan I told ye what happened. Tell her, and she'll confirm it all. I swear. I swear it.'

'Keep your eyes closed. I'm not done,' William snaps. 'After the man ran off, were there any sounds?'

'No. There . . .' He stops. 'There was no car,' he says suddenly, getting to what William wants from him. 'I never saw a car. Or if there was, it was parked a bit away.'

Another nail in Ben's coffin, I think.

'Any other sounds you remember?'

'No.'

'All right, you can open your eyes now,' William says, as he massages the bridge of his nose. 'Larry, read back Devon's statement to him, will you?'

Larry does so. Despite trying to remain objective, I can hear the defeat in his voice as he goes through it. We'd all been hoping for a confession of guilt. Instead, we get this. And the awful thing is, it fits. It fits what I've learned about Devon and Megan, what I've gleaned of their relationship. It fits the evidence we've found so far. And if it is the truth, and I think it is, it's the bits that don't fit that we have to concentrate on now.

After Devon signs his statement, the live feed ends.

'That was unexpected,' Susan says, rubbing her face. 'I really thought we had something.'

'We do,' I say, trying to buoy them up. 'We know now that the crime was committed by a man, acting alone. That it occurred between two and three in the morning, that this man did not use a car.'

'Ben didn't have a car,' Kev says, what we're all thinking.

'Look, we are not investigating Ben. What we need to do now is investigate the bits of evidence we have that don't fit. Number one, Sandra was allegedly scared by a man in a red jacket with a yellow crest. He was driving a black petrol car, mid-size with a scratch on the door of the driver's side. We need to locate it. We need to locate that driver. Kev, you are on *Crimecall* on Monday, so make sure to highlight these facts if we have made no progress.'

'I will.'

'Number two, our SO may very well have come in by boat.

Push those neighbours, Susan. More than one of them must have seen that stationary light on the hill. Also, get back on to that fisherman, Dotey—'

'Dotsy,' Susan says.

'Yes, Dotsy. Ask him if he knows what lights are used as a transit to get boats in to the pier? What was the old transit? Is it still there? Is there a new one? That sort of thing. Also ask him for names of anyone he ever remembers using that pier. Local or further afield, I want a list. If they've done it in the dark, chances are they've done it by day. See if anyone leaps out.'

'I'll help Susan do that,' Kev says.

'Let's do some good old-fashioned police work,' I say. 'It's under our noses, let's go.'

They hop to it, Kev dumping the remains of his sandwich in the bin, Susan pushing her glasses further up her nose and straightening her jacket. She reminds me of a character from an Enid Blyton novel.

'I'll get Jordy to bring Megan back up,' Dan says, as he makes for the door.

'Rob sent me a bunch of dead flowers yesterday,' I say, stopping him in his tracks. 'What do you think of that?'

'He what?'

'Got a shop to deliver them to my mother, who, of course, thought they were from a secret boyfriend. Honestly, does she think I'm that hard up to like dead flowers?'

Dan studies me, then says quietly, 'That is really weird, Lucy. What are you going to do?'

'I've been . . . Well, it's a long shot.'

'What?'

'I might ring him. I'm not sure if he still has the same mobile number from when he went to jail, but I'd say he has. He told me once that he'd never change it in case I needed him. He said that as he was being led away. As my career nose-dived. Arrogant shit.' Oh, God, I'm getting upset again. Dan's concerned gaze almost undoes me. 'What do you think?'

'Do it. Fuck him.'

His certainty galvanises me. I search my pockets for my phone.

'On the table, Detective,' Dan says wryly.

I flick it on, changing my number to private. 'Okay, here goes nothing.' My finger jabs out Rob's old phone number. Yep, I still remember it. It connects at the other end. 'What if it makes things worse?' I ask, as it begins to ring.

'We can arrest him. How nice would that be?'

The ringing stops. 'Hello, Robert Ganley Photography.'

His smooth-as-caramel voice makes me jump slightly. How many people did he con with that silky timbre?

'It's Lucy,' I snap.

There's a moment of silence, then a cautious 'Yes?'

'Lucy, your ex-wife, so we're clear. I'm warning you that if you pull any more stupid stunts like you did yesterday, I will bury you.'

'What?'

And there is something in that denial, in the way he's trying to make me sound like a lunatic, that sets the fuse to the dynamite I've refused to light for so long. I only wish he was standing in front of me so I could thump him. I should have done it in Castlebar the other day instead of trying to maintain my dignity. Dignity is overrated. 'You are unbelievable. Don't try to gaslight me, you absolute shit. Own your bloody stupid piss-arse actions, for God's sake.'

Dan gives an impressed thumbs-up.

'You have officially lost it.' Rob has the gall to sound amused. 'I wish—'

'The flowers. You sent me those dead flowers and I swear, if you try anything else, I'll come after you with every bit of officialdom I've got. I will invent stuff to put you in jail. How's that now? Fake evidence. Understand? Good.' I disconnect.

Dan claps and whoops, then says, his lips twitching, 'Piss-arse actions?'

'Yeah, well, I—'

'I sincerely hope you didn't intend to carry out that last threat, Lucy?' William says, from the door where neither of us had spotted him.

Christ.

'Eh, no. It was . . .' I open my mouth to tell him who I'd been yelling at. Then, like a horse about to bolt, I rein myself in. William is not a man for personal-life stuff. It's all about the job, as I found out to my cost only the other night. 'No, Cig. That call, it wasn't . . . Look, I'd never plant evidence or fake results or intimidate a witness or even, God forbid, quash driving fines or . . .' Shut up, Lucy, I think, but I can't '. . . or bribe people or do deals with drug dealers in exchange for drugs to sell or steal from—'

'Just go back in to Megan,' he interrupts loudly.

'We're on our way.' Dan virtually pushes me out of the room. 'Jaysus' sake, Luce,' he whispers as we head down the corridor, 'how much corruption could you think of in two seconds?'

'I couldn't stop myself.'

Dan chuckles, then stops and says, 'Proud of you.'

And I am proud of me too.

★★★

An hour later, we've got the same story from Megan as told to us by Devon. 'It was my idea to cover it up,' she says. 'I just thought . . .' She pauses. Then, sounding defeated, she says, 'I thought, in the heat of the moment, that he'd done it. I didn't want to think it, but I did and, honestly, I wouldn't have blamed him. She really was difficult this time. It was as if she was hyped up about something, and poor Mammy dead.'

I don't inform her that Devon is still on the radar. He may very well have done it. The only thing saving him now is that we know Ben was in the house and we have to take in the possibility that Ben is lying about the time he left it. He says it was just after midnight, but it could have been later. There is nothing to back up Ben's story. We haven't even found a motorist who saw him on the road. That Devon didn't notice any car makes the case against Ben look worse. In Ben's favour, there are no traces of him in the bedroom or on the T-shirt Sandra was wearing.

When Megan is released, Leo and Devon are waiting for her in Reception. When she sees them she bursts into tears. 'I'm so sorry, Devs,' she says. 'So sorry.'

Devon stands up, 'It's . . .' he begins, but then it's like he can't find the words.

Megan moves closer. 'I'm sorry for everything. For Sandra, everything.'

He swallows hard, his face a map of loss.

'It's my fault you walked into the sea, isn't it? It's my fault—'

'Let's go home,' Leo interrupts, wrapping an arm about her. He looks at Devon. 'What about you, eh?'

After a second, Devon nods and Megan hiccups out a sob. Then, looking battered, they all make their way out of the station.

Back to the beginning.

36

I don't leave the station until eleven that evening. It's been a dirty day and the night is not much better. Dark and overcast, cold and blustery, rain spits on the windscreen of my mother's car as I plough my way homewards. I do enjoy driving this car: it's nifty and comfortable and—

A vehicle that had pulled away from the kerb as I drove out of the police station is still behind me. It's been sticking close the whole way. It had followed me across the Matt Talbot bridge, onto the island, driven with me past the shops where Sandra and Maudie had their argument. It had followed me through Keel and past the beach and the caravan park and on, out towards Keem, where I live. Not many people will attempt these roads in the dark so it had to be someone familiar with them.

I shake it off.

I'm getting spooked because of the dead flowers and Rob. It was all very well with Dan alongside me, making those threats to him, but here, out in the dark, the drop to the Atlantic close by, it's a different matter. The car is only metres behind me, if I were to stop, it would crash right into me. My testimony had put Rob in prison and, at the time, I hadn't been afraid. But I do not know this man any more. A man who'd lost his son and granddaughter. Maybe he blames me for it and he'd be right. I had done nothing to encourage Luc to rebuild a relationship with his dad just like – the thought worms its way into my head – Megan had steered Devon away from Sandra. Maybe the anger at what he thinks is an injustice will—

And then the car indicates left and heads on up towards Slievemore.

I exhale.

My mother is up when I get in. She throws a sod of turf on the fire as I enter and the sweet smoky scent of it comforts me. It's the smell of my childhood. I flop down on the sofa beside her, throwing my coat over the back of a chair. On TV, the highlights of some ridiculous reality TV show are playing in which you have to guess what plastic surgery the contestants have had done.

'Eyes, ears, head and neck,' my mother says, with confidence. 'And left finger – see, see there, Lucy, that little scar. That's a tell-tale sign. Gives it away. Not a great surgeon there, God bless her.'

'D'you mind if I see the late news, Mam? We've put out a call to the media to run a mugshot of someone we want to talk to. I just want to see if it's on.'

'Is it of Ben?' She hands me the remote.

'No, not Ben.' The news has just started and the headline is about another gangster killing in Dublin. Does it ever bloody end? Solving crime is like trying to get rid of ants from a house: the little shits will always find another way in.

'I had a great day today,' my mother says, as I try to raise the volume on the TV, without her noticing, or she'll talk all over it, 'because I have no car, the women from the ICA called around to the house. It was great in a way, not having to stir outside, them all coming to me. Of course,' her voice dips, 'they were wanting to know if Ben had been charged yet but I told them I wasn't privy to that at all.' She sounds very proud of herself.

'Good.' I'm only half listening. Two men shot in O'Connell Street, barely alive.

'I mean, I know you'd tell me if he was charged, but I've learned my lesson now.' She mimes zipping up her mouth.

'Good.' Next item is that a large-scale documentary is being made about Ireland's islands.

That's not news, I think.

'That's great news,' my mother says. 'A film about us. We could be in a film. Anyway, you'll never guess who's getting married?'

And then, as my mother starts to give me hints, the newscaster says, 'The guards in Achill are very anxious to trace this man.'

'Shush, Mam!'

'I beg your pardon.' She sounds annoyed.

I ignore her.

The picture is not much better than the CCTV.

'Who on earth would know who that was?' My mother snorts. 'Sure he wouldn't even recognise himself.'

'The guards are hoping to speak to this individual as they believe he might be able to help them with their enquiries. This footage was taken from a garage in Crossmolina on January the third last. The man was wearing dark jeans and a red jacket with a yellow crest.' The newscaster gives out a phone number and once again stresses that the man isn't in any trouble.

'I bet he is in trouble, though,' my mother says. 'Isn't he?'

'No, he's not.' And then, because I have to, just in case Rob makes a fuss or something, I say, 'I met Rob the other day, Mam.'

Her silence tells me she's shocked.

'It wasn't a planned meeting. I met him on the street in Castlebar. We had words.'

'*A stór*,' she says.

'Those flowers yesterday, that was him.'

There's a deep pause before she half whispers, 'I could kill him.' She clasps my hand. 'I could kill him, Lucy.'

'I know. I rang him today and told him to keep away so that should be an end to it.'

'Good.' A firmer hand squeeze.

'Yeah.'

'Good,' she says, pulling me into an embrace. 'He knows he's not wanted. He'll go away soon.'

'Yeah.' I so want to believe her. But this is Rob.

'And he still had the same phone number,' she says, after a bit.

'He still had the same number.'

'Will you tell Luc?'

'No. Him and Tani don't need that.'

And so, decided, we sit, her arm about me, until the fire goes down and the dark conquers the room.

Sometime around six in the morning my personal phone bleeps. It's a text message and, heart thumping, I open it. Something has to be wrong with Luc. He and my mother are the only ones—

I never sent anything. Luc told me to stay away and I have. RG

The liar. All the lies he told me when I began to suspect him of fraud. How he had me believing him. Never again. The blood rises in me and I'm about to reply but then decide I won't.

He might think the phone is out of action.

But I screenshot it.

Just in case.

37

20 January

It's been decided that, for now, our main resources will be used to track down petrol-pump man, and William assigns Dan to work with Larry on CCTV. The rest of the team, bar Susan, Kev and Mick, are retracing Sandra's steps, interviewing everyone she came into contact with during her last weeks on Achill. Mick is tasked with locating anyone who might have known Sandra at her other addresses in an attempt to track down any boyfriends, as well as keeping abreast of forensics. Kev is doing the same with Richie. Susan is meeting with Dotsy again to ask him about the transit lights that were used back in the day to get into Dugort. I can tell she's dreading it: she says Dotsy is weird.

'You'll talk to a lot of weird people in this job,' I tell her.

As conference ends, Dan motions for me to join him.

'Bit of a development,' he says. 'Chloé rang – the girl from the garage? She says one of her flatmates who used to work in the station served petrol-pump man a few months back and might have information for us.'

'I thought we interviewed all the staff?'

'This girl left the job and only copped it this morning after talking to Chloé about it. I told Chloé someone would be out to take her statement in an hour.'

I wince. Two witnesses talking to each other is never a good idea. 'And this information?'

'Chloé said they'd meet us at the café.'

'I bet she did. Right, come on, Kev,' I shout across the room to him. 'Interview with me. Mick, take on Kev's work with Richie, would you, please?' I ignore Mick's look of anguish. 'Enjoy the CCTV, Dan.'

Dan tips me a salute and lopes off to join Larry.

A delighted Kev trots at my heels out into the car park. The only DDU car left is an older version of the one I normally use, with a hell of a lot of miles on the clock.

Kev kicks the wheels in disgust. 'My flipping Micra is better than that.'

'I hear you.' I unlock the doors. 'Come on, get in. The sooner we arrive and do the interview, the sooner we can go for lunch.'

'Oh, wow, and we can claim it on expenses, can't we?' Kev rubs his hands, excited at the prospect of a free meal, and I remember when I'd been as innocent and as ambitious and as enthusiastic as him.

Five minutes later, we're heading towards Crossmolina and, in fairness, the car is comfortable enough. Kev puts the heater up full blast and sticks his face into it. 'My ma doesn't believe in central heating,' he tells me. 'She won't put it on so the house is always freezing in winter. She says it makes people soft. She'd hate this.' He holds his hands to the blower, like it's an open fire.

I don't know much about Kev, except that he's always hungry,

is a good swimmer and has a girlfriend who likes him in uniform. 'Is your dad not around to tell your mother to turn on the
heating?'

'Naw. He just keeps his mouth shut. They don't have the best
of marriages, to be honest,' he rolls his eyes, 'always bickering
about things. My mother is only happy when she can get her
own way in everything.' And he gives me a big happy grin. 'How
about you, Luce?'

'My mother is still alive, but my father died when I was eight,
off a fishing boat. I barely remember him, which is weird. I mean,
I was eight. His body washed ashore about a week later.'

'That was a shock for your ma?'

'Yeah, it must have been.' I've never actually asked her. How
did she cope when the love of her life was torn away from her
like that? And, again, I have that flash of memory, the piles of
Tupperware that lay about the house, the coffin in the good front
room, the parade of neighbours and the prayers. And me, playing
with my cousins, delighted to have them over. Oblivious.

The road whips by. I wonder if Sandra and Megan ever think
of their father. I suppose they do: they were both older when he
died. I'd left the island by then, carving out my Dublin career.

I'm suddenly aware that Kev is talking. He tells me about his
older brother, who is a fireman and has just got married to a girl
his mother hates. 'My mother and my brother don't really get on.
In fact, I think I'm the only person she does get on with. I haven't
introduced her to Kylie yet because she'll find some fault with
her, and I like Kylie.'

'Then you stick to your guns.'

'I will.'

I let his chat roll over me as the journey unfolds.

★★★

Chloé is sitting at the same table as last time with another sleek and chic companion. Isn't it strange how the same types of girl always hang out together? These two are like mini-clones of each other. From the corner of my eye, I observe Kev straighten his spine, square his shoulders and pat down his cow's lick. I wonder how his preening would go down with Kylie.

Chloé spots us and waves and then, with a look of confusion, she asks, 'What is this man here for?' Her lip curls as she stares at Kev.

'I'm Garda Kevin Costelloe,' Kev answers cheerily, sliding into a seat. 'How are yez?'

'And Dan?' Chloé looks to me.

'He's on another job.' I'm brisk, sitting down too. 'Now, I believe your friend has information for us?'

'Yes. This is Monique. We have order breakfast. Is all right?'

'Well, I didn't—' Her friend attempts to interject.

'Sure,' I interrupt, admiring Chloé's nerve. 'That's what we're here for. The public feed us information and we feed them.'

'Can I—' Kev begins.

'No. Two coffees for us. Go on.'

He moves away and I chat with Chloé and Monique. By the time he arrives with the coffees, the two girls are tucking into their full Irish.

'So, Monique, you believe you saw petrol-pu— this man we're trying to trace?'

'Definitely,' she says. Her English is better than Chloé's. 'It was when they described the jacket on the news, that's when I knew he had come into the garage. It takes a certain type of man to wear a red jacket with, eh, style, don't you think?' Then before we can answer, 'And this was not the type of man to do it. That's why I remember him.'

'Right.' I can't help wondering what these two fashionistas think of me and poor old gangly Kev.

'This is good.' Chloé looks up from her fry. 'She has good information for you.'

My heart quickens. 'Go on, Monique. Try not to interrupt, Chloé. Ideally, we'd have preferred you not to have discussed it between you, but—'

'Then we never would have found out it was the same man,' Monique says, as she spears some black pudding.

'Exactly,' Chloé agrees. Then, using her fork to jab towards her plate, she says to Kev, 'Have some. You is very thin man.'

Kev looks at me but I deliberately don't meet his eye. 'Eh, just get on with the story,' he says. 'Thanks anyway.'

'Very thin,' she says again, with a little nose wrinkle. Then, 'Off you go, Monique.'

'I am not sure of the exact date,' Monique says, 'but it was a cold day, I remember. It was the morning shift, so before nine o'clock, and he came in to pay for petrol. I notice the jacket. It was shiny material and had a yellow circle with a triangle and maybe writing. And he paid and then he leave.'

'This is good bit.' Chloé sits back as if she's waiting for a show to begin.

'He leave his money by mistake,' Monique continues, 'and so I run out after him and he climbing in his car and I give him the money.' A pause. A look to Chloé. 'There is jackets in back of car.'

'Jackets?'

'Yes.'

'No,' Chloé says. 'Not his same jacket, other jackets.'

'Chloé, please, it'd be better if Monique tells us herself.'

They look to each other. Converse in French. Shit, I should have brought an interpreter.

'Life jackets,' Kev says, and the two women look at him in approval.

'*Oui.*' Monique nods. 'Life jackets for the swim. Two.'

'Great.' Though I wonder what it means. Maybe this guy is a sailor or fisherman or both. 'Anything else stand out? What was the car like?'

'I think is black,' Monique says. 'Big. I do not know type. But big scratch on the shiny part of back.'

Oh, yes! 'That's great, Monique. Now, think hard, do you remember what his voice sounded like? Hard, raspy, soft?'

She looks at me blankly. Then wonder-cop Kev babbles to her in French.

She babbles back.

'He had a nice voice,' Kev translates. 'She thinks he sounded like a DJ. But his face didn't match it.'

I flip my laptop towards them and show them a picture of Devon, plus eight other guys from Viper. Though Devon doesn't drive a black car, he's still a suspect. 'Do you recognise anyone here?'

Monique shakes her head almost immediately. 'This man, he is old,' she says. 'Fifty, maybe. Older even.'

'Anything else you remember?' I ask, as I log out of Viper.

'No. It is months ago. I just recall jacket.'

'All right. Thanks so much, ladies. Enjoy the breakfast.' I throw twenty euro on the table, then Kev and I leave the café, Kev looking longingly back at the menu.

'That was good. Life jackets, eh?' Kev says, as we head back to the car. 'Maybe he did come in by boat. Maybe that's why there was no car. Maybe that's why Devon didn't hear anything.'

I wonder if the sound of a boat in the harbour would carry up to that house. But with all the panic, Devon most likely missed it.

'Phone it in.'

Just as Kev is calling the station, my own phone bleeps. It's Susan. She sounds as if she's in hell, a howling wail accompanying her voice down the line. 'Hi, Lucy, I hope you don't mind.'

'Where are you?'

'I'm at the top of a hill, somewhere behind Sandra's mother's house. I talked to that Dotsy fellow and he brought me here and he's left me and I'm not sure what to do. And I'm freezing.'

'What are you doing at the top of a hill?' I have her on speaker. Kev is grinning broadly.

'Dotsy said that in years gone by Sandra's grandfather erected a transit light on a hill behind the house. He showed me where it was – well, he pointed up the hill and I saw it and it was a very steep hill, Lucy. My legs are in bits. Anyway, I had a look at it. It's a metal thing with a holder for a torch or something. And there are bits of rubber in the holder, like as if a torch was used recently. Will I take a sample or do I need to get SOCO or—'

'Jesus, don't get SOCO. We have no proof of anything. Have you your evidence kit on you?'

'Yes.'

'Then take a scraping and label it. You know the drill. And the other light? Did Dotsy tell you about that?'

A small shriek, before she says, 'That wind is almost taking me off my feet. Christ.'

I bite my lip to stop myself laughing and talk her through taking the sample.

'The other light?' I press.

'Oh, yeah, that was disappointing. Apparently, Sandra's mother always left the porch light on and they used that. So,' a moment as she rights herself against the breeze, 'maybe this isn't important at all, this light. Maybe he didn't come in by sea.'

'People saw a light on the hill. This is our only explanation so far. You think it's been used recently, take some pictures too. Bring them all back. We can ask for the sample of rubber to be tested if we need it. Now, get back down that hill safely and go get some lunch. Thanks, Susan.'

'It's eerie out here, Lucy. All big white rocks and bog and that fecking fisherman just . . . just fecking off and leaving me. Bastard.'

Kev can't contain himself. He snorts out a laugh.

'And you're a bastard too, Kevin,' Susan snaps. 'I'd have liked to see you climb this hill.'

And she hangs up.

'Can we get some lunch now?' Kev says. 'A good laugh always makes me hungry.'

'What I can't figure out,' Kev says, as he pours copious amounts of salt over a salted pile of fish and chips, 'is where all these guys Sandra supposedly slept with are.'

'What do you mean?'

'Well, there was this girl in school with me, right, and not trying to be offensive but she was banging everyone. And everyone knew and everyone could say I was with her and there was no dispute about it. But, like, I've been talking to locals about Sandra on the door-to-door, just trying to get a feel for her and though everyone says, oh, she was wild and she slept with loads of lads, I've yet to meet one lad she actually did sleep with.'

'She must have slept with someone because she got pregnant.'

'Yeah.' He picks up a chip and pulls it apart. 'I'm just think-ing that, you know, say she wasn't like that, say she only slept with the one lad but that he knew she was pregnant so he put a rumour around saying she was with everyone, and lads of that age, they want to be seen to have done the business.' A look at me. 'Speaking as a lad who was that age once.'

'He puts out the rumour so he doesn't have to take re-sponsibility.'

'Yeah.'

'But she never said who the father was,' I counter. 'If she'd known, wouldn't she have said?'

Kev thinks about this. 'Unless it suited her to keep quiet. Maybe, I dunno, his family gave her money not to say.'

'Probably cheaper than bringing up a baby.'

'Yeah. He could have been married or anything. Who knows?'

I start to let that train of thought unspool in my head. Unless she'd come back to demand more money to keep her secret and been murdered for it. But who would murder over such a thing nowadays? And twenty years on, surely it would have lost its power.

'I talked to one fella on the door-to-door,' Kev says, laying on more salt. 'He told me he'd been in the same class as Sandra in school so I said to him I believed she'd had quite the reputation and he just laughed. Said he tried to shift her once and it would have been easier to shift the Eiffel Tower. Another lad said she was way too crazy for him, always going off on one. So, like, I began to wonder who all these fellas she slept with were.'

I think back. When was the first time I'd heard about Sandra sleeping around? And though I can't say for sure, I really don't remember anything being said about her before I left for Dublin. She would have been about fifteen then, so that was when it had started. I know when I heard she'd been pregnant, I'd rung Megan to ask if it was true and she'd been distraught. She said she couldn't believe it. So where had it all started? Had it actually begun when she'd become pregnant? Maybe it had, and then it just embedded itself into the story of Sandra.

'That's a good point, Kev.'

He looks up from his chips. 'If we could find out where all that stuff about her started, we might find out who wanted to do her harm.'

It's an interesting theory but I wonder how on earth we'll ever do that. And, sure, maybe it was said as an aside by someone in a shop and it grew legs.

'There's a lot said about Sandra that hasn't added up,' I tell him. 'And I don't know how it all grew but I do know that her family never disputed it, never once. Never stood up for her. That's odd, isn't it?'

'Not if they want it to be true,' Kev says.

And just as I'm thinking what a truly special guard this young fella is, just as I'm about to say how insightful he is, he says, 'Does this free food stretch to a dessert?

38

When we get back, I'm informed that William is out on another case and that I have to chair the conference, which is something I hate. I position myself at the top of the room, lay my files on the table. 'All right, what have we got? Kev, can you give the team a run-down on our enquiries today?'

Kev does, and because the Cig isn't there, he takes off the two girls, especially Chloé, and has the room crying with laughter. 'Anyway,' he finishes, amid hilarity, 'life jackets in the back seat, so we think he must use a boat of some sort.'

'Thanks, Kev,' I eventually say as, to loud applause, he sits down. He's quite the performer. 'Susan?'

'I can't follow that.' She giggles, and people start to laugh again. She's obviously forgiven Kev.

If William was here, there's no way he'd allow this to continue. 'What did you find out?' I ask, more firmly, and Susan being Susan, she flinches. It's enough to rein the rest of them in.

She gives a run-down on the light and says she sent the rubber scrapings to be tested.

Mick hops up after that. 'I've contacted Sandra's other addresses. They were in flatland, so it's proving difficult to find

258

anyone who really knew her because it's so transient. I did track down two landlords and they said there was never any trouble from her and never any complaints. She always paid her rent on time, but one landlord said she ran off owing him a month's. As for Richie, nothing as yet. He's provided us with a list of his passwords so Computer Crime is examining his laptop now and will have some sort of preliminary results by tomorrow. His phone yielded nothing out of the ordinary, bar those texts to Sandra, and so far we haven't managed to trace . . .' He trails off as attention is diverted by Peter Glynn arriving in.

Peter shrugs an apology and I flash a quick smile back. But the sight of him causes dread deep in the pit of my belly. What is he doing here? 'Mick, carry on.'

'Just to say,' Mick eyes the newcomer uneasily too, 'that we haven't managed to trace any of Richie's other girlfriends.'

'Keep on it. Dan and Larry?'

Larry stands. 'Eh . . . we're making progress. Harvesting feeds from along the route of that black car. We've picked it up but haven't had much luck with the reg. It's been identified as a Mondeo, though. Hopefully we'll have more tomorrow.'

'Great. Good. Pat?'

'I had a preliminary look at Sandra's bank accounts. We knew she was getting money from Maudie, but I was surprised to see that she was receiving a regular payment of two hundred and fifty euro a fortnight from her.' A look at us. 'How much pension money does a retired teacher get?'

'That's an interesting point. She had a lovely extension done on her house and the furniture in the place wasn't IKEA. Did you get her financials?'

Pat nods. 'Yep. I'll look at it ASAP.'

I scan the room, wanting to put off what I suspect is coming. But no one else has anything to contribute. 'Peter, have you anything to add?'

'Yes.' Peter stays by the door. 'Just to say that I got a call ten minutes ago.' He glances at Mick. 'You probably missed it because of conference, but that trophy in Megan and Leo's house has been identified as the murder weapon. Furthermore, Ben Lively's prints were found on it.' He has the grace to look uncomfortable. 'So, William has decided to arrest him. We've also requested that the forensic tests on Sandra's T-shirt be redone.'

The shock in the room is so strong, I can almost touch it. Prints on the trophy that killed her, along with the circumstantial evidence, is damning. 'Were there any other prints on the trophy?' I ask.

'A few,' Peter admits. 'We've identified the ones from the family but a couple of partials remain a mystery. They could have come from the time Devon was presented with the trophy. You know yourselves that prints can be there for years. However, we do know that the only time Ben Lively was in the house was on the night Sandra was murdered. It is therefore extremely likely that the prints were deposited that night.'

'Are you still tracing any cars that were about that night?' Larry asks. 'Cars that might have spotted Ben?'

'We do know how to do our job,' Peter snaps. 'That's our update, Lucy. I'll let you know how the interview goes.' So saying, he turns on his heel and leaves.

Everyone looks at me. The disbelief in their eyes mirrors mine, I'd say. I take a breath, wonder what the Cig would do, and know he'd point out that the evidence will speak, that we just have to go doggedly about our task, and if Ben is innocent, the cards will fall that way. But will they? Damn it, I think, I'm not the Cig and these are Ben's colleagues, for God's sake.

'Look,' I gulp out, 'this is a shock, especially for us because we know Ben. But we just have to keep on keeping on. My gut says that Ben Lively could no more have murdered Sandra Byrne than—' I can't think of an analogy '—than . . .'

'Than William will tell me and Susan we're the best,' Mick offers.

The laughter that follows helps ease the mood. Then, turning serious, I say, 'We need to find this man in the black car. Let's see who he was and why Sandra was scared of him. Did he murder her? Get the search of Richie's laptop prioritised, is there anything on there. Ger, money lenders?'

'Yes, Lucy. It seems she did have a loan she defaulted on but she has been paying it back in the past year. The interest is huge so she would have been paying it off for years to come, but she was paying.'

'Good work.' That rules out the money-lender theory, not that it had been a serious one, really. 'Keep at it,' I tell Ger, 'just in case she had another loan or something. We can't rule it one hundred per cent out.'

They get their job sheets and the conference breaks up. The mood is downbeat, the conversation muted. It's the sort of investigation where we seem to be taking two steps forward and four steps back. And now to have Ben arrested on top of it all . . .

Dan joins me as I'm clearing my files from the table.

We leave the room in near silence. I glance into William's office but he's still not back, which is weird, though knowing him, he'll probably ring me at some horrible hour in the morning looking for a run-down. I think about calling him but decide against it. 'Just leave the files on the desk,' I say to Dan. 'I'll stay here in case William turns up. See you in the morning.'

'Grand, see you tomorrow.'

39

It's almost time, he thinks, as he readies himself. He has hired a car for the occasion. He really doesn't care much what happens after this. If he gets away with it, he'll keep going, knocking off anyone who hurt him during those years in prison. But if he doesn't, he'll have taken his revenge on her in the best way possible by hurting the boy. And her. Oh, he'll bloody torture her.

The boy is home. He saw him arrive back, late, in a taxi. A girl with a baby on her lap kissed him. Then the boy got out and he saw the old woman hug him, then bring the boy into the house. He heard chat and music and saw lights pop on in the windows.

He looks at his watch.

He wonders what time she'll be back.

The bitch who ruined his life. Who took his family from him.

Who killed the woman he loved.

Who made his son a stranger. An almost-orphan.

He'd cut the wires on her car, spooked her with dead flowers and now . . .

Lucy Golden is in for a shock, he thinks, as he strides towards the house.

40

I spend a few hours with Larry at the CCTV, waiting on William to return. Finally Larry leaves, and half an hour later, when William still hasn't arrived, I pick up my jacket and say goodbye to the two guards left in the incident room. Both are reviewing the statements gathered so far.

Outside, the car park is deserted, barely lit by a single street-lamp, but the sky is clear and studded with masses of stars, the moon a sliver of yellow. Out beyond, the ocean's eternal beat mixes with the thump of music from a function in the hotel up the road. I put the car in gear and drive out of the station.

I'm five minutes from home when my personal phone rings. Glancing at caller ID, I see Rob's number pop up.

What the hell is he playing at?

I flick off the phone and keep driving.

The cheek of him. Who does he think he is that he can just ring me? Who? With every kilometre, my grip on the steering-wheel gets tighter, anger making my knuckles whiten. How dare he? I'm so busy cursing him in my head that I almost don't see the car pulled up on the grass verge just before the final bend for home. It's a dangerous place to pull in so I get out, ready to knock on the window to tell whoever it is that, if they park there, they might just get a smash in the rear from oncoming motorists.

There is no one inside.

That's weird.

Maybe it broke down.

'It was a man,' a voice says, from the other side of the road, startling me, making the hairs stand up on my arms and the blood rush to my head.

It's Rob, half hidden by shadows.

Jesus Christ tonight. Can he not take a hint?

'Get out of there. Come here where I can see you, arsehole.'

'I'm only trying to say—'

'Don't! Don't say anything to me.' I march towards him, head thumping, hands clenched. 'Are you fucking spying on me? First thing tomorrow, I'm going to make a complaint against you.'

'If you could get over your anger for one second, I can—'

'Me? Get over my anger?' I shove my face into his and he takes a step back, stumbling a little. 'You've a better chance of getting over your arrogance. Piss off home. Now.'

He holds up his hands in surrender. 'There was a man in that car and he went into your house.'

'Fuck off. Fuck off. It's not your car, I suppose?'

'No, I got a taxi and—'

My hand shoots out and I shove him. He stumbles again. 'Don't play your mind games with me, you little shit. I'm not the idiot I once was. Piss off back to the hole you crawled out of.'

He calls something after me, but I don't even hear it. I get back into my car, slam the door and fire the engine. I think my skin might erupt in boils or blisters or something. Bastard. Bastard. I slide the window down as I pull off, 'Get it through your head. We don't want you in our lives.'

'Lucy—'

And I give him the two fingers.

41

The house is in darkness when I scorch into the driveway, dust in my wake. Jesus, my mother normally stays up and now, when I want a good vent, when I want to vomit out my bile about Rob, she's gone to bed. And I can't wake her because Luc is here tonight, having come back from college. My head is hopping. I don't think I'll be able to sleep. I fire my coat onto the chair in the hall and fling open the kitchen door.

It's as if I've been plunged into an alternative universe.

My mother and Luc are bound hand and foot to two chairs, gags in their mouths.

I can't take it in. It's like my mind has flipped three-sixty.

'Lucy, we meet again.'

A man steps out from behind the door, a large, serrated knife in his hand. Horror crawls from my feet to my scalp. He's changed from the gawky kid I once knew but his voice is the same and it makes my legs buckle. I grab the door handle to stay upright.

Dessie McKenna, my one-time informant.

Rob was telling the truth.

I can't show fear, I know that much. I need to appear in control until I figure out what the hell I can do.

What can I do?

And how can I not show fear? He'll hurt my child. My mother.

A hammering at the back door. Someone is kicking it in and making a shit job of it.

'The fuck is that?' Dessie shouts, heading for the back door.

A final kick and Rob stumbles through, like a man possessed, straight onto Dessie's knife. He collapses onto the floor, clutching his stomach. Dessie backs away, shocked, I think. My mother lets out a muffled scream.

'Shut up, you stupid biddy,' Dessie snaps at her. 'Who the hell is this fella?' A bit of a laugh, forced. 'Not a guard anyway, that's for sure.' Then without waiting for an answer, he says to me, 'Sit down.'

'He's seriously injured.' I indicate Rob, who now has blood pooling around him at an alarming rate. 'We need to get an ambulance.'

'We'll need another ambulance if you don't sit the fuck down,' Dessie says.

'Rob, put pressure on it.' I move to a seat. But I can't let him bleed out on the floor in front of me. I take the chance, kneeling down beside him, placing my hands about his wound. I glance up at Dessie, who looks truly terrifying. 'Just let me help him and I won't try anything, I swear.'

Dessie scrutinises me for a long moment, the boy I remember battling the man he now is. 'You do and I'll gut the old woman and your son, Luc, like - like chicken fillets. Actually, I'll probably do it anyway.'

My stomach heaves. 'I'll do whatever you want.' My hand is soaked in Rob's blood.

Dessie looms over me, invading my space as I try my best to staunch the flow. Then, in one abrupt movement, he refocuses his attention on Luc and my mother. 'I have to tell you why I'm here,' he says. 'This woman,' he twirls his knife like a baton, jabbing it in my direction, 'this woman, who you both probably think is bloody wonderful, pissed all over my life. Do yez know that?' At my mother and Luc's lack of response, he slams the knife on the table and leans towards them. 'Do yez know that?'

They shake their heads quickly. My mother trembles all over. Luc is doing his best to be brave, though his eyes are wide with fear. White-hot rage at seeing them put through this starts in my belly but there is nothing I can do. I just have to wait for an opportunity.

'Stay with me, Rob,' I whisper.

'I will. Just keep touching me,' he jokes, on a gasp, before his eyes roll back in his head.

'Rob!' I cry, pressing harder on the wound.

Dessie jumps slightly.

I take a chance. 'Dessie, come on. D'you want murder on your conscience?'

'You've lived with murder, you stupid cow,' Dessie says, eyes darting between me and Rob. 'And very nicely too.' He moves towards Luc. 'Your mother, she fucked me over.'

My mother tries to say something through the gag.

Dessie immediately focuses on her. He tips her chin up with the point of his knife.

'Leave her alone!' I think I might vomit. 'If it's me you want, take me,' I say, with as much calm as I'm able. 'I saw your car on the road outside, just drive me anywhere.'

'Not until I tell all these people how you played with me,' Dessie says. 'How you used me and then threw me off like some kind of rubbish you needed to get rid of.'

'I'm—'

'Don't say you're sorry.' He slams the butt of the knife onto the table and spit flies from his mouth.

My mother jumps.

'Sit still, old woman,' he snarls, his anger soaring. 'Your daughter is a bitch. I was only a kid, like you,' he turns on Luc, 'a stupid little kid who needed to make a few bob to put himself through college. Doing engineering I was. I was clever.' He eyeballs me. 'You knew that, though, didn't you?' And when I don't answer, he yells, 'Didn't you?'

'Yes.' I had. I'd known everything about him. It had been easy to use him because he had so much to lose.

My hand is sticky with Rob's blood. He's still breathing, though, still hanging in there.

'I had a girlfriend. She was pregnant,' Dessie goes on, pacing, breathing, twirling his knife. 'I needed money. I needed money for college because my folks struggled. I needed money for my girlfriend. I just fucking wanted a better life, so I was dealing, just small scale, making a quid here and a quid there, paying college fees. I was in my final bloody year when your mother nabbed me. A little ambitious bitch she was.'

'You'd been nabbed before then,' I say. I can't let him skew this story. 'You'd been warned you might go to jail.'

'Shut up!' His gaze is malicious, and I know he believes his narrative. I know any compassion I sensed in him has fled amid his growing anger in the recounting of his story. 'Her,' he jabs once more in my direction, getting right up into Luc's face, 'and this other lad told me I'd never get a job with a conviction, told me they could make it go away if I went undercover. Help flush out the real dealers. They said it wouldn't be long but four years

270

she had me doing it. Four years of shit and stress and then,' he looks at me, 'what happened then, Lucy?'

'You turned state's witness, put away a mass-murderer drug dealer,' I say back.

Rob groans and his eyelids flicker.

'I lost my bloody life, that's what happened.' Another slam of the knife on the table, and my mother and Luc jump. 'Your mother,' he howls at Luc, 'she took away my wife and my kid and my life. That's what happened.'

Luc looks at me. I don't think it had ever occurred to him before what I did for a living, how I operated, the sort of people I was dealing with.

'Your wife was offered state protection too and she chose to turn it down,' I say calmly. Rob has paled, his forehead clammy. Is he going into shock? 'And if you hadn't gone, you would have been killed along with your wife and son. It was for your own good.'

He upends the table, almost smashing it into me. My mother screams.

'That is not true. I lived my life without ever seeing my kid again. I missed them.' He advances on me with the knife. 'My wife is dead. Did you know that?'

'Yes. I know. She gave me my scar.'

He backhands me and I go flying into the door. I feel no pain but know that I've banged my head because the world grows fuzzy and sickness crawls in my stomach. Dessie charges towards me but slips on Rob's blood, the knife flies in a high arc out of his hand and he lands on top of me. Luc howls like an injured animal.

It galvanises me.

I try to get up but Dessie is on me, hands coming around my neck to choke me. I am vaguely aware that my mother is trying to get up, that Rob is bleeding out and that Luc is straining against his ties. Dessie's hands tighten on my neck and, all of a sudden, my training kicks in as I wrap my legs around his waist, control his elbows by crossing my arms over his wrists and holding onto them. I push away with my hips, his elbows bending. In one swift movement, I bring my legs around his shoulders and heave. Then, crack, his elbows snap and he shrieks in pain. I push him away from me and jump up, scanning the room for the knife.

It's by the table. I scramble towards it, Rob's blood coating me too.

Dessie stumbles to his feet.

'Don't you come any closer.' I wave it in front of me, like a madwoman. 'I will kill you. I swear.'

'You bitch,' he yells. 'You—'

Behind him, the back door is smashed in and two guards from the ASU in full tactical gear, both armed with H&K MP7s and Tasers, rush in, shouting, 'Armed gardaí!'

It's surreal.

Have I been knocked out?

Dessie lunges at me again.

I jab the knife out, nicking his arm.

He yells.

The first armed guard grabs Dessie about the neck and restrains him, all the while cautioning him.

The second guard makes for the hallway to see if it's clear.

'We need an ambulance,' I say, snapping into work mode. 'There's a man with a knife wound to the abdomen. Two people suffering from shock. Otherwise it's all clear.' I don't know where they've come from or how, I'm just weak with relief to see them. I turn to my mother and Luc and use the knife to cut through their ties. As they free themselves, I pull them close, hard against me. Luc moves away first, hunkering down beside Rob.

I join him. 'Rob?' His eyes flicker though his face has got the pallor of poached chicken. His breathing is laboured.

'Rob!'

Nothing.

Luc takes Rob's hand. 'Dad? Dad, are you all right?' A shake. 'Dad.' Anguish in his voice. 'Dad, please, don't go. Dad, stay!'

'There's an ambulance coming.' William arrives through the back door, pocketing his gun as he takes in the situation. 'Make that two,' he says into a receiver.

I can't catch what's going on at all. I wonder if I'm badly concussed, or if I was knocked out and don't realise it. How are they here?

'William?' I say. 'What are you doing here? How did you—'

'Later,' he says. He turns to my mother. 'Are you all right, Mrs Golden?'

'It's Mags and, yes, I think so. Just . . . shocked.' She can't control her trembling.

'And Luc?'

Luc shrugs, his gaze fixed on Rob. I move to caress him but he shifts away a little under my touch.

'We'll need to take statements from you all,' William says. 'As soon as possible.'

'Dad!' The word tears out of Luc as Rob's breathing stops momentarily before resuming in a gasp. 'No! No!'

I push Luc out of the way and press hard on the wound. Rob's eyes flicker open briefly. 'Knew dead flowers was bad,' he says, the end of the sentence fading away in a whisper. 'Hard to—'

'Save your energy, save your energy.'

I am aware of William standing above me, and I see in his eyes what I haven't acknowledged. Rob might not make it. William knows it by his colour, by the position of the wound, by the size of the knife. My tears fall unchecked onto Rob's light blue jacket.

'Will he be all right?' Luc asks.

I catch William's eye. 'We just have to wait and see, son,' he says.

The ambulance arrives a couple of minutes later and, with Rob attached to tubes and an oxygen mask, it goes screaming off into the night.

Dessie, who has been cautioned and cuffed, is bundled into the next one.

'Hurry up,' William says, grabbing his arm and pulling him towards it.

'Mind my arms. The bitch broke them,' Dessie cries out.

'Pity she didn't break a bit more,' William snaps. 'Now get in before I push you in.'

Dessie throws him a poisonous look.

After the ambulances are gone, the questions take over. We are led into three different parts of the house to give our statements.

And then, much, much later, after I've told my mother and Luc to leave the house for tonight, Luc to stay with Tani and her parents and my mother to stay with one of her many friends, after I've given my clothes over for testing and showered, I join William in the sitting room. The fire has died down but the room retains its heat. It looks the same as it did yesterday and the day before but somehow it will never be the same. This house was my safe space, a refuge against the evils of the world, but it's been invaded and by something I thought I'd left behind a long time ago. I stand in the doorway, staring about, the worn sofa, the plump cushions, the family pictures, a photo montage to Sirocco on the wall, and the love for the room dies a little in me.

William gives the fire a bit of a poke, but it's beyond saving. 'How did you know?' I ask him.

He places the poker carefully back in position, then turns to me and gestures for me to sit down. My head is banging but I'll survive if I take it easy for a day or two, the paramedics said.

William waits until I've sat on the opposite end of the sofa to him and drawn my feet up under me. 'Jordy thought he recognised him when he was questioning people coming to and from the island in connection with Sandra Byrne's death. He came to me with it and I tasked him with getting an official whereabouts on Dessie McKenna and it turned out that he'd gone AWOL a couple of months back. We spent the last two weeks trying to track him down. There was a sighting near here the other day but the guard was thrown by a different name. Still, he called it in but he'd gone to ground. In the end, we thought, well, if he was targeting you, we'd track your movements. You nearly caught us the other night so we stayed back further tonight. It was only when we saw the car on the road outside your place and tried to ID it that we realised he must be in the house.'

'You should have told me.' I haven't the energy to feel mad.

'We would have but we had no real proof it was him. I'm sorry we left it so late.'

I stare into the dead fire. 'The hospital said they'd operate tonight. I have to go in.'

He doesn't ask why or tell me that Rob ruined my life or say that I've to take it easy. Instead, he unfolds himself from the sofa and jangles his car keys. 'Come on, then.'

42

21 January

Rob has been transferred to ICU, having had major surgery to repair the wound. The knife had punctured some vital organs and the nurse on duty, Izzy, her name tag reads, tells me that the next twenty-four hours will be critical. 'It's up to him now,' she says, as she writes a note in his file, then taps the pen off her front teeth.

She points me in the direction of the relatives' waiting room. I'm reminded of when I was here a few days back. It seems ages ago now, another lifetime.

That night unfolds like thick treacle falling off a spoon. Slow, every part of it etched into my brain. I buy tea from a vending machine and let it go cold, I watch other anxious relatives come and go. I don't know how to feel. I watch Rob, hooked up to machines, through the small ICU window, willing him on. William stays with me, silent, occasionally checking his phone.

Gradually, daylight creeps into the waiting room, banishing the dark and heralding a new day. Eight fifteen. Luc texts, wondering how Rob is. I reply, *Hanging in there.*

'Come on down and I'll get you breakfast,' William breaks his silence. 'You've had a rough night. Don't burn out.'

I'm tempted to say I'll be fine, that I'll eat when I'm ready, but I know he's right. It's what I would say to a relative. I haul myself up from the chair, legs creaking, arms stiff, head hammering still. I follow him on leaden feet towards the canteen.

The hospital has woken up too. The smell of food wafts down the corridors, and I hear the rattle of cups and plates as breakfast is dished out to patients.

In contrast, the canteen is deserted: just us two and three doctors, who look no older than Luc. They're all scrolling their phones, eating eggs and bacon and filling up on tea. They look wrecked. I hope they're coming off a shift.

William orders me to sit down, then goes up to the counter and comes back with a large pot of tea and two enormous plates of fry. 'Eat what you can,' he says, handing me a plate. 'I got a bit of everything because I don't know what you like.'

'Thank you.'

'No bother.' He digs in, polishing off his food in minutes while I jab at a sausage, poke at some scrambled eggs and do my best to eat something. Finished, he pours us both a cup of tea and butters another slice of toast for himself. 'Does he have any family I can contact?'

'A sister. She won't speak to me because I let, her words, Rob go to jail. I texted her last night but she might not open it.'

'Give me her name and address and I'll get one of the boys to call out. If she's not there, we'll give her a ring.'

'Her name is Clara Ganley, unless she's married and changed it. She lived out in Stillorgan in Dublin, in an apartment.' I try to remember the address but I can't. 'It was near the shopping centre there.' I call out the phone number, which I have never deleted. I never thought I'd be using it in these circumstances.

'We'll find it,' William has been tapping notes into his phone as I talk. 'Now you,' he puts aside his phone and leans towards me, 'stay off for a couple of days. I'll have Jordy back on the investigation now so he can take up some slack.'

'I'll be back once I know about Rob,' I say. 'You can't take me off the case.'

'I actually can,' he says, though not unkindly. 'You've had a terrible experience, Lucy.'

'I see it all the time in the job,' I say.

'But not at your own door, with your family. Take time off, all right.'

I know it's an order not a suggestion and I could weep. Work is the only thing that will stop me thinking of the horror I faced, the only thing that will keep the demons at bay.

'I've to go. I'll be in touch, right.' William stands up, grabs his jacket and pockets his phone.

'I'll be keeping tabs on the investigation,' I warn him. 'Just so you know.'

He looks at me in exasperation. 'Fine. But stay away, right? This sort of thing, this experience, it stops you being as detached as you need to be.'

I give what might be construed as a 'Fine,' and he leaves.

I call Luc and there is no answer, so then I ring my mother who, of course, asks how I am, and when I tell her I'm fine, she tells me she's fine too but that she might stay away from the house for a few days.

'That's grand, Mam. I understand. I might see if I can crash somewhere else too.'

'Lorna said you can come here. There's plenty of room.'

Lorna is my mother's best friend and, while I'm fond of her, she and my mother together would test the nerves of a fighter pilot. 'It's grand. I'll only cramp your style.'

My mother laughs, then asks, 'How is Rob? What was he doing there anyway?'

I answered that question for myself last night. 'I think he got worried when he heard someone had sent me dead flowers. He told me it wasn't him when I challenged him but sure you know Rob. You can't be believing him.'

'And yet he risked his life . . .' Her voice trails off.

'Yeah,' I say, choking up a little. 'People surprise you.' They surprise me every day in the job. The kinder the person, the worse the damage when they snap, I often think, and maybe the colder the person, the greater the sacrifice when they care enough, too. People are rarely all good or bad.

And, the thought squirms inside me, maybe Dessie wasn't so awful once. He had a partner he loved, a child he loved, and I took him away from all that. He has every right to be mad at me. And he's correct: I was so ambitious back then. Still am. And there's nothing wrong with that, is there? Is there?

'Lucy? Lucy, are you still there? I can't—'

'Yeah. Yeah, I am. Have you spoken to Luc today?'

'He rang to see how I was,' she said. 'He sounded fine. Was he not in touch with you?'

'No.' Hurt, sharp as a knife, pierces me.

'Well . . .' she says, as she scrambles to think of what to say '. . . he probably thought you'd enough on your plate.'

'Maybe.'

'When will I see you?'

I tell her I'll call over to her once I know how Rob is. She blows me a kiss down the line and hangs up.

I try Luc again.

Nothing.

He arrives in at three o'clock, just as I've hung up on Dan, who I've made promise to keep me abreast of all developments in the case. I don't trust William to do it. Dan, however, is more easily swayed. He'd told me that, so far, they've managed to get a few numbers on the black Ford Mondeo reg plate, so that's good. It's a 2-2-1, he says. They're running a pulse trace on all black Ford Mondeos of that half of the year. See if any belong to locals or, indeed, anyone connected to the island.

'If you pass me the list, I'll be able to see if there's anyone on it I recognise, you know, who might have had connections to the Island.'

He hesitates, obviously having been warned by William not to include me.

'You know it makes sense, Dan.'

'Not if you were attacked in your home last night and—'

'—and trying to find a distraction from it. Come on. William doesn't need to know.'

'All right.' He gives in because he knows there's no point in holding out on me. 'How's Rob?'

'Not great.' The words catch in my throat. There is something about speaking things aloud that makes them real. 'There's no improvement since last night apparently.'

A pause. 'I'm sorry, Luce.'

'Yeah.'

Neither of us knows what to say after that. We'd both despised him and there are no words now to cover how we feel. There was decency in him, after all, and I'm reminded again of why I'd fallen for the brash, flash guy he'd been. And it proves, too, that my gut hadn't been all wrong.

Just then I spot the gangly, spiky form of Luc slouching up the corridor in his over-sized jeans and black jacket. I bid Dan a hasty goodbye and wave a little as Luc crosses towards me.

He plonks down beside me and barely returns my greeting, preferring instead to stare at the floor, looking utterly morose and miserable.

I reach out to touch him, to assure myself that he's all right, that he's in one piece, but he moves away slightly and my hand falls.

Finally, 'How is he?'

'Not good,' I answer, as gently as I can. 'They operated on him last night and the hope is that he'll start to recover, but so far . . .' I shrug. 'Nothing.'

A slight sob escapes him and, bending, he covers his face with his hand. This time, I touch him lightly on the back and caress his shoulder before he shrugs me off.

'I wasn't nice to him,' Luc says, after a while, his voice a whisper. 'I told him that day in the gallery that I was ashamed of him. That every time I thought of him I wished I wasn't related to him. Oh, God.' He wipes his eyes viciously with the palm of his hand.

'Aw, Luc, look—'

'And he said,' Luc interrupts, gulping, 'he said it wouldn't always be that way and I said, yes, it would. Yes, it would. That there was nothing he . . .' A ragged inhalation. 'I can't take it back.'

'Your dad almost ruined the country, Luc. He took money from vulnerable people. Of course you were ashamed of him.'

He doesn't react.

'He showed no remorse because he thought those people were stupid. And for that, he deserved to go to jail. But last night,' I shake my head, 'last night he did a good thing. And he did it because he loved you so, yes, you're proud of that. And you can tell him when you get in to see him.'

He gets up and walks away from me.

At four thirty, I'm allowed into ICU. Rob is at the very end of the room, by the window, and I have a stupid thought that at least he has a nice view. He looks grey, though his breathing seems stable.

'Rob,' I whisper, as I take his hand. 'It's Lucy.'

Nothing.

In all the years I spent with him, and in all the years apart, I've always imagined Rob as a force of nature, for bad mostly, but still, a force of nature that pulsed with energy, vital and alive. And this shell of a man is not him. Even the last time I saw him, standing on the slight rise of grass by my house, black eyes glittering in the dark, he had a vibe about him. I wish I'd listened to him. I wish . . . There's no point in going there. I would never in a million years have listened to him. 'Rob,' I whisper once more, as the machines hiss and whump, 'thank you.' I squeeze his hand harder. 'Thank you for being there last night. Thanks for Luc.' I stop. Rack my brain for more to say and come up empty. 'There's not much else I can thank you for, really. You made my life a misery,' I half laugh, choking back a sob, 'but those two things you did for me, they're the most import-ant things one person can do for another. And I will always be grateful.'

A rustle as a nurse appears beside me. 'Your son is outside waiting to come in,' she says. 'I hate to hurry you but—'

'No, it's fine.' I'm relieved Luc's back. I'm relieved he won't have the enormous regrets Devon will have. I turn to Rob. 'Luc is here.' I touch his face, let my palm caress it. 'He's very proud of you.'

When Luc arrives back out of ICU, his eyes are red. I have a can of Coke and a packet of crisps waiting for him.

'Did you really ruin that man's life?'

The question comes out of the blue and wrongfoots me.

'Rob's life?'

'No. That guy last night. Did you ruin his life?'

I can't tell if he sounds accusatory or not.

'He thinks I did,' I answer carefully, not sure where this is going.

'But do you think you did?'

Do I think I did? Was he on track to ruin it anyway? 'It's not as straightforward as—'

'You either did or didn't.'

'Luc—'

'Did you ruin his life? Did you just use him like he said?' His voice rises, hurt and confused, and I can't believe this is happening.

'Luc, running informants, it was part of my job back then. And if I hadn't done what I did, one of the biggest gangsters would be roaming the streets right now, selling to youngsters like you. People would be dying.'

'But he was going to college and—' He stops. He looks at me like he doesn't know me, 'Say it was me and I had to leave Tani and Sirocco behind.'

'Jesus, Luc—'

'I've smoked joints. I've even done a bit of cocaine.'

'Jesus, Luc!'

'I've been high. I've—'

'JESUS!'

A silence. People are looking.

'Are you saying,' I whisper furiously, 'that you feel sorry for that man last night?'

'No.' Luc shakes his head. 'I just never thought you'd do something like that to someone.'

And it's the disappointment in his voice, the disillusionment, that kills me. 'It's my job.'

He seems about to say something else, the words balancing in the air before he pulls them back. 'I'll see you tomorrow,' he says.

My mother arrives in later, carrying a flask of coffee, some paper cups and a bag of sweets. The cups have balloons on the side and say 'Congratulations'. 'These are the only ones I could get in the shop,' she says, as she hands me a coffee. 'How are things here?'

I tell her about Rob and then Luc. 'Please will you talk to him for me?'

'I will. But I have to say I was a bit shocked when I heard you'd done those things, too, but you're a guard and I suppose you have to do all that sort of stuff. It's a bit ruthless but—'

'I'm not ruthless.'

'Let me finish,' she says, and pauses, waiting for me to break, the way you would when you tell a dog 'Leave it.' Finally, satisfied, she continues, 'It's a bit ruthless but I can understand it because it's for the greater good.'

'Thank you. Can you say that to Luc?'

'If I see him.' A hesitation before she says, 'I don't think I'll go back to the house tonight, Lucy. Lorna has said I can stay with her for another night or two.'

'I get that. Look, I can arrange counselling for us and—'

'I don't need counselling, I just need to talk to someone.'

'Yes, exactly, and—'

'Lorna is a good listener.'

That's put a lid firmly on the counsellor idea.

'I'm looking for Robert Ganley.'

The voice carries and my mother and I glance towards it. It's Clara, Rob's younger sister. We watch as she has a brief chat with the nurse, who then points her in our direction.

Clara freezes briefly at the sight of us, then hesitantly approaches. She looks better than she did twelve years ago: she's had her hair cut quite short and it suits her tiny features. She has the same dark looks as Rob but none of his charisma. She was always a bit off with me – I think she was jealous because up until I arrived it was her and Rob against the world. Clara's clothes are as bohemian as ever: wide-legged trousers with some crazy, psychedelic pattern, teamed with heavy boots and a loose top with over-large sleeves that I'd imagine would keep getting caught in a plate of food. Still, the look suits her.

I, by comparison, don't have a look, unless it consists of black trousers and white shirts.

'Hi, Clara,' I say, sounding squeaky and anxious.

'Hi, Lucy. Hi, Mags.' Her voice is rich, a lighter version of her brother's.

'Sit down beside me here, *a stór.*' My mother pats the seat beside her as if twelve years haven't passed since we last saw this woman.

286

As Clara uncertainly takes her seat, my mother unscrews the top of her flask. 'Would you like some coffee? I have biscuits too.'

'Black coffee would be nice,' she says. 'Thanks, Mags.'

My mother pulls out her cheery cups and hands one to Clara, who looks at it in bewilderment. 'Hold it steady there,' she says, as she pours. 'Now, how about a biscuit to go with that?' She waves a packet of shortbread.

'I'm vegan. Thanks, though.' Clara wraps her hands about the warm cup and takes a sip.

'There's no meat in the biscuits.'

'I don't eat animal products either.'

'But biscuits aren't animal products,' my mother says gaily.

'There is butter in shortbread,' Clara explains. 'That's an animal product.'

'Oh.' My mother pulls away. Screws up her face. 'So, you wouldn't be partial to an egg then?'

'No.'

'Or a sponge cake?'

'Not unless it had a flax egg and sunflower butter.'

'A flax egg?' My mother is baffled. 'Right.'

'Made with flax seed and water.'

'That's hardly an egg.' She pulls a biscuit from the packet and chews. 'Would you eat . . .' she frowns '. . . a fruit salad?'

'Yes, I suppose. If there was no cream or yogurt on it.'

'Carrots?'

'Yes, carrots are fine. All vegetables.'

'But not biscuits?'

'Mam.' I hold up my hand. I think I might laugh and that would be awful in an ICU waiting room. 'Clara doesn't want to spend the next two hours talking about her diet.'

Clara's eyes fill and she tries to blink away her tears.

'I'm really sorry about Rob, Clara,' I say. Tears start to trickle down her face and plop into her coffee.

'Aw, now, you've upset her,' my mother chides, carefully taking her coffee from her and setting it on the floor before enfolding her in a hug.

43

22 January

There is still no change in Rob's condition the following morning, which is neither good nor bad. Clara tells me that she will
stay and send me a text if anything happens.

Dan rings and tells me the list from Pulse has come through
and is being examined by Susan, who will call me if I'm needed.
Then he offers me a bed in his place after first accompanying me
home to collect some clothes. 'You can't stay in your house on
your own,' he says. 'Wait until your mother and Luc go back too.'

I'm secretly glad he's said that. When I unlock the front door
and stand in the hall, I'm glad that the kitchen door is shut. I don't
want to see that room just yet. I run down to my bedroom and
pull clothes from the wardrobe. Ten minutes after arriving, we're
back on the road to his cottage.

Fran has stew in a big crockpot waiting for us.

'Comfort food,' he says, as he ladles it onto my plate. 'Just what
you need.' He wraps an arm about me and kisses the top of my
head – I feel about twelve again. I reach up a hand and hold him
close for the briefest moment.

'Thank you, you two.'

Fran chats easily about his day as we eat. He's a landscaper. It's not too busy as it's winter but he paints funny pictures of his clients and their weird requests. His stories relax me. Then, when we've glasses of hot whiskey in hand, he talks about his mother, of how lonely she is since his father died.

'She's angling to move in with us,' Dan says.

'She's angling to move in with Dan,' Fran says. 'Not me.'

Dan chortles and I let their chat and banter slide over me, feeling a pang that I don't have this easy love any more. I hope what they have lasts for ever.

That night, I dream of being hunted down. I'm in a house and the light is shining out into the night and it's a beacon and all the wild things are coming and I can't turn off the light and—

I jerk awake, heart hammering.

My phone says it's five in the morning. I lie there, staring into the dark, knowing that sleep has deserted me. Feck it, as quietly as I can, I pull on my socks and tiptoe downstairs to grab a glass of water.

Dan is not a guard for nothing. Five minutes later, as I'm finishing, he appears in the doorway. 'All right?'

'Did I wake you?'

He waves me away. 'How are you?'

'I'm all right. Have they interviewed Ben yet?'

'Yesterday.' He pours himself a glass of water. 'Aw, Jaysus, Lucy, it looks bad for him. He says he did touch the trophy. He said that while he was waiting for Sandra, he saw it and wondered how heavy it was and lifted it up. Said he even tried to lift it with one hand - you know Ben.'

I can imagine him doing just that.

'I could get in shit for this, Luce,' Dan says, flicking a look at me, 'but, sure, seeing as you're not working with us, do you fancy having a read of Ben's memos and Devon's statement again and seeing if there's anything, anything at all, you can find that will either prove it was Ben Devon saw that night or someone else?'

I'm grateful to be doing something. 'If William asks, I'll say I pressured you into giving me a job, pulled rank on you.'

Dan raises his eyebrows, 'No one will believe that.'

'It doesn't matter what they believe.' I grin. 'It's what they can prove.'

'I'll email them to you.'

'Thanks, Bud.'

He offers me a half-salute.

44

23 January

At eight, the documents pop into my secure email folder. I've three hours to study them before I've to relieve Clara at the hospital. I print them all out and then, with a strong cup of coffee and some high-quality biscuits, I set to work.

Three hours later, nothing has jumped out at me. Devon saw a man, in black, running down the driveway of his grandmother's house. This man didn't have a car or any visible means of transport. He appeared to be of similar height and build to Ben. When he went inside the house, Devon found the trophy alongside his mother's body.

Ben states that he left Sandra as she was tearing her mother's kitchen apart. That he sneaked out of the house and down the driveway. That he wore black. His phone had died so he didn't call a car or anyone to pick him up. That he walked for miles to Tonragee, with no definite sighting of him on CCTV, and spent the night, soaking wet, in his friend's barn.

The only person ruled out in this scenario is Richie, as he would have needed a car, though I suppose he could easily have parked it somewhere else. But chances are we would have picked it up on CCTV somewhere that night. I read until the words dance in front of my eyes. Then I pack it all up and head to the hospital.

When I get there, Clara is chatting to Luc in the corridor. It looks as if he has just arrived. He hasn't even bothered to call and tell me he was visiting. I could have given him a lift.

'Hey,' Clara calls out, as I approach, 'I can't believe my only nephew is gone so tall. What have you been feeding him all these years, Lucy?'

'Good country food.' I smile. 'How's Rob?'

Her sunniness dips a little. A shrug, but she can't say the words.

I touch her hand and she squeezes mine back.

'I'll hang on until five,' I say. 'Then I'll get something to eat and be back.'

'No need,' Clara says. 'I've taken time off work. And he's my brother and . . .' She lowers her gaze and I know she was about to say that Rob is nothing to me now, not really.

'You can't do it all on your own.' I'm matter-of-fact. 'Me, my mother and Luc are happy to help out and we owe him, you know.' My own voice falters a little. 'Plus Luc is his son.'

'I am,' Luc agrees.

Clara swallows hard and I can see her doing her best to stop herself sobbing. 'You know, since he got out of . . . well, prison, he just tried his best to be as good as he could. Tried really hard to get back in with you all. Taking pictures of Mayo, moving down here. I don't know what he thought he was doing. I mean,' she laughs a little, 'he hated the country. And I told him, "You've burned your bridges there," but, you know him . . .' she says, half in exasperation, half tearfully. 'He just ploughed on with his own thing.'

'He bought Sirocco a present for her christening,' Luc admits to her, like confession. 'I threw it back at him in the middle of his photo exhibition.'

For a second she looks hurt on Rob's behalf but then maybe she puts herself in Luc's shoes or mine, I don't know, but she says, 'I told him at the time it was a bad idea. He really shouldn't have done that, Luc. You were right to give it back.'

'Yeah, I thought that at the time but now, with him in there,' he looks uneasily towards the ICU, 'and what he did and—'

'And nothing,' she says. 'Don't beat yourself up over it. Sure, he laughed about it afterwards, told me you had guts.'

'Did he?' Something heavy leaves Luc: I can see it in the slight shift of his shoulder, in the straightening of his spine. 'He said I had guts?'

'Yep.' Clara shoots a look at me and I mouth, 'Thank you'.

Later, after she and Luc have visited and left, it's just me and Rob and the bleep of the machines and the grey dullness of the day outside his window. I take his hand and rub it, marvel at the well-kept nails and smooth skin. He still has the trace of a scar on his thumb that he got when he tried to hammer a picture onto the wall. He was shit at DIY. The memory comes up sparkling clear. I watch his chest rise and fall, hear the whoosh of the machine breathing for him, and the silence of the place almost lulls me to sleep. I jerk myself back to wakefulness. Then, because the nurse has told me that they think people in a coma can hear, I whisper, 'I was half dreaming just now, Rob, of how we met. D'you remember us both queuing up for tickets to a Springsteen concert? And I missed the last ticket by one and you turned around and told me you'd get me in anyway.' Halcyon days tinged with grief. We'd both been so young, so full of . . . joy. 'And I said I didn't believe you and you said that if I met you on the day that you'd get me in. And I was so desperate to see Springsteen that I did.' I half laugh, half sob. 'I didn't tell my mother - could you imagine? Me meeting a strange guy? And I turned up and there you were, and we were both in the same T-shirt and you said it was a sign. And you took my hand and said that you'd a ticket for me and you waltzed me in and the machine went off and we kept walking. And it was only after that you told me the machine was bleeping for us. That neither of us had a ticket, that you'd sold yours and made a fortune. Confidence gets you in anywhere, you said.' I remember feeling an illicit thrill at what we'd done, even though I was in Templemore garda training college at the time and he'd known that. 'I should have guessed then, Rob, what I was getting myself into, but you blinded me. I couldn't see anything but you.' Oh, the glory of those heady days. The giddiness of loving someone that hard. And the laughs we had. And afterwards, after the arrest, I'd tortured myself with wondering if he'd ever loved me or not. Was it all a show to seem normal while he conned people I cared about? But now, with what he did, he's answered that question. 'I missed the laughs when you got put away.'

The steady bleep of the monitors is the only response.

Outside, the sky darkens quite dramatically and, within seconds, thunderous rain hammers on the windows and bounces off the paths. And—

Oh, my God. Oh. My. Good. God.

It's so obvious.

I squeeze Rob's hand. 'Rob, I've to make a few calls. Don't go anywhere.' I know Rob would appreciate the joke. 'I'll be back tomorrow.'

Out of the ICU. Down the corridors.
Into my car.
And making calls.
I know how to check out the truth of Ben's story.

45

By the time I finish making the calls, two hours later, I have it all mapped out. To dot all the *i*s and cross the *t*s, Devon and Ben's interviews would need double-checking but I have no reason to doubt that they'd change at all.

I need to get to the Cig with my findings.

I head to a print shop in Castlebar and print out the documents that have been sent to me on my email. And finally, at around three, I drive to the station in Achill Sound and hang about, out of sight, until I spot William leaving to go to his favourite pub for his four-o'clock sandwich. He always eats there when he's in Achill and, as a result, none of the rest of us visit the place until he leaves. It's just too awkward eating with the Cig. Mind you, the pub is no great shakes, old and battered and a bit smelly.

I wait for about five minutes, until I'm sure he's found a seat and ordered, before I push open the heavy oak door. The interior is almost as gloomy as the elderly barman at the top of the room. His name is Dickie, not because his name is Dickie, but because he wears a bow-tie all the time, usually teamed with a white shirt that has seen better days. Dickie is a bent, wispy-haired, contrary fecker, who castigates any customer that dares enter the premises.

William braves him daily and I think they have an understanding of sorts.

'Hi,' I say brightly. 'Fancy bumping into you here, William.'

He looks up and instant suspicion crosses his face. 'You are meant to be on leave.'

'I am. But imagine if I came up with something that could help. Well, I'd have to pass it on, wouldn't I?'

He leans back in his seat and crosses his arms. 'And how could you come up with something that would help when you're not near the case?'

'I just remember detail,' I say. 'Like you. And it just so happens that today I remembered a tiny detail and chased it up and guess what?'

He raises his eyebrows.

'It proves that Ben couldn't possibly have been near Sandra when she died. That the man Devon saw was not Ben or that, indeed, there was any man at all.'

He indicates for me to sit down. Dickie shuffles over with the Cig's order, a tired-looking tomato and cheese sandwich with coleslaw on the side.

'You?' Dickie says. 'What are you havin' to ate?'

'Nothing, I—'

'You're using up space in me pub, taking advantage of me heating, sitting on seats that I paid for and you think I'm doing it all for your good?'

'I'll have a coffee then, thanks.'

He remains.

'And a cheese sandwich.'

He shuffles off.

'How can you stand this place?' I say. 'The food is rank.'

He looks mildly surprised. 'I think the food is grand.' He bites into his sandwich and chews appreciatively. 'And Dickie is a straight-talking man. I like that. You were saying.'

'I was going over the different interviews in my head this morning and I was thinking about Ben's statement and also Devon's. Now, if you'll remember, Devon said that when he went into his mother's house it was about three a.m. Five minutes before that, he alleges he saw a man running down the driveway. Right?'

'Yes.'

'Now Ben says he left Sandra at around twelve forty-five and walked to his friend's house just outside Tonragee. His first memo says that it started to lash just as he got there, which, at the speed Ben said he walked - impressive - would mean it was about four to four thirty in the morning. Ben alleges he spent the night in the barn in wet clothes. So, I checked with Met Éireann, Cig. I asked them if they could send through a weather report of the Tonragee area on the thirteenth of January and it turns out that there was heavy rain from four fifteen until four forty-five, which would lend credence to Ben's story. Now, if Ben had been the man Devon saw, who had left Pauline's house at three, and if he had walked to his friend's house from that time he would have been dry when he got there as there were no other showers reported between Dugort and Tonragee from two a.m. until seven. Ben was where he said he was, when he said he was. He didn't do this, Cig.'

'Have you got both statements there?'

'No. How would I—'

'Give them to me.'

Shit.

I hand them over.

'I will not even ask who gave these to you. For Jaysus' sake, Lucy, can you not obey a simple order?'

'I was, I just . . . Well, I have nothing else to do.' Gently I push another printout toward him. 'The weather reports, Cig.'

He grunts what I hope is 'Thanks,' before flipping through the statements. I sit on my hands to force myself to stay quiet.

Finally, after what seems ages, he looks up. 'Good work. I—'

'Here.' A shrivelled sandwich is placed in front of me along with a knife and one sachet of mayonnaise. 'Enjoy that now.'

'I shall enjoy presenting this to Peter Glynn,' William continues, when Dickie has shuffled off to fetch my coffee. 'He's gung-ho to get Ben for this. Well done, Lucy.'

'Can I do anything else? Honestly, William, I'll go mad at home and time off isn't any good for me.'

He pulls a tomato out of his sandwich and pops it into his mouth. Chews, studies me. 'Look, we've made some progress, there really isn't any need for—'

My phone rings. It's Susan.

Shit.

'Is that your work phone?'

'Eh . . . well, yeah.' I try for surprise. 'Whoever it is probably thinks I'm still on the team.'

'I told them all yesterday that you were taking time off. They bought you a card and signed it. You'll probably get it in the post today. Give it here.' He holds out his hand.

'Aw—'

'Now.'

Reluctantly I hand him my phone.

William answers without saying who he is, which is mean. I can hear Susan blabbing away, thinking it's me.

'Susan,' William finally says, when she draws breath, 'this is William. Why are you calling Lucy?'

A silence from the other end.

'Susan?' he says nicely. 'Are you still there?'

She says something.

'Why are you calling Lucy?'

'Leave her,' I hiss. 'It's my fault. I wanted to be kept in the loop.'

Susan is still babbling on to him. Making up a story.

'Apparently,' William hands the phone to me, 'Susan is calling you not because you're a guard but because you're a local. And that's just as well because you're not on the case.' He takes another bite of his sandwich, drains his coffee, pushes his chair back. 'See you, Dickie,' he calls up the room. 'Put the two sandwiches and the drinks on my tab, will you?'

'I will certainly, William,' Dickie calls, almost bowing before William. Then after the door closes behind my boss, Dickie shoots a sour look at me and goes back to polishing glasses.

'Susan,' I say, 'I'm so sorry about that. I had to give him the phone. Just keep with your story. Don't veer from it, no matter what.'

'It is the truth,' she says. 'I like you, Lucy, but there is no way I'd go against that fella's orders. He's too scary. I do really want your help with some names. The lads handed me the Pulse registrations for the black Mondeos. No one in Achill has one, so I'm scrambling to try to see if anyone has any connections to Achill. And with Matt off the case, I thought I'd call you. Anyway, I'd better just—'

'Send it to me.'

'Oh, I couldn't. William would kill me.'

'All right.' I think hard. 'Don't send me the full list. We know this guy is in his fifties to sixties, right, so for now get rid of the women off the list. After that, look at the address. Narrow it down to people who live near the coast, because this guy sails. Then, have a look, cross-check those names with anyone who lives on the Ballina side of Crossmolina. That's your starting point, your most likelies. Tell me those names and I'll see if they ring a bell.'

'Brilliant.'

She rings off and I feel a quiet satisfaction. She hadn't acted like I wasn't part of the investigation.

I sit in the gloom of the pub and chew the sandwich. Thankfully it lacks any sort of taste.

Thirty minutes later she calls me back. 'Two names,' she says. 'A Glenn Ryan and a Brendan Walsh.'

Oh. Something snags. Brendan Walsh. It hovers, just out of reach. 'Okay, Susan, if I get anything, I'll be back to you.'

I google 'Brendan Walsh'. Millions of results. I add in 'boat' and it narrows but not significantly. I add in 'Achill' and nothing useful.

Balls.

I call my mother.

'Is everything all right?' she asks, sounding anxious.

'Fine.' Another bite of the sandwich. 'I've two names here. I'm wondering if either of them rings a bell, as in did they ever live in Achill one time? Maybe have a connection to Sandra. Glenn Ryan?'

'Glenn Ryan,' she ponders. 'Glenn Ryan. *Glennnnn Ryyyyan.*'

I bite my tongue as she repeats it a few more times, slower and slower.

'There are the Ryans out in Keel,' she says eventually, 'but there's no Glenn. No. No bells. What does he look like?'

302

Instead of answering, I ask, 'How about Brendan Walsh?'

'No.' A moment. 'Unless you mean Brennie Walsh?'

My heart knocks about a bit in my chest. 'Brennie Walsh. Yes.' I know why it seemed a familiar name now. 'He saved Sandra from drowning.' I'm hit with disappointment. It can hardly be the same man as in the garage. Why would she be afraid of him? Unless he reminded her of that time. Or she was afraid Richie would find out the truth about her? But why would Brennie kill Sandra? Unless . . . 'He was engaged to Maudie, wasn't he?'

'For a while anyway. It ended a couple of months after Sandra came to stay with them, around the time they found out she was pregnant. After the poor creature lost her father, and her mother dumped her on Maudie. Fair play to Maudie, holding everything together.' Then she says, 'Don't tell me you're working. Shouldn't you be resting and—'

'Mam, I've got to go. Thanks for that. It was great.'

Without waiting for her to say goodbye I hang up.

Like a dog on the scent, I'm running now, in and out, examining every angle, side, thinking hard.

I google Brennie Walsh. And Achill.

And bingo.

It's an *Island News* piece that's been digitised. And they want five euro for me to read it. Now that's a crime. It's more than the cost of the complete paper. I pull out my purse and—

'Another sandwich, perhaps?' Dickie appears beside me, looking pointedly at my empty plate. 'Only you can't just sit there and eat nothing and use up my heat and my seats and everything.'

I'm tempted to tell him to shove it, but it's cold outside and I can't go into the station or William will blow his top. 'I'll have a toasted cheese,' I say, hoping it'll be an improvement.

'Right ya be.'

I sincerely hope the tourists that descend on this island in summer don't encounter that fella first. What a welcome. I wait until he's made his slow, shuffling way back up the room before keying my credit-card details into my phone. And I'm in.

Mr Brennie Walsh yesterday was hailed a hero for braving the treacherous, stormy waters around Inishbiggle to rescue teenager Sandra Byrne (14) who had reportedly got into difficulties in the sea.

The currents around Inishbiggle are treacherous and stormy and are the very worst in Europe. Indeed, in winter months the island, only ninety metres from our own lovely Achill, can be inaccessible.

Pauline Byrne, Sandra's mother, who was shaken but relieved, said that she will be forever in debt to Brennie Walsh for saving her daughter from the treacherous seas. 'He's a hero and what makes it even better, he will soon be my brother-in-law as he's engaged to my big sister. He's been very good to Sandra, bringing her out on his boat, showing her the ropes. She's even thinking of taking up sailing.'

You can't ask for a better brother-in-law than that!

June Kilbane, a woman who lives near Bullsmouth, described the moment she saw the young girl in the water. 'I was down by the Bullsmouth, it was a wild day and I spotted the young girl swimming out in the water. I think she fell in or something, it was fierce windy at the time. I took my jumper off for her to grab a hold of but she kept swimming out. I was screaming and next thing Brennie was there and he started yelling at her to come back, to get out but she didn't listen to him either. He left and next thing I see him in his boat, rowing out after her. Both of them were being flung about. It was a nasty day. There were moments when I thought that Sandra was gone. I was praying the rosary the whole time. Next thing, I see him drag her back onto his boat and it looked like she was fighting him off but then she gave up. She's lucky to be alive. I hope she knows that.'

Brennie Walsh is an experienced sailor, having won many competitions. He's a native of Strandhill in Sligo. He's also a keen Gaelic player and plays senior football for Sligo.

Sandra Byrne is recovering at her aunt's house and was unavailable for interview

God, I think, the journalism is awful. Underneath there is a picture of Brennie flanked on either side by two ladies instantly recognisable as Pauline and Maudie. Maudie, dressed smartly, as always, in a tight skirt and clingy jumper, is beaming up at him. She looks softer, more human. Even in the grainy black-and-white of an old image, her pride and happiness dominate the picture. Brennie, slightly taller than the others, has an easy confidence that is evident from his nonchalant stance, an arm draped loosely about each woman's shoulder. Pauline, in contrast to her sister, is wearing a shapeless skirt and a jumper that looks as if it's been through the wash too many times. Her hair is wild and her face looks impossibly sad. In the background, I recognise Bullsmouth harbour, the blur of Inishbiggle in the distance.

I log out of that site and back into Google. There are two more articles on the rescue, one of which describes Sandra as a keen sailor, but other than that, neither of them says much more than the *Island News* piece. I glance at the date of the incident. It was ten months before Sandra gave birth. So, she hadn't jumped because she was pregnant. If she'd jumped . . .

Next thing, I google his name. *Brennie Walsh. Strandhill.*

Walsh's Sailing Club, Rosses Point, Co. Sligo was established by Strandhill native Brennie Walsh almost twenty years ago. Today it is part of the vibrant tapestry that makes up our part of the world. Almost every school-going child is enrolled in the Walsh's Sailing Club and within a few weeks they know the basic skills of sailing. They work with our fabulous instructors and Brennie is always on hand to offer his advice. He also coaches our more serious students, affectionately known as 'the elites'.

One-on-one classes with any of our coaches are also available.

And there it is. An up-to-date picture of Brendan Walsh with twenty or so young people, mostly teens, all beaming into the camera. But the icing on the cake is what they are all wearing.

Red jackets with a yellow crest.

46

Chloé and Monique need to ID Brennie now for us to be able to question him. And Susan needs to confirm that it's the same Brennie who owns the Ford Mondeo. And some key dates need to be nailed down. Rather than go into the station, I give Brian a call on the hotline.

'Hello, Garda Brian O'Neill here. How can I help you?'

He sounds good, I think. 'I'd like you to put me through to Detective Dan Brown, please,' I say, disguising my voice as best I can. The less I can involve people the better.

'Lucy, how are you?' Brian says. 'I was terrible sorry to hear about what happened. We all bought a card for you and signed it. I couldn't think of anything to write so I just put best wish—'

'Brian, can you put me through to Dan?' I interrupt. 'And don't mention to anyone that I called.'

Brian does as instructed.

Dan half laughs when I tell him what I want. 'I'll be fired,' he says. 'Hang on. Susan!' he calls. 'Come in here, will you? Have you got the Pulse details?' I hear a muttered conversation before Dan comes back. 'The car is a Sligo reg all right.' I hear him

307

tapping some keys. 'Well, what do you know?' He chortles. 'It's a Strandhill address. It's got to be the same guy.'

'Great. Now, call out to Chloé and get her and Monique to ID him, if they can. Then get Susan to present the lot to the Cig.'

'You should take leave more often,' Dan says. 'You're on fire. William is crowing about how you got Ben off the hook.'

At that moment, my second sandwich slides under my nose. It looks even more unappetising than the first, which I didn't think was possible. He has the cheek to add, 'Enjoy,' with it.

'I want to go with you,' I say to Dan, sensing he's about to hang up. He takes a breath, about to protest, so I jam in, 'I'm not due back in the hospital at all today – I'm supposed to be sleeping – but I'll go out of my head if I have to sit on the sidelines.'

'You can't.' Shit, he sounds adamant. 'Look, I'll keep you in the loop. Sit tight. I'll let you know if we get an ID. If we do, I'll present it at conference this evening.' A slight hesitation. 'It's at four,' he says.

By three o'clock, I've eaten three horrible toasties, drunk some foul coffee, made a few phone calls and re-examined the pictures from Sandra's crime scene. If it's Brennie, he came in by boat. But how? He couldn't have done it in the dark.

I look at the pictures from every angle. I drive down to Dugort Pier. I look again. And then I see it.

I bloody see it!

I mean, I'll need to prove it, but I see it.

I call Susan and ask her to give me Dotsy's number. I call him. He's hard to understand because, as Susan warned me, he has no teeth, but I assume his 'yath' is 'yes'. I tell him someone will ring him later.

After I hang up, Dan rings to tell me that Monique was unable to offer an ID and that Chloé identified two men, one of whom was Brennie, before pointing to the other man, telling Dan she was almost positive it was him.

I tell Dan not to worry.

By four, I'm outside the station.

I wait until I think all the team are assembled upstairs before heading into Reception. William rarely uses this entrance.

Matt is on the front desk. 'Lucy,' he says, with some surprise, as I hurtle through. 'I thought you were off. We got you a card—'

But I'm behind the counter and through the door and up the stairs in seconds. On the second landing, there's a bit of activity. I hide in the bend of the corridor and am just in time to hear Dan present his evidence. He finishes with the fact that neither Chloé nor Monique could give a positive ID.

'So, two of this man's number-plate digits match the ones you and Larry identified,' William summarises. 'His car is the same make, he has a direct tie to Sandra Byrne in the past, he sails, runs a sailing club whose members wear red jackets with yellow crests, and he lives in Strandhill, which would put him on the road to Crossmolina, should he ever visit west?'

'That's it.'

'But he saved her life? Have we any reason he might have killed her?'

And that's my cue. 'He might have been Devon's father,' I say, startling them all as I bounce through the door. 'The timelines fit. According to a newspaper report he was teaching sailing to Sandra on a one-to-one. He was there when she tried to drown herself. I looked up some documents in the registry of births,

309

marriages and deaths and Sandra's father died in November. She was presumably sent to live with Maudie soon after. Devon was born in the August. Sandra was underage when she got pregnant, which means he could have been abusing her. And if she was going to spill the beans, maybe because her mother had died and wouldn't be around to hear it, it gives him a great reason. You're welcome.'

People laugh. Someone claps.

'Dan, Susan, Larry, good work on the car. Kev.'

He has ignored me. There's an uncomfortable silence.

I plough on.

'I re-examined the crime-scene pictures too. I know how he came in. I know who else might be involved.'

William glares at me.

The room holds its breath.

Someone says, 'Bloody hell, that's impressive.'

Someone else giggles but the tension grows.

Finally, William nods for me to continue.

'He did use lights. One on the hill, which Susan located and which we believe was used recently as there were rubber marks on the inside bracket.'

'Susan took scrapings, Cig,' Kev pipes up, and I smile at his attempt to support me.

'And the second light Dotsy said was normally a porch light, but we know it was off that night. Broken. The pictures of the scene confirm it. However, this light,' I hold up a picture of the exterior of the house, 'was on. It's an illuminous light installed by Leo in the week before Sandra's death, supposedly to stop her falling when she'd come home in the dark.'

'That's right, Cig,' Dan agrees. 'That's in Megan's statement.'

A bright bubble of hopeful chatter erupts.

'Leo had an alibi for the night,' the Cig says.

'He did, but he could easily have flicked on the light on the hill. It was on his way home. Though it could have been turned on anytime. Who'd notice it shining during the day?'

William sits back and eyes me. 'And can we prove it lines up with the other light?'

'Dotsy has agreed to go out on the boat to check it tonight.' I hesitate. There is no way I will go with him. My father was killed off a boat. I have no love for the sea. 'Someone needs to go with him.'

'I will.' Kev's hand shoots up, as I thought it would.

William nods. 'All right. Susan, you go too.'

'On a boat?'

'Yes, is that a problem?'

'No,' she says miserably.

'We'll get some sort of a light rigged up so as not to tamper with the bracket,' William goes on. 'Then as soon as Dotey—'

'Dotsy,' Kev, Susan and I say simultaneously.

'—the fisherman gives the go-ahead, we'll put it on. You,' William looks at me, 'see me in my office after. Pat, keep going with Maudie's bank account. Try to find out where her money is coming from. Mick, any more on forensics?'

'There was nothing on Richie's laptop of note, bar the tracking he did of Sandra's phone. But Forensics said it wasn't serious. The trophy yielded prints that didn't belong to anyone we'd identified so far but they're running them through the database anyway to see if there's a hit. Maybe they are this Brennie Walsh's.'

'Okay. Right, this is great, people. Keep me briefed.' With a nod to the team he walks out, not even glancing at me.

There's an embarrassed silence. I turn on my heel and walk out too.

I hesitate outside William's door, hand raised to knock. Then, without bothering, I open the door and face him.

47

He sighs in exasperation and glares at me.

'Please.' I slide into a seat before he can tell me to leave. 'Cig, you know it and I know it, if you put me off the case, I'll just keep at it anyway. It's my case. I got the leads. I can't leave it. If you put me off, then . . .' I can't say his name, it sticks in my throat '. . . that crackpot will have won. He'll have robbed me of the satisfaction of putting this sick bastard away. Please, don't do that to me.'

'I was in your house the other night,' William is surprisingly measured – I thought he'd bawl me out, 'where that man attacked your mother and your son and put Rob in a coma and—'

'Rob's still hanging in there and my mother and Luc are fine. Please, Cig.'

There's a knock on the door and Kev pokes his head around. 'Are you back on the case, Lucy?' he says brightly. Then, seeing the look on William's face, he flushes. 'It's just, Cig, it'd be good if she was, like.'

'Have you asked him to do this?' William snaps at me.

'No.' Though I have to admit, I couldn't have arranged it better. 'What's up, Kev?'

William doesn't tell me to butt out. I take heart.

'It's just . . . it's only a long shot but, like I said, I knew that fella, Brennie Walsh.'

'How well?'

'Vaguely, like. I grew up in Sligo and he's a genius. Everyone loves him up there. I was always good on a boat, Cig. And I was a good swimmer and that. And, like, you know he runs the boat club up by Rosses Point. It's all gone upmarket since I was there, I never knew they had jackets and that, and Brennie only takes the best kids himself. Now, I wasn't the best but this girl in the club, Darina or something her name was, she was brilliant. And one day she just left. She was a bit older than me, so I rang my mother to ask her where Darina was now and, well, she's just out of rehab, Cig. She's not had a good life. And no one knows why she left the sailing. Even her own mother doesn't because I asked my mother – at the time, we were all so disappointed and that. And I thought, Well, maybe there's something there. Maybe she left the sailing because of him.' Then sensing that maybe it's a bit thin, he says, 'It's worth checking out.' A beat. 'I mean, if Gary O'Toole hadn't—'

'Enough,' William snaps. 'Gary O'Toole had proof that swimmers were being abused. We have a man who called into a petrol station to buy some petrol and of whom our IP was allegedly afraid. This man saved our IP's life once upon a time. Yes, no one has come forward to claim Devon but that does not mean he was the father. And, Kev, people leave clubs all the time.'

Kev swallows hard.

'You know what happens with thin theories?'

I wince. Kev bows his head, and a slow flush creeps up his neck.

'They break. They don't stand up in court. Right, Lucy,' he stares hard at me, 'go home, get some sleep—'

314

I open my mouth to protest and he holds up his hand.

'I'll be in touch later.'

I want to ask him to promise, but I'm not six. 'All right.'

'And after this you're taking a break. I'm not going to be responsible for burnout.'

'The budgets take care of that, Cig.' I feel safe enough to joke now.

He grunts in reply and waves a hand at us to leave.

48

'You were right about the lights,' William says, without any pre-amble, later that night when he calls. 'Dotey—'

'Dotsy?'

'—whatever he's called - brought Kev and Susan out on the boat this evening. We placed a torch above the bracket on the hill and, using that and the light at the house, he was able to navigate the boat in. Good call.'

Fran has just fed me my dinner and I've barely been able to eat it, pacing around like a tiger in a cage, just wanting to be let loose on the case.

'And?'

'What's Leo's connection to Brennie?'

'I don't know. What's the next move?' I want to ask if I'm part of it, but I'm afraid I'll annoy him.

He sighs. 'I've been thinking about that. Sending SOCO to the light on the hill might warn whoever that we're on to them. So, Kev is going to meet you in Keel and I want you and him to have a chat with Leo and Megan. Put out a bit of bait. Say we believe the murderer came in by boat. Ask them if they'd they have any idea who it might have been, and if they're aware of any

316

transit. It might panic Leo into doing something stupid if he's involved. He might call Brennie. He might leave and come up to the light, where we have a few of our lads, to check there's no evidence. He might try to dispose of whatever torch he used on the night.' A pause. 'Plus that hill, it's way too exposed, I'm not sure about getting too many forensics. And if we get Leo's prints or anyone else's, they can say they were there years back.'

'What if Leo panics and warns Brennie?'

'I've rung the lads in Sligo. They're going to keep eyes on him. And if we do end up arresting him and Leo, we can check their phones and see if Leo did call him after your visit. It's better evidence than what we can get from here. I've fast-tracked Susan's rubber scraping anyway. Fair play to her.'

I smile. Susan will be thrilled with the endorsement. 'Okay. Is Kev in Keel now?'

'He's on his way. Get over to Leo and Megan's and put the frighteners on.'

'Thanks,' I gulp out. 'Thanks for including me.'

He doesn't reply, just hangs up.

49

Driving through the rain, across country, towards Keel to pick up Kev, as the wipers flick-flack clearing the windscreen, my head is flooded with images of Megan. Those bright, hazy, long days of summer holidays on the beaches when we were young. Megan the sandwich-maker, the drinks-provider. Megan the go-to girl for plasters and sun cream. Megan the great older sister with the troublesome Sandra. Megan the fantastic 'help to her poor mother'. Megan who sat on the rug while we all splashed and dived, who told us to be careful and always left at a sensible hour to make her mother's dinner and because she had to be sure that her younger sister didn't get too tired and cranky.

Good-natured Megan, who never complained and whom we never missed if she didn't come along. Megan who, with me, found Sandra half dead up Slievemore. Megan who screamed into her sister's face, who shook her, who told her she was fed up. *Fed up.* FED UP. Megan who scared me that night, whom I had to pull off a comatose Sandra. Megan who sobbed all the way back in the taxi I called to bring us to my mother's house.

It all unspools like a film, days we can't get back, questions we can never ask, time slipping by and leaving only an imprint of what we should have done or said.

I pick up a buoyant Kev, who regales me with his boat journey, tells me how Susan had to go below deck for most of it, how Dotsy let him press buttons and how it was great altogether. Before I know it, I'm pulling up outside the entrance to Megan's farmhouse. In front of us, the crescent of a winter's moon hangs bright.

Sadness for all I didn't do presses in on me and I must sigh because Kev turns to look at me. I wave a hand at him. 'Don't mind me.'

'You've had a bad couple of days,' he says matter-of-factly. 'But you need to be on this team.'

'Thanks, Kev.' I open the car door and hop out. 'Come on.'

He joins me in the yard.

In the house someone, Megan I think, pulls a dirty net curtain across to peer out.

The wind picks up; the rain gathers pace.

A few seconds later, Megan arrives around the side of the house, drying her hands on a tea-towel. 'Oh, it's you, Lucy.' A frown. 'Is there news?'

'A little. Can we come in? We've a couple more questions.'

'Of course, no problem. Just me or all of us?'

'All of you, if that's all right. Devon is here?'

'Yes, moved back when . . . well . . .' The memory of that day in the station makes her uncomfortable. 'This way, come on.'

'This is Garda Kevin Costello.'

'Hello.' Megan leads us into the house, which is slightly more inviting than it was the last time as a fire burns in the stove in the kitchen. 'It's so cold outside, we thought we'd splash out,' she says. 'Sit down. Tea?' Before we can answer, she bellows, 'Leo! Devon! Come down here.'

Devon arrives in, stops when he sees us. 'Do they have news?' he asks Megan, sounding apprehensive.

'They've just a few more questions, pet,' she says. 'Leo!' Then to us, mouthing, as if it's hilarious, 'He's a bit hung-over.'

Leo arrives in, half dressed. 'Sorry.' He blushes, buttoning up a tatty shirt. 'I was - I was in bed.'

'That's fine. Look, if ye can sit, we won't take long. We have a couple of developments in the case to talk ye through, see if you can offer up any help.'

Megan sits down opposite me. Of the three, she is the brightest looking.

Leo sits in beside her. Devon, arms folded, leans against the kitchen sink.

'We're working on the assumption that Sandra's murderer may have used a boat.'

'Really?' That's Megan.

'Yes, he or she would have used Dugort Pier and walked from there to the scene. Would any of ye know someone who would have access to a boat and also have a grudge against Sandra?'

Silence. Blank looks.

'A number of people close by also reported an odd light up near the hill beyond the house in the weeks before the murder. We're working on the assumption that this could be a transit light—'

'There was a transit light,' Megan pipes up. 'My grandfather put it in years ago but it hasn't been used in decades. And it was on the hill.'

'Great. We think, and this is only a theory, that the murderer used that transit light and lights from your mother's house to get into the harbour.'

'Mammy used to leave the porch light on,' Megan says. 'I remember now. But, Jesus, that light has been broken for a long time. And sure, Sandra,' her voice wobbles on the name and Leo places a hand over hers, 'Sandra would never have thought to fix it.'

I smile, feign disappointment. 'Okay. Well, we'll keep looking and, sure, if we find another light, we'll let you know.'

'That's why I heard no car,' Devon says, from his position at the sink.

'Exactly. Anyway, if ye think of anything, it doesn't matter how small, tell us. We'll investigate it. Thanks.'

None of them stirs as we leave. In fact, Megan looks suddenly shell-shocked.

In the end, Leo calls out, 'Goodbye' and 'Thanks.'

'Now we wait,' I say to Kev.

50

The evening turns into night. The car, which we've parked down from Megan and Leo's, grows cold and I'm colder still but to put the heater on would give us away. The only thing keeping me warm is the pulse of adrenaline under my skin, the jumpy feeling when I'm waiting for something to break. A few cars pass on the road, an occasional dog-walker, but nothing else stirs.

Kev and I talk about random stuff. He tells me about his girl-friend, the one who likes his uniform. He met her in a sweetshop on holidays. 'One of those old-fashioned ones,' he says. 'We both ordered a quarter of cola bottles. Do you like them, Luce?'

'I did when I was eight,' I reply, with a grin.

He tells me once a cola-bottle fan, always a cola-bottle fan. She's tall, taller than him, so she must be about six three, with long brown hair that she plaits and puts ribbons through. She also weight-lifts.

'I cannot wait to meet her,' I say.

At one point I ask him what the coverage in the local paper said about my attack.

'Eh . . .' Kev shifts, obviously uncomfortable with the topic. 'There was a fair bit. Like the whole paper basically. Stacy was even on RTÉ – Matt was very proud of her.'

'What?' How the hell had I missed that? 'Stacy? National news?'

'Yeah,' Kev says, like it's obvious. 'Sure, you were attacked in your home, you're a guard. Your ex was knifed. Of course, it'll be on the news. They sort of put an "Is no member of our security forces safe any more?" spin on it.'

'Oh, for Christ's sake. Did they say why I was attacked?'

'No. They think it's to do with Sandra Byrne's murder. William has told the press office not to answer any questions.'

'Good.'

'Yeah, he's got your back.' After a second, casually, 'We all think he fancies you.'

I gawk at him. 'Are you mad?' Then, 'Who is all?'

'Me, Matt and Susan. Mick thinks he's a robot and incapable of feeling and Jordy—'

A flash of something catches my eye. All thoughts of William, his feelings and my infamy drop away as a car pulls out of the farmhouse gate. 'Radio in. Tell them we're on the move.'

As I fall in behind Leo's battered car, Kev calls it in. 'He's got no lights on,' he says, as he disconnects. 'He'll kill himself.'

Despite not wanting to be noticed, I flash Leo, the way any motorist would do, to tell him to turn on his headlights but he either doesn't see me or chooses to ignore the warning. His car picks up speed and seems to be veering all over the road. It's almost as if he doesn't care whether he crashes or not.

Kev grabs hold of the dashboard as I push the accelerator. 'What the hell is he up to?'

'I don't know but it doesn't even look like he's heading for Dugort or the hill.' I accelerate again, trying to keep up with him without putting myself or Kev in danger. I flash him again but again he ignores me. He drives straight through Keel and on. 'It looks like he's going the Keem road,' I say, 'but he'll come off it driving like that up there.'

My phone rings and it's Leo. I answer. 'You'd better slow down - you're going to kill someone.'

There's a moment's silence. Then, panicked, he says, 'Megan is gone. She's after taking my car and she's not answering her phone. She was acting funny after you left.'

'What?' All my certainties start to crumble.

'Megan. Is gone.' He says it like I'm not understanding, which I'm not. 'She was screaming and shouting and crying after you left. None of it made sense. Please find her, for God's sake. I just have a feeling . . .'

'Okay, Leo, calm down. Are you at home?'

'Yes. She took the car. She said nothing, just went off in it. But it's not like her. She usually . . . Just find her. Or get someone out looking.'

'All right. Look, I think we see her. She's just in front of our car. Now, tell me, why would she do this?'

'I don't know. It was after you came, she just . . . she went mad. And Devon walked out and she screamed at him and she never— Oh, God. Please. Find her.'

'Can you remember anything she said?'

'How will that find her?' he almost screams into the phone. 'This is an emergency. Christ, I'm ringing the station.' He disconnects and, cursing, I tell Kev to try to call him again.

It's engaged.

I ring William and give him an update. 'She's heading to Keem, but the way she's driving, she'll go off the road. We need a car to cut her off. I don't know what's after happening.'

'I'll get Keel station to send a car out and block her off on the road there.'

'Tell them to be careful – she's got no lights. She'll ram them.'

I hear him relay the information back and then he comes on again. 'All right, they're actually on the Atlantic drive now. They're turning back and going to close off the road until she's safe.'

'Great. Any news of Brennie Walsh?'

'Nothing so far. He's at home, inside. I'll send a car for Leo, if we have any sort of an emergency with Megan. He might be able to talk to her. I'll get back to you.'

He rings off and I accelerate slightly to keep behind Megan. What is she playing at? What will I do if she decides to drive her car off the cliff face? What can I do?

'What'll we do if she plunges off the cliff?' Kev voices the question.

'Let's just play it by ear,' I say, as Megan's car begins to climb.

I get Kev to try ringing her but she won't answer.

We plough on. Darkness has been thrown over the world and we're caught under it. On and on, twisting and turning up familiar but dangerous roads. Hedges, bushes, glimpses of the sea below flash in and out of our headlights.

And then she veers off to the right.

And, shit, it's Maudie's place she's going to, I think. Maudie lives up here in her fancy house with her big extension. Bits and pieces start to slot themselves into place.

'Kev, call back. Tell them it's Maudie she's going to. Dan will know the address.'

Kev does as he is told, and we follow Megan up the road to her aunt's house. She's a bit of a distance ahead. If I drive any faster, I'll only invite trouble.

I don't think she's even noticed us behind her.

Smash!

The sound roars in our ears.

It's followed by a series of other bangs.

Someone screams.

I gun the car forward, up Maudie's driveway.

There is no sign of Megan's car, but from behind the house, someone is roaring.

I draw my gun, flinging a silent prayer that I won't have to use it, and run around the side of the house, indicating for Kev to take the other side, keep his phone on and keep out of sight. Megan's car is buried in Maudie's extension. Great sheets of glass lie smashed on the ground. Megan, like some warrior queen, in her matronly clothes, stands among the debris, bleeding from the forehead, a shard of glass in her hand. Maudie cowers, her body pressed deep into one of the bright kitchen chairs. Megan strides through the kitchen, kicking up glass and brick as she does so.

'You bitch!' she thunders, in a voice I've only ever heard once before. 'You bitch! You using, manipulative, greedy bitch.'

Maudie tries to stand but her legs won't support her and she collapses back into the chair.

'Megan,' I point the gun at her, 'put down the weapon, please. You can still get this back.'

'Get it back?' She whirls on me, then moves to the side so she has me and her aunt in her sights. The glass shakes in her hand. 'Get it back? Are you joking me? Get my fucking life back? How can I do that?'

I don't know if she knows that she's crying.

'Don't hurt anyone, Megan.' I have to stop her using that glass until the others get here. 'I understand you're angry and—'

'You understand nothing,' she says, a bitter laugh rising into the air. 'Nothing. You with your – your great fucking mother and real son and grandchild and great career. God, even when you get attacked in your home, it makes the bloody news.'

'Megan, you have to calm down. Please.'

'Nothing like that for Sandra, was there, Maudie?'

'I don't know what you mean,' Maudie says. Then to me, 'I don't know—'

'This woman,' Megan overrides her as she stalks towards her, 'she had such power over my mother. Such power over us. Maudie says this. Maudie says that. Maudie says get lights in Sandra's garden, Megan, save her from falling. And Megan does. Megan gets her husband to do it.'

'To help Sandra,' Maudie says.

'To help yourself!' Megan snarls. 'You never liked Sandra. Bringing shame on our family and—'

'No! It was never that!'

'Yes. And then you show me where to put the lights and I thought it was because you cared about Sandra. Put them here, Leo. You bitch!' She runs towards Maudie, who screams.

'Megan!' I yell. 'Stop!'

The order shocks her to a halt. She faces me, tears bouncing down her face. Jabbing the glass in Maudie's direction, she cries, 'She set us up. I see it now. All our lives. Sandra just needed help and—'

'You've got it all wrong,' Maudie cries. 'Sandra was going to ruin us. You don't know. It would have been disastrous for Devon and—'

'And this isn't? This isn't? Oh, my God. Oh, my God.' Her body seems to convulse with sobs.

I move forward slightly, the gun still aimed at her. Four more feet.

'You took Sandra from Mammy. I shouldn't have let that happen.'

'You don't have a clue,' Maudie says, with such bitterness that Megan flinches.

Three more feet.

'Who did it for you?' she demands.

'Did what?'

'She said,' Megan jabs in my direction with the glass, 'that the murderer used a transit. Our porch light was always a transit, along with my grandfather's light on the hill. That light you got Leo to put in. That—'

'It was a light, nothing more!' Maudie snaps.

'It wasn't.' Megan shakes her head furiously. 'And you won't lie to me any more. I won't let you. I depended on you, Maudie. And all you ever did, I see now, was tell me what to do. Leo said it for years, and did I believe him? No. You told me Sandra was an unfit mother, even though she wrote every two weeks. She was a good mother. A good mother. You made me lie to Devon. You made me burn Sandra's letters. You asked me to make Leo put that light in Sandra's garden, Maudie. You did it because you knew how stupid I am, how gullible, how fucking nice I am. I'm sick of being nice. I've lost everyone. I don't care any more. I don't—'

'Enough!' Maudie's voice is feral. 'You have no clue.'

Two more feet.

'You've been lucky, you've—'

With a howl, Megan slashes the glass across her wrist and, despite my training, I cry out.

Kev barrels towards her.

Behind me, Leo roars out his horror and pushes past to cradle his wife in his arms.

51

The following two days are busy, so busy I don't have time to think. I like the racing, the chasing. The blanking-out of everything except the investigation. We follow up evidence trying to stitch it all together, but there are holes: we need confessions and to get a confession we need compelling evidence.

In between it all, I talk to my mother and Luc and, together, we make a hesitant plan to return to the cottage once this case has been put to bed. My mother, I think, is under the impression that it will be a while yet. Tani sends me a video of Sirocco blowing me a kiss and telling me she 'boves' me. And I watch it every night before I go to sleep in Dan's spare room.

I visit Rob in the hospital and he's not looking good. I don't voice my concern to Clara, who is convinced that his body is just trying to repair itself after the trauma. She is always there, holding his hand and whispering to him, and I feel a bit of a fake voicing my concern for him when up to a week ago the very thought of him made my skin crawl. But he tried to save me and Luc, and for that I love him. For that, I start to remember all the reasons I'd fallen for him in the first place, and in doing so, I find little bits of myself that I had lost along the way.

Finally, Dan and I are given the Maudie interview while Larry and Peter, the detective from Dublin, are tasked with interviewing and arresting Brendan Walsh once Dan and I have got what we can from Maudie. I always think that the end of an investigation is like that card game you play where you have to turn over the matching pairs. The closer you get to the end, the more rapidly you can find the pairs. If we can understand why Brendan did what he did, probe him and Maudie to develop a motive, we are probably home and dry. After that we can, with prints, hopefully put him at the scene, match his prints to the partials on the murder weapon.

Finally, on 26th January, Maudie, who has spent the last few hours in a cell, is brought into us in Interview Two. She acts as if she's just come from a day's shopping, though the black circles under her eyes tell another story. Her solicitor, a trim man, perches in a chair alongside her. I don't think he'll have much say in what happens.

'How is my niece?' Maudie asks, a slight quiver in her voice, though whether that's from anxiety at what Megan might have said or concern for her, I can't tell.

'She'll live,' I say. I don't add that she's too ill to be questioned just yet. Better for Maudie to think we might have talked to her.

I flick on the first DVD and remind Maudie that she's still under caution and that the interview is being recorded. Then I introduce everyone, and before I can get a question off or build any kind of rapport, she says, 'You must be loving this, Lucy. Interviewing your old business teacher.'

'I interview anyone I think might help with the case,' I say mildly. 'Do you miss the teaching?'

'Miss dealing with dunderheads like yourself? No.'

I can totally understand how she controlled that family. In school, hardened students quaked when she turned that flat gaze on them. 'I wasn't great at the subject but, sure, I found my calling here.'

'Let's hope so. I'm innocent and you've arrested me.'

It dawns on me then that she's still treating me as if I'm fifteen, as if nothing has ever changed between us. That's sort of pitiable. I make one last attempt to engage her. 'Are you feeling up to talking after what happened the other night?'

A flash of some sort of emotion, before it disappears with a regal inclination of her head.

'And you understand why you're here?'

'I won't even dignify that with a response. I'm not stupid.'

I ask her once again to confirm where she was the night Sandra died and she trots out the same story.

'All right. I'd like to talk about the other night, the twenty-third of January. You admitted to persuading Megan to ask Leo to put up lights in Pauline's garden.'

'Yes. It's not a crime, is it, to want your niece not to trip and kill herself on the way home from the pub?'

'Indeed it's not. But we believe that this light had another purpose.'

'Yes. That night Megan said you believed it to be a transit light.' A slight arching of her eyebrows.

'And you understand what a transit light is?'

'I grew up by the sea. My father was a fisherman.'

'I'll take that as a yes. Exhibit SB39.' I push across a picture of the two lights, one of them the garden light, taken from various angles on a boat on the way in to Dugort Pier. 'One of our team went out with a local fisherman and tested this light and another, which is located up the hill from Pauline's house. See the way this top light and the light from Pauline's house align?'

'Yes.'

'Used this way, they offer safe passage to any vessel coming in to the pier.'

'So?'

'This other light,' I point to the one on the hill, 'was found on the hill above the house. Do you know anything about that?'

'My father put it there when my sister Pauline married Paudie. It was his wedding present to them. Safe passage into Dugort.'

'That's right.' The foundry stamp had been on the bracket. We'd traced it right back to Maudie's father.

'After Daddy died no one sailed. The light was never used. You of all people should know the pain of going out on the water when you lose a loved one to it.'

I flinch. Dan, sensing it, nudges me with his foot to tell me I'm doing great. 'As I said, your father placed it there. And your sister, we believe, always kept her porch light on as a second light. Now, when we searched your house, we found this. Exhibit SB40,' I narrate, showing her a large torch. 'Recognise this?'

'Yes. It's my torch. I use it at night.' A flat look.

'And see this here, Exhibit SB41, a picture showing abrasions down the length of the torch?'

'Yes, wear and tear.'

'We matched these abrasions up to traces of rubber found on the bracket of the light on the hill. They are an exact match. The composition of the rubber is an exact match. This torch was in that bracket. What do you have to say to that?'

She shrugs, looking at me as if I'm some kind of swamp creature.

'Anything?'

'No.'

'Moving on from that,' I pretend to shuffle some pages, 'how well do you know a Mr Brendan Walsh of Rosses Point sailing club in Sligo?'

Now she shifts slightly on her seat. Carefully, she says, 'Brennie Walsh was engaged to me once. It fell apart, largely due to Sandra's uncontrollable behaviour.'

'Have you had contact with Brendan since?'

'Now and again, yes.'

'As in?'

'Phone calls. We meet sometimes. A Christmas card. That sort of thing.'

I hadn't expected her to admit that. 'In the days after the funeral, he rang you, didn't he?'

'Yes, to offer his condolences. He couldn't make the funeral.'

'I see. All right.' I frown, feigning puzzlement. 'Can you explain, then, why he pays you four hundred euro a month?'

Her mouth opens and shuts and opens again. 'Were you poking your noses into my bank accounts? How dare you?'

'We dare because it's legal if we have suspicions about someone. Why does he pay you four hundred a month?'

'Because . . .' a long moment '. . . the two of us started that sailing club in Rosses Point years ago. Then we broke up. It's profitable. I still get money from it.'

'We found no paperwork to that effect in your house.'

'It's between friends.'

'And yet you've no relationship with him?'

'*Romantic* relationship.'

'Is there anything to say you lent him money?'

'I can't recall.'

'We'll be talking to him so we'll see if he says the same.'

She smirks. 'I'm sure he will.'

If she's lying, she's good.

'I'd like to ask you again about the last time you saw Sandra. Do you remember, it was the day she died? You met her on the bridge?'

'Yes.'

'Tell me about it.'

She does so, finishing, 'As I said, she wanted money and I refused to give it to her. I was already giving her money, which I'm sure you know. She was a greedy girl.'

'Exhibit SB9. This is a still taken from the CCTV of that day. Is this you and Sandra?'

'Yes.'

'There are two passers-by in this picture, see.' I point them out. 'We tracked them down and they remember the two of you quite well. We interviewed them separately and they came up with remarkably similar stories. They said that they distinctly heard you say to Sandra to lay off, that it was in the past and that she'd regret it.'

'Yes. Yes, I did. She was threatening to contest the will. I told you that.' A high flush across her cheekbones. Slight panic.

'And then they said they heard Sandra say,' I turn to my notes, '"We have to confess, tell everyone what happened."'

Maudie's mouth opens in an 'Oh'. It's hard to gauge what it means.

'Have you anything to say to that?'

'I don't know what those girls heard. But they misheard.'

'Both of them?'

'Obviously.'

'What did you mean the other night when you said to Megan that Sandra was out to ruin you all?'

'What I said. I meant what I said.'

'How would Sandra have ruined you?'

'By contesting the will.'

'How would that have ruined you specifically?'

'It's not nice to be involved in a court case.'

'You'd hardly be ruined, though.'

'That depends on how much you value your family name,' she says, in a tone that suggests I wouldn't know about any of that.

I let it go. 'Right. I'd like to talk to you now about your sister's funeral. Tell me about it.' Stay pleasant, Lucy, I tell myself.

'If you'd bothered to go, you'd know about it.'

'Tell me about the hotel and specifically what you remember about Sandra.'

'It's common knowledge that Sandra had to be brought home. She drank too much.'

I wait but she doesn't say any more. 'Can you elaborate?'

'I brought her home. She was being quite loud and aggressive.'

'According to the priest, she seemed perfectly sober. His account is that she was talking to him, albeit loudly, about forgiveness and that you appeared and dragged her away.'

'She was not sober. Trust me.'

It is such an arrogant thing to say that I want to slap her. Instead I let my silence do the talking. Finally, when the air has calmed, I say it. 'Talk to me now about when you took care of Sandra as a child.'

'For God's sake, what has that to do with anything?'

'Humour me.'

She's balled up her fists, her mouth in a grim line. She's going to blow. Dan can sense it too. I tread carefully. 'What happened that you took charge of her?'

'Her father died and her mother was not able to cope. Pauline was always a delicate creature. No resilience. What's the word these days? Snowflake? Well, she was the original snowflake.' It's said with a sense of satisfaction that makes my stomach curdle. As if she knows how everything should be done. 'I offered to take Sandra from her because she was a difficult child. I under-estimated how difficult, though. It was one thing after another. And then she ended up pregnant. It was too late to do any-thing then. She had to have it. Brendan left me around that time too. I was heartbroken, and sure she had the baby and we were run off our feet. We sent her to school in Dublin then, to keep her safe and where no one knew her. But nothing we tried worked.'

'You sent her off to an addiction clinic.' I can't resist it. 'Let's tell the truth here.'

'After the clinic,' she grinds out, 'we sent her to a school.'

'How long had she been with you when you discovered she was pregnant?'

'What has that to do with anything?'

Oh, snappy. 'Well?'

'I don't know.'

'Think.'

Her eyes narrow at my tone. 'I did. I don't know.'

I fight to keep the passive tone, 'All right. Tell me, how long before she had the baby did Brendan leave you?'

'A couple of months.'

'Why was that?'

'It was hard for him, being around her. He cared for her. He saved her life. He did a lot for her.'

'Who is Devon's father?'

She jerks, flushes. 'Like I said, it could be anyone.'

'In the past couple of days, we've chatted to a lot of men who were in school with Sandra. None of them had sex with her.'

'Who'd admit it, for God's sake?'

'Who is Devon's father?'

She eyeballs me, a slow look of dread passing across her face.

'We have reason to believe it could be Brendan Walsh.'

And slowly, unbelievably, a smile spreads its way, like butter, over her face. 'I've never heard anything quite so ridiculous in my life.' A look at me. 'Once a dunderhead, always a dunderhead.'

52

We terminate the interview shortly after that. My head is reeling.

When we get back, Larry is in the office, leaning on the desk, arms folded. 'She's lying,' he says. 'Why else would he kill Sandra?'

'She's not lying.' I sink into a chair and groan. 'She knows who the father is, no doubt, but it's not Brendan. She lied about pretty much everything else but the only time she relaxed was when she called me a dunderhead.'

'I kind of get that,' Larry says, with a smirk.

I fling a pen at him and he dodges out of the way, laughing.

'Bingo,' Mick announces, as his laptop pings. 'Some results from Forensics.' We crowd around the screen and he opens the email titled, 'Boots analysis/Sandra Byrne scene'.

It's a long email, not easy to understand, but it's comprehensive. It identifies the make of boots based on the tread pattern and goes into detail about the distinguishing marks on the soles. There's another email that analyses the substances found in the blood at the scene. It's a mix of sand and soil.

'We'll have to arrest Brendan and conduct a search to locate those boots,' I say. 'But the only thing we have to go on is a chance meeting at a garage and we can't even get a positive ID on him.'

'I bring tidings of great joy.' Kev bounces into the room with William. He starts peeling off a large multi-coloured scarf. 'My mother knitted it for me,' he says, by way of explanation. 'It's handy in the cold.' Then, with glee, 'I had this brilliant idea this morning. Dugort is a quiet pier, right, but Rosses Point, where Brendan sails from, is not. And guess what? Brendan Walsh was spotted getting off his boat in Rosses Point on the night of the murder. One of the lads on the lifeboat crew saw him and remembers the night particularly because they had just come in from a job on the sea and it's logged, so there is no mistake on the date or the time. And I even got CCTV of him on his way to the boat and on the way back. It's too dark to make out the finer details but it definitely looks like him, and Larry can work on enhancing it. Then the Cig told me to hire a fisherman and ask him to ferry me from Rosses Point to Dugort and back again, and guess what? The time frame is as near perfect as you can get.' A grin, a bow. 'And thank you very much!'

'The kid has a brain,' Larry announces, clapping him on the back.

'It still might not be enough to arrest him,' William says. 'The DNA we get will either prove or disprove his paternity. Though I agree with Lucy, having seen the interview. I think Maudie was telling the truth about that. Now,' he eyeballs us all, 'even if he was at the scene, we can't conclusively prove he killed her, though Devon's testimony will go a long way to establish that someone did so around that time. However, if we find a good strong reason for him to have done so it will help the case against him. This we know. And if we find that, we'll be able to probe him for a confession and make it a whole lot easier on ourselves when it comes to court. I want everyone combing those files, those witness statements. I want Megan talked to as soon as she's able. We have time to turn this around. Go.'

Just as I've picked up a few statements to read over, my phone rings.

'Ma,' Luc says, when I answer, 'I'm at the hospital. You need to get in here now. Like, now.'

'Why?'

But he's gone, hung up.

'Everything all right?' Dan asks, in an undertone, as I pocket my phone.

'I don't know. I have to get to the hospital. I don't know.' I haphazardly reach for my jacket.

'Come on,' Dan says, standing. 'I'll drive you.'

I'm about to protest, but he says sternly, 'It'll be safer. You look like you might crash.'

'I won't cr—'

'Ah, ah.' He holds up a hand. 'Come on.'

'Thanks.'

While Dan drives, I try to reach Luc again, then my mother, but neither is picking up. To distract myself, I talk about the case with Dan.

'We won't find anything significant in the next few hours,' he says. 'I can see us having to let her go until something turns up.'

'Yeah.' I wonder where she'll go. Her house is destroyed, and I doubt Leo will offer her a place to stay. Maybe she'll move into Pauline's house. Maybe when she sees the place where her niece was murdered she might relent and tell us what happened because she knows. Maudie is the family recorder. The one who remembers everything. Some people recall only bits and pieces of their childhood, others more, but each person's recollection is coloured by their own memories. Maudie, I suspect, has the clear-eyed memory of the master manipulator.

A while later, Dan drops me off outside the hospital. 'I'll be in the car park,' he says. 'Give you a lift back. I've got a few files I can be looking at.'

'Thanks.'

'Let me know what's happening, yeah?' Then, in a rare touchy-feely gesture, he pats me lightly on the back. I think it's meant to be supportive. He immediately looks embarrassed.

'I'm glad that moment's over,' I joke, as I climb out of the car.

Racing towards Reception, I try to rein in my spiralling thoughts. Luc is waiting for me just inside the door, his eyes hollow. 'It's Da— Rob.' He crosses towards me. 'He - he had a clot, Mam. He's had a stroke. He's . . . he's . . .' A big tear falls from his eye and breaks my heart. I catch him in an embrace and he falls against me. 'He never even met Sirocco,' he gulps out.

I hug him harder but don't comment. In time, Luc will know that we would probably never have trusted Rob enough to allow him to meet Sirocco. 'Come on,' I say, my arm around his shoulder, determined not to cry. 'Where is he?'

He leads me upstairs and through a maze of corridors. On the third floor, I spot my mother halfway down one. She hurries to meet us. 'I thought you'd never get here,' she says, taking my hand and pulling me towards a room. 'He's fading, the nurse told me. Clara is there with him now but she said for you to go straight in.' She scans my face. 'Do you want to go in?'

My answer is to push open the door into Rob's room. Clara

turns at the sound, before motioning me towards the bed. Her eyes are puffy and swollen, her voice choked up from snotty tears. 'Thank God.'

'How is he?' I ask stupidly, taking the chair beside her.

She shakes her head, unable to put it into words. Then she takes his hand in hers and strokes it, smoothing out his long fingers.

'I'm so sorry,' I say.

'It was a clot.' She gazes at her younger brother with such love that my heart almost shatters.

Finally, after a moment, she releases his hand, placing it gently on his chest. 'Talk to him, Lucy. He'd like that you're here. I know he would. He was . . . He did really care about you.'

I say nothing because Rob had a talent for getting people to take his side. It's not that, in this moment, I'm not sad: I am. I can feel the grief setting up a tent in my heart, but it's grief for what might have been. Grief for the wonderful man he could have been, the one who appeared only in brief flashes. A criminal who saved my life. And killed it too. As Clara softly exits, I wait a moment before taking his hand in mine. It's warm. His nails are trimmed. I see a tiny pulse in his wrist.

And the room is peaceful.

'Rob,' I try to summon the right words, nice words, meaningful words. 'I . . . well . . . look . . . well . . .' Christ, nothing's coming. I've gone blank. I have to say *something*. But too much has happened. Too much hurt and so much love. But he's dying and he can't leave without me saying how I feel. Only it's too big and too muddled and too much . . . 'There are no words for right now,' I choke out, my grip tightening on his hand. 'There's too much to say and it's too big a moment, yet it's too short to jam everything into. You're dying, Rob, and I can't believe you are because you were so alive. Always. And . . . that's it. That's all.'

And the tears come. Sad, messy, complex tears. For a man I loved and yet despised. For a bad man who wasn't a bad man. For the stories I told about him that were true but only shadows of the truth. Behind me, Clara comes in and my mother and Luc, and we all stay there, and then there is one final gasp before the pulse in his neck, that tiny beat of life, fades.

He's gone.

Just like that.

Later, Clara accompanies us back to my house in Keem. We want to be together and there is nowhere else we can go. Someone, probably a friend of my mother's, has been in and cleaned up the kitchen, tidied things away. The heating has been switched on and, standing in the hall, staring about, I feel as if this place is the only familiar thing in my world right now. Yes, it's too tidy but it's my house.

But will it ever feel like a home again?

I push aside the thought that my long-ago chance meeting with a small-time drug dealer led to this carnage.

There will come a day when I'll have to testify against Dessie in court. There will come a day when I'll have to face up to what I did. And my part in it.

But not right now.

'Come on.' My mother, as usual, takes charge, and I find comfort in her badgering. 'Let's all find somewhere to sleep. Clara love, I'll put fresh sheets on my bed and you take that and—'

'She can have my room,' I say. 'I'll take the sofa.'

'Are you sure?' My mother looks relieved.

'Yes.'

'Thanks, pet.' She gives me a quick hug.

A good while later, after Luc has updated Tani, after Clara has stopped sobbing, after my mother falls asleep, I'm still wide awake. Too much has happened, from Rob to our disastrous interview of Maudie. So, to relax, I stare at the ceiling and run over the case. Sandra Byrne. Thirty-nine years old. Murdered in her mother's house. Didn't look as if it was planned. Stalked by her son who hasn't exactly been ruled out as a person of interest. Main suspect, a man who once saved her life. No reason for it, though a lot of the evidence so far points to him.

Why? Why now? What changed in both their lives?

Pauline died.

She was the victim's mother and the suspect's hoped-for sister-in-law.

They also saw each other at the petrol station unexpectedly.

Did that light a spark for Sandra?

It affected her so much she ran back into counselling.

Why?

Aside from an abuse angle, which we're close to ruling out, nothing.

I go over all the other statements from all the other witnesses in my head. I log on to my laptop and read them again. Maudie has probably been released by now.

I sit in the dark and silence of the house, going over and over what I know until my head fuzzes. The problem with the case is that Sandra was the source of so much gossip it's hard to tell the truth from the lies. And she lied so much and—

And something shifts. I scroll back to Richie's statement.

And as I read it, I think, Oh, my God, how we assumed.

How we *assumed*.

Without even looking at the clock, I call William.

He doesn't know yet about Rob and I swore Dan to secrecy because I'm seeing this case out. When William answers, sounding all fresh and awake, without even a hello, I plunge into what I'm thinking.

He listens and I can tell he's buying it. 'Right, get your arse over to Richie and, in the meantime, I'll have a look at that. If it pans out, we might just have found our leverage. Also, task Dan with talking to Leo, if he's up to it, about the contents of Pauline's house. That's crucial.'

'Will do. Can I take the Brendan interview?'

He laughs. 'Let's see what we find first.'

Just as I put the phone down, I notice my mother in the doorway.

'I have to go in to work later.'

'No, you have to be here,' she says.

'I can't.' I just can't. I can't mourn Rob in the normal way. I don't know how to mourn him. All I know is that work calms me, and that maybe I'll find the answers there when I'm not looking for them. But I don't know how to express this and I lower my gaze as my mother looks at me in disappointment.

'All right,' she says. 'If Luc or Clara asks, I'll say it wasn't your choice.'

'Thanks.'

She walks out of the room.

53

29 January

Brendan Walsh is dressed in slim-fitting dark jeans and a blue sweatshirt with the crest of his sailing club emblazoned on the left-hand side. He's bald, his complexion ruddy, his face roughened by the weather. Short thick fingers drum the table-top that divides him from me and Dan.

He's shell-shocked but doing his best not to show it.

He'd been in the process of packing when he'd been arrested. Ready to run, we think.

The search of his house and boat is ongoing, and we'll be updated immediately with anything of interest that they find. So far, we've located a ledger which seems to back up Maudie's claim that they're in business together. His DNA has also come back negative for paternity.

It all hinges on what we found out in the last two days. Dan is taking the interview: if it goes badly, I don't want anyone saying I wasn't emotionally able for it.

The DVD recorder is on, Brendan has been cautioned and, so far, he has hesitantly told us about his sailing club, about how many students he has, about his plans to expand and about how much he loves his job. His voice is soft, gentle, and he's got a meekness about him that would irritate me.

'Is it fair to say that that sailing club is your whole life?' Dan asks.

'Yes, I guess.'

'Great to have a job you're passionate about.' Dan shifts a few files about. 'What is it they say? If you work at something you love, you'll never work a day in your life?'

'Yeah, I guess,' he says again. 'Look, can we just get this over with, whatever it is?'

'Sure,' Dan says easily. 'Now, like we told you, we're investigating the murder of Sandra Byrne. Do you know her?'

'I did. She was a kid when I knew her. She stayed with Maudie, my fiancée, for a bit. She was her niece.'

'That's right, go on.'

'Maudie and I broke up soon after but we stayed good friends. She helped out with the sailing club.'

'Tell us why the relationship floundered.'

And there it is, just the tiniest tell. His mouth opens and closes and then the lie: 'The usual. We weren't right for each other.'

'Good to find out in advance, eh, before the big day?' Dan says, and he agrees, a little too eagerly.

'Sandra was murdered in the early hours of the thirteenth of January. Can you account for your movements that morning?'

'Eh . . . Not sure. You took my phone and it'd be on that.'

'We checked,' Dan says pleasantly. 'iPhones are amazingly good on detail. And your iPhone seems to have nothing at all on it from about nine the previous evening until the following morning.'

'Probably went dead. I'm pure useless at keeping it charged.'

'Really? You were carrying a mobile charger when we arrested you.'

'I was organised today, is all.' He laughs, stops, laughs again. Drums his fingers.

After a moment of silence, Dan opens the door and asks the exhibits officer to come in. He does so and produces some items of clothing, all individually packaged. 'We'd like you to identify the following items of clothing that were removed from your house,' Dan says. He reads out the exhibit numbers and narrates, 'A red jacket with a yellow crest, which reads "Rosses Point Sailing Club", a pair of Caterpillar boots and a blue shirt with white stripes.'

'I'd have said a white shirt with blue stripes,' Brendan says, 'but, yes, all mine.'

'Can you tell me, Brendan, about the last time you saw Sandra?'

He scratches his head in a pantomime of remembering. 'Oh, years ago, I'd say. Before I left for Sligo.'

'Are you sure?'

'I, eh, think so, yes.'

'Exhibit SB10.' Dan places a still from the garage CCTV in front of him. 'Is this you in Crossmolina garage on January the third?'

Brendan jerks, fingers stilling on the table. After a second, he pulls the image towards him, peering at it. 'Oh, yes,' he says, in an 'I'm-an-awful-eejit' way. 'That's right. I saw her that time. She . . .' He glances at us, then back down. 'She acted really strangely, actually.'

Dan waits.

'Really strange,' he says again. 'She ran off. Yes, that was the last time I saw her.'

'Ran off where?'

'To the back of the shop. I'm sure you know that, you having the CCTV image and all.'

'Any reason why she would run off?' Dan asks.

'I don't know. I said hello to her and she just ran.'

'We have a witness who says she was so shocked she couldn't speak when she saw you.'

'Yeah, she did seem shocked, all right.'

'Why would she be shocked?'

'I don't know. Maybe seeing me made her think of home and she didn't get on too well at home by all accounts.'

Dan studies him, his head to one side. Brendan attempts a smile.

'Maybe,' Dan agrees, causing Brendan almost to collapse in relief.

'After that day, did she contact you?'

It was just a question we thought we'd ask, seeing as Donna had said that Sandra had expressed a desire to write to this man. Brendan's reaction is interesting. He doesn't answer immediately. Instead he seems to be gauging us. Figuring out what we might know. Finally, 'She wrote to me, actually. I, eh, ignored it. The letter was just sad, sort of.'

'In what way?'

'It made no sense. I tore it up, didn't even finish reading it. I can't remember what it said, only that it was rubbish. And that was the end to it.'

'Where did you put the letter after you tore it up?'

'In the bin, where else? I was hardly going to frame it.'

'All right, we'll move on. Talk to me about leading lights.'

A defiant jerk now. 'Leading lights?'

'Yeah. Would you know if there are leading lights for Dugort Pier, for instance?'

He clasps his hands together, fingers knotting themselves in and out, in and out. 'There used to be, years back, but I don't know any more.'

'So, years back,' Dan says, 'when you were sailing in Dugort, what would you have looked out for?'

'Well, 'twas Pauline's house at the time, Sandra's mother, you know. Pauline and Paudie actually. And Pauline was in the habit of keeping a light on in her porch at night, and there was also a light on the hill above the house – her father had it put in.'

'That's interesting,' Dan says, 'because in recent weeks some-one has started using that light again.'

'Really?'

'Yes.' Dan changes the subject once more. 'Let's move to Pauline's house itself. Were you ever in it?'

'Years back when I was going out with Maudie.'

'Were you in it recently?'

'I'd have had no cause to go in.'

'Can you remember much about it, back then?'

'No.'

'Describe the place from what you remember.'

'I'm not great with detail. It was a long time ago.'

'Give it a go.'

So, he does, growing more confident as he describes what he remembers of the kitchen, the flooring, the way the place was always cluttered with knick-knacks. He finishes, 'I was never in the bedrooms, but I believe there were three upstairs.'

'That's right. Are you sure you were never upstairs?'

'Why would I go upstairs?'

Dan pushes another image towards him. 'Exhibit SB14, a partial boot print in blood found at the top of the stairs after the murder of Sandra Byrne. This print matches the sole of your left boot.'

'Most every fisherman in the country has boots like mine.'

'Not every fisherman has a crack right down the middle of the sole. See here.' Dan points to a seam in the print. 'But you do. See your boots. The ones you told us you owned. And what's more, see this?' He points to a dot on the image, where the heel starts. 'That corresponds with a nail right here in your boot. When you had them repaired.'

'I wasn't in that house recently,' Brendan says. 'I told you.'

'Then how would you explain the fact that a partial finger-print of yours was found on a trophy that has now been identified as the murder weapon?'

'I could have touched it years ago.'

Bingo! Dan says casually, 'It wasn't in the house years ago. It was won by Devon two years ago in an athletics competition.'

'Then I made a mistake, I was actually in that house the year before last. With Maudie.'

'I see.' Dan taps the image of the bloody boot print again. 'Do you know there were tiny particles of soil on the sole of the boots, which subsequently got deposited along with the blood on the floor of that house? That soil matches soil found at the end of your boot, which, get this, matches soil found onboard your boat. Can you explain that?'

'I really can't.' Brendan shrugs. 'This is a set-up.'

'We also have a witness who claims she saw you at five a.m. on the morning of the thirteenth of January disembarking from your boat in Rosses Point. She said you seemed in a hurry and didn't stop to talk.'

'I was not there. It's a mistake.'

'Exhibit SB15. I am now showing the witness a CCTV image taken from the camera of Rosses Point lifeboat station at five a.m. on the thirteenth of January. Is this you, Brendan?'

'No.' He doesn't even look at the picture.

Dan lets a pause develop, then says, 'We all lose it from time to time and things happen. Things we regret.'

'Nothing happened,' he says, with grit. Then, 'Why on earth would I kill her? I saved her life years ago, for God's sake. I'm a decent man. I've come from nothing, nothing. I had nothing, and I built up my sailing club. I worked hard. I've taught children how to be safe in the water – I've probably saved their lives. I've held charity galas. I've done the right thing always. I am a decent man.'

'Tell us why she tried to kill herself that time you saved her.'

His little monologue derailed, he looks a bit shaken. Then he says, 'She didn't try to kill herself. She just fell in.'

'That's what you thought at the time, all right.'

He pales.

'But you found out later why she did it, didn't you?'

He pulls back in his seat and swallows hard.

'You found out around the time her father died to be exact. Let's talk about that.'

'About what?'

'The death of her father. More specifically, how he died. Tell me about that.'

'Nothing to tell. I ran Pauline into Westport on the boat, and when we got back, Paudie was dead at the foot of the stairs.'

'That's right. He fell down the stairs.'

'He did.' Pause. 'He was a drunk.' Bitterness laces his voice.

353

'And here's a photo taken of the scene at the time, from the inquest report.'

Brendan avoids looking at it.

'In recent years, blood-spatter analysis has really come into its own. Do you know what that is, Brendan?'

'No.'

'We examine the way the blood has been dispersed around a crime scene in order to determine what happened. Back then, when Paudie died, it was investigated, and while the coroner expressed concern that his fractured nose might not be compatible with falling down the stairs, it was ruled death by misadventure, probably because it couldn't be proven that he hadn't acquired it by falling down the stairs. Probably because he'd been drinking heavily the night before, as was confirmed by the local publican. And you, Maudie and Pauline all sang from the same hymn sheet. You were out in Westport, shopping. You came back and he'd fallen. But we decided to have a little look ourselves, and when we gave this to the guys in the lab, they had a good hard look at it, and do you know what they think?'

'How would I?'

'They think that this man was pushed. That he tumbled down the stairs, clambered up and someone hit him on the nose, causing a spurt of blood. He fell back, banged his head. That someone was standing here.' Dan taps the picture. 'See the way the spray from the nose isn't in an arc, the way it should have been? It's blank, right here, where the person was standing.'

'Maybe he was punched. We weren't there.'

'Do you know what we think happened back then, Brendan?'

'No, and I don't want to.'

'That carpet in the hallway was only bought last year.'

Brendan's mouth opens like a hinge. 'What?'

'That carpet. Only bought a year ago.' Dan, with his unfathomable stare, is making Brendan uncomfortable. If asked later, Brendan won't be able to pinpoint why he was so uneasy, because Dan is the very personification of polite and affable. But he's deadly too. 'I asked you to describe Pauline's house to me, the one you hadn't been in for thirty years. No, sorry, two, wasn't it? You talked about the hall carpet. It's only a year old.'

'Maybe I was in the house a year ago, then.'

'Sandra went to AA. Did you know that?'

He winces, wrongfooted again. 'What?'

'Sandra Byrne went to AA and we have a statement from her partner, Richie. He says that when she was asked to tell her story in AA, she said, "My father was murdered, and I lost my mother."'

'Sandra was a liar.'

'I don't think she was. I think she always wanted to tell the truth and she decided to start with AA before confessing and asking forgiveness. That's what I think.'

'That's nothing to do with me.'

'Do you own a pet?'

'Yes. A dog.'

'There was a dog hair found on Sandra. We're running tests against your dog's hair now. That'll be interesting.'

Brendan stiffens.

'We also know, because we tested DNA on a cap belonging to Paudie Byrne, which was found packed in a box in the house, that he was most likely the father of Sandra Byrne's baby, Devon. Was Paudie Byrne raping his young daughter, Brendan?'

The words have a power all their own. 'Rape' especially.

'Young daughter.' They conjure up images too horrific to deny if you're any kind of a decent person.

Brendan closes his eyes and starts to shake.

'Tell us what happened, Brendan,' Dan says. 'Did you try to help Pauline and it spiralled? Were you all doing the impossible in an impossible situation?'

And as we hold our breath, as my hands clench in anticipation, Brendan whispers, 'None of it was meant to go like that. It's been a nightmare to live with and then Sandra wanted to blow us all out of the water.'

54

'You are not obliged to say anything unless you wish to do so but anything that you do say will be taken down in writing and may be given in evidence. Do you understand?'

Dan reads Brendan's memo back to him:

> 'I met Maudie through sailing. She was a great oarswoman and we were a good team. We got engaged and I met her family. Her sister Pauline was married to Paudie Byrne at that time. He was a big man, rough, but welcoming. They lived in an old house they renovated down by Dugort Pier and they showed me the transit Pauline's father had put in for the boats. I didn't use it much back then as Maudie still lived in her family home near Keem, with her brother Dom. Also, I was never that easy in the house. Paudie liked a drink and could get cross. It was obvious that Pauline and the younger girl Sandra were afraid of him. Megan less so as she was older and out more, working and that. So, I used to take Sandra out on the boat, get her away from the house. Megan was very protective of Sandra, I remember.
>
> 'Anyway, one day, I was with Maudie and she gets a call. Pauline is in an awful state, saying she had pushed Paudie

down the stairs, and that when he had got up, Sandra had punched him. He looked like he was dead, she said. At first, you know, we thought 'twas a joke, like, only it wasn't. When we got to the house, he was lying at the end of the stairs. He wasn't dead. I think he was still breathing, and I was all for calling an ambulance, but then Pauline turns around and says no way was she calling any ambulance. She told us then what he'd been doing to Sandra because she was pretty. She'd caught him and warned him off but he wouldn't stop. He had to be made to stop. And how would they ever live with the shame of it all? The whole family would be dragged down and Megan about to marry Leo and maybe he wouldn't marry her if he found out and, sure, she'd be in trouble for pushing him down the stairs and so we just, well, I suppose we were all in shock, but we . . . I don't know where Megan was, maybe work or something. Yes, work, I think, and Sandra was home, out sick from school that day.

'So, we, well, Maudie really, decided that Sandra would go with her, and that Pauline and I would go sailing to Westport for shopping and just leave Paudie there, and if he was alive when we came back we'd call the ambulance, and if not, we'd say he fell down the stairs. And that's what we did. When we came back, he was dead. I remember how glad Pauline was. And we told Sandra she had to keep her mouth shut or we'd all go to jail on account of letting him die. And we told her that Megan could never know. And then, sure, we discovered the child was pregnant. Maybe that's what Pauline knew already. I don't know, she never said. But we made our statements and because he was roaring drunk anyway, people believed he fell. Maudie is convincing anyhow.

'And then, I don't know . . . Sure, when I was scouting out places for the new sailing club, didn't I run into Sandra again, years later, after saving her life and all, and she is afraid of me or whatever, I don't know, maybe not afraid, but she writes me a letter saying she needs to come clean. That it's eating away at her and she has to let it go. That she'll keep me and Maudie out of it but, sure, how can she? And I panic, I do, and I ring Maudie, who says she'll have a word with her and then, sure, doesn't Pauline die, and I know, I just know that Sandra will tell all. Sure, what's to stop her now? She only kept quiet on account of Pauline and now she doesn't have to. And at the funeral, Maudie tells me she's going on about forgiveness and that, and Maudie and I know she's gearing up to tell someone. All I wanted was to talk to her. I wanted to meet her and tell her not to – how will Devon take it? How will Megan cope? And me and Maudie? But she wouldn't talk to me. So, I tell Maudie to have that word with her quick smart or I will. I've got my boats to consider and my life, and all them years ago, I was only doing what was best.

'So, Maudie talks to her, but next thing, she asks me if I'm stalking Sandra and to stop it and I say I am not, and she says that Sandra is after putting a complaint into the guards only she hasn't named me. Also, she thinks that Sandra is writing a confession. So, I went to find it. Maudie sorted the transit, gave me a key and I let myself into the house. I was just looking for her phone or computer or just to beg her not to do it, but . . . but . . . when I go in, I hear her upstairs, pottering away, talking to herself. So, I go up to her and every step I feel madder and madder. This mess is all because she can't live with herself. She wasn't thinking of us. Or Devon.

'So, I go upstairs. I think I have the trophy with me. I barge into her room. She screams and this object was fired at me. I ducked or it might have been me that was murdered. Next thing she's picking up something else. I swing the trophy at her. Hit her. And maybe I hit her a couple more times, I can't remember. Next thing I remember is that she's on the floor, just lying there. I tried to feel for a pulse in her neck, like, and there was nothing and I couldn't believe I'd done it. I didn't mean it and I'm not a murderer. I saved her life before. I'm not a murderer. I just ran in the end because, well, that's like two deaths, isn't it? I never meant it.

'Ends.

'This statement has been read to me by Detective Dan Brown and I have been invited to make any corrections thought necessary in it. It is correct.

'Signed: Brendan Walsh

'Witnessed Dan Brown D/Gda 2357M

'Witnessed Lucy Golden D/Sgt 1457F'

The statement is dated and signed, and the DVD is turned off. Brendan Walsh is taken back to his cell.

'Good job,' I say.

'Good job, you.'

I bide my time, waiting until Dan is ready to leave before I say, 'William will be down in a minute and I'm off the next few days, so I'm just going to say this now. Go and see your father.'

The look of surprise on his face is almost comical.

'Luc is distraught about Rob. Devon never got the chance with

Sandra. Don't be an idiot, go and see him, curse him, do whatever but, Dan, there will come a day you won't get the chance.'

Then, before he can reply, William, Kev, Susan and Larry arrive in, and the drab interview room is filled with the sounds of congratulations and back-slapping. I feel detached from it all, the joy of a clean confession just hitting off the edges of me.

William takes the file and says he's going to call and press the DPP to charge Brennie.

It's always a tense time, waiting for a charge, hoping we've done enough to keep a man behind bars. Because when you know someone has done a terrible thing and the DPP disagrees, it's horrifying to see them released, back out to live their lives until another little nugget of evidence can be found. It's like sifting for gold in the muck.

The six of us, unable to do any more except wait, mosey on up to the kitchen. Susan fills the kettle and asks us if we want tea or coffee. Kev finds a bar of melted chocolate in his pocket and offers it around.

'That's even worse than the sandwiches in the bar across the road,' Larry mutters, as he takes two squares and pops them into his mouth. 'Rank,' he says then, nodding.

Kev gives him the fingers.

Larry musses up his hair. 'Little buckshee detective man,' he says.

'Piss off,' Kev says, unruffled.

Larry smiles. 'You did good.'

'I know,' Kev agrees.

Susan hands us all a cuppa.

Silence descends. No one can think of anything to say. The minutes tick by. Outside, rain starts to spatter on the window. Jordy and Matt arrive.

We wait, like expectant relatives at a birth.

And finally William comes back in.

We all turn to look at him.

A slow smile spreads its way across his face and he nods. The room erupts in cheers, the clinking of cups and laughter and joy. And the evening is rearranged so we can all go for a drink.

And I'm happy but I can't feel it.

William beckons me out. In the corridor, he says, 'You can have the honour of charging him. That was great work you did.'

And all I can think is that the father of my boy has died. 'I think, Cig, that Kev should do it. I know he's not a sergeant but he's done Trojan work and he deserves it.'

'Are you sure?'

'Yeah, give it to him. Make his day.'

As he goes to break the news to Kev, I leave. Today won't be a day for celebrating in the pub. Today I have to go home and help Clara bury her brother and Luc bury his father.

55

31 January

Rob's funeral is a humanist one and it's a small affair. It's held on 31 January, the last day of winter in the Irish Celtic tradition. Tomorrow is St Brigid's Day, a day of fertility and rebirth. The first day of spring, my mother used to tell me, though I would argue black and blue that spring didn't arrive until sometime in March. It used to drive her mad and make me laugh. Anyway, winter, it seems, wants to go out like a lion. Wind wails around us in the graveyard as Rob's coffin is lowered into the ground just at the foot of Slievemore in Achill. It's what Clara wanted for him, to be near his son, and how could we refuse?

The press is here, snapping from a distance, but they mostly keep out of the way.

Clara sobs, as does my mother, who is basically the chief mourner, no matter whose funeral she goes to. Luc, Sirocco in his arms, remains stoic. Tani, dressed like she belongs in Paris fashion week, clings to Luc. I'm glad he's got her – she's a great kid. And it's good to know he has some support because he's barely spoken to me since the attack, and it hurts. Beside them, Katherine, Tani's mother, and Johnny, her father. They seem to be on good enough terms, having separated a while back. Both of them hug me hard. I'm touched they're here because, years ago, Rob swindled them out of their life savings.

A couple of Rob's friends also come, including the owner of the gallery to whom Rob sold his photographs. He's really upset and, as he rocks to and fro, he intones the prayers in a very loud and mournful voice, which makes Tani giggle and earns her a puck in the ribs from Katherine.

William and Mick represent my colleagues. Some of the others had come to the removal the previous night and had shuffled by awkwardly, offering me their condolences. It was weird to see them away from work but I appreciated their support. Ben had arrived and enfolded me in the biggest, tightest hug and whispered a shaky 'Thank you,' to me. I whispered that it was my pleasure. Dan and Fran had come, Dan saying they were heading to Dublin to his father the following day. 'I'm going to introduce him to Fran,' he said. 'If that doesn't kill him, there's hope he might survive.'

We'd had a bit of a laugh over that, before he'd unexpectedly pulled me into a bear hug and told me he loved me. And then he was gone.

The prayers at the graveside end and people come up to offer their condolences again, but I slip away, walking instead, between the graves, reading them, wondering about the people buried there. It soothes me. Some were blessed with great long lives, others had barely taken a breath. All with a story to tell.

'You all right there?' William says from behind, falling into step beside me, hands buried deep in the pockets of his jacket.

I nod a hello.

We mooch on, feet sinking into boggy soil.

'See that poor fecker was only twenty,' William points to

a grave to his left and we pause, reading the inscription. *Chris McDaid. 1980–2000. Missed by his heartbroken parents.* A picture of Chris underneath the writing. A young man with a wide white smile and no idea how short he had to live.

On we walk. White headstones, black, wooden crosses of the newly buried.

'I'm sorry I didn't tell you that Rob had died when Dan and I did the Brendan interview,' I blurt out.

'I knew he was dead, Lucy.'

I turn to him in surprise and our eyes lock. I'm the first to turn away. Of course, he knew. He knows everything.

'I let you do it because I knew you had to. I'd have been the same. It helps, yeah?'

Just the fact that he understands sends tears to my eyes. I blink hard, so he won't see, and utter an 'Uh-huh'.

'My bonsai tree,' he says, apropos of nothing, 'was my mother's. She tended that tree as if, by looking after it well, she could keep us all safe.'

I steal a glance at him from the corner of my eye. His voice is low. He's staring straight ahead. I want to tell him I don't need to know but he wouldn't tell me if he didn't want to.

'My father, Patrick, had mental issues and where we came from, which is the cess pit of Limerick city, there wasn't much help out there, and back then, even less. He was in and out of hospital and one night he set our house on fire. My mother, brother and sister died, my father too. I was the only survivor mainly because I slept downstairs. Afterwards, one of the firemen found the tree. He gave it to me, and I've had it ever since.'

The weight of his grief finds me. I turn, open my mouth to say something but there is nothing to say.

'The work helps,' he says. 'I know that.'

He must have been a child himself when it happened, I think.

'I was twelve.' He reads my mind. 'Long time ago now but it leaves its mark.'

'Lucy!' my mother calls, breaking the moment as she hastily makes her way over. 'What are you at? Are you reading those gravestones again? We've—'

Then she realises it's William I'm with. 'Sorry,' she says, recognising him. 'I just . . . I . . . Look, thank you for your help that night.'

'How are you, Mrs Golden?' He smiles at her, his face transformed. No wonder witnesses trust him.

'Mags, please. And grand. Grand. Getting there, you know yourself.'

'I was just congratulating Lucy on the Sandra Byrne case. She did a great job.'

'She did,' my mother says staunchly, even though I haven't told her the details. 'She's very dedicated.'

'She is, but now she's taking a couple of weeks off, aren't you, Lucy?'

And so saying, he strides away, his head bent against the wind, the aloneness I always recognised in him more obvious now somehow.

'Isn't that lovely, a couple of weeks off?' My mother's bright voice comforting me despite everything. 'You should go somewhere nice, a hotel or a spa or something. I'll go with you.' She links her arm in mine. 'Come on, we're going back to the hotel for a bite to eat.'

'I'll be along in a minute.'

She must sense that I want to be on my own, so she squeezes

my arm, and moves off. I watch the crowd around Clara dwindle until she's alone at the grave, my mother a respectful step behind her. Luc and Tani are heading off with Katherine, Johnny trailing behind, not sure if he's wanted, until Tani turns to him and he runs to catch up. Voices float in the breeze. Someone laughs. Someone else joins in. The Irish funeral, sad but a great bit of craic all the same.

I notice, suddenly, that I'm at Pauline Byrne's grave. A small wooden cross is hammered into the ground as the earth isn't ready yet for a headstone. A mound of clay with some dead flowers. Sandra will be joining her soon, her body released now that the investigation is finished.

The legacy of what happened so long ago finding its way into her present.

How it always does.

'Lucy!' my mother calls. 'Come on. Never mind those other graves, pay your respects to your father.'

And I join her. *Patrick Golden. 1953–84. Missed by his loving wife Margaret and his daughter Lucy. For ever in our thoughts and hearts.*

And though I barely remember him, I think he's been with me throughout this case. Thoughts of him flashing in and out of my mind. I reach for my mother's hand and she squeezes mine.

'Oh, how he loved you,' she says.

In the distance I see Luc and Tani crossing towards Katherine's car, Sirocco in Luc's arms. I watch as he bends his head and kisses her, a simple unconscious gesture. A thing neither of them will recall if ever quizzed on it but a gesture that cements the future for her as best he can.

I realise that my mother is looking at Luc too, maybe thinking the same thing.

Sirocco is a lucky little girl.

There's a lot of luck involved in life.

And all we can do sometimes is tend things as best we can.

'Come.' My mother links her arm in mine. 'Let's get food and then book that holiday.'

I turn to her. 'I love you, Mam.'

'I know you do, *a stór.*'

And she pulls me close.

Acknowledgements

Thank you to everyone who has helped get this book onto the shelves.

Firstly, my family. Honestly, what can I say that I haven't said already? Colm, who has championed me through it all. I could not have done ANYTHING without your support.

My two children – adults now. Love ye more than you will ever know.

My family and extended family.

Taylor and Haro: two dogs who make sure I always get my morning exercise. It means I don't feel guilty sitting around all day trying to write!

My friends and everyone who came to the launch of *The Branded*. Such a wonderful, fun night. Thanks to Maynooth University Library for allowing me to use their fabulous facility. And thanks to Elaine Bean and all who helped her on the night; I am indebted to ye all. Thank you, too, to Clare Dowling and Claire Joyce for their magnificent launch speeches. (Was it me ye were talking about at all??) I am indebted to Zoë Miller, Debbie Thomas and Patricia Gibney for their writerly support.

The guards and detectives who have advised me on procedure.

Thanks also to the reader detective who makes sure I get it absolutely right, every time.

A huge thanks to my old school pal Seamus Butler of the Bellacragher Boat Club, Mayo for explaining all the sailing terminology to me. He gives great boat tours!

Eilish Power and Dave Curtis of Achill Island RNLI for their help with the book and information on harbours.

Martina Burns, McGowan's Funeral Directors, Ballina, Co. Mayo for her help while researching funerals. (Honestly, you learn so much when writing crime.)

Caroline Hardman at Hardman Swainson for being a really great person AND a great agent.

All at Little, Brown: Krystyna Greene, Hazel Orme and Rebecca Sheppard. Legends, all.

All in Hachette Ireland for looking after my books in Ireland.

Achill, my muse. And to Mary, Caroline and John in the Achill Island tourist office for supporting the book.

And thanks to you, the reader, for picking it up and taking a chance on it. Your support, emails and letters are what keep me going.